"I learn as I teach."
Aristotle (384–322 BC)

To Janet,

Best Wishes,

(signature)

(P.J. VANSTON).

CRUMP

P. J. VANSTON

Matador
5 Weir Road
Kibworth Beauchamp
Leicester LE8 0LQ, UK
Tel: (+44) 116 279 2299
Fax: (+44) 116 279 2277
Email: books@troubador.co.uk
Web: www.troubador.co.uk/matador

The characters and educational institutions described in this novel are entirely fictitious
and any similarity to any individuals and institutions is entirely coincidental.

ISBN 978 1848762 855

British Library Cataloguing in Publication Data.
A catalogue record for this book is available from the British Library.

Typeset in 11pt Book Antiqua by Troubador Publishing Ltd, Leicester, UK

Matador is an imprint of Troubador Publishing Ltd

Printed in Great Britain by the MPG Books Group, Bodmin and King's Lynn

For my Mother,
Marjorie,
A Good Teacher

CHAPTER ONE

Starting Out

Kevin Crump was happy – and because Kevin Crump was happy, he smiled.

He smiled when he woke up early that morning in his dark and smelly bedsit; he smiled as he splashed through the puddles and the drizzle to the train station; he even smiled at other commuters on the platform, though no-one smiled back. In fact, he only stopped smiling when a spotty youth with diamond earrings in the crowded carriage told him, in very specific and street-wise terms, that if he didn't do so immediately he'd get his head kicked in and worse. But then, after a couple of minutes, when both he and the other noisy and uniformed school kids had got off the train, Crump started smiling again – only to himself, this time, just in case someone else got the wrong idea. He knew that like most, if not all, males of the species, he looked dangerously like a pervert when he smiled, but he just couldn't help it. Kevin Crump was happy, so Kevin Crump smiled.

He looked out of the window at the passing cityscape, past the reflections of the long faces of the grumpy commuters in the window glass, and smiled – for today was truly a happy day for Kevin Crump and a wonderful day to be alive. As if to agree, a shaft of sunlight peeked out from behind a cloud, and he blinked into the bright, beautiful sunshine. He would make the deliberate mental effort to lodge the memory of that moment in his brain so that, in future years, after he'd achieved his academic ambitions and made something of himself, he'd be able to look back to that very moment, the moment when he, Kevin Crump, had sat smiling on that train, when it had been bliss to be alive at the dawn of a new and better day.

Crump – for that is what Kevin had been called by everyone but his mother since he was eight years old – was not usually a 'smiley' person, not at all like one of those girls at the supermarket he went to, whose vacant cheery faces looked like they'd been sprayed on. He liked to think his usual lack of smiling was because he was intelligent and intellectual, and even when he was thinking of pleasant or happy – or even sexual – things, he didn't smile all that much. He tended to agree with the mediaeval idea that smiling was a sign of idiocy, so wasn't too displeased at his natural unsmiling visage. The truth was he just wasn't a 'smiler' – but he wasn't a grumpy person either. Neither a frowner nor a smiler be, he thought. He was just, well, somewhere in between. Not too happy, not too sad. Just average. In the middle, nothing special, but nothing bad either. A blank slate. Not a bad thing to be, really – average and blank. After all, he smiled a bit when he was happy, and he frowned a bit when he was not, and what was wrong with that?

Today, Crump was happy and smiling because he was starting a new job. And not just any job either, but a post as a lecturer at Thames Metropolitan University. That is why he was travelling, via two crowded rush-hour trains, via Waterloo to historic Greenwich, a World Heritage site, home of the world-famous Mean Time and, quite literally, zero hour – or at least zero longitude – and famous throughout the world. He smiled again at the thought of his starting his academic career: he was now, officially, a university lecturer – and if that wasn't a reason to smile he didn't know what was, even though he had got the job at the last minute. Today, it would not be inaccurate to say, Kevin Crump was perhaps the happiest that he had ever been in his entire adult life. And so he smiled. Today was a beginning – a beginning of a new beginning – and a beginning he would remember for the rest of his life. And he knew it.

Crump, twenty-nine years old, slightly scruffy and lost-looking like a stray mongrel puppy come in from the rain, with thick ginger (he preferred 'strawberry blonde') hair and wiry thick glasses balanced on a long thin nose – today, Kevin Crump, an average achiever at school and university, an average teacher at a further education college, a man of average height and build who was so average he could have put that in his passport if his passport had been interested – today, Kevin Crump, a boy born and brought up in the dull suburbs of London, son of a nurse and a union official, and grandson of a Welsh miner – today Kevin Crump was joining academe, was actually becoming a lecturer at a university – a real, proper, British university, and consequently respected internationally as one of the best in the world.

It was the first step on a university career that could lead him, well, who knew where? Anywhere – perhaps even to the very top. To a senior lectureship and beyond – maybe one day even to a head of department job, and eventually on to an elite university – in Britain or anywhere in the world. And it would give him a regular and secure income for the rest of his life too – eventually that is, when he had a long-term contract at a university and not the short-term one he had accepted. It would also allow him the respect that he had always yearned for but which he had never enjoyed in any job, ever. It would, in other words, set him up for life.

It really didn't matter that he had originally been rejected for the job in favour of another candidate after attending an interview before the summer break, or that he had been fully expecting to be teaching full-time again that autumn term in his usual job at West London College. All that mattered was that he'd got a phone call two weeks earlier offering him the position at Thames Metropolitan University due to 'unforeseen circumstances.' Crump had no idea what this meant specifically – he didn't ask, and wasn't told either. He only had

3

a two year, 0.8 fractional contract and the pay was at the lowest end of the scale, meaning he'd still have to work a day a week at the college on his free day. He'd also accepted that he'd have to be as flexible as possible and take any classes he was asked to take – or in other words be a bit of a dogsbody – but it was an opportunity that he just couldn't miss and a great first step on the journey of his new university career, so dogsbody was fine. For now.

Everyone had to start somewhere. And didn't all great journeys start with but a single step? Thames Metropolitan University was that single step – a foot in the door, and a good place to start for a novice lecturer. And when in the future he was teaching at a better university, one that was not languishing at 116th position out of 123 in the university league tables, he would be in the fortunate position of being able to compare the two, to learn from both experiences, to cross-fertilise as it were.

Thames Metropolitan University was 'diverse, vibrant and inclusive' – or so it said in the prospectus. He liked that – it made life more interesting. He was used to teaching both foreign and ethnic minority students at the college, as well as 'challenging' students and those with dyslexia or other learning difficulties – such as the difficulty, or even inability, to read or write or speak or string a sentence together in any comprehensible way. It certainly didn't mean that the students, or the teachers for that matter, were any *worse* than those at any of the top twenty universities – like the redbrick northern university he had scraped into more than a decade before through clearing, having flunked one of his A-levels. If the students had got into university, especially from inner city comprehensive backgrounds, then they must have some brains at least – and quite probably more than those born with silver spoons sticking out of one of their orifices who'd had the usual behind-the-scenes benefits of such a background, from private tutors to parental expectations. It didn't matter either that they could enter the university with low A-level grades – or even with no

4

exam passes at all if they were over the age of 23 and classed as 'mature' students. It didn't matter at all – to think it did was petty and elitist. Nobody was 'thick' – people just didn't achieve due to their lack of opportunities and bad teaching. Everyone had potential and he, Kevin Crump, university lecturer, was there to unlock it. It was his job. It was his duty. It was his mission. And he would do it to the best of his ability.

But none of these silly details mattered. What did matter, and mattered in a real way, was that he was here, now, getting off the train at Waterloo, rushing over to the smaller Waterloo East station to catch his connecting train, and then, after arriving at Greenwich, making his way down the High Street through the September drizzle to the university.

Today was, without any shadow of a doubt, the day that Kevin Crump had gone up in the world, the day that he really and truly had become a middle-class professional – an achiever, a winner, one of the team; the day he had grown up and become a man, a man going places, a man ready for anything life or the world could throw at him – except, that is, the little globular bomb of bird shit that, at the precise moment he passed through the gates and entered the impressive university campus, fell silently from the sky and baptised him with a long white streak on the sleeve of his jacket. He felt it hit his arm, saw the white shit-mark, and cursed the unseen feathered shitter somewhere in the sky as he wiped it off with one of the tissues he always carried in his pocket. But no matter how much he tried to rub it off, there was still a dirty white stain in the fabric of his jacket – in fact, he had made it bigger by rubbing, though it had faded and was less visible than before.

Can't be helped, he thought. He'd put it into the dry cleaners on the way home and wear his other jacket tomorrow, the tweedy one – he only had two, being more used to wearing a T-shirt or a jumper as a teacher at the college. He wasn't sure about the dress code at Thames Metropolitan University, but thought it best to wear a jacket and a shirt and tie, at least at first. He had learnt from his teaching that if you wore smart clothes for the first week the students would respect you more, even if you changed into casual clothes for the rest of the year. It was all about image and gravitas, but it worked.

The campus was beautiful. It deserved to be. Thames Metropolitan University now occupied the buildings of the Old Royal Naval College in Greenwich – a baroque riverside masterpiece designed by Christopher Wren in the 17th century, just like St Paul's Cathedral some way off on the other side of the Thames. The university had only taken over the site seven years earlier after moving from a depressingly dirty-grey tower block in one of the less salubrious areas of South-East London – an eyesore of a building that, like so many others, had won armfuls of awards on its construction in the late sixties, but which had now been demolished to make way for an equally hideous shopping mall that had won armfuls of awards too.

The architectural splendour made the university look ancient (which it wasn't), prestigious (which it wasn't) and elite (which it wasn't either). When the university was called plain old South-East London Polytechnic it had been one of the worst polys in the country, right at the bottom of every applicant's list, a sanctuary for all those who scraped a couple of low grade A-levels, if that. But then, just like all the others, it had metamorphosed into a university in 1992 and now occupied one of the most stunning historical sites in London.

Crump had been to the campus at Greenwich before, but only once – for the interview before the summer for the other job. After getting that phone-call a fortnight before offering him his new job, the head of department had requested that he not visit before today, so as not to get in the way, he supposed – it was always hectic in the run-up to the start of term.

Having grown up in the suburbs of London, he'd naturally been to Greenwich before, with the school – to see the Royal Observatory, the Meridian line and, of course, the Cutty Sark, the last surviving 19th century tea clipper now in dry dock just a stone's throw from the campus. It was a pilgrimage all children growing up in London and its environs were almost obliged to make, but he had only been a kid when he had last set foot on the ship's decks. He made a mental note to visit again, now he was going to be here four days a week – perhaps for several years.

My God, the buildings of the Old Royal Naval College were magnificent! Even in the morning drizzle the honey-coloured stone shone. Well, not shone exactly – but it had the age and quality that looked elegant and beautiful in any weather. It *glowed* is what it did – glowed with the pride of history. What it had, quite simply, was class. Pure, well-bred, well-proportioned, history-drenched, good old-fashioned class.

He would enjoy working here, he could tell. He knew it. He felt it. Crump had always thought that he should have been born into a more, well, refined and cultured background. It was, he decided, 'him', though he had never admitted this feeling to anyone for fear of ridicule, or worse.

Standing in the middle of the campus, on the car-less road, equidistant from each of the four elegant buildings that the university occupied, Crump looked out over the dark slow-flowing river to the new-built apartments on the old East End dockland site on the other side. He closed his eyes, sighed and smiled at the *rightness* of it all. Inhaling deeply, he smelt the air – it tasted sweet, of history. Crump was exactly – precisely – where he was meant to be.

Where would he be this time next year, he thought, or in five years, or ten? The future lay open like a... like a... like a what? Like an oyster perhaps? Crump thought. No, too clichéd. Like a... road? An open road? Weak simile that. Like a... box? A door? A...vagina? The future lay open like a vagina? He'd heard worse similes in award-winning novels, but even though...

NAH! NAH! NAH! A loud beeping blasted his ears. He opened his eyes.

"Oi you fuckin' ginger twat!"

Crump looked round. A dirty, white delivery van was behind him, the stocky driver leaning out of the window and making a wanking sign, his large biceps looking as though they were stretching his white T-shirt to near-ripping point as he did so. A bit like Mike Tyson, he thought. The van man was now smiling broadly at Crump who was not, by now, smiling at all. The driver had large white teeth, three of them gold, two diamond-effect stud earrings as well as large gold chain around his thick neck and a zig-zag design cut into his close-cropped hair. Crump knew that this man looked 'hard' – like a rapper or a gangsta – in fact, this was the kind of look sported by the kind of person Crump went out of his way to avoid.

He also knew his own face bore the dazed expression of a frightened rabbit staring into the headlights as he stood there, despite there being no headlights for him to stare into, but he didn't know what else to do, so did nothing except raise his eyebrows quizzically, as a rabbit would no doubt do, if a rabbit had eyebrows. The hard-looking driver frowned and slowly shook his head in an expression half-way between pity and disgust, as though he had been confronted by some escaped mental patient wandering in the road. Crump, for some reason, smiled – albeit weakly – and the driver suddenly stopped smiling, and now looked very angry indeed.

"Yeah you, white boy," he said, "get out the fuckin way ya ginger cunt!"

The driver spat a large globule of spit out of the window onto the road without taking his eyes off Crump. It plopped in a puddle.

As if following a barked order from a sergeant major, Crump jumped out of the way and the white van sped past narrowly missing him, the driver staring at him and shouting obscenities which included, Crump noticed, the phrase 'white cunt' several times. Should complain about that really, he thought, but then how would that look on his first day at a new job? Don't want to make a bad impression or frighten the horses – or rabbits. How bad would that look? First day and already a troublemaker.

And he *had* been standing in the road – well, not road

exactly, not a public road for the general public, but how else were people to deliver things to the university if not by that private access road? No, he had been stupid, standing there dreamily taking in the atmosphere, enjoying the baroque architecture, the view of the Thames and the promise his future held. It was, he decided, his own stupid fault that the van driver had nearly run him down and called him a 'ginger twat' and a 'white cunt'. He would try not to get in the way in future. Lesson learned.

There were four main buildings on the Greenwich campus of Thames Metropolitan University. Each building was identical – a rectangular block with an inner gravelled courtyard onto which corridors and rooms looked out. Crump's new place of work would be in building two – the 'Mary Seacole' building.

The other three buildings were called 'Nelson Mandela', 'Marcus Garvey' and 'King Abdullah', the latter named after a generous beneficiary and home to the newly-established Centre for Islamic Studies. There was also the 'Stephen Lawrence Learning Zone' which everyone called a library, because that was precisely what it was. These buildings had previously been called after Kings and Queens – Queen Anne, Queen Mary, King William, and King Charles, due to the extensive Royal associations of the area – but soon after moving in, the University Council had made the bold and pioneering decision to change these outdated Royal names to names of relevant significance which also, happily, reflected Britain's, and especially London's, multicultural society and the diverse nature of the university's staff and students.

There was nowhere else in Britain that had all its buildings named after people of colour, though the councils of not a few towns and cities had got a bad case of Mandela-itis in the 1980s, naming every new-built concrete monstrosity, whether a school hall, a student union building, or any council office block, after a black South African leader who had never set foot in their town and would be unlikely to ever do so, or even know of its existence.

Crump was not entirely sure what connection Nelson Mandela, or Mary Seacole, or any of the others, had with Thames Metropolitan University or its buildings – he would do some research later – but he certainly wasn't going to question the wisdom of the name change which would, the report said, make the university 'more inclusive' and 'give black and minority ethnic students a sense of ownership'. It would hopefully also encourage applications from cash-rich foreign students as well as helping the university meet its targets in widening participation – attracting as many students as possible from low-income households, many of whom were black or Asian, thereby improving the university's place in the league tables via value-added diversity scores.

This was obviously the right decision in 21st century Britain, especially as more than half of Thames Metropolitan University's students were BME (Black and Minority Ethnic). The abbreviation had recently replaced 'ethnic minority' as the preferred term for 'non-whites', but always reminded Crump of BMX bikes, and, no matter how hard he tried, whenever he heard the phrase his mind's eye saw an surreal image of Nelson Mandela frantically pedalling a BMX bike through some South African township on the way to freedom after his years of captivity. He also wondered what on earth was wrong with the phrase 'ethnic minority' anyway, but knew how the manufacture of new words and phrases, especially referring to race or gender, was a thriving industry in the world of academics, think tanks and government departments.

As he ambled along the Wren-designed colonnade towards his destination, Crump remembered his interview earlier that year, and how he had passed several students smoking and spitting and swearing, and generally hanging around outside the Seacole building. Not one of them, he noticed, had moved out of the way to let him pass, and he had been pushed and jostled more than once as he passed students on the campus that day. The students there seemed to have no manners at all – he was sure that students would never have been so rude at his old university. But then, that would be his job: to mould those smoking and spitting and swearing students into the leaders and productive citizens of tomorrow – to build a new, equal society where anyone, of any race, from any background, could achieve and help make the world a better place. It was just a shame they couldn't all do it with good manners, that was all.

But Crump believed absolutely in his mission. He had said so in the interview as he'd discussed how he had managed diversity at his college teaching job – (this actually took up most of the interview) – and had gone into a long, detailed, explanation of why all white people were intrinsically racist, even if they didn't know it, and should feel guilt at the terrible burden of slavery that all black people had to bear, so should accept 'positive action' in all its forms even if that meant blameless white people would be disadvantaged and racially discriminated against due to their skin colour. It had gone down well, as had his statement that all institutions were guilty of institutional racism. He knew it would, and that's why he had said it. Whether or not he actually *believed* what he was saying was neither here nor there – he knew the way interviews worked and what the panel expected, and he knew the education system well too, albeit at a college and not a university.

The interview panel consisted of a bored-looking middle-aged man with a red face and a weary seen-and-heard-it-all-before look in his eyes, an obese black woman with huge white teeth in colourful African dress and hat, and a tiny, nervous, bird-like Asian woman who sat between her colleagues rather as though she were their stunted and deformed child. They were duly impressed by Crump's performance and beliefs, or so it seemed. And they never once asked about his qualifications or intelligence or education or knowledge, or whether he loved his subject, but just about how he would manage diversity through differentiation, what he knew about the latest research on learning styles and, most important of all, how he would promote equality of opportunity in his teaching – they asked him about this again and again. He gave text book, fashionable, politically correct answers, and he knew it. This is what an old friend, also in teaching but now abroad, had told him to do in his last letter – especially the bit about slavery and how all white people were racist and therefore 'positive action' was needed to redress the balance. The friend had worked in a secondary school for several years before leaving to go and teach English abroad, so knew what he was talking about.

Crump also stated that, in order to better reflect the society we live in, women should be positively encouraged to go into management, as they were 'under-represented' in senior roles, through similar programmes of 'positive action', so to more truly reflect society. He didn't agree with this kind of discrimination either, believing that people should achieve through merit and merit alone – and as a white male he was also aware that the belief that he should become a victim of racism and sexism for his gender and skin colour was not only very unfair and wrong, but would also mean that unfair discrimination against him personally was justified and right! But he wanted the job. God, he wanted the job. He gave what he thought were the right answers and, then, he got the letter two days later telling him he hadn't got it. He didn't know why.

"You could be anyone, innit?"

The obese female security guard with dyed, dark-red hair and lipstick to match stood at the entrance to the Seacole building and was refusing to let Crump in. Embarrassingly, he had forgotten his security pass – and on his first day too. A couple of young students in hoodies pushed past him, flashed their cards and swaggered into the building.

"B...but... I'm a member of staff," he said, hoping this would sort things out.

"I don't give a toss if you fink yer the master of the bleedin' universe, mate. If you ain't got no security pass you ain't comin' in."

Crump would have loved to correct her sloppy English – he

12

could even have shown her that her tautological use of negatives actually derived from the Old English Anglo-Saxon syntactical pattern, and he was sure he could have even taught her how to pronounce her Ts properly – but thought better of it. She was very large security guard woman.

"C...couldn't you, y'know, check with the department upstairs? They are expecting me..." he said.

"What, with *my* knees?"

Your knees look just as obese as every other part of you, Crump thought, but he hadn't meant for her to actually climb the stairs personally.

"No, I mean, couldn't you...y'know...call upstairs with your...?" He put his hand to his ear to signify a phone.

The security guard rolled her eyes, sighed and shook her red-haired head. Her jowls wobbled.

"Look, we're short-staffed 'ere today – I gotta check students' passes."

A couple of students rushed past without her even glancing at their passes, Crump noticed.

"Come back later, innit? Then I can call upstairs for yer," and then she added, somewhat facetiously Crump thought, the word 'sir'.

Crump really hated it when people used the word 'sir' to him, and also wished they would stop saying the word 'innit' – the obese security guard woman had just managed to use two of his most hated words in the English language, and almost in the same breath! She was clearly enjoying the power she had to pettily prevent Crump from entering the building – he felt that she could easily have called upstairs, or even let him in without calling anyone.

With his briefcase and his glasses and his jacket and tie, he hardly looked like a terrorist or a thief, but he knew that the more he protested, the more the security guard would be enjoying watching him squirm, like a big fat spider watching a fly struggling into paralysis in its web.

Embarrassingly, he felt a sudden, momentary, and

unexpected, urge to cry, but managed to swallow hard and steel himself against the adversity he was facing. He felt, bizarrely, as though he were five years old on his first day of school. It was intimidating, overwhelming and somewhat confusing, and he had a gut-wrenching knot of anxiety in his stomach – and he hadn't even entered the building yet. It was all just *so* frustrating!

"But..." the pitch of his voice was higher now, he could tell, "but... I'll be late. It's my first day."

The security guard looked at him as though he were the most pathetic man ever to walk on the face of the earth.

"Well you shoulda foughta vat when yer forgot yer pass," and then she again added, with a sneer, the sarcastically spat out word, 'sir'.

"But I..."

"What part of the word 'no' doncha understand?" she interrupted.

The security guard gave a smug smile of intransigence as she let several students into the building, again without even looking at their security passes. Just to spite him, he thought. Her flabby white cheeks wobbled as she shook her head and Crump noticed that he and the security guard were the only white faces amongst the crowd of students waiting to enter the building. He hadn't noticed until then. That was fine, though. Crump liked diversity in all its forms – his views on diversity had been what had got him the job, after all – but he couldn't help feeling that this security guard woman – this *white* security guard – was not letting him into the building *because* he was white, or, rather because his skin was *not* brown or black. Could that be true? Was he being treated in a racist manner by a white person for being white? Was that possible? Or was he just getting paranoid and frustrated? More paranoid and frustrated than usual, that is.

It was best not to jump to any conclusions. After all, he didn't actually have a security pass so she was only doing her job, and had a legal duty not to let those without passes into the building. He could have been some Islamic terrorist hell bent on blowing up students of English language and literature, for example. Not likely, but possible. It was just a shame this security guard couldn't just bend the rules a little and accept that the be-suited, bespectacled, ginger-haired man with a suitcase in front of her was almost certainly not a member of Al-Qaeda.

That damn security pass! He knew there was something else he needed to bring in on that day, but he'd been in such a rush that morning he hadn't realised that he'd forgotten anything at all until he'd reached the entrance to the Seacole building and seen the security guard asking to see people's passes. Perhaps he'd been too busy smiling to think clearly? He just knew that all that smiling would end in tears.

The security guard was now laughing and joking with a couple of students – both muscular black men of about twenty – and then she let them into the building in a way that was, Crump thought, almost sexual. In fact, it was very sexual, and there was definite body contact as the men rubbed past her. She noticed him still standing there watching her, his hair dampening in the rain. Crump felt a cold trickle of rainwater run down the back of his neck.

"Look – I can't let you in, an' I can't call upstairs coz I'm too busy – so either go home and get yer pass or come back later when I got time to call upstairs."

How long did it take to call upstairs? She had time enough to chat to students, after all. Crump couldn't help thinking that, as a security guard, she should perhaps be showing him some deference for being a university lecturer, or at least some politeness and/or helpfulness and/or respect. But as soon as the thought came into his head he was ashamed at what he recognised as snobbery on his part. It was he who should be respecting the security guard – she was, after all, on a far lower salary than him or other lecturers, and was probably struggling to afford to live in London. But then he was struggling to afford to live in London too. In fact, everybody in a normal job, and especially those on a single income, was struggling to live in London. But he knew what he meant, anyway. And, even though she was white, she rather bizarrely had the distinctive strains of Jamaican patois somewhere in her heavy London accent, which somewhat unnerved him. Was she trying to sound *black?* If so, *why?* But she had probably been very oppressed in her life, because of her class and gender, and had probably been brutalised by men too, which was why she was oppressing him. It was his duty to understand her natural reaction to a man like him, not her duty to conform to his patriarchal assumptions of superiority. But even though... She could have at least called upstairs to the department and asked if he was expected. That would have sorted everything out in an instant.

I'll be back, Crump thought – though he didn't say it. He decided he'd go somewhere to have a coffee – (he'd noticed several cafes on the High Street) – and then try and find a call box to call the department from. He didn't have a mobile phone any more – he had accidentally dropped it into the washing up a couple of weeks earlier, and even though he'd tried to dry it out it still didn't work. He hadn't got round to getting a new one yet and wasn't even sure he'd bother – he had to admit as well that he hardly ever got calls from anyone anyway and had only got the mobile in the first place for emergencies, like being attacked or kidnapped or mugged, or stuck in mud when the tide was coming in, or if his car broke down. But he didn't have a car, never went anywhere near mud, and doubted whether an attacker or kidnapper or mugger would allow him to make a call for help before any attack or kidnap or mugging took place.

And some people said mobiles could cause brain cancer – (the 'jury was out' on the matter) – so, even though he wasn't able to call his department due to his lack of a mobile phone, at least he would not be even slightly statistically increasing the probability of his getting brain cancer either, which was a plus.

There is always a bright side if you look hard enough, he

thought, as he stood getting wet in the rain. The stress of it all, however, may well have cancelled out any health benefit – Crump could feel a little nerve starting to twitch in the corner of his left eye. He reached up to hold it still and could feel it twitching under his fingertips, like a tiny insect trapped under his skin.

"It's Kevin, isn't it?" a deep voice boomed.

He turned round and saw a large red face smiling at him – it was the middle-aged man from the interview panel before the summer. Crump smiled – a friend at last.

"Y...Yes," he said, "well...people...call me Crump... actually... usually..."

"Then Crump it shall be! The name's Sandy," and with that he grasped Crump's hand and shook it hard.

Sandy looked at the security guard whose ample adipose frame was now blocking the entire entrance to the Seacole building.

"Oh for fuck's sake Tracey you old tart – let the boy in!"

"He ain't got no pass, Sandy!"

For some reason Crump couldn't remember any of the names of those that had interviewed him in June. But Sandy was one of them and now Sandy was here, and Sandy was his friend. A big boy on his first day of school to keep the bullies at bay, to show him the ropes, to be his protector, and Crump would owe him one for the favour. He wouldn't forget this, though he had to admit he was somewhat shocked at the rather sexist language usage – the word 'tart' was surely not in keeping with the gender equality policies of Thames Metropolitan University? He'd have to check, but it was unlikely that such language was ever acceptable in an academic context, except perhaps in the food technology department, which used to be domestic science, which used to be the cooking and catering department before that. But far from being offended, the security guard was *smiling* at Sandy, who, Crump now decided, smelt distinctly of alcohol – whisky, if he wasn't mistaken. The red face grinned.

"Trace, he works here – so let him in, eh?" And then, plaintively: "Look at him, he's a lost puppy."

They looked at Crump, who looked back and blinked, slightly startled at being called a 'lost puppy'. He was twenty-nine years old, an experienced college teacher about to become a university lecturer and, most importantly, he was human, not canine. What did Sandy mean, 'lost puppy'? A dribble of rainwater ran down his nose and formed a droplet at the end of it. Crump wiped it off and sniffed. He almost whimpered.

"Now what kind of a welcome is it when a grumpy bint like you makes his life difficult? Abuse of power... 'innit'!" Sandy said to Tracey the security guard, enunciating each syllable like an old roué of a Shakespearean actor.

He then smiled at Tracey and winked, and she smiled back coyly. Again, the use of the word 'bint' perplexed Crump. He had the utmost respect for women and would never call his girlfriend that, if he had one. But Sandy's charm seemed to be working.

"Don't worry 'bout Trace – she's a star really," Sandy whispered to Crump, before turning and winking again at the security guard "she's just got a thing about big black men – ain't ya Trace – so always tries to get revenge against all the white men in the world for not satisfying her in her youth."

Tracey let out an enormous rasping smoker's cough of a laugh. Sandy grinned at Crump who was somewhat confused at this change in the security guard's demeanour – she now seemed like a happy friendly person, when a moment before she'd seemed like a pain in the neck, to say the least.

"*I* satisfied you though, didn't I?" leered Sandy.

Tracey smiled widely, blushed the colour of her hair and shook her head. She seemed to be enjoying being leered at by this man, even though if Crump had behaved like that he was sure he'd be up on a charge of sexual harassment. He knew a bloke at the college who'd got into trouble for calling a female colleague 'love' and only managed to keep his job by convincing the disciplinary panel that it was a term of address to both women and men common in his native Sheffield.

Tracey shifted her vast bulk out of the doorway, with all the casual yet oft-rehearsed insouciance of a hippo rolling over in mud.

"OK Sandy – just for you then," she said, and with that she waved them into the building. "But don't – forget – yer security pass – again," she barked.

"Oh, yes...er no...er thank you," said Crump, but Tracey just rolled her eyes and sucked air into her teeth in the manner he had observed amongst black teenage boys at his college – very rude, perhaps, but an Afro-Caribbean cultural mannerism to which one must be sensitive.

But Tracey the security guard was white. Pasty, even. Perhaps she *had* been obstructive to him because he was white, after all. Perhaps she *did* hate white men? But she didn't hate Sandy, and Sandy was white. But then, Sandy had 'satisfied' her, apparently. An image of Tracey the obese security guard standing naked squeezed itself into his mind and Crump suddenly and momentarily felt rather queasy.

"Don't worry about Tracey – she may look like an ugly fat-arsed cow, but she's not so bad really."

"Oh," said Crump, not knowing what else to say – and really rather taken aback by the words 'ugly', 'fat-arsed' and 'cow', though acknowledging that he had thought exactly the same things about her moments earlier.

He followed Sandy along the ground floor corridor of the Seacole building and past the lifts where a large crowd of students was hanging around. The doors of one of the two lifts opened and some waiting students pushed their way into the lift, with no consideration for queuing or who was nearest the doors, or for letting the lift's occupants out first. Two Chinese-looking girls looked particularly frightened as they just about managed to leave the lift in one piece. Crump looked on at this scrum and Sandy shook his head.

"Welcome to the glorious seat of learning that is Thames Metropolitan University," said Sandy, "Don't ever bother with the lifts – we're only on the first floor anyway – and the last thing you'll want to be doing is standing in a confined space with some of *our* students." And then he added, loudly, "Bloody animals!"

Sandy laughed and one of the small, frightened-looking girls turned round – she looked like she was about to cry. Crump looked back at her, wanting to help, but not knowing how to. The students in the lift stood silent and staring at him. A couple of them started smirking and laughing as the lift doors closed. One of the Chinese girls burst into tears and ran off, comforted by the other.

"Come on Crumpet, up the stairs," called Sandy.

Nobody had called Kevin Crump 'Crumpet' since school. He hated it – hated it so much he couldn't say; hated it with all his heart and every fibre of his being; hated it because whenever he heard that word it all came flooding back – those times at school, all the name-calling, the bullying, all of that. The past. The pain. And he didn't even like crumpets very much!

But Sandy had saved him, got him into the building and was now, he had decided, his one and only friend at the university. Crump decided to say nothing. He would mention it later, when he was settled in, if Sandy continued to use the nick-name. He was Crump, and Crump he would stay – he would make that clear from the start. But not just now. Even though now was the start. He would make it clear soon, anyway...

He was rather surprised to see Sandy bounding up the stairs two at a time. It was a job to keep up with him, and Crump was out of breath when he reached the top. Amazingly, the middle-aged, grey-haired, red-faced, grinning man standing in front of him wasn't in the slightest bit breathless and stood at the top of the stairs waiting for Crump like a cocky teenager waiting for his out-of-shape, middle-aged, flabby dad.

"My name's Sandy and I'm an alcoholic," Sandy bellowed at Crump as he climbed the stairs, "that's why I'm as fit as a flea."

"Oh, right," said Crump, panting and out of breath, and not knowing what else to say.

"Joking, old boy, joking – I just likes me tot o' whisky from time to time – I'm not a *real* alcoholic."

"Oh, right..."

"And I'm absolutely bloody determined to live for as long as possible – I've got two years to go to retirement, and I want every single fucking penny of that pension I've been waiting for – for nearly thirty fucking years..."

Crump finally reached the top of the stairs, wheezing like a sickly child.

"So there's absolutely no bloody chance whatsoever of my drinking myself to death, no matter how much they'd all like me to."

Crump had just had time to register what he'd said and wonder who 'they' might be exactly, and why they would want him to drink himself to death, and whether he had really been a lecturer for thirty years, when Sandy was off again, marching down the first floor corridor to the right of the stairwell.

"Follow me, my dear boy! Follow me!" he called as he strode off.

Crump scurried after Sandy, who was now walking down the corridor at speed and humming, for some reason, the theme from Indiana Jones. He didn't know why, but Crump felt like a naughty eight year old following his headmaster to his study to be punished. Sandy marched to the end of the building, turned a corner and continued marching down an identical corridor.

The name and number of the room he was meant to go to was on the letter the university had sent him, but Crump had forgotten to bring it with him, together with his security pass – and he had also forgotten to bring his welcome pack, which had details of where his office was located and where the staff room was, though it wasn't called a staff room at all – it was called a 'team room'. It was the same at the further education college – the staff room was called a team room there too, and had been for couple of years, though Crump had mistakenly called it a *tea-room* for his first term there and only noticed his mistake when a colleague facetiously pointed out with a smirk that he could have coffee, too, at break time if he so desired.

'Why couldn't things be called what they were any more?' thought Crump, as he hurried after Sandy – it would all be so much easier if they were. How does the phrase 'team room' improve on the phrase 'staff room' in any way whatsoever? But Crump knew why and how these things happened. A manager would go on *'a course'* and come back pumped up with American-style corporate management psychobabble and all the latest buzz-words, and everyone would have to stop using the perfectly good words and phrases they were all used to, and replace them with silly new phrases which made no sense. This, allegedly, was called progress.

After reaching the end of the second, longer corridor, which ran parallel to a busy road Crump could see from the window, they emerged into the foyer of the department – more specifically, the Department of Cultural, Creative and Communicative Studies where he was now a junior lecturer. There was a very modern-looking glass door and partition through which Crump could see the department's two secretaries at work on their computers. He remembered these from his interview too – they were both large, middle-aged women, one white, one black, and were clearly not to be messed with. The withering look the white one had given him when he had got lost before his interview the previous June made him feel about three feet tall, probably smaller. Crump suspected that this particular secretary, with short hair and a gruff, sneering manner was probably a lesbian, but he certainly wasn't going to risk enquiring, and it wasn't relevant anyway, of course – she would be just as intimidating whether straight or gay. There were easy chairs and a rack of leaflets and magazines in the department foyer, and a couple of worried-looking young students were leafing through magazines nervously as they waited.

"Come on, come on! Don't want to be late for our first departmental meeting now, do we?" boomed Sandy, emphasising the 'mental' of departmental loudly as he said it.

All in all, Sandy seemed rather a cynical man, but he was clearly at home in the department and Crump was sure he could learn a lot from him: everybody needs someone on their side.

Crump had no idea that there was to be a meeting that morning. He had expected just to arrive at his office – (though he couldn't remember the exact number of the office, but he could always ask someone) – and get down to the business of settling in. He had an appointment with his immediate manager and mentor, as well as with the head of department the next day, but hadn't expected any meetings at all on that day. Crump was sure that this hadn't been mentioned in any information in any letter or welcome pack he had received, but maybe it had been. He would have to check at home later, but surely he would have remembered something like that? Surely they would have let him know about it? If not, then why hadn't he been informed?

He followed Sandy down a corridor leading off the foyer, and suddenly felt rather annoyed at not being told of this meeting, but decided not to mention it to anyone. It was his first day, after all – he didn't want to get a reputation for complaining. He had to accept that he was a last minute stand-in for this job – and, unlike everyone else, he hadn't had the whole of the summer to prepare for the new term either. It was best, in such situations, to keep one's head down and try not to be noticed, although he was aware that the smeary white bird-shit stain on his jacket may have been having the opposite effect.

Sandy swung open a door marked 'TEAM ROOM' and held it open. He was here at last, in his department, in the bosom of academe. The future, Crump thought to himself smugly, was wide open. Like an oyster, a door or a box. Or possibly, even, a vagina.

He went inside.

CHAPTER TWO

Settling In

Crump was sitting alone in his new office, thinking.

He hadn't really been expecting to share with three other junior lecturers, or to have so little space – his desk was both tiny and wobbly, rather like something that could have been picked up in a jumble sale, and he had to share one grey metal filing cabinet with another lecturer too. Even worse, there was only one narrow bookshelf on the wall. How would he manage that? He had piles of books at home. But he would just have to make do, somehow – bring in some boxes – pile up a few books under the desk perhaps. Or limit the books he kept at the university. Of course, they were bound to be pushed for space in such a successful department. By that logic, it would have been worrying if he'd had plenty of room for his books and an office all to himself – that would probably mean that the department wasn't thriving at all. So, in a way, it was a relief that there wasn't enough room to swing a lesson plan.

At least he had a computer, though it did look rather old. He turned it on – it whirred and crunched and took ages to warm up, like an old black and white TV – but without a password couldn't access the system, so he turned it off again. He'd ask his mentor for a password later. He didn't want to make a bad impression by complaining about the details of his office arrangements, especially on his first day; he knew he was lucky to be working there at all.

At West London College nobody in the English department had their own office. The more senior full-time staff had a desk in a large aircraft-hangar-like room which looked like some Kafka-esque nightmare and made him depressed whenever he stepped into it to collect things from his pigeon hole. The more junior full-time staff and part-timers just had to use any available surface in the 'team room' where the full-timers also went to have coffee or have a chat, or even go downstairs to the staff canteen. Crump had never had a desk at the college – in fact, never in his working life had he had his own desk before. But there it was, in front of where he sat – a desk. *His* desk, in *his* office. It didn't matter at all that he would be sharing the room with three others. Actually, it would be good to be able to get to know some other members of staff. He hoped they'd be good company.

One day he'd have his own office to himself anyway, so there was no need to rush. This office was just fine for now. And his desk *was* by the window, so there was rather a nice view. Not that he had chosen it – when he entered the room after the meeting he had found a little card on the desk with his name on it to show it had been allocated to him. But he probably would have chosen this desk for himself if he could have – he much preferred to be sitting at this desk, by the window, than one of the others, by the door.

Looking out from where he sat he could see the rustling trees outside, and when he stood up he could see past the black, metal railings marking the university boundary, past the pavement, past the cars and buses trundling by on the busy road, and on to the greenery of Greenwich Park beyond. This, he decided, would be a perfect desk at which to think, ponder and work. It was an *intellectual* desk.

"Good morning, I am Rajdeep," a voice said behind him in an Indian accent.

Crump turned round.

"But you can call me Raj. I am new lecturer here".

Crump had seen him earlier at the meeting in the team room.

"Oh....yes...me too. I'm Crump," he said, "Kevin Crump."

Raj smiled widely.

"I am very pleased to be meeting you, Kevin Crump. We are both new lecturers starting on same day! Now we are neighbours eh?"

And with that Raj shook his hand so enthusiastically that he thought a small bone in it might have been broken. Crump winced, but with a smile, and he hoped Raj hadn't noticed that the expression on his face was one of mild, but not insignificant, pain.

"Neighbours...yes," said Crump.

Raj examined the desk adjacent to Crump's and tried out the chair, sitting down hard and noisily on it several times. Although rather short, Raj was also noticeably plump, and Crump feared that the rickety wooden chair might splinter under the strain.

"Nice view," said Crump, nodding to the window. Raj looked out of the window momentarily, but seemed unimpressed at the trees.

"This is good chair," said Rajdeep cheerily, bouncing up and down on it, "I am liking this chair."

"Good," said Crump, baffled at why such a shabby chair should inspire such pleasure.

He was not a chair-expert, he would be the first to admit, but the chairs they had been given were most certainly nothing special. They were actually just bog-standard, crappy, old wooden chairs – the kind that a school or a college would probably put on a bonfire and replace with something more comfortable so as not to be sued by their students for chair-induced injuries. Not that he was complaining – he was happy with his chair too. It had four legs, a seat and a back, and could be sat on. It was, in short, a *successful* chair.

"Not much space, isn't it?" said Raj looking around the room and at the narrow bookshelves attached to the wall.

"It's going to be tricky to find space for all my books," Crump said, nodding at his own limited bookshelf space.

Raj frowned, deep in thought, then smiled brightly.

"Maybe we could... say something. Report it. To university managers."

"Maybe we could," said Crump, deliberately non-committal.

Raj grinned widely, then looked around the room, blinked and then gave a little yelp of pleasure. Crump smiled at his cheerful new colleague.

"You know, ever since I was little boy – in India – I was dreaming of coming to England – to London – world city – and now, well, look at me – I am a lecturer at British university – and everybody is knowing Great Britain is having some of best universities in whole world!"

Raj sighed with pleasure and sat back in his happy chair. His enthusiasm was infectious, and Crump felt better that he was not the only one with a knackered old desk and a rickety chair in a cramped office. Like new boys starting at a new school at the same time, they would be firm friends, Crump knew. They would have to stick together, give each other support and advice – that sort of thing.

Suddenly, the door flew open. Two young women came into the office together and sat down at the desks near the door. They'd been in the meeting too. One of them – a short, dark-haired, plumpish woman of about thirty – smiled at Crump and he smiled back, shyly. He knew from experience at the college that some women could take an innocent smile the wrong way – even as a leery, sexist gesture – so it was best for any man to keep a distance until he knew his colleagues better. The other woman was older, in her forties Crump thought, and had long, lank, platinum blonde hair, which may have been grey – Crump couldn't tell. The most noticeable thing about her, though, was that she was pencil thin – she looked skeletally underweight and dangerously pale. She didn't make eye contact with anyone and remained unsmiling as she sat at her desk, frowning and pale, like a ghost, or a corpse, or something in between. If she'd been cut she probably would have bled white. Crump thought it only polite to introduce himself. He stood up.

"The name's Crump," Crump said, extending a hand to the dark woman who had smiled at him.

"Hi. I'm Athena," and she shook his hand with a broad, warm smile, "from Greece, originally."

Raj introduced himself too with his usual cheery enthusiasm. This woman seemed friendly and easy-going, and Crump instantly liked her. She also spoke excellent English, with only a slight accent, and he secretly hoped she might teach him a few words of Greek at some time. He had been planning to visit a friend in Greece at some stage, and it would be good to have a few words of the lingo.

It turned out that all four of them were starting their first lecturing jobs in their first universities on the same day, including the ghostly-pale skeletal woman who, although she seemed too old to be beginning her career, was taking up her first appointment too – she had come to lecturing as a career change having just graduated from Thames Metropolitan with a Master's in 'gender representation in the media'.

Crump thought it would have been better to have put some more experienced lecturers in with new staff, but then the university obviously knew what it was doing. If he'd been a lecturer there for years he'd want a private office all to himself too – and he would surely get one in time. It's just that there would be nobody on hand to ask if they needed any help or advice of any kind – but then, the other lecturers, as well as the department secretaries, and managers, were only a short walk down the corridor. It wasn't as though they'd all been 'dumped' into the fray without any support.

"Hi, I'm Crump," said Crump to the skeletal blonde, extending a hand.

She looked up at him from her desk with cold blue eyes that reminded Crump of splinters of ice, but which, paradoxically, seemed to be burning with hatred for some reason. She turned away without taking his hand and looked terribly upset and put out. For a horrifying moment Crump thought she was about to cry. Then, suddenly, and purposefully, she stood up and stormed out of the room, rage in her eyes, and slammed the door behind her. A baffled Crump looked at Athena.

"Cecilia is not happy about sharing an office," she said.

"We would all be liking a little bit more room," said Rajdeep, "but the beggars cannot be the choosers!"

"No, you don't understand – she has special needs."

Crump and Raj simultaneously wondered what these special needs were that made the skeletal ghost woman so rude and aggressive. Perhaps she was anorexic – he'd heard eating disorders and other mental illnesses and disorders could cause emotional outbursts, as could medication. Perhaps that's what he had witnessed?

"Oh, special needs," said Crump, nodding thoughtfully.

From his time teaching at college, he was well used to the educational obsession with special needs and learning 'difficulties' such as dyslexia – a catch-all term for difficulty with reading and writing which, controversially, many eminent experts believed did not even exist. He also knew that assigning behaviours to 'special needs' or 'disorders' had become the new orthodoxy, not to mention offering career options and profit-making opportunities to a great many individuals and companies.

He was, he had to confess, guilty of using the label to give unfair advantage to his college students in the past – such as extra time in exams. But why shouldn't he work the system? All the most famous private schools in the UK were expert and adept at using such tricks to rig the system in their favour, and thereby get better results for their students and a better placing in the league tables, so why shouldn't he? These days, there wasn't a private school in the land that didn't have a large percentage of pupils with special needs – usually dyslexia, dyspraxia or dyscalcula, and quite possibly dystopia and dyspepsia too – and they were advantaged because of it. The state schools and colleges didn't play the system nearly so well, but were rapidly catching up, labelling ever more students as special needs every year. They were *learning*, which was rather appropriate, considering their *raison d'être* being other people's learning.

Crump had even considered claiming that he had special needs himself – all you needed was a certificate from a psychologist, and clinical judgement was notoriously subjective and subject to fashion, not to mention income. He'd known several people, including some very well educated and literate teachers, who had deliberately got such a certificate in order to claim special advantage and perks, such as a free laptop from the college, or employment and training opportunities. It was, quite simply, a racket, and people played the system shamelessly, whether or not the 'special-needs-ification' of education was valid or not.

"What *kind* of special needs is she having exactly? asked Raj.

Athena sighed, and sat down at her desk.

"Well... I don't know really...but... I think it may be some kind of phobia."

"Phobia?" said Crump.

Some kind of phobia? What did that mean? His mind flicked through the common phobias he knew of: claustrophobia, arachnophobia, agoraphobia, acrophobia – (the fear of heights usually confused with vertigo) – as well as the more political and modern, semantically incorrect ones: Islamophobia and homophobia, the latter always conjuring images in Crump's head of a person frightened and hateful of mobile homes. There were literally thousands of phobias out there, he knew, and plenty of ancient Greek words left to name thousands more. The human brain was so complex and mysterious that it would, he was sure, be possible for somebody to have a phobia about anything at all – even phobias.

"What... *kind* of phobia, exactly?" asked Rajdeep, looking puzzled.

Athena seemed slightly uncomfortable, making Crump

wonder what phobia the skeletal ghost-woman could be suffering from. Food? People? Politeness perhaps?

"Well," said Athena, "it seems that Cecilia has a phobia of...men."

They looked at Athena, who shrugged and smiled back weakly.

"Men? But that is absurdity," laughed Raj, "how can anybody be having phobia about half of human race?"

"Less than half actually," mumbled Athena, but Raj ignored her.

"Maybe she just... doesn't like men?" said Crump.

"Oh no, it's a real phobia – she has a certificate from a psychologist," Athena pronounced the p in psychologist, he noticed, "and the university has recognised her special needs – and told her they would make arrangements to accommodate her."

"But she can't *not* talk to any men at all – she has to teach male students, surely?" said Crump, slightly uncomfortable with the double negative.

"I know, and she said she could do that so long as she could mentally prepare herself for the shock of teaching them before lessons," said Athena, "... but... she was promised an office sharing with women, not with...well...you...or any..."

"Men?" said Crump.

"Yes," said Athena.

"Perhaps," said Rajdeep, "she shouldn't have been becoming lecturer – perhaps she should be becoming nun or some such?"

"I know, I think it's very strange," said Athena.

"Isn't there a place in Greece where you are having only men?" asked Raj.

"Yes, Prince Charles went there on holiday, didn't he?" added Crump, remembering a news story from years before.

"Oh you mean the Orthodox monastery on Athos, in the north of Greece – only men allowed, and only male animals too – it's tradition – except cats – the females are better at killing –

mice...not... men..." Athena's words trailed off and she looked a bit embarrassed, "You must think we are very weird in Greece."

"Maybe it is shame they are not having place like that for women in UK – then Cecilia would be happy as the pig in the poo-poo."

Raj had momentarily lost his cheerfulness and looked quite cross.

"Why everyone in this country is having 'special needs' nowadays? Were British having *'special needs'* when they were building greatest empire whole world was ever seeing? No. So why they are needing them now?"

He had a point, and there was no answer Crump could give him. Even though he was relatively young, he couldn't remember so many people being diagnosed as having any kind of special needs when he was at school either. It seemed a very modern thing, probably originating in America – like rock and roll, drive-by shootings and enormously fat people.

"Why people are not just being normal anymore," asked Raj slumping on the chair at his desk, as much as it was possible to slump on a small and rickety wooden chair.

"What's normal?" asked Athena, and for a moment they all sat staring at each other in silence at the profundity of this quandary.

Both Crump and Raj were thinking the same thing: whatever normal was, Cecilia wasn't it. And they were simultaneously hoping that they would never be forced to share an office with such an unpleasant and disturbed individual too.

Half an hour later, after organising their desks, the three of them decided to go and have lunch together in Greenwich. Cecilia had not yet returned to the office, and would not have joined them anyway on account of two of them being disgustingly and irredeemably male. No doubt she was being relocated to another office in the building, and was probably at that moment demanding a female-only space because of her 'special needs' which, Crump admitted silently to himself, didn't seem to extend beyond being a bitter and twisted man-hating head-case.

On Raj's suggestion, they decided to cut through the public gardens in the direction of the Thames, where the tourist attraction of the Cutty Sark was in dry dock. They wouldn't pay to go on board but just have a look from the outside – they were now going to be working only a short distance away so they'd be able to have a proper look at any time. They all decided to go for a pub lunch, especially now that the drizzle had stopped – the sun was peeping out from clouds now and again, making the honey-coloured stone of the campus buildings look exquisitely beautiful.

As they walked along, Crump thought how lucky he was to be working in such a superb location – a campus comprising historic buildings in a World Heritage Site, right next to the river and just a short hop from central London and all that had to offer. He knew he'd be happy here – he just knew it.

"There," said Raj, "there she is!"

Raj pointed at the sky in front of them and Crump followed the direction of his pointing finger – he could see the Cutty Sark's masts too, standing proud against the white and cloudy September sky. Raj was as excited as a special needs schoolboy on exam results day, and both Athena and Crump smiled at his enthusiasm.

"You haven't been here before?" asked Athena.

"No," said Raj, "this is only second time I am coming in Greenwich – once for interview for job, and today. Oh look!"

And with that, Raj could contain his excitement no longer and started to run towards the Cutty Sark as quickly as his little legs could carry him. Crump and Athena hurried after him – his excitement was infectious – and both were trying not to laugh at the sight of Raj, a short and rotund man, attempting to sprint towards the river.

"How about you...er...Crump?" asked Athena.

"Of course," said Crump, "when I was about ten, with the school, and then again when I was about... fifteen I think."

"Oh really?"

"I'm originally from the London suburbs – and everyone from there has been to see the Cutty Sark – it's tradition," said Crump, "but I haven't been on board since that last time – when I was a teenager."

"We should go on board sometime – you can show it to me, as you know all about it."

"Oh I wouldn't say I knew all about it..."

Crump suddenly realised that Athena was, perhaps, asking him out on a sort-of date, even if it was to wander round an old ship that, quite frankly, Crump found rather dull when he was ten, and even more so when he was fifteen, and would no doubt find less than scintillating on his next visit. Truth was, Crump was not in the slightest bit interested in maritime things – a bit of a shame really, what with his now being in Greenwich, but it just wasn't his bag. History, yes – but there were more interesting places to visit than the Cutty Sark because, bluntly, once you've seen one ship you've seen 'em all, though he realised that ship enthusiasts might disagree. But he tried his best to empathise with Raj's excitement – if he'd never been there before perhaps he would be excited too. Maybe. A bit, anyway.

"OK," said Crump.

Athena smiled.

"It'd be great for Raj too – to go on board a ship like this."

Crump suddenly realised that when she said 'we' she hadn't meant only the two of them, but Raj too. After feeling momentarily annoyed, most of all at his own misunderstanding, he agreed with her – it would indeed be good for the three of them to get to know each other seeing as they'd be sharing an office for the foreseeable future. Perhaps soon there'd be a fourth lecturer in their office who could join them too?

The Cutty Sark was the last surviving tea clipper from the 19th century – it was, essentially, the jumbo jet of its day, able to transport goods, mostly tea, from the Far East to Europe at what were high speeds for the day. A dry cargo of tea would make a handsome profit too for investors – (at today's prices, tea cost £800 a pound three hundred years ago, or about £8 a teabag) – provided that the ship made it back to Europe with a dry cargo, at least.

Crump remembered his first time there as a ten year old in the third year of primary school. He had left his packed lunch on the coach so, while the rest of the schoolchildren sat on the grass, probably in the garden they had just walked through, eating their sandwiches and crisps after viewing the ship, he had had to sit watching them, pangs of noisy hunger growling in his tummy. His teacher at the time, a horrible spiteful woman, had told him he deserved to go hungry as a lesson in life, and said he would make sure he wouldn't leave his packed lunch on the coach again, wouldn't he? No, actually – he did exactly the same thing five years later when he visited with his secondary school. He had never got on with packed lunches really – something always seemed to happen when they were involved. He didn't know why.

Raj could have stayed there all day, looking up admiringly at the Cutty Sark in its dry dock, with its masts and the brightly-painted figurehead, reading every single word on every single notice he could find. Crump could tell Athena was getting bored or tired or both, so suggested going for lunch, and as it was his first day in his new job, he said he'd treat them too. Raj was, happily, just as enthusiastic about this as he had been about the Cutty Sark, and judging from his build, Crump could tell he was no stranger to substantial and regular meals. There was a pub visible from where they were standing so they thought they might as well try there. The drizzle was starting again too, so they walked quickly over to it and went inside.

Crump offered to buy them all a drink, and was happy to see that Raj was not teetotal, although he wasn't sure if he was Muslim or Hindu or if he had any other religious affiliation. If he had been teetotal, Crump wouldn't have minded, but the fact that he wasn't would mean that they'd be able to go for drinks after work, nursing their pints and relaxing as they discussed academic issues – the mismatch of the sober with the drunk is always starkly annoying to all concerned. He'd actually been expecting more change from a twenty pound note for the drinks but then everything was expensive these days, especially in London.

They all sat down at a dark wooden table in the corner. Crump took a large sip of his lager – perhaps more of a glug. It would do him good, he thought, after all the stress of the morning, but his relaxation was not to last long.

There were no menus on the pub tables, but the day's fare was chalked up on a board on the main wall. Raj and Athena were already looking at it, but when Crump looked at it he almost spat out his lager at the prices. Bangers and mash – or, as the pub menu described it, two organic farm sausages with Dijon mustard mash, was £9.99. Ten quid for bangers and mash! Worse, fish and chips – or as they called it, beer-battered Atlantic cod and organic hand-cut potato wedges – was £11.99! But there at the bottom of the extortionate menu, past the organic lasagne and the vegetarian options – (a salad for £8.99!) – was the stuff of nightmares: organic T-bone steak with organic hand-cut potato wedges and organic Tuscan-style broccoli for £19.99! He knew, just knew, that Raj would choose this, after a waitress brought two plates of said steak to a neighbouring table. It looked good. Small, but good. And expensive. Extortionate, even.

"The steak is looking quite delicious," said Raj, licking his lips.

"Fish and chips for me," said Athena, "Can't get more British than that!"

"And also side salad – this is always going well with steak," said Raj, "Healthy eating eh!"

Crump smiled, his mind spinning through the calculations – the lagers had already cost over ten quid, and the steak, and the fish and chips plus salad would cost him over fifty quid!

Fifty flipping quid! With his order – he would have the fish and chips too, so that was another £11.99 – that would be over sixty quid for a pub lunch! He certainly wouldn't make the same mistake again by eating there – it was a tourist area after all, what with the Cutty Sark and the Royal Observatory up the road. Crump finished his drink – he noticed, however, that the others had not even drunk half of theirs, so wouldn't be buying a round, so he'd have to get himself another pint too.

They ordered their meals from a waitress whose English sounded more like rough Spanish with an occasional English word thrown in for luck – even as a specialist in English language and literature, and having taught many foreign students, Crump struggled to understand her. She also had a large, tight, pus-filled spot – on her eyebrow of all places – that Crump couldn't stop focusing on. He hoped she had understood the order but, if he were to be truthful to himself, he didn't much care any more – whatever it was it would be expensive. Beans on toast would probably be called Tuscan-style beans with organic tomatoes on hand-made bruscetta, and cost ten quid. It was with some relief, and feeling slightly queasy, that he dragged himself away from the view of the enormous yellow zit on the Spanish waitress's brow, and went to order another drink at the bar.

The barman was foreign too – he sounded East European, probably Polish from the accent and the Slavic features – but spoke adequate and functional English, Crump was pleased to discover. While his drink was being poured he looked around at the other people in the pub – something was a bit odd about them, he thought, as he surveyed the scene.

And then he got it – he realised he was in a pub entirely populated by foreign people – in short, a tourist pub. After listening to the languages spoken and the accented English, he also realised he was the only native English speaker in the pub. This, in itself, would have been fine – but what it meant was that he had stumbled into a pub that was, more or less, a tourist trap.

He had forgotten that, to most people, Greenwich was not a place to work and live, but a touristic place to visit, with correspondingly inflated prices. The mistake was costing him over sixty quid! For lunch! He made a mental note to explore the area at a later date to find pubs and eateries that were more in the price range of a new and aspiring lecturer – there had to be some normal reasonably-priced pubs skulking somewhere in the south London side streets.

Crump sat down at their table and took several large mouthfuls of his lager. Fortunately, it was starting to make him pleasantly mellow and he felt the stress of the day, even the stress of the eye-watering prices, evaporate through the pores in his skin like steam. He smiled warmly at Athena.

"This is nice," he said, stupidly.

"Yes," said Athena.

"Most agreeable," said Raj.

It was, in an average and expensive way.

After lunch, Crump was pleased to see that Tracey the security guard was still at the door and, with nothing more than an annoyed 'don't-do-it-again' look, she let him into the department despite his still not having his security pass. He would buy Sandy a drink at some time to say thank you for his help in getting past her that morning.

"You should never go in there, old boy," Sandy said later when Crump passed him on the corridor, "Strictly for the tourist fodder – full of bloody foreigners doncha know! We'll go out for a real session one night."

"Oh – a pub crawl?" said Crump.

"Of course a bloody pub crawl!"

"But... I live miles away," said Crump.

"Well I don't – you can crash at my place. Always room chez Sandy."

Crump agreed – it would be great to get an introduction to what Greenwich had to offer from a local, and an experienced drinker at that. They would make arrangements later.

It was annoying to live so far away. He would have to do

something about that – get somewhere closer to the university. The rent for the dingy bedsit in West London took almost half of his college salary anyway, so he doubted he'd have to pay more for the same somewhere in South-east London.

Back at the department, Crump decided to familiarise himself with both the staff and student handbooks, as well as the university prospectus. He had read through the staff handbook before – he'd been sent it before the interview and also another copy a fortnight earlier. It was at home with his security pass, his keys and his letter from the university on the sideboard. But it was never a bad thing to read these things several times, as Crump had learnt from his time teaching at the college. If one was familiar with all staff procedures, the range of courses offered, and the makeup of the student population, one would have a better idea of any issues that may arise before they did. 'Be prepared' as they used to say in cubs, and they were not wrong.

That afternoon, the new staff from all departments had a separate meeting to welcome them to the university. It was held in a lecture hall in the Mandela building, and was attended by around forty people. Crump sat at the back with Raj and Athena – he always liked to do this, so he could survey the scene and see who was present at the lecture. He noticed from this vantage point that he was not only one of the few male staff present – he and Raj were two of only seven men, he counted – but also one of only five white people there, and the other four were women. This could only be a good thing, thought Crump, at a university where more than half of the student body was BME and with so many international students too.

There were, Crump also noticed, several women present wearing headscarves and one was even covered from head to foot in a burqa – a black whole-body and face covering, with just a little slit for the eyes. He wondered which department she would be teaching in and whether the inability of anyone to be able to see her face would be conducive to successful learning outcomes. How could anyone actually teach with their face masked like that? He knew research showed that around 70% of comprehension by a listener relied on visual clues in the shape of the speaker's mouth and their expression, and only around 30% on what was actually said – (this was always an issue when it came to testing the listening skills of learners of English as a foreign language) – so anyone trying to understand someone without being able to see their face would be severely disadvantaged.

The lecture was given by a large, depressed-looking woman in a trouser suit with a monotonous, male-sounding voice that droned on for what seemed like hours, though the lecture lasted less than half an hour according to Crump's watch. Perhaps it had stopped. Or perhaps time did really move more slowly sometimes, and Einstein was right all along. The woman was the head of staff welfare, she said, and was called Mandy. Unbelievably, it turned out that her surname was 'Pandy'. Mandy Pandy? Crump stifled a giggle when he read the name at the bottom of the handout and coughed to hide it – especially as Mandy was at that very moment talking about the undeniably downbeat issue of the high suicide rate amongst lecturers, and the counselling services available to them at the university. No wonder she looked depressed, thought Crump, if she'd had parents who'd named her Mandy Pandy. Though perhaps she was lucky not to be a boy, or he would surely have been christened Andy, or Sandy – or perhaps even Randy.

After Mandy Pandy's lecture, they were handed the obligatory feedback questionnaire that they were encouraged to complete there and then. All universities did this now, aping the corporate world in its obsession with customer feedback. Crump gave her 'extremely satisfied' for everything, partly because he thought she needed cheering up, and partly because the two pints of strongish lager had put him in a good mood – though he was a bit baffled about the question about how well the lecturer had 'promoted equal opportunity and diversity'. She was giving an introductory talk to new lecturers on staff welfare, not giving a lesson on equality policies. He gave her an 'extremely satisfied' anyway – well, she had given exactly the same tedious, droning lecture to everyone, irrespective of race or gender or age or sexuality or disability, so that was equality, in a way – it was equally dull and tedious for all.

Afterwards, they all followed Mandy Pandy over to the 'Stephen Lawrence Learning Zone', which everyone called a library, because that is what it was. There, they were greeted by a nervous young Asian woman in a headscarf called Miss Sharma who proceeded to show them around every part of the library in what Crump thought was a very patronising manner, as though they had never been in a library before or knew how to use one. That is, until he heard some of the questions his fellow new lecturers were asking her. They ranged from details about how one took a book out, to how to find a book in a particular subject on the shelves – Crump remembered having the same sort of lecture when he was a teenager starting university. In fact, he remembered having the same kind of talk when he started secondary school at the age of twelve.

Hadn't these people – these new lecturers at a university, these tyro academics – used a library before? He was somewhat perplexed. One man in particular, a young black guy in a hoodie and a baseball cap who introduced himself as Kwame, seemed utterly amazed that he could take several books out of the library at once. He knew a lot of the staff were from developing countries, which used to be called the 'Third World', and maybe Kwame was too – but surely the few universities they had there had libraries that lent out books too?

Crump had never been to a developing country – in fact he always wondered what exactly developing countries were supposed to be 'developing' into – but from what he'd heard they had some very good and traditional schools and, perhaps due to a permanent lack of funds, had a great respect for books and education generally.

It was only after they'd been on the tour and were walking

together out of the library that Crump realised, after eavesdropping on a conversation between Kwame and another new lecturer, that he was not from a developing country at all. He was London born and bred, and Crump had only struggled to understand him due to his extremely thick, 'street', inner London accent. Crump also learnt that this man would be teaching English language in Crump's department which was, frankly, ridiculous, if not incredible. How could someone who spoke such bad and unintelligible English, and who didn't know how to use a library, teach English at a university, especially in the Department of Cultural, Creative and Communicative Studies? P.E. or 'sports studies', yes. Woodwork and metalwork and food technology – well, why not? Geography, business and media studies, quite possibly. But *English*?

Back in the department, Crump organised his desk as best he could – he mentally mapped out where he would put his books, and which to bring in from home. He'd have to be very selective – there was only space for about ten books maximum on the shelf space allocated to him. Raj and Athena had already brought some of their books and papers, so busied themselves organising their desks, both of which looked less bare than his own – but then, they had been able to prepare over the summer. It would all come together in time, thought Crump, and soon his bookshelf would be bulging with books and his desk would be a veritable hive of academic activity, piled no doubt with essay papers to mark, lesson plans and lecture notes. He would also be able to use his computer when he got his password, which would be a plus.

If he were honest with himself, he had to admit that the stress of the morning and the alcohol of lunchtime hadn't exactly made him eager to get down to work. At that moment, what he felt like doing more than anything else was going back to the pub – or *a* pub, at least, and a less expensive one – and knocking back a couple more pints, and then having a little snooze. He had been sitting at his desk looking out of the window at the trees with his hands behind his head for perhaps several minutes when he was awoken from his daydream by a loud knock at the door.

He looked round to find that he was alone, even though he couldn't remember Raj or Athena leaving the room. Perhaps he'd even been asleep? Or having one of those micro-sleeps that cause car crashes? It unnerved him that he couldn't remember and felt momentarily that he was about to be cross-examined about his whereabouts that afternoon, as though he were some psycho who'd gone on the rampage but hadn't been able to remember a thing about it. But at least he hadn't been driving a car, so that was a stroke of luck.

Crump looked at the door blankly. The loud knock came again – the same three loud raps as the first time. Then he remembered that, in fact, this was his office, even though it was shared, and that he was actually meant to be there and not an imposter. He sighed in relief.

"Come in," Crump called, for perhaps the first time in his life.

The door opened and the guy in the hoodie with the baseball cap – Kwame – from the library poked his head round the door.

"This Two-Oh-Four?" the young man said.

"Yes – yes, it is," said Crump.

"Thank fuck fer dat – I's been all round diss place innit."

He came in and looked around. Crump sat up in his chair. Apart from his accent, which was heavy London street-speak, Kwame sort of slurred and mumbled the words together when he spoke, making him difficult to understand. Crump, usually so good at understanding people with strong accents, strained to hear what he was saying. He wondered if Kwame might have some kind of speech impediment – a special need to be considered. Or maybe he'd had a stroke? Crump felt guilty for failing to understand every word Kwame said.

"Sorry, but..." Crump said.

Why was this illiterate from the library there, in his office?

43

"Oh right yeah," the man smiled at Crump, "I come ta join ya innit."

"You have?"

"Yeah man – dis my office innit! Dey tell me come here coz like woman teacher like move an shit coz of some beef an ting – so dey give me dis innit?"

Amazingly, Crump understood most of what he said this time.

"Oh – you mean you're replacing Cecilia?"

"Das what I said innit?"

"Oh OK – that was Cecilia's desk there," and Crump gestured to the desk near the door.

"Oh... right – das shit innit. But das cool."

"I...I...think all the desks are all the same," said Crump, pointing at his own.

Kwame nodded in agreement. Crump introduced himself and Kwame did too. Even though Crump already knew his name from earlier at the library, he decided to say nothing as it would have seemed rude to have been listening into others' conversations.

It turned out that Kwame had been born and brought up in Newham, East London, and had done a degree, and then an MA, in Communications and Media. Crump wondered how he had managed to do this – partly because his English was so strongly accented and sloppy as to be almost unintelligible, but also as he had seemed utterly baffled earlier as to how to use a library. Anyway, he seemed pleasant enough, but by now it was getting on for four o'clock and Crump decided that he'd had enough of introductions for one day – it would take him the best part of an hour and a half to get home and he wanted to prepare for the prearranged meeting he was having with the head of department the next day. He bade farewell to Kwame, and Kwame said something in response that was completely unintelligible. It could have been Klingon for all Crump knew, and perhaps it was.

It was on his way down the corridor that he passed Sandy

who grinned as soon as he saw Crump, who smiled back. He was sure Sandy was going to ask if he wanted to go for a beer and had mentally prepared his negative reply, so was surprised when he didn't.

"They've found him, old boy," said Sandy.

Crump looked puzzled.

"Found...who?"

"Finch."

Crump was baffled.

"Who?" he asked.

"Freddie Finch."

Crump looked blank.

"Freddie Finch – whose sudden disappearance created your job vacancy," and then he added with a big smile, "old boy."

Crump was stunned. He looked stunned too, like the frightened rabbit he had resembled when he had almost been run down by the van driver earlier that day. And it was no wonder he was stunned – nobody had ever mentioned to him that he had got his job at the last minute because of another lecturer's disappearance.

"What?" said Crump in amazement.

Sandy peered at him closely.

"You don't mean to say you didn't know?" asked Sandy.

"I...I..." Crump stuttered, unsure at this point whether to lie or not.

But what was the point in lying? It was hardly his fault if he'd been offered the job of a man who'd disappeared. He had no idea why he felt a knot of anxious guilt tightening in his stomach.

"Now that's just typical of this place," tutted Sandy, "they never tell you anything!"

Crump was wondering what would happen to his job now that his predecessor had reappeared. Would he be sacked – be asked to leave? Would he have to resign? Or should he resign, as a gentlemanly act of magnanimous self-sacrifice? Or would they be able to employ both him and the mysteriously disappearing then reappearing Freddie Finch. Crump needn't have worried.

"Shame really," said Sandy, accidentally burping loudly after what was no doubt a liquid lunch. Crump could smell a mixture of cigar smoke and whisky on his breath, with a slight tang of garlic.

What, thought Crump, was a shame? But he said nothing and just looked blankly at Sandy.

"What a waste..."

Sandy noticed his colleague's bafflement.

"Oh, of course, you don't know."

Crump shook his head and Sandy nodded.

"They dragged Finch's body out of the Thames this morning."

Crump was stunned and didn't know what to say, but eventually said, stupidly:

"You mean... he's dead?"

"Course he's bloody dead, old boy – he's been in the river for a month. Topped himself, the damn fool."

Crump felt a sense of shock, followed by intense sorrow, followed by anger that no-one had told him, followed by guilt at his anger, followed by a horrible sick feeling in the pit of his stomach. Sandy looked wistful but generally unconcerned.

"Course he's pretty badly decomposed – no face left apparently – bloody crabs...always go for the eyes first..."

The image made Crump wince.

"...but, they know it's him. Dental records – and he had an identity bracelet, you see – diabetes I think. Ma and Pa ID-ed him too, or what was left of him, poor sod. Prob'ly had a birthmark on his cock or his arse or something."

Sandy laughed loudly at this, but Crump found it in extremely bad taste. He also felt really rather sick all of a sudden.

"Fancy a quick snifter, old boy, perk you up a bit? You're looking a tad squiffy."

It was no good – Crump could hold it in no longer. With one enormous emetic heave he bent over and vomited up the beer-battered Atlantic cod and organic hand-cut potato wedges and two pints of very expensive lager onto the clean, corridor carpet.

Sandy seemed completely unfazed – he had no doubt been here many times before – in fact, he smiled knowingly as Crump straightened himself up and surveyed the enormous splodge of puke that covered a good two metres square of the corridor and had even sprayed and splashed itself up the walls. Crump suspected that vomiting incidents were not unusual in the life of Dr Sandy Buttery.

But all Crump could think of, he was slightly ashamed to admit to himself, was not his predecessor who had just been found dead and decomposing in the Thames after finding his life one of so much misery and despair that he threw himself into a watery grave.

No – all Kevin Crump could think of when he looked down at the semi-digested lumps of potato wedge and fish and batter in the large puddle of beery puke he had just created, was that he was looking at the best part of twenty quid's worth of reconstituted lunch on the floor before him. What a waste, he thought.

What an awful, terrible waste.

CHAPTER THREE

Breaking the Ice

Crump's first lesson was going as well as could be expected.

He was teaching a group of twenty-two students in the Seacole building and was spending much of the lesson on introductions and ice-breaking activities, as well as outlining the socio-linguistics module he would be teaching them that term.

Using student booklets, Crump went through the university rules on attendance, behaviour and academic issues such as plagiarism. He would give the same introductory 'lesson' to all his students for all the courses he was teaching, in both English language and literature, and all other courses he was expected to teach in the Department of Cultural, Creative and Communicative Studies. The same, or at least a similar, ice-breaking lesson was always the first lesson he gave to every class he had ever taught at the college, and he knew it so well he could almost do it in his sleep. It was important, though, to build a good rapport with students and to make sure everyone knew what was expected of them.

The students seemed a pleasant lot, if a bit quiet, and mostly just sat there listening to what he was saying. There seemed to be no real academic 'stars' in any of his classes, unfortunately, though several students seemed to think that they were, and there seemed no lively characters either – which was a shame. Perhaps they were just shy. The icy reserve would soon be broken, he was sure, and it would melt like a snowman in the sun as he got to know his students better, and they, him.

Crump knew from experience that a quiet class was sometimes worse than a class containing individuals who could be a bit wild or even disruptive – he didn't really mind teaching those as he knew how to deal with them. True, such classes needed careful management, but he had plenty of experience of that from the college, though he never remembered students being so rude and potentially disruptive when he was doing his A levels as some that he had taught there – but then this was a different world, a world of multimedia noise and instability in every field of life.

This university was, Crump knew, one of the worst in the country according to results, so he wasn't really expecting exceptional intellectual curiosity or ability in his classes. It attracted a large number of students, especially ethnic minorities, from deprived backgrounds and from the poorer parts of London, for whom just getting to university was an achievement, as was getting a couple of low grade A levels – even though the pass rate these days was 97%, and 25% got A grades, and it was almost impossible to fail unless you didn't turn up to the exam and/or failed to submit coursework.

Still, it was great that these young people were choosing education over a life of underachievement on the streets or getting into trouble. They had taken a large step in just deciding to go to university, even if it was a former polytechnic that was stubbornly languishing at the bottom of all the league tables.

There was, happily, no trace of the previous day's vomit visible on the corridor carpet, Crump noticed, even though a stale and bitter beery odour lingered in the air. His nostrils twitched and sniffed slightly at the pong wafting up from the carpet, and he blushed ever so slightly at the memory of the day before. Everyone had been very understanding, but Crump was perhaps more worried about the smell of the puke being distinctly alcoholic than anything else, and wondered if he'd get called in for a 'word' about it – he was mentally preparing himself for defending his decision to go the pub the previous day, just in case. If asked, he would say that he didn't make a habit of drinking at lunchtime, but as they weren't teaching yet and were simply getting to know each other, it seemed justifiable. Giving such a bad impression on his first day was worrying though, so he would say, if asked, that there had been something in his lunch that had disagreed with him – mention 'food poisoning' perhaps. It seemed some kind of poetic justice anyway, considering how much he'd paid for the fish and chips he'd regurgitated – he may as well get his money's worth, after all.

Several staff members came up to him and asked him whether he was alright that morning – something he found intensely irritating, though he tried not to show it – but not Cecilia, who walked straight past him in the corridor. She somehow seemed even skinnier than she had been the day before and looked even paler too. Crump wondered what the reaction would have been if he'd had a phobia about women to the same extent that she had an extreme phobia about men. He was sure he would have been called a male chauvinist pig and a sexist bigot, and probably would have been asked to leave the university.

In his office he arranged the books he had brought from home on his bookshelves and saw that Raj and Athena had already done this. Some of his bookshelf had been taken up by Raj's books, but he decided not to say anything – after all, he hadn't brought all his books to the office yet and there was no point creating an argument out of nothing. Kwame had settled in at his desk but, surprisingly, and after unpacking a large cardboard box, he seemed to have only three books on his shelf, although he had brought a lot of CDs as well as his own computer – a flashy, metallic blue laptop – as well as a compact hi-fi unit and an expensive-looking pair of wireless headphones.

Crump decided he would have to tell his office-sharing

colleagues about Freddie Finch's body being found, though he knew scant details himself. It would be humiliating if they found out from someone else that he'd stepped into a dead man's shoes and that he'd been given his job at the last minute – quite possibly, Crump was starting to think, because he'd been the only candidate available at such short notice. He told them of Freddie's probable suicide.

"But that's awful," said Athena.

Kwame shrugged at the news of Freddie Finch's death.

"Man was coward innit," he mumbled like a sulking teenager, "An' I di'n't know dat geeza so whassit ter do wiv me yeah innit?"

"We shall never know what sorrows are residing in human heart," said Raj, sounding almost mystical as he said it, like some guru dispensing advice to stoned and wide-eyed gap-year hippies.

"The thing is," admitted Crump, "well...it seems that...if Freddie hadn't disappeared and then...well...then I...sort of...wouldn't have got the offer to work here."

Rajdeep and Athena looked at him, and he smiled back, weakly.

"One cannot be thinking like that," Raj admonished him, "One *must* not be thinking like that. What is happening, is happening."

"That's very kind of you Raj," said Crump.

"It is chaos of universe – this is all!"

"But obviously I feel bad – stepping into a dead man's shoes..."

"No – no, you shouldn't say that," said Athena, "you should have got the job before the summer, like us, so obviously you were meant to be here."

Crump wondered who had got the job instead of him at the June interview.

"I think Raj got that job," said Crump.

"Oh no – my position here was being arranged for long time," said Raj.

Crump looked at Athena.

"I didn't come to an interview here at all – my university in Greece arranged for me to be interviewed there. They have contacts with this university – send a lot of Master's students here."

Crump looked at Kwame who was now sitting at his desk with his eyes closed, nodding to himself at the music coming through his headphones – it was so loud that the bass of the rap music could be heard by all of them.

Kwame reminded Crump of some of the more difficult teenagers at the college. He just didn't seem like a university lecturer somehow – he was even wearing a hoodie and a baseball cap for goodness sake! Surely, this man hadn't succeeded at the interview that Crump had failed? Surely he, Kevin Crump, well-read and educated, committed, hard-working and intelligent – an *intellectual* – couldn't have been beaten by Kwame, a man whose English was so bad he was hardly intelligible and who didn't even know how to use a library? Perhaps, thought Crump, Kwame was some kind of imposter. He'd heard of people pretending to be paramedics or nurses – perhaps Kwame was the academic equivalent?

Crump sat up with a start. He was embarrassed at the thoughts that were going through his head and how he was making assumptions about Kwame – for being black perhaps, for listening to rap music, for wearing a hoodie – and for speaking English with a strong London accent. In fact, he was embarrassed to be doing everything that he always tried to stop his students doing – making assumptions without knowing the full facts. He was ashamed of himself. It was as though he was a racist or something, which was certainly not true at all. If Crump had had a hair shirt he would have worn it, after whipping himself with an instrument of torture, if he'd had one handy, and rubbing salt into the wounds, if he'd had any wounds or any salt to rub into them. He knew that the human mind only really worked properly and at its best when it was open – like a parachute.

But there were, it was true, only three books on Kwame's shelf. Three books! He expected that more would appear later when Kwame had finished settling in. And he told himself to stop pre-judging people as well – he would, he was sure, find out from Kwame himself at some later date if he'd got the job Crump had been interviewed for in June. Anyway, what did it matter now? They all had jobs at the university after all, and they were all being extremely badly paid and on short-term contracts. Same boat. All in the past. Forgive and forget.

The meeting with Fiona Windrush later that morning went well. She was a tall, erect, bold-looking woman with long dark hair, slightly greying at the temples, sharp beady eyes and a permanent wry and supercilious smirk on her red lipsticked lips. She looked like the kind of person who would succeed in climbing the greasy career pole to its top – the kind of person who wouldn't give up, but also perhaps the kind of person who would use whatever she could to get to be where she wanted to be.

In Crump's experience, those who got into management jobs – like those at the college – had done so by manipulating others, sometimes subtly, sometimes blatantly, always ruthlessly. If Crump wanted to climb the career ladder of academe he would have to learn how to do the same, he thought, however unnatural it would be for him to do so. There was no other way. Fiona Windrush would have used every weapon in her armoury to win her little career ambition war, and he wondered how many people she had stepped on, put down, and crushed, to get where she was.

Fiona had attractive Mediterranean colouring and Crump wondered if she had any Italian blood. Or perhaps she had a Greek or Turkish parent – there were plenty of those in London. She spoke English in slow and certain tones – a fairly standard English, but sometimes a rough north London vowel sound would give away her roots and she was obviously not as posh as she aspired to be. The tone of her voice was warm, even sultry, and she spoke in a slow, quiet, deliberate manner, keeping her slow steady gaze fixed on his as she spoke. It was the kind of steady, hypnotic voice that you would stop and listen to. Because it was there.

Today all the new staff in the Department of Cultural, Creative and Communicative Studies were having a short interview with Fiona, and Crump was glad to be able to meet the person who was, ultimately, his and everyone else's boss.

She welcomed Crump to the department and hoped he would be a success there. Crump reciprocated by saying how keen he was to contribute to the success of the department – for which Fiona Windrush thanked him and said she was sure that that would be the case. They both knew this was all cobblers and that this interview was one of the motions that had to be gone through at the beginning of term, like a little courtship dance. It was doubtful that he would have much to do with Fiona Windrush during the year – she would have far more important management and strategic issues to deal with. The head of English, Wendy Webb, would be his direct line manager, as well as his supervisor and mentor. The meeting with her was later that day, so Crump spent some time looking at the trial timetable that Athena had printed off her computer for him. He still didn't have a password to access the computer system, which was a bit annoying to say the least, because everything he needed was on the staff intranet.

Wendy Webb's office was on the same corridor as that of Fiona Windrush, but it was about half the size – though that was still double the size of Crump's shared office. It was a nice office though, with a large, heavy-looking desk, swivel-chairs and two sleek and expensive-looking computers.

Crump had been early for the meeting so had waited in the foyer, from where he could see, through the glass partitions, the two formidable secretaries working in the department office. He used the time to glance through some of the leaflets and brochures provided – the prospectuses, the guidance booklets, the usual advice leaflets on alcohol, drugs and various issues. Crump picked up a colourful leaflet on STDs and decided to read up on Gonorrhoea and Chlamydia – just in case.

He wondered how much good such leaflets actually did – as if a student sitting in a glorified waiting room like the foyer, perhaps waiting for an interview or a disciplinary hearing, would suddenly decide, when faced with a leaflet on STDs, not to have a one-night stand as planned with someone at the local nightclub, or to use a condom because of reading it. If all these leaflets were banned would there be any difference? The UK, after all, had the worst rates of STDs and teenage pregnancy in Europe, but the UK also seemed to have the most sex education leaflets about not catching STDs or getting pregnant too. Statistically, that meant that there was at least the possibility that the profusion of leaflets about sex was one of the causes of STDs and pregnancies in the first place. But then, statistics was always one of the more dodgy subjects on the curriculum.

Crump's mind wandered as he waited. He pondered why and how the abbreviation VD had somehow become STD in the last few years – although he hesitated to call it a seminal development. Was it another example of an academic influencing the semantic conventions of a government department? What was wrong with VD anyway – in a linguistic sense, that is? It seemed a perfectly good abbreviation, and also rather poetic, being derived from Venus herself, rather than the clinically cold 'Sexually Transmitted Disease', shortened to STD, perhaps in the KFC manner and in the odd vogue for abbreviations for everything.

But then, why did 'half-caste' suddenly become 'mixed race', when the latter term was so vague and nebulous, and the former, derived from the British Raj, so specific? And why did 'tidal wave' suddenly become 'tsunami' when the first description was so complete and understandable – was it the exoticism of the foreign term that made it more attractive? As a specialist in English language and literature, Crump found all this fascinating.

He stood up and walked over to the rack, putting the STD leaflet back. If he kept it on him and it fell out of his jacket at some later stage it would look to everyone as though he may have an STD and was reading up on it, which would cause all sorts of embarrassment. There were several attractive postcards in the rack, advertising products and advice lines, and with blank spaces to write a message rather than promotional text, so he took out a couple and put them in his jacket pocket – he would later send a couple to his friends, including those abroad, to let them know he was in a new job.

His eyes were drawn to a postcard with a Union Jack design, and he pulled one of them out of the rack. The design showed the red, white and blue of the Union Jack rearranged so as to form a swastika – this postcard, according to the blurb at the back, was part of the university's 'FIGHT RACISM' campaign.

Crump looked at the Union Jack swastika design and felt both sad and slightly cross. Was it really necessary, in order to 'fight racism', to mock and insult the flag of this country – the country which abolished slavery before almost any other, and well before most? The country which fought the Nazis for six years suffering a terrible toll to its population, economy and infrastructure – it was, shockingly, only in the 21st century that Britain had finished repaying its war debts to the USA. The country whose people fought alone against those who fought under the swastika and all it stood for, saving the world from itself in the process. The country which was and is, in most ways, more tolerant that most others in the world, which has welcomed millions of incomers from the Commonwealth and elsewhere, which has laws both ancient and modern giving everyone equal protection against injustice, the right to a jury trial and an assumption of innocence until proven guilty, as well as more specific laws against racial discrimination too.

As though any passing racist would suddenly change their mind when confronted by a postcard like that! As though some skinhead on his way to 'bash a Paki' would suddenly catch sight of that postcard and think 'goodness me, I see it now – I can see the error of my ways so I shall work with others to achieve racial harmony and not go a-Paki-bashing on this fine

evening, and all because I have seen this colourful postcard!'
On the contrary – that skinhead would probably be so incensed
at the deliberate insult to his country that he'd probably bash
that Paki a little bit harder for having seen the postcard in the
first place. In most countries of the world you could, and
would, be arrested for defacing the national flag – in many
you'd be tortured or killed – but in the secure and stable and
un-nationalistic UK the defacing of the national flag, if it
happened, was treated by everyone as just a bit of silliness –
just a joke. But that did not mean it should be supported by the
university as part of its 'fight racism' campaign. Surely they
could campaign against racism without insulting anyone or the
country whose people's taxes were funding them in the first
place? Or perhaps that was just the intention.

"So sorry about the lateness, Kevin..."

Crump turned round. The short, plump, and rather plain
form of Wendy Webb, the woman who was to be his supervisor
and mentor, and also head of English language and literature
in the department, was standing beside him in the foyer.

He had been convinced Wendy Webb was a lesbian from
the first time he had seen her at the meeting on Monday – she
looked, he thought, like a short fat man in a wig and a dress,
though he was a bit embarrassed at the thought, even though
he was sure her mass of blonde hair just had to be a wig. She
also wore clothes that made her look like a member of the WI,
so not the stereotypical masculinised trouser suit that many so
inclined are supposed to favour. Not that lesbianism bothered
Crump at all. Why should it? It just, quite simply, *intrigued* him,
and the vast majority of heterosexual men too. There was
almost certainly an evolutionary explanation in there
somewhere.

He wondered if Wendy had a girlfriend. But he wouldn't
assume anything – he had got into trouble like that before,
assuming a masculine-looking gruff woman on the teaching
staff at the college with short cropped hair was a lesbian. He'd
even asked her about the tennis when Wimbledon was on –

until he'd met her husband, a very large and muscular lorry driver called Colin who had stared at him hard when they had met at a Christmas do. Crump would not make the same mistake again. There were vaguely masculine women and vaguely feminine men, and that didn't necessarily mean they were gay, or less 'womanly' or 'manly' than anyone else. It was all just labels anyway – masculine, feminine, gay, straight. What did it matter, so long as someone could do their job well and treated others well too?

"Oh it's not a problem, really," lied Crump, who hated lateness, even if it was from his direct boss and line manager, "but call me Crump please – everyone does..."

"Ah, but I'm not everyone," said the rather croaky and deep voice of Wendy Webb, raising her bushy eyebrows "but don't worry, we'll call you Crump if you like. Nickname from school, eh, and it stuck?"

"Oh... no... I've always been called Crump, by everyone, except my mum that is..."

Wendy nodded, knowingly.

"Mums always know best, don't they?"

"They do," said Crump.

"Shall we?" Wendy Webb gestured towards the corridor.

Crump followed her to her office. Just as he was leaving the foyer, he could see the white van driver who'd nearly knocked him over on his first day entering the department office – he didn't notice Crump, thank goodness. What was he doing there, apart from delivering something, presumably? It put Crump off a little bit – and, if he were honest with himself, the man frightened him. He'd never been one of those boys at school who liked fighting, and was now a man who disliked it too – consequently, he had always tried to avoid situations that might lead to fisticuffs whenever possible. He felt his heart pump that little bit faster as he thought of it.

Crump followed Wendy into her office. He looked around and the first thing he noticed was that there were a great number of spider plants in the office – on the desk, on the shelves, on the window-sill. Wendy noticed Crump looking at the vegetation.

"Oh I see you've noticed my spider plants," she said, "problem is, they grow and grow and grow, making lots of little babies, which I re-pot, which then grow and grow and grow again!"

Crump nodded and smiled. Well you could always chuck them away, he thought, or give them to someone. Perhaps he would have taken one of them if he'd had the room in his office, which he didn't.

"It's never-ending – they're too successful you see, and just grow and grow and grow. Just like Thames Metropolitan University," sighed Wendy Webb, placing a file on her desk and opening it.

"Right," she said, "Kevin...Crump..."

"That's me," said Crump, stupidly.

Wendy smiled weakly and looked down at the file.

"Welcome to the team, Kevin...oh... errr...Crump'."

"Thank you, Ms Webb." Crump deliberately buzzed the 'Ms' so it couldn't be mistaken for 'Miss' – he knew how seriously some female teachers took such nominal trivialities.

"Oh Wendy, please. We're all informal and friendly here."

Crump smiled. It was good that his mentor and line manager was so approachable. Things like that could make a real difference in the workplace. Best just to smile and sound positive about everything, thought Crump, except perhaps the death of his predecessor. As if Wendy were somehow reading his mind, she mentioned him:

"Such a shame about Freddie Finch," she said, sadly, "He was such a...unique... part of the department team."

Crump, of course, had never met Freddie. He hadn't even seen a picture of him. What on earth had made him do himself in, throw himself into the cold dark depths of the Thames rather than shine the light of education and enlightenment on his students? Crump just didn't get it. Perhaps he had some family or girlfriend/boyfriend problems, or some kind of mental illness – Crump had known people who had suffered with severe depression, and that was certainly no laughing matter, except for the ones who wrote comedy for a living, that is.

"A great loss," added Wendy before adding, cheerfully, "But, you wouldn't be here if he were still with us, would you?"

Crump didn't know what to say – it was true, yes, but she didn't have to say it!

"We probably would have employed you after your interview in June if the other candidates hadn't been quite so strong," Wendy continued.

Was it Kwame she was talking about now? Had *he* got Crump's job? How was he, in any cerebral or academic way at least, 'stronger' than Crump?

"Truth is, you're very well qualified – and well experienced too, in college teaching." She leaned forward and added, "Most university staff aren't, you know – haven't got the foggiest how to teach. They love doing research – but teaching's just an irritation for far too many academics."

Crump thought he'd better say nothing. Just smile – it was safer that way. For all he knew he was being tested in some way, and she was trying to entrap him – catch him out. He knew a manager at the college who always used just this technique on candidates and staff. It worked, apparently – the victim was drawn into the web by agreeing with the interviewer's opinions, only for the interviewer to suddenly change direction, leaving the helpless victim entangled and struggling and forced to defend their captor's views. This interview technique was best practice in HR departments these days, apparently.

"And you can teach here with us – on all courses – as well as popping in to the School of Education and Training every week to teach those PGCE students training to be English teachers."

"Yes," said Crump.

Accepting this arrangement had been part of the job offer, and though he knew he might be being a bit used as cheap labour, his salary being about half that of an established lecturer, it didn't really bother him – he knew he had to make sacrifices if he wanted a university career.

"And you're on a 0.8 contract?"

"Yes, I'll still be teaching at West London College on Fridays," said Crump, cheerily.

"Excellent, yes..." said Wendy, "so long as it doesn't interfere with your work here."

"Oh no, it won't interfere at all – in fact it'll complement it perfectly."

Crump wondered if he'd overegged the pudding a bit there, but smiled none the less. If they want no other job to interfere with this one, then perhaps they should give him a full-time contract so he wouldn't have to teach a day a week at the college? Wisely, he kept his thoughts to himself.

"Yes," said Wendy, looking unconvinced.

"And I'll be doing research on the teaching of English language and literature and the representation of the British education system in 19th and 20th century literature and film."

"Ah yes," said Wendy, reading the file in front of her.

It was a file which, Crump realised, was his – or at least about him. It was very thin indeed.

"I intend to get articles published in journals – as many as possible," said Crump, knowing it would be music to Wendy's ears.

Since the introduction of the new RAE – (Research Assessment Exercise) – system, the more articles an academic published the better, irrespective of whether they represented original research or were just rehashed, mediocre pieces of waffle. Better still, academics could publish a lot if they clubbed together, which is why so many pieces of research had multiple authors. It was all about quantity and not quality, and the RAE verdict would determine both funding and ranking for the department, so Crump knew that he had to spend any free time he had this year doing research and trying to get it published.

He also knew that many, if not most, senior academics got their PhD students to do much of the work in the articles and books they then published and got both the credit and the payment for – rather amoral, if not immoral, but that was the system, and he hadn't made the rules. He was determined, however, that when he became a senior academic he would never do such a thing – instead he would produce quality, original work that he had done himself. A life spent exploiting others was not what he wanted – if he'd wanted that, he would've got a job in a field like business or law. Or worked in TV, perhaps.

"Just one thing," said Wendy, gravely, "and I say this to all new staff..."

"Yes?" said Crump, looking expectant.

"Equality of opportunity is taken very seriously indeed at this university."

"Yes, of course," said Crump as seriously as he could, and he was about to say that he had known a lot of black and gay people in his life too, but thought better of it.

"It is our aim to embed equal opportunity in all that we do and to celebrate our diversity, in all its forms, and we expect all staff to do so too."

"Absolutely," said Crump.

"Freddie Finch..." she started, then hesitated.

Crump wondered why.

"Freddie Finch was, unfortunately, not prepared to celebrate diversity and equal opportunity to an acceptable level at this university..."

This was news to Crump – no-one had told him his predecessor had done anything wrong.

"...so he paid the ultimate price."

It sounded as though they had executed Freddie, not that he'd thrown himself to a watery death in the Thames.

"But then that's what happens," said Wendy, "when people have a lack of commitment to our equal opportunity policies."

Crump nodded. What did she mean? What had happened to Freddie Finch?

"Not that they all choose the easy way out – some staff have had their contracts terminated or have left of their own accord," she said, somewhat triumphantly, "So best really to fully support the ambitions of the department to celebrate diversity and equal opportunity and embed it in all that we do – and I do mean 'all'."

Crump agreed. Wendy smiled. They both nodded. They understood each other.

It was annoying that Wendy couldn't give him his password for the computer system, but she did give him directions to the office responsible for all ICT at the university, over at the Marcus Garvey building, where he had to fill in three forms to get one. As he was a late appointment to the university, it appeared that the usual password allocation process hadn't been initiated, so a password hadn't been issued. It would have been helpful if someone had told him that earlier, but there was no point in making an issue of it now.

The rest of the week went by in a flash, what with all the ice breaking in classes and students getting used to everything. It was annoying that it took him three days before he got a password – three days when he was unable to access his computer or the department intranet, three days in which he felt as if he were getting further and further behind his colleagues, three days when he was left 'out of the loop'. But at least he had one now.

It was also a struggle to learn all the names of the students in his classes, but then Crump was used to this from teaching at the college and, even though his memory was not brilliant, he always managed to remember everyone's names in the end, especially if he wrote them all down – and especially if he explained to his students at the beginning of the year that he was bad at names so not to be offended if he got their names wrong. He did this with every class he taught. A great many of the students were foreign too, so often had names unfamiliar to British ears, which made everything even more tricky.

A lot of the overseas students were so quiet that Crump wondered if they could understand what he was saying to them at all. It was difficult to know for sure really, and he did understand that it could be very difficult for a student from a completely different culture to be immediately open and confident in lessons. It would take time – he knew that – and his ability to understand things from a student's point of view was, he thought, one of his strengths as a teacher.

It was agreed, with Wendy, that he would not introduce himself to the School of Education this week, or take any classes there, but wait until things had settled down a bit first, which suited him fine.

Sandy later told him all about Freddie Finch. He was a young man of twenty-five who had just completed his postgraduate studies, and whose parents had been well-off intellectuals and academics. He'd been both to Oxford and a redbrick university before accepting the teaching job at the former polytechnic, partly due to his political opinions, apparently. He could have gone for a teaching post at a top university, but wanted to help the brightest kids from poor families to make it in the education system and get a first class education, so had chosen Thames Metropolitan from the many offers he'd had. Then it had all gone wrong somehow. He had started drinking, and was going missing for days on end before that final, fateful day a month earlier when he hadn't come back at all. A suicide note had eventually been found, so no-one had been hopeful. After a few weeks with no news, they had offered Crump his job.

Why had Freddie Finch cracked up? What exactly had happened? Crump wanted to ask Sandy, find out why this young man of promise had decided his life had not been worth living – but he didn't really know him, or anyone else at the department, well enough to pry further. He would, though, ask more questions later. He had to find out what had happened to Freddie Finch.

The week whizzed by, as the hectic starts of terms always do, and almost before Crump knew it, Friday had arrived and he was back teaching at the college. Crump had been teaching at West London College for seven years, initially part-time but full-time for the last four. Now his one day a week would boost his income, as well as allowing him to do primary research on representations of the education system and sociolinguistics – teenagers always loved creating their own argot and slang. He was well-experienced at teaching A-levels and also enjoyed teaching that age group. Yes, the 16-18 year olds could be annoying and irritating – infuriating even – but they had a freshness and an honesty that Crump liked, and he was a popular teacher too. He had to admit to himself, too, that he actually preferred their company to that of many of his teacher colleagues.

Friday was a busy day at the college. He had so many things to do, in addition to teaching classes, that he didn't leave until 7pm that evening – and he had arrived at 7.30 that morning, and hadn't taken a lunch break either. He'd only be paid for five hours' teaching time for that.

The day went well but was exhausting, and he was glad to go home with a take-away and a few cans of lager to mark the end of his first week. He had turned down Sandy's offer of a Friday night drink – he was just too tired. Lots of Chinese food and drink, followed by a long deep sleep, would be celebration enough for his first week in academe. It would all settle down in a few weeks, as it always did, at both the college and the university. The start of the academic year was always hectic and exhausting.

Crump lived in a dump and he knew it. Not only was it a dump, but it was a dump an hour and a half's commute from where he was now working four days a week in Greenwich. And it wasn't cheap either. Nowhere was in London, and he lived near Twickenham, an area which tended to be pricey. His bedsit was convenient for the college, but inconvenient for the university, so he would have to move. Fortunately, there seemed to be a lot of accommodation available at a reasonable distance from the university, especially in Eltham, a working class suburb in southeast London. He had made a couple of phone calls during the week and made appointments to see three separate rooms.

The first two rooms Crump saw were awful. The first, near New Eltham station, was over a kebab shop and stank of stale grease. The second room was tiny, little more than a box room with a window looking straight out onto a brick wall, and smelt as though someone had died in there. They probably had. So he was not optimistic when he approached the third. The address was a semi-detached house near the train station, and, coincidentally, was also near to one of the student halls of residence of Thames Metropolitan University, which was set in parkland.

The lady who showed him round wore her grey hair in a bun and looked as though she were in her late sixties. From her accent and demeanour, she seemed to be one of London's original white working class of the type one rarely meets in London any more – there are probably far more in the south of Spain these days. She seemed pleasant enough, and the room she showed him was, Crump was delighted to see, a whole flat – the entire first floor. There was a living room, a kitchen and a small bathroom, all of which hadn't been mentioned in the advert. And it was cheap too – a flat for the price of a room. He checked the price, just in case the landlady had made a mistake, but she said that it was correct and that he was the first to view it after her previous tenant had moved out.

The landlady, who introduced herself as Mrs Glidewell, said she had others coming to view it later that day, so Crump accepted the 'room' on the spot and paid her there and then, part cash and part cheque, for the first month's rent and deposit. The only downside was that she lived in the ground floor flat – he had no idea if she would be an interfering landlady or not, but really had no choice so would have to take the risk. She told him that her husband had died of *'prostrate'* cancer some years before – Crump almost corrected her but thought it would be too cruel – and so she now needed to make ends meet by renting out the first floor of the house. She seemed to like Crump, and was impressed by his respectable job at the university. The flat was perfect. Mrs Glidewell was harmless. Life was good.

It was with a happy heart that Crump returned to his dump of a bedsit slum that night. He immediately called his landlord, and gave notice that he'd be leaving in four weeks – he'd be gone well before then, but would still have to pay rent on the room for that time, which would be a bit of a struggle, but worth it.

Crump spent the rest of the weekend trying to clean up his bedsit and get organised, and had put most of his possessions in cardboard boxes by the end of the weekend – he'd move out in stages during the next week.

He prepared his lessons for the week and got his things together in good time, so sat down on Sunday night to watch some TV and relax. An early night would do him good.

It would be a busy week. And a lot more stressful then he could have ever imagined too.

CHAPTER FOUR

Complaining

"There's been a complaint," said Wendy Webb.

Crump was sitting in her office in the Seacole building at 8.30am on what was a very dull and rainy Monday morning.

He had gone into the department as usual that morning and made his way to his office, but could tell by the way the secretaries had peered at him through the glass partition that something was wrong, and had found an urgent email on his computer stating that he should go and see Wendy Webb immediately. He had no idea why. The word 'immediately' was underlined and in bold.

Perhaps he was going to be given some more classes? He knew that he was expected to be flexible and was prepared to be so too – he would probably have taught lessons in anything they wanted, if they'd asked, even things he didn't know anything much about. There were plenty of teachers at schools, colleges and universities for whom this was not an unusual state of affairs at all.

"Did you or did you not use the word *'nigger'*?" said Wendy, sternly, annunciating the N word with a sharp, and perhaps unnecessary, nasal clarity.

Crump was shocked – shocked at the very sound of the word, especially from Wendy's lips, but also shocked that he'd be accused of using the word. His felt his jaw fall open.

"Of course not," he said, somewhat startled "I don't think I've ever used that word in my life'.

"Why then," Wendy Webb continued, "have three students complained that you used the word in a lesson?"

Crump was baffled. How could they complain about his using a word he hadn't used? It was bizarre, and he had no answers.

"I... don't... know," he said slowly, trying to think, as Wendy peered at him closely with narrowed eyes, "Maybe they misheard me in some way..."

He looked at Wendy Webb blankly, unsure of what else to say – he was telling the truth, after all.

"We take racism very seriously indeed at this university", she went on.

"Yes", said Crump, "of course – so do I."

"And we do not tolerate any use of racist language of any kind."

"No," said Crump, "nor do I," trying to look and sound as innocent as he was, "I have no idea...what..."

"The account of all three students is remarkably similar," Wendy Webb interrupted, "though I shan't, of course, be revealing their names."

Crump wondered who they were, these students making false allegations about the use of racist language against him. His mind flicked through all the faces and names of the previous week – they all merged into a blur after a while, as students always did – but he could not think of a single incident or use of language in any class that could merit any accusation of racism. He was completely flummoxed – he was stumped – his flabber was completely and utterly ghasted. Wendy Webb read from the piece of paper she was holding.

"'Mr Crump said we should not be *niggerly* on two separate occasions...' says one of our international students – Chinese actually – and I don't need to remind you, I'm sure, how important they are to the financial health of this institution..."

Crump agreed that he didn't need to be reminded of this –

even though he had just been reminded, and for the umpteenth time too.

"'We all earn a *niggerly* salary here' – that's what you said, according to your students,'" Wendy quoted from the piece of paper in her hand.

With some relief, Crump realised how the misunderstanding must have happened.

"Oh – I didn't say *niggerly* – I said '*niggardly*', as in 'we all earn a *niggardly* salary here'."

What a relief – it had all just been a silly misunderstanding, after all. Wendy Webb raised her eyebrows at him. He reiterated:

"*Niggardly* – that's what I said – *niggardly*, not... It means meagre, stingy, ungenerous..."

"Yes, I know what it means, Mr Crump," she said, sounding stern, especially using the formal title. She looked very grumpy, even though Crump had just explained the reason for the misunderstanding.

"So, you see, it wasn't *niggerly* – I don't even think that's a word, actually – it was *niggardly*, meaning 'in the manner of a *niggard*' – from the old English *hneaw*, meaning stingy, I believe, though I may be wrong..."

It was a rare day when an extensive knowledge of etymology could lessen the stress and misery of human existence, but today may well have been that very day.

"The question," continued Wendy Webb, "is not only why you used such a word, but why you would be complaining to students in class about your salary – which, actually, is perfectly acceptable for a beginning lecturer."

Crump was baffled. Firstly, he was not a beginning lecturer, having taught for years and in what were almost certainly far more difficult circumstances than most of the lecturers at this or any other university. Secondly, his salary was rubbish, as she well knew, though he would have preferred that his words had not got back to her. Thirdly, he was baffled because he had used a perfectly good English word, and was now getting into trouble because some students had misunderstood what he had said. He was, quite simply, been punished because of the ignorance and illiteracy of others!

"It was a joke," said Crump, half-truthfully, "about the salary."

Wendy Webb looked at him as though he was a guilty schoolboy caught looking at dirty magazines.

"A *'joke'*?"

"Yes, you know, a joke," Crump was beginning to doubt that she did know actually, then added: "moaning about one's salary – everybody does it..."

It was a stupid thing to say and he knew it.

"I don't," said Wendy Webb.

He knew she was being truthful, though on her salary – plus perks – he wouldn't have been moaning either. Crump tried again.

"I didn't use the word *'nigger'* or *'niggerly'*; I used the word *'niggardly'* because it is a perfectly good English word..."

"No it isn't."

"Sorry?" said Crump, baffled.

"It is not a good word at all."

"Oh," said Crump, "isn't it?" even more baffled than a moment before.

"No, it isn't. And the reason why it isn't a 'perfectly good English word' is because it *sounds* like *'niggerly'*, which *sounds* like *'nigger'*, which is a word we most certainly do not use at this university. Is that understood?"

"But..." said Crump, weakly, "but... I didn't use the word *'nigger'*."

"No, but you used a word which sounded almost the same as the word *'nigger'* which, in a way, is even worse, because that means your students didn't understand clearly and accurately what you were saying when you were teaching them."

"But..."said Crump, "but..."

But nothing came out.

"I am afraid I have only one option," said Wendy Webb,

"and I would like to express my great disappointment that we have reached this point so early in the new term. You are hereby given a first warning, which will be kept on record."

"A first... warning?" said Crump. He was stunned.

"Yes, a first warning regarding your failure to adhere to the equal opportunity policy guidelines at Thames Metropolitan University. You will be written to in due course."

"But," said Crump, startled by this turn of events, "I haven't actually done, or said, anything wrong."

Wendy Webb looked at him with a hard stare and raised her bushy, greying eyebrows.

"Denial is never a pretty thing, is it? Of course, if you wish you may contest my judgement, in which case you will have to attend a tribunal after a period of suspension..."

"Suspension?" asked Crump.

"These things usually take three to six months to resolve."

Three to six months! Crump certainly didn't want to be suspended for that time – he doubted the suspension would be paid either, and he wouldn't be able to teach elsewhere while it was ongoing – but that would mean he would have to accept that he had done something wrong in using the word 'niggardly', when he hadn't.

"But all I did was use the word 'niggardly', a perfectly good word, which the students misheard as something else, and...and..."

Wendy Webb just stared and scowled at him and he knew at that point that he could never win. He would just have to accept the first written warning, even though he had done nothing wrong.

"So," Wendy Webb said, "are you prepared to accept a first warning for your use of racist language?"

"I did not use any racist language – just the word 'niggardly'!"

Crump was exasperated.

"If I could draw your attention to section three, subsection seven, paragraph five of your staff handbook – you may wish to refer to it later – you will see that the *perception* of racism or the use of racist language is considered to be sufficient evidence for disciplinary action."

Crump had read the staff handbook but didn't remember that bit. But then the staff handbook had rather a lot of important, unmemorable 'bits' in it, so he wasn't all that surprised.

"But," said Crump, "that's absurd. People's perceptions can be wildly wrong. You can't decide someone is racist on the basis of someone's perception!"

"Oh but we can," said Wendy Webb, "and we do. Your taking up your teaching position was conditional upon your acceptance of the rules and regulations of this institution in their entirety, as detailed in the staff handbook and in your contract."

"I know, and I do accept them," said Crump, "but..."

By now he was worn out and could think of nothing more to say. Wendy Webb smiled and repeated her offer:

"Are you prepared to accept a first warning for your use of racist language? If your answer is 'yes', we can end the complaints procedure today. If not...well, there will be a full tribunal in due course, after you are formally suspended, of course."

Reluctantly, Crump solemnly nodded his agreement.

"I accept," he said, sadly.

"As part of your acceptance of a first warning, you will also have to attend regular counselling sessions at the staff welfare centre – standard procedure."

She had said nothing about this before, but it now seemed part of the punishment 'package'.

"Counselling?" asked Crump, "for how long?"

"For as long as it takes," smiled Wendy Webb, "Many staff attend regularly anyway – it helps to talk things through sometimes."

What, things like being falsely accused of racism, Crump thought, and being cornered into accepting those false allegations as fact?

He had been to a counsellor only once before, in his first year at university when he'd attended several sessions with a counsellor about his shyness and his difficulty in getting to know people. He found the experience utterly hopeless – the young, friendly counsellor just sat there nodding like a dog, which was rather appropriate as she had a face not dissimilar to that of an Afghan hound – so he overcame the problem himself, with the aid of cheap beer and vodka. He soon made some friends, and had his first girlfriend too – literally – though the details of his sexual initiation were a bit vague and hazy due to his total drunkenness. But he had decided there and then that the fashion for counselling was just some enormous scam that allowed nosey people to interfere in others' lives under the guise of being 'helpful'. In Crump's view, the vast majority of counsellors should be sacked and the money spent on something more useful. Alcohol perhaps. Or fireworks. Or ice-cream. That would cheer everyone up enormously.

Wendy Webb put a statement in front of him and he signed it, though he didn't read word for word what he was signing – it could have been his own death warrant for all he knew – his mind was a blur. He had just admitted, in writing, that he had used racist language in class, and had also accepted that he would now have to have regular counselling. It was all absurd – utterly ridiculous – but he had to do it. What choice did he have?

He had to go with the flow – it would look utterly awful if he'd been suspended after only a week in the job. He'd brand himself a trouble-maker and perhaps ruin his whole academic career! Best to just accept what had happened – try and be stoical about it and just get on with things. Keep calm and carry on.

He could be thankful at least that the university had a strict policy of confidentiality – only he and Wendy, and he supposed Fiona Windrush, need know about this at all. Apart from senior management it would be strictly hush-hush – if his colleagues thought he was some kind of closet racist, they might not even talk to him, despite his protestations. As it was, he could be sure that his accepting the first warning was the end of the matter and it would never be spoken about again – he'd be like some wayward relative around whom shocking rumours, known to only a select few, swirled. His counsellor, Crump realised, would be Mandy Pandy, the gruff, depressed-sounding counsellor who had given all new staff a lecture the previous week.

* * *

After morning classes, Crump went for a walk around the campus – the rain had cleared, and here and there sunlight poked out from the clouds, seemingly taunting him with its erratic optimism. Outside the Abdullah building there was a small gathering of bearded men and veiled women in burqas standing in two segregated groups. He wondered what was going on. They just seemed to be having a break between lectures like ordinary students, except they were in single-sex groups and didn't seem to be talking much, but just standing together in silence, contemplating. Perhaps that's what students of Islamic studies did? It made a change from some of the loud and ill-mannered behaviour of other students, that's for sure.

Crump knew very little about the Abdullah building – it was the only campus building he had never been inside and the only one he had not been led around on his tour of the university. What exactly was housed inside the building? The sign outside simply said: 'Centre for Islamic Studies'. Did that mean the *whole* building was given over to that department? All of it? The building was apparently entirely funded by Saudi Arabian money courtesy of a university agreement and a generous donation from the House of Saud, but Crump didn't really know what that 'agreement' entailed. He could ask Sandy later.

He also hoped that he wouldn't be working with any veiled women in burqas in his department, although he had seen one at the introductory lecture. How on earth, he thought, can anyone who is fully veiled with a little slit for the eyes possibly communicate effectively with a class? Apart from anything else, it was extremely rude to mask one's face like that, doubly so if one was a teacher. But mainly, it was just impractical and a barrier to communication. Whatever had happened to 'When in Rome' anyway?

He had never had a veiled student in his college classes, but had already decided that he would refuse to teach any student wearing a veil – it was a sexist, backward, and essentially political, garment. It was a principle he had never had to defend, thank goodness. He also knew that there was nothing in the Koran saying that a veil had to be worn either, and the wearing of the burqa was really just a backwards village-based cultural tradition, so his attitude was in no way bigoted or against any religion, even the literalist interpretations of them.

Personally, he thought that such attire should not be allowed in any college or university, but he knew that those in senior management were keen to bend over backwards to accommodate any ethnic or religious group in the name of multiculturalism, mainly because more students equalled more funding and turning them away therefore never made financial sense. Also, any policy seen to discriminate against Muslims held the added danger of the college being picketed, boycotted or even attacked – possibly even bombed – by the more radical hotheads in that community. It was far easier to allow anyone to wear whatever they wanted to wear, especially if there was a religious, ethnic or cultural reason for it, though that did not seem to apply to any non-Muslim who wanted to wear a Halloween mask or a Viking helmet all day long, of course. But how on earth could anyone learn or teach when wearing what was, to all intents and purposes, a one-woman tent?

Crump walked around the outside of the Abdullah building – in all the windows were heavy curtains or blinds so he couldn't see into any of the rooms. He also noticed a dark-suited figure following a short distance behind and observing him closely, so he thought it best to walk back over to the main concourse. He'd had quite enough stress for one day, and certainly didn't want a security guard suspecting him of being some kind of thief or pervert as well.

After walking around Marcus Garvey and back around Mary Seacole, he decided to walk down to the Stephen Lawrence Learning Zone to look at some educational journals – it would help his research in education in literature and film to read a lot of back issues. Also, seeing as he was soon to start teaching lessons in the teacher training department, a familiarity with modern educational thinking and theories would certainly do him no harm.

As he approached the library, he could see a group of people outside, seemingly protesting about something. They were shouting in unison – Crump couldn't hear what exactly – and were waving placards. He could see, as he got nearer, that the placards had swastikas on them, and union jacks too – including the same union jack twisted into a swastika design that he had seen on the leaflet in the university foyer.

Suddenly, the shouting seemed to get louder and the protesters turned and looked at him, as though they were acting as a single organism. Some were pointing at him as he drew closer, though he had no idea why. Perhaps they were welcoming him as a protester against whatever it was they were protesting about – he would have to tell them, as politely as he could, that he wasn't coming to join their protest but going to the library. He hoped they wouldn't mind.

Then something hit him on the head and his legs gave way below him. Later, he was told that he'd collapsed on the ground and passed out at this stage, with blood running from a wound on his scalp. He'd been hit by a piece of wood from a placard and was utterly oblivious as people crowded around his fallen frame.

He woke up in a bed in Lewisham hospital some hours

later, feeling rather dizzy, it was true, and couldn't remember much – just a memory of his walking towards the library, people shouting a lot, and then... nothing. An utter blank. He looked around the ward. In the bed to the left of his was a man of about sixty who was snoring loudly. On the right was an old lady who looked so pale and motionless that it was only her occasional groaning in agony that assured him she wasn't dead.

This, Crump discovered, was the observation ward, which made perfect sense after the nurse told him that he was being kept in overnight for observation – they thought he had concussion but just wanted to make sure it wasn't anything more serious.

How anybody was able to sleep in the ward was a mystery – it was brightly lit, constantly noisy and nurses were constantly walking around this way and that too, chattering, nattering and laughing. It would probably have been quieter on the street outside. He had a splitting headache, and still felt rather dizzy, so it was likely that he did have concussion, however mild.

The department at the university was bound to know where he was, and he was sure they'd be able to organise cover for his classes – his time at the college had taught him that all educational institutions could cope with sudden absences remarkably well, despite the endless moaning from managers and teachers alike. Needs must, and all that.

Lying back on the pillow and closing his eyes, he decided to treat his little stay in hospital as an opportunity for rest and to catch up on some shut-eye, and before long, despite the noise and the activity, he was asleep.

The nurse woke him up early the next day – he'd been asleep for more than twelve hours. Breakfast didn't look particularly appetising so, after a cup of tepid, weak and flavourless tea, and a quick examination during which a doctor looked into his eyes with some contraption and gave him the all-clear, he left the hospital and caught the bus back home. He was told to take the rest of the day off. The university department would be sure to understand.

When he arrived back at the flat, Mrs Glidewell was scrubbing the doorstep outside. He told her about what had happened and she insisted on inviting him in and making him nice cup of tea and a bacon sandwich for breakfast.

The bottom floor of the semi-detached where she lived was neat and tidy, though estate agents no doubt would have said it needed modernisation. There were photos on the mantelpiece of what was surely Mrs Glidewell's late husband, and pride of place was given to a wedding photo in which Crump could see the face of a young woman peering out coyly from a wedding dress and standing next to her groom – he guessed it was from the late 1940s or early 1950s.

Mrs Glidewell clearly enjoyed Crump's company and having someone to talk to. It must be difficult, thought Crump, after living with someone for so many years, to suddenly be on your own again – like losing half of yourself. People of Mrs Glidewell's generation had gone straight from living with their own families to living with their spouses, so Crump doubted if she'd ever lived on her own before. Her husband had been her whole life. Crump made a mental note to look in on Mrs Glidewell regularly for a cup of tea and a chat.

She insisted on having a look at the cut on Crump's head and dabbing some TCP on it. It made Crump stink of disinfectant, but he could easily wash it off later. Mrs Glidewell told him of the time her husband Stanley was bitten by a *rabbit dog* – one of 'them what foams at the mouth' she said – and how he'd had a fever and was in bed for a week. But she said that neither of them trusted doctors so avoided them as much as possible – according to Mrs Glidewell a nice cup of tea, some bed-rest, a couple of aspirin, and some TCP would solve most ailments and illnesses, and who was to say she was wrong? But the *prostrate* cancer she said her husband died of, however, could not be beaten by either his wife's care or that of the doctors and hospitals. Against such an opponent both the quack and the physician are equally useless.

Mrs Glidewell was shocked that no-one from the university had gone to see Crump at the hospital or even called to ask how he was. And when Crump thought about it, he was annoyed – even hurt – by this too. All those people in the department who would drop everything to attend a bureaucratic meeting but who could not even manage to find five minutes to enquire about the health of a colleague who had been violently attacked – and attacked at the university too! This behaviour was typical of educational institutions though, as Crump well knew from the college. The first concern of any manager was how to cover classes and tick boxes, not the welfare of any absent teacher. There was surely something very wrong about that.

Crump was happy to get back to his flat and was glad he'd now finished moving in. It was all a bit spartan, and he could still have done with more furniture, but it was comfy enough. Out of the corner of his eye, he could see the light on the answer phone flashing – there were seventeen messages, all of them from people at the university. Five messages from Wendy Webb asking where he was; one from Fiona Windrush; two from Many Pandy asking him to make an appointment as soon as possible; three from Athena, who had heard about his injury and wanted to know how he was; two from Raj asking the same; two from Sandy asking if anything was wrong; and two from one of the office secretaries asking, rather snootily, where he was.

Surely, someone must have realised he wasn't in the department for good reason? If Athena and Raj knew about his injury – as they clearly did – then surely the department as a whole did? From experience, he knew that it really wasn't that difficult to find short-notice cover for absent teachers – he had covered enough lessons for the ill or the maternal over the years to know that. As a last resort, a class could be doubled up or even cancelled. It certainly wouldn't be the end of the world if students missed one or two lessons anyway, especially if they could be made up at a later date.

First of all, he called Athena. No answer, so he left a message. The same with Raj. Sandy was there, however, and expressed surprise when Crump told him he'd been in hospital.

"Thing is, old boy," said Sandy, "your absence has rather buggered up the timetable here."

"But... I was unconscious...I was hit on the head..."

"Hit on the head?"

"Yes."

"Oh dear boy – but why?"

"I have no idea – there was some protest or other outside the library. That's all I remember."

"Ah I see..."

Sandy told him all about the protest.

Apparently, one of the new undergraduates at the university that year was a mature teacher training student called Nick Craven who had been active in the National Front in the 1980s and had gone on to be a high-up member of the British National Party in the 90s. Despite the fact that being a member of any legal political party should arguably not have been any business of the university's, it seems some student activists, especially from ethnic, religious and left-wing organisations and societies had found out that he was starting a course at Thames Metropolitan University and were determined to stop him. Fascists who promoted intolerance like Craven had to be stopped expressing themselves at all costs in a tolerant and decent society.

The unlikely irony was that Nick Craven had, about five years before, become a born-again Christian and renounced his former life of extremist politics – in recent years, he had dedicated his life to charitable works and campaigning against extremism and bigotry of all kinds. He was studying education at the university with the aim of becoming a teacher with a Christian charity and spreading his message of peace and harmony throughout the world.

Crump was not exactly sure what had happened, but it seemed likely that the piece of wood that had struck him on the head had been intended for Nick Craven. Apparently, it was a case of mistaken identity – both Crump and Craven were about the same age, with the same gingery colour hair, and someone at the protest had assumed he was Nick Craven and attacked him. He would have assumed that in the circumstances he might be offered some sympathy – but then, assumption is the mother of much misunderstanding.

"I'm afraid Wendy wants to see you urgently – she seems rather angry, if truth be told, old boy..."

Surely, they must have realised where he was? He'd been knocked unconscious on the university campus, after all. He took a deep breath and phoned Wendy Webb – she answered after one ring.

"...so that's why I wasn't at the department yesterday and won't be in today either," he said.

"But you said you'd been discharged from hospital..."

"This morning, yes. The doctor ordered me to stay at home and rest today."

There was a pause during which Crump could hear Wendy sigh heavily.

"It is extremely inconvenient when staff go absent without giving us any notice in advance," said Wendy Webb.

Crump felt a throb of pain in his head.

"It would have been very difficult for me to have given you notice in advance about being knocked unconscious by an angry mob," retorted Crump, slightly crossly, "right outside the university library actually."

"We prefer to call it a learning zone these days – it's more inclusive and creates a sense of ownership amongst our diverse students, we find."

Crump blinked. Was it really relevant what the building was called?

"We rely on lecturers letting us know these things – we cannot be expected to read minds."

Before Crump could answer, Wendy asked a question:

"And what were you doing being attacked by an anti-racism protest anyway?" she asked, suspiciously.

"I think it was an accident," said Crump.

"An *accident*?"

"Yes – I mean, I don't think I was attacked on purpose – I think it was a mistake... of some kind..."

"A *'mistake'*?" said Wendy Webb, her voice dripping with cynicism, "Or perhaps some anti-racism protesters attacked you because you're a racist."

"I am *not* a racist," protested Crump.

"You willingly accepted a first warning for using racist language, so some people may be of a different opinion."

"Opinion is not fact," said Crump – he always told his college students the same thing.

There was a moment of utter silence. Then Wendy spoke:

"Now, when can you come into the department?"

"I'll be in tomorrow," said Crump, matter-of-factly.

"But there are classes today," she protested.

Crump told her that he was following the hospital doctor's advice. Wendy Webb tutted and sighed audibly over the phone.

"And have you contacted Mandy Pandy and the staff welfare service about counselling?"

"I haven't had the chance."

"You could have called them yesterday morning, straight after our meeting," she suggested.

Crump's head was really thumping with pain now. Why couldn't she just accept what he was saying?

"We all have responsibilities, Mr Crump," she said, again using her usual snide formality and first person plural sanctimony.

He told her that he would call staff welfare services later that day, and made an excuse about someone being at the door just so he could put the phone down and get some peace. She did say, happily, that there was no need for him to phone Fiona Windrush – Wendy herself would let her know what had happened. After another cup of tea and a sandwich, he felt a bit stronger so called staff welfare and made an appointment for later that week.

How could people not know what had happened? He had been hit by a missile and knocked unconscious a stone's throw from his department and his direct manager and mentor didn't even know! More than that, he was now being blamed for it!

Crump remembered Wendy Webb – and others – mentioning the importance of empathy in the teaching process in the interviews and lectures he had had at the university, and wondered why these people seemed incapable of showing any whatsoever to someone who had been the victim of a violent assault. What on earth was wrong with them?

He took it easy for the rest of the day, and did some re-reading, especially of the staff handbook, paying particular attention to the clause Wendy Webb had mentioned at his meeting with her. At just gone seven, the sound of the phone ringing woke him up – he had fallen asleep on the sofa and now had a pain in his neck to match the one in his head.

Athena was relieved to hear he was feeling better. Most of his lessons had been covered by other lecturers, including her and also Rajdeep, and no, she said, they didn't mind at all. She was also surprised that neither Wendy Webb nor any of the management had heard about his being injured or the fact he had gone to hospital – they had assumed the management would know. Apparently, or so Athena had heard, his being hit on the head by the stake from a placard was a clear case of mistaken identity – Miss Sharma the librarian had seen it all and had been the one who had stopped Crump being beaten on the ground by the protestors. She had stayed with Crump, helped by the veiled Muslim women Crump had seen standing outside the Abdullah building, until the ambulance had arrived. He made a mental note to personally thank them all as soon as he could.

The next day, Sandy was the first person he saw when he went into the department.

"Ah, back from the wars are we, old boy?" he said, looking at Crump's scalp for evidence of injury and seeming disappointed at the smallness of the wound.

"Something like that," said Crump, "Apparently, I look a bit like an ex-racist called Nick Craven, and..."

"Ah yes, I can see the similarity," interrupted Sandy, peering closely at Crump's face.

"You know this Nick Craven then?"

"He's a student in the education department so you may even be teaching him if you're doing some hours in that madhouse of mediocrity."

Crump still wondered why this student – or any other – was not allowed to have any belief they chose, however extreme, so long as they weren't being offensive or discriminatory to anyone in the university, but he didn't say anything in case he sounded sympathetic to a known racist, even if he was an 'ex' one.

Sandy suggested that they go out for a few drinks in the pubs around Greenwich on Saturday night and Crump accepted, especially as he could also crash at his house nearby.

He then went to see Wendy Webb – she was glad he'd made an appointment with the staff welfare department, but was very unhappy with his absence over the previous two days, despite his protestations about being unconscious and in hospital. Happily, she said there was no need for any further action to be taken against him.

Perhaps it was he, Crump thought, who should be taking action against the university – after all, he had been violently attacked on university property by university students – but thought that if he did so, it would look as though he were a troublemaker. He was a new lecturer after all, and he didn't want to get a bad reputation, especially as he already had a first warning.

Crump told Wendy that he would find time to teach extra classes if necessary to any students who missed lessons due to his absence, and that he was known at the college for his excellent attendance record – she seemed satisfied with that. She then reminded him that the next day he was to go and introduce himself to the education department and teach some classes there, and Crump said he was looking forward to it. It all went as well as could be expected.

During lunch, Crump thought it better and safer if he stayed in his office instead of venturing out onto the campus – he thought that may be tempting fate, especially if the protesters were still around, so he logged into the computer and the staff intranet, and got on with preparing some lessons. He was glad to see Athena and Raj again, but Kwame was nowhere to be seen.

"Oh he is at important conference," said Rajdeep.

"Lucky him," said Crump. The only conferences he'd ever been to – all about further education – had been extremely dull affairs full of extremely dull people with massively inflated ideas of their own importance. Academics, in other words.

"Hip-hop studies," added Athena, "it's a very popular option now, apparently."

"Especially in USA," said Raj, "Kwame says it is big conference in East of Anglia – many visitors are coming from black universities in United States."

Crump remembered that, probably because of the tradition of segregation and slavery, not to mention a significantly large African-American population, all-black universities and organisations were common in the States. Whether hip-hop studies was a valid field of study, on the other hand, was something of which Crump was less sure – but he certainly wasn't going to risk expressing that view in case it was misconstrued as somehow being racist. He noticed that there were still only three books on Kwame's bookshelf. He could have done with that space too – maybe he'd ask Kwame for it when he got back.

For the rest of that week, he got on with his classes, teaching lessons on Shakespeare, media interpretations, and 19th and 20th century literature, and they all went rather well, he thought. Only occasionally did he feel angry that some of his students had complained about his using supposedly 'racist' language.

One problem was that so many of the students were so quiet that he found it hard to judge how much of his lessons and language they were able to understand. In order to gauge their levels, he set them all essays for homework – he would be able to assess their intellectual and language ability more easily once he saw what they were or were not capable of writing.

Later, he went to see Mandy Pandy at the staff welfare office. It was situated in the Marcus Garvey building, and the waiting room was a tranquil shade of sky blue, with pretty landscape watercolours on the walls, and supposedly soothing but utterly irritating panpipe music playing incessantly in the background. Why did people think panpipes were so relaxing? They always made Crump think of the jungles of South America, with all their snakes and spiders, not to mention Mayan human sacrifice rituals and people getting decapitated and having their still-beating hearts cut out with obsidian knives. Still, it could have been worse – it could have been bagpipes.

There was only one other person in the waiting room, but Crump recognised her immediately – it was the tiny nervous bird-like Asian woman who had been one of those who had interviewed him the previous June. She didn't recognise him. In fact, he doubted if she even noticed him entering the waiting room at all – she was huddled up on one of the comfy chairs, weeping. It was somewhat disconcerting for Crump to sit there with the woman in such distress sitting just two seats away, and he wondered if he should ask if she was alright – a stupid question, because people weeping uncontrollably tend not to be 'alright'. Perhaps she just didn't like panpipe music either. And what could he do anyway? Recommend that she saw somebody about her problem? That's surely why she was in the waiting room of the staff welfare office in the first place!

Mandy Pandy looked as depressed as she had looked when she had given the lecture to staff the previous week. She seemed weary and uninterested in anything, and her voice had the same bland droning monotone he remembered from the lecture.

Crump explained why he was there. Mandy Pandy sat opposite him nodding at his words.

"So that's it really – I'm not a racist and I was sent here for being misunderstood," he said.

"Do you often feel misunderstood?" she asked.

"Only when people misunderstand me," he said, smiling, and she wrote something in her notepad, unsmilingly.

Crump always hated it when people wrote things he couldn't see. What was she writing about him anyway? Good things? Bad things? What?

"That must be very frustrating," she continued, sounding bored.

"Yes," said Crump, and she wrote something else in her notepad which was, actually, very frustrating indeed.

"Do you often feel people are telling lies about you?" she asked.

"I'm not paranoid, if that's what you mean," said Crump, and he watched her write again in that damn notepad, "I was unfairly accused of racism so, as a condition of my first warning which I accepted because I had no real choice, I have to come and see you."

Mandy Pandy looked at him, nodded, then scribbled something in the notepad again.

"We may be able to help you," she said.

"In what way exactly?" asked Crump.

Mandy Pandy smiled, sympathetically, with that empathetic face people like her always wear to fake concern. It must have taken a lot of practising in front of the mirror to get it right.

"Many people find it helpful to talk to somebody – about the stresses and sadnesses in their lives..."

"Well I don't," said Crump, "I'm completely cynical about counselling and therapy."

"That's very common in those who've had a bad experience in the past, and are in denial" said Mandy Pandy.

"I'm not in 'denial' – or 'de Thames'," said Crump, smiling at the joke.

Mandy Pandy didn't smile – he wondered if she had understood the joke. Perhaps she had – perhaps that was the problem.

"It's just I think it's not at all helpful to most people. It's just a fashion, and makes a lot of money for a lot of people, and gives those people a lot of power over others, without any responsibility whatsoever."

Mandy Pandy looked at him, nodded, then wrote something in her notepad again. It was all Crump could do to restrain himself from grabbing that bloody notepad and ripping it up. What diagnosis had the woman written about him? Or perhaps she was drawing a doodle? Or writing her shopping list?

"I'm sensing a lot of aggression," said Mandy Pandy, "which is also common in those with issues of various kinds."

"I have no 'issues'," said Crump.

"We all have issues," said Mandy Pandy, "and we could all do with someone to talk to sometimes."

Crump couldn't deny that this, if nothing else, was a brilliant marketing strategy for the very profitable counselling industry to expand its customer base.

"Do you have issues then?" asked Crump, bluntly "and do you have anyone to talk to?"

"We're here to talk about you, not about me," said Mandy Pandy, predictably, "Now, tell me a bit about your background."

"My 'background'?"

"Yes, you know – your mother and father, your family, your childhood..."

An hour later, Crump emerged from the consulting room

feeling depressed. He had told Mandy Pandy far more than he had intended – about his visit to the counsellor in the first year of university, about his overbearing mother, about his father's death, about his problems with girlfriends, even about his sexual fantasies. The lot.

How did that happen? He hadn't meant to do anything but stop the counsellor prying into his psyche, and now he felt as though his mind had been filleted, battered and served with chips.

Mandy Pandy had given him some relaxation tapes and visualisation exercises which, supposedly, would help him think more positively about things – which was ironic, really, as he had left the counselling session far more depressed than when he had gone in.

Crump couldn't help thinking that it was rarely, if ever, useful for anyone to delve too far and too deeply into their past – human beings were meant to bury bad memories, and that's why the human brain did so. If people wanted to improve their lives or their moods they should concentrate on being stoical about their lives, accepting what they couldn't change and working hard to make better what they could. They should try and get some balance in their lives – some sense of proportion – and, perhaps, just perhaps, think about people other than themselves for a change. But most of all, they should save the time and money they were spending on counsellors, therapists, psychiatrists and quack alternative 'cures' on something far more useful and enjoyable, such as a hobby or a holiday. Ice cream, perhaps. Nobody ever seemed sad while eating ice cream.

The next day, Crump went over to the education department in the Mandela building. He had agreed to teach anything and he really didn't mind teaching any classes that he was asked to take. He was sure that this willingness to be some kind of 'educational prostitute' would give a good impression of his willingness to work hard and be flexible, and that certainly wouldn't harm his prospects later on.

It would be a change to teach teacher training classes anyway – most of these students would be mature and already have degrees, so he would get some experience of teaching graduates too. He was also looking forward to teaching students of a higher level than the usual undergraduates. Variety was essential in any teaching job – to preserve one's sanity, if nothing else.

He would be teaching in the department of post-compulsory education. The head of this department was a man in his late fifties called Edwin Wittering, and Crump was sitting in his office admiring the decor and the watercolours on the walls.

"We're a very successful department," said Edwin Wittering, in perhaps the most unpleasantly irritatingly nasal voice Crump had ever heard, "I've been here for over thirty years, in various capacities."

The man's smile and manner were oleaginous and irritating, and Crump was doing his best not to show his distaste, so he simply nodded at what the man was saying. There was also an extremely unpleasant odour in the air. After a while, Crump realised it wasn't coming from outside as he originally thought, but from Edwin Wittering himself. It was a sickly, pungent, heavy smell of decomposition – a putrid odour of rotting fish and flesh – and it was starting to make Crump feel physically sick.

"I've taught in a further education college for several years," said Crump, "so I'm sure I'll enjoy teaching classes to those wishing to enter the profession."

"Quite," said Edwin Wittering, smiling to show two rows of yellow, stained teeth.

Even from where Crump was sitting he could smell the sickly odour of bad breath emanating from the man's mouth. After receiving his timetable from Edwin Wittering, he left the room in relief.

In the staffroom, aka teamroom, there were several teacher trainers – all female – most of whom didn't even acknowledge his presence when he went in. Only one of them said hello, and he introduced himself to her and explained what he was doing there. Some of the teacher trainers looked round to peer at him suspiciously, but apart from that, none said hello. Crump had met some rude teachers in his time – being stuck-up, institutionalised, and obsessed with your place in the hierarchy was a large part of being a teacher for many – but this was the rudest bunch of teachers he'd ever met. And that was saying something.

It was with some relief that he left and headed for his classroom. He had decided to give his first teacher training lesson about his experiences of disruption in a further education college.

He entered the classroom at two minutes to the hour and was surprised to see only two people sitting there. It was not until quarter past the hour that most of the twenty-five teaching students turned up. None of them offered an apology for lateness.

More worrying, however, was the gradual realisation that many of the students, all of them graduates, and all aiming to teach *English* in further education colleges, had such a low level of education that Crump was surprised they'd even passed a GCSE in the subject, let alone an A-level or degree. Their spelling and grammar were utterly atrocious, several of them had never studied a whole Shakespeare play, they said, despite having good degrees in English from British universities, and a few couldn't even speak the language properly. One had such a strong London accent that Crump couldn't understand a word she said; two others had heavy African accents that were almost unintelligible; and an Irish student spoke with such a heavy brogue that he sounded like a comedy leprechaun. Still, at least it all proved how flexible and international the English language was, if nothing else.

Half the class was made up of foreign students, and amongst them was what Crump had always dreaded – a Muslim woman in a full veil. He would address the issue with the department later because he was unhappy that a woman wearing such clothes was in his class – and, to be honest, was amazed that anyone would think such a woman would ever be fit to teach English in the first place and allow her on a course to study it. It was a logistical and practical issue, as well as a liberal one. He wouldn't say anything to the student, however, so as not to embarrass her – and this was his first lesson, after all. He'd wait a while before raising the issue with the department – as he had a first warning for racism he'd have to choose his moment carefully.

Later on, Crump found out that all PGCE students now got a bursary of thousands of pounds to study on teacher training courses, and that many people apparently did the course just to get their hands on that. He also discovered that to get onto the course, all a student needed was a degree – (and not even that if one was doing a teaching certificate – Cert Ed – rather than a PGCE) – and to get onto a degree course, especially at one of the lesser universities, one needed no qualifications whatsoever.

In recent years, something called APR – Approved Prior Learning – had become prevalent at universities, allowing those with very low levels of qualifications to get on degree courses by using their life-experience itself as a 'qualification'. So, for example, someone could say that they had run a home, gone shopping and watched documentaries on TV on the APR form and that could be used for university entry, especially for mature students, as evidence of proficiency in English, maths, and a whole range of skills.

As some degrees were entirely coursework-based and modular these days, and tutors were often encouraged to practically do the coursework for their students by correcting and re-correcting their essays, it was perfectly possible that somebody who wouldn't even get a low grade at O-level could get a good degree and be studying for a postgraduate qualification or a teaching training certificate, and could then become a teacher or a university lecturer themselves.

How, thought Crump, did the British education system become so devalued that degrees – and Firsts and 2:1s at that – were being handed out to students with such low levels of thinking, ability or intelligence?

He decided to say nothing to Edwin Wittering or any of the other teacher trainers about his concerns, but just to say the lesson had gone well and the students were fine – anything else would have been perceived as moaning or causing trouble, and Crump had seen quite enough of that lately. Feeling somewhat depressed and disillusioned, he made his way home, but was at least looking forward to having a drink on Friday night with Sandy.

The next day, Friday, he was back at the college. He enjoyed teaching his A-level students again, and helped the new teachers as much as he could. It was annoying that everything these days was about targets and outcomes and exams and teaching to the test – it would have been great to have had the freedom to try and convey his love for the subject he was teaching, to *educate*, instead of just being a robot, going through the motions, ticking boxes and following the curriculum like an automaton.

The kids – young adults really – liked his lessons and he got on well with them. He did, to some extent anyway, manage to convey his love for the subject and teach well – but this was *despite* the curriculum, not because of it. Sometimes he thought that no-one in charge of the British education system had the faintest clue what they were doing or cared a jot about education at all. But he did, and he knew it. Perhaps that was the problem...

Crump also had a good chat with his friend Becky in the college staffroom about the previous week at the university: 'Keep your head down', she had advised him, 'and before you know it, it'll all come good.'

He knew this anyway – he had been in a similar position at the college when he'd started, and some of the other teachers had treated him very rudely indeed. A few had been real shits, and he hadn't forgotten it – they were still there, these shits, plodding along in their mediocrity towards retirement. Becky had always been friendly, though, so had become a good friend – they had metaphorically cried on each other's shoulders many a time.

He decided to follow her advice. It would all get better – that was for sure. It would all come together in the end. It would all 'come good'.

* * *

"Don't worry, old chap," said Sandy, "you'll get the hang of it after a while. Cheers!"

"Cheers," said Crump and took a large sip of his lager.

He was sitting with Sandy in a slightly grotty, but happily inexpensive, pub in Greenwich. Well, more Deptford really.

"Thing is, old boy," said Sandy, "if you're working in the university system, you just have to remember a couple of things."

"Only a couple?" asked Crump, smiling wryly.

"The two golden rules."

"Sounds mysterious," said Crump, although it didn't really.

He prepared himself for a lecture by an old timer. Sandy cleared his throat.

"Rule number one, the education system is just a business like any other – never think it's anything better or more special than that. It's not, old boy. It's all about money in the end and is ultimately market-led – get lots of students in, any way you can, give 'em good degrees in any subject they like, which in turn will mean your university will be higher in the league tables and so will attract more students and earn you more money – 'specially from those lucrative foreign student cash cows."

Crump nodded and took a sip of his pint. Sandy smiled at the attention his advice was receiving – he was on a roll.

"Turn a blind eye to anything that may hinder that process,

such as plagiarism of any kind, an inability to speak English, or a complete and utterly staggering level of stupidity and ignorance."

Crump thought about how real 'education' was, or should be, so much more than a business – that it should be about developing the intellect, learning how to *ask better questions*, keeping alive the bright torch of the Enlightenment in the darkness of an ignorant and brutal world. But no, now the education system was just a business – like Tesco's, or Sainsbury's, or BT, or Enron, or any fraudulent bank you could name – all about profit and making money, and nothing more. He was about to say something in defence of his principles when Sandy moved on to golden rule the second:

"And rule number two, remember – it's all just a game – you play it by their rules and you'll win by their rules – try and challenge the powers that be and you'll end up on a sticky wicket, by golly."

So that was Sandy's advice: it's all just a business and it's all just a game. Sandy sensed his colleague's disappointment at his cynicism.

"You can't fight the system, old boy – I know, I tried to, years ago, when I first started teaching – tried to make society better too, naive little twerp that I was."

Crump wondered how Sandy had tried to 'fight the system'. It seemed unlikely, somehow.

"Remember – you are only an insignificant little cog in a giant monster of a machine – you do not matter and you are utterly dispensable – disposable even – like a...used tampon..."

Sandy guffawed at the simile. Crump pondered the unpleasant imagery and winced.

"You see that was his problem – Freddie Finch – didn't play the game and look what happened. So, just play up, play up and play the game, and don't try and change the rules. I promise you, Crumpie boy, you'll lose if you try to change the world – because the world's not for changing, and the times they are most certainly not a-changing either – not now, not ever."

Crump was still not exactly sure what Sandy meant by 'the game', but certainly the cynicism of Sandy was all-consuming and absolute.

"Could you... not call me that, please," Crump said.

"What?" said Sandy, "Oh – Crumpie?"

"My name's Crump," said Crump, because it was.

"Actually it's Kevin, isn't it? Your first name, I mean." Sandy smiled.

"You know what I mean."

Sandy laughed loudly.

"Only joking, dear boy – just pulling your plonker! Course I'll call you Crump, if you want. Top up?"

They continued drinking at that pub, and then several others – Crump couldn't remember exactly how many. The conversation started fairly sober and rational, with Crump asking about what Sandy meant by his concept that it was all 'just a game', and Sandy giving a lot of examples about what he meant, including stories about Freddie Finch who didn't 'play the game' and whose funeral was to take place the following week.

After a while, and drinks at three or four more pubs, Crump wasn't really able to take in what Sandy was telling him, though he later remembered it all seemed very interesting at the time. Sandy knew everything about the way the place worked – where the money came from, who was in charge, how things would change in future – and he knew everyone's secrets, he said, though he wasn't telling. It seemed the future of the university was foreign students and foreign cash, especially outsourcing degree courses to colleges in China, India, Russia and the Arab world – essentially, all Thames Metropolitan would have to do was sign off the courses and leave everything to the foreign colleges, and the money would roll in.

According to Sandy, this was the way the campus would go too – they already had a large new Islamic Studies Department in the Abdullah building thanks to a massive injection of cash from Saudi Arabia, and there would quite possibly be a department of Chinese Studies soon too. Sandy mentioned lots of figures and statistics, but they swam through Crump's brain like pissed little fishes through a net full of large holes – he would have to ask Sandy about the details again at a later date.

By the end of the evening, Crump was well and truly plastered – so much so that he had trouble standing up – but Sandy seemed merely a little tipsy. Perhaps he was just more used to the booze – that's what happened with heavy drinkers, Crump supposed.

After closing time, they both staggered back down Greenwich High Street, stopping at a takeaway where they bought large greasy kebabs, scoffing them as they stumbled down the street with the noisy drunks and happy herds of binge-drinking youngsters.

Crump followed Sandy, and soon found himself stumbling past the Greenwich theatre and up a hill lined with large, posh townhouses. To his surprise, Sandy stopped at one and got out his keys. He can't live here, thought Crump, not on his salary – but Sandy opened the door and they both fell in.

The house had three floors and no doubt several bedrooms too, and it must've been worth a million at least – maybe two. Looking around the hallway, Crump saw that the place was crammed with antiques – there were original oil paintings on every wall, and old-looking, beautiful furniture all around. It all looked elegant and expensive. Crump followed Sandy through to the living room which was similarly furnished with antiques and hung with original pictures. Sandy smiled at him. Crump looked overwhelmed at the opulence.

"Bought at the bottom of the market," said Sandy, "so old Sandy's done rather well for himself on the proverbial property ladder."

"S'a lovely place you got 'ere," said a very drunk and envious Crump – he knew a small flat in the area would cost over ten times his annual salary. Maybe fifteen.

"Oh I know it is! Boy like me who grew up in a council house – and now..." He waved his hand majestically in the air, "I've got all this, but..."

"But?" asked Crump, on cue.

"Sadly I have no beautiful maiden to share it with, and no son and heir either..." and he added, "Just never seemed to get round to it somehow..."

"I'm sureyacan get-a-girlfriend," slurred Crump.

"Oh I have plenty of girlfriends, old boy," said Sandy, "rich men tend to, but I would've liked to have a wife and kiddiwinks too..."

Crump knew what he meant. He also sometimes thought it would be nice to have a wife – at least a partner – and children, a thought that had increased with age. But he was only twenty-nine so he had plenty of time, and anyway, there was no way he could ever have afforded to give his kids a good standard of living on his salary. He would be bringing them up in dire poverty, and he would never want to do that.

How could he, Crump, get up to Sandy's level of living – have a house like his? Just thinking the thought confused his drunken brain and started to make him maudlin, so he banished the thought to the dark recesses of his skull, making a mental note to hook it out at a later date for depressive consideration.

Sandy opened a bottle of whisky – 12-year old single malt – and poured them each a large glassful. Later, Crump remembered talking with Sandy and drinking whisky, and then... nothing. Nothing at all in his memory bank.

Nothing more until he woke up early the next morning in a smallish room furnished with antiques and oil paintings. His head was pounding like a piston and his mouth tasted of metallic sick. He spent some time listening to the twittering birds and heaved himself up to look out of the window – he was on the first floor of the townhouse and was looking out onto the road, but felt rather dizzy so went back to bed and dozed.

Sometime later, Sandy brought him a cup of tea. Apparently, he'd fallen asleep on the sofa the previous evening so Sandy had, somewhat impressively, carried him upstairs to bed – Crump was pleased to see he was still clothed, at least. Sandy seemed not to have even a trace of a hangover – how could anyone drink so much alcohol and be so unaffected? Crump, on the other hand, felt dreadful – he had a headache, a stomach ache, a back ache, and he even thought his aches had aches – but somehow managed to struggle out of bed and get the bus for home, thanking his host for his generosity before he left.

Later on that day, after a shower, and much the better for a couple of paracetamol and a change of clothes – plus a hair-of-the-dog glass of whisky – he got the bus back to Greenwich and met Athena and Rajdeep next to the Cutty Sark as they'd arranged. He still felt rather ill, but was glad to be going sightseeing in London, especially on such a sunny and beautiful day – the weather made him feel better after all the rain of the previous week. Were human beings really so superficial that a glimpse of sunshine could lift their whole mood so much? Yes, actually, they were.

After a visit to the Cutty Sark, which Raj enjoyed tremendously, and which brought back painfully vivid unhappy schoolboy memories for Crump, they got on the Docklands Light Railway and made their way to the Tower of London where they caught a river cruise to Westminster. Raj was as excited as a child again and Athena was clearly enjoying herself too.

It was while on the river cruise that Crump started to feel a little sick, although he didn't actually vomit – a bit of deep breathing and swallowing made the sick subside, and after a few moments he felt fine again and enjoyed the sights they were passing on the Thames. They got off the boat at Westminster Pier and stood gawping at the Houses of Parliament and Big Ben with all the tourists before heading off towards Trafalgar Square.

Both Raj and Athena were taking a lot of photos with their digital cameras, and Crump was happy to take some pictures of them in front of the sights too. Athena promised she'd email him the best ones, and smiled at him in the way he loved – he thought he even blushed slightly. There was no doubt about it – he liked Athena very much indeed.

In Soho, they had some tasty Chinese food, most of which Raj and Athena enjoyed he was pleased to see, and Crump soon felt much better for the sustenance. It was a jolly day out, all in all, and Crump was more than delighted to see that Athena was really enjoying herself. He decided he would wait until another day before asking her out on a date – it was something he was chronically awful at, so he wanted to get it right.

They all agreed that the day had been a success and they should do it all again soon – after all, there was so much in London that they could go sightseeing every day for a year and still not see everything.

But Crump was tired and so turned down the offer of watching a film that evening. Instead, he went home and went straight to bed. He was asleep as soon as his head hit the pillow. He dreamt about sailing down the Thames on a boat with Athena, who was naked, and they were being pursued by some sinister unseen force – a dark malevolent force that smelt of putrid, rotting flesh, crawling up from the depths to capsize their boat and drag them under to their doom...

In the middle of the night, Crump woke up with a start, ran to the bathroom and vomited into the toilet bowl. Judging by the volume of vomit, it seemed he had puked up the entire Chinese meal he had eaten earlier. It seemed that every time Crump had a nice meal out, he ended up puking it up, and he made a mental note to try and kick his emetic habit in future.

He went back to bed and slept deeply. He would rest up on Sunday and take it easy – the following week would be busy as usual and he wanted to be prepared. Because, as it said on his staff handbook, in a phrase no doubt lifted from some corporate American guide to management: 'fail to prepare, prepare to fail'.

And Crump was determined that he was not going to fail to prepare, and he was not going to prepare to fail either. Not now. Not ever.

CHAPTER FIVE

Learning and Doing

Students applying to Thames Metropolitan University had a vast array of degree courses to choose from. Especially at the newer universities, there were all kinds of subject combinations in a modular system – a pick-and-mix, smorgasbord menu that allowed students to choose any concoction of subjects they desired.

It was all entirely market-led – so if there was a demand for a degree course in, say, the study of TV soap operas, then you could be guaranteed that some universities would offer degrees in 'soap opera studies', or at least offer modules in this as part of a general media or TV studies degree course.

If a subject was unpopular – perhaps because it was difficult, required great effort and a high level of intelligence, and especially if it offered a lesser possibility of high marks and good degree results – then universities would attempt to replace it with a more popular one which would get the grades and bring in the students and the accompanying cash. That, ultimately, was *what it was all about.*

The terrible flaw with this on-demand, market-led system was that it led naturally to difficult, but important, subjects being dropped from the syllabus entirely and easy, popular, 'fun' subjects proliferating exponentially, irrespective of whether they were actually useful to either the students or the economy. Nobody seemed to even bother to ask the question any more about what a good education should actually be, let alone attempt to find an answer.

This system also naturally led to massive grade inflation and a terrible dumbing down which meant that there were students now graduating with good degrees who would probably not have passed an A-level or even an O-level thirty years ago; there had been massive grade inflation in the last decade alone too. But then, no university these days really gave a fig if its graduates were ignorant, uncultured and woefully uneducated, so long as the money kept coming in, and the students kept enrolling. It was all a business and a game – of survival – in the academic jungle.

The science departments at Thames Metropolitan University had been closed two years previously. The physics and chemistry departments were just not attracting enough applicants onto their courses. Students found the courses too difficult, especially with the narrowness of knowledge required for A-levels these days – (even students with straight A grades usually didn't know the basics) – and students doing these courses got fewer First and 2.1 degrees than those doing other subjects, which looked simply awful in the stats.

Everybody knew that low degree results fed through into the university league tables, and that foreign students – and their teachers and parents – looked at those league tables online when deciding where in the UK to study. So, the managers of Thames Metropolitan decided that things would have to change. The science departments were closed, and in their place the Islamic Studies Department was opened in the former science building. It now attracted students from all over the world who each paid thousands of pounds into the university's coffers to study there. As a mark of respect to King Abdullah of Saudi Arabia, where most funding for the department had come from, the building was renamed in his honour. Everyone at the university was happy with the name change, as well as the most generous donation by Saudi Arabia of many millions of pounds.

Other closures included the departments of engineering

and of mathematics. These were attracting fewer and fewer students, so it was best to let other 'research-led', traditional universities offer these subjects. Moreover, there were plenty of foreign graduates in engineering, maths and the sciences, so if the country needed graduates in these subjects for its economy there was a ready supply emanating from India and China anyway – and as they had so many people in those countries who could emigrate, it hardly seemed worth worrying that British students were no longer becoming qualified in these subjects in any great numbers.

The closure of departments was not bad news – in fact, quite the opposite, because new, exciting and diverse departments replaced these tired old out-of-date academic ones. As well as the new Department of Islamic Studies, there was a successful and expanding business school, which students from all over the world were keen to attend. Its results were amongst the highest in the UK – amongst the new universities, that is. There were also the expanding departments of education, health and social care, as well as psychology and counselling – and whole new departments in media and TV studies, diversity and human studies, and environmental and green studies. The forensics course had also proved popular, especially after the popularity of TV detective dramas, as had the new department of complementary medicine, with its exciting courses in aromatherapy, colour therapy, and homeopathy, as well as skincare and aesthetic medicine (which used to be called 'putting on make-up'). One of the most exciting and popular modules on all the university courses was the module on celebrity studies which, if a student so chose, could comprise up to forty per cent of a degree in media and TV studies. The internet pornography module was especially popular, apparently.

These policies were clearly working – the university had attracted many more students this year than last, and the number of overseas students, especially from China, was up by 20%.

The university could charge what it liked to students outside the EU, so instead of the rather measly £3000 it got per UK or EU student, a Chinese student would pay at least £10 000, and up to £18 000, depending on the course. Consequently, the university's finances were in rude health, and the university's exciting and innovative approach had been rewarded with a Queen's Award for Industry presented to the Vice-Chancellor, Baroness Bloodstone, by Prince Charles earlier that year.

"Don't piss off the Chinkies, old boy," said Sandy sternly.

Crump wasn't sure he approved of the use of that term, even in jest – it seemed rather casually racist, really – but he decided not to make an issue of it. Sandy was a senior lecturer, after all.

"But, look at these!"

Crump was holding up the homework he had got back from some of his students on the undergraduate degree courses.

"I know I know, and don't assume I approve," said Sandy, "but we all have to play the game."

"What, even if we award degrees to students who can hardly string a sentence together in English?"

"Yes."

"And even if we pass work that is clearly a fail?"

"Oh yes."

"And even if we pass work that's obviously just been copied and pasted from the Internet?"

"Yes, yes and yes again. We have to be sensitive to cultural differences – in many countries, copying is an acceptable educational practice. *That* is university policy."

Sandy smiled wryly. His eyes twinkled.

"Perhaps, old boy, it is the British tradition of valuing original thought that is the exception to the global rule. Perhaps the time has come to realise that it was we in this...*septic* isle...we in these...*irony* towers...who have been wrong all along. Perhaps," he smiled, somewhat wistfully, "we need to join the club – fit in – do what every other bloody university in every other bloody country in the world does, and stop being so damn bloody British, old boy!"

Crump was unsure whether Sandy was joking or not. Was he advocating cheating? Was he suggesting that's what they did in other countries? Wasn't that *racist*? Or *xenophobic*, at least? Or was what he was saying actually *true*?

They were in Sandy's office, and Crump had gone to him for advice. Strictly, Wendy Webb was his mentor, but Crump neither liked nor trusted her – he much preferred Sandy, and would in future take any problems he may have to him first. Sandy handed him a cup of coffee.

"Remember the two golden rules?"

"Of course," said Crump, "It's a business, and..."

"It's a game. Precisely. And if a player on your side in the World Cup final accidentally *on purpose* scores a goal to put you in the lead by using his hand to nudge it in, or by faking injury to get a penalty, are you going to rat to the referee?"

Crump thought hard. He hated football, and all sport come to that – he just didn't see that point. But that wasn't the point – the point was that the sporting analogy was not a good one.

"But this isn't a game of football, this is the British higher education system!"

"And we are following good practice in being sensitive to the needs of international students and their cultural diversity."

"But Sandy," said Crump, exasperated, "some students in my classes can't even speak or understand basic English – let alone read or write it – and the educational level of some of the others... it's practically..."

"Retarded?" said Sandy.

"Well...yes," said Crump, somewhat embarrassed at the thought.

The word sounded so insulting somehow – dirtied by history, misuse and insult – but he had to admit that it was both accurate and succinctly descriptive.

"Except we don't say retarded, do we?" said Sandy, admonishing himself.

"No?" queried Crump.

"No," confirmed Sandy, "we say 'learning difficulties' and pass students' work for the effort shown and the process they've gone through to write it."

"Even if we have to communicate to them in class by using sign language or pictures?"

"Especially if we have to use pictures," said Sandy, "because that's good – that means we are using differentiation and have correctly identified a visual learner and are personalising the lesson for them."

Crump sipped his coffee and winced – it was bitter, and tepid, and had a sour aftertaste.

"But what if a student simply copies and pastes stuff from the internet?" asked Crump.

"We pass it and say we are being sensitive to 'different cultural norms' because that 'paraphrasing' would be acceptable in some cultures and countries," said Sandy.

"Which countries, exactly?" asked Crump.

"Countries which send a lot of juicy fee-paying foreign students to Thames Metropolitan," Sandy smiled. "Remember, my dear boy, play up and play the game – it's all just a business and a game at the end of the day. Remember that – if nothing else, remember that."

"But," said Crump, "isn't it all just...well...cheating?"

"Shhh!" said Sandy in whisper, "You must *never ever* use that word! Remember – what used to be called cheating in the golden olden days isn't called cheating anymore."

"No?" said Crump.

"No," said Sandy, "it's like...we don't say 'working class' anymore, we say 'middle class', and we don't say 'worker', we say 'manager', for almost everybody – do you see?"

Crump saw, but wasn't sure if he liked what he saw. Actually, he wished he'd never seen it at all. He finished his coffee – it tasted as though there'd been alcohol in it somewhere, but he couldn't identify the drink, exactly. Something bitter, cheap and harsh.

"Giving the buggers what they want – that's what it's all about – and they want good degrees, 2:1s or Firsts. It makes them happy, it makes us happy – we get the moolah, they get the pretty certificates and letters after their name, and so it goes around and around, on our mad little merry-go-round..."

Sandy grinned and poured himself a large whisky. It was just gone 8.30 in the morning.

"And remember Crump, old boy – never piss off the Chinkies – or the Arabs – and never fail them, or anyone else come to that. The worst student gets a pass as minimum. And always give extra marks to the internationals – at least 20% just for being foreign and fee-paying – more if necessary. Never ever fail them for cheating or anything else for that matter."

Crump really couldn't believe what he was hearing. Was the British higher education system really like this? A corrupt sham and scam on an enormous scale?

Sandy sensed his shock and put a reassuring avuncular hand on his shoulder.

"Play the game, Crumpet old boy, and you'll be fine. Trust me."

So Crump did.

* * *

Later that morning, Crump was trying to explain to a baffled-looking Chinese student called Ernest – (the Chinese students always gave themselves English names that often sounded similar to their Chinese names, but which were often comically old-fashioned, so there were many Mabels, Marjories, Arthurs and Alberts amongst them) – that he had found his essay very interesting, despite the fact that the young man had only written three rambling sentences in barely comprehensible pidgin English. Something about a beautiful house and family, and about his wanting to be in business and to travel. Or something. Perhaps. It was hard to tell, really.

In class, Crump simply mimed his pleasure at reading Ernest's essay, and another Chinese student, a cheerful bright girl called Mabel, translated. Ernest smiled and nodded at this translated compliment, and also at his C-graded mark, and Crump died a little inside at the absurdity of this – he had given a pass mark to a piece of writing that he himself would have failed as a ten year old at primary school. And how this student, and many others, would be able to follow the course in English literature he would be teaching was anybody's guess. How would it be possible? Crump had no idea.

In the UK these days, it was your teacher's duty to spoon-feed you, tell you exactly what to write in essays, pre-mark your essay, correct it for you, mark and correct it again and again as you revised it until, eventually, and despite the essay showing no independent thought or learning or intelligence, all the boxes would be ticked and all criteria met and the essay awarded an A-grade. It was almost impossible to fail. This was called 'good practice'.

"I was reading," said Rajdeep, through a mouthful of samosa, "that it is more difficult for Chinese to be getting in to the university in China so that is why we are getting lot of worst students in UK."

"Really?" said Athena, "I didn't know that."

"Nor did I," said Crump.

Kwame, back from his conference, was sitting at his desk and nodding his head to some repetitive thud in his headphones. Apparently, his paper at the conference had gone down very well, and he'd been given an award, too, for empowering the African diaspora. It now hung on the wall beside him in the form of a certificate with an image of Martin Luther King on it.

"Oh yes, this is quite true. For emerging Chinese middle class, who are having one child only because of admirable population control policies which sadly my own country India has not yet been using – because of this and the growing prosperity there are very many who are wanting to attend the university."

Raj took another bite of his samosa, as did Crump of his. Generously, Raj had offered everyone one of his home-made samosas – delicious, though a little spicier than the usual.

"But they are not having enough universities in China and they are only taking best students who are passing difficult entrance tests with the flying colours. Others come to UK."

Raj seemed to know what he was talking about. Crump knew next to nothing about Asian education systems, which was not necessarily a bad thing – just trying to understand the British education system was enough to drive anyone to drink.

"Also, many are cheating in English language tests and some certificates are forgery too. I was reading this on internet."

Raj tapped on his keyboard to find the website.

Crump and Athena stood behind him and looked at the screen – it displayed an article on an educational website. It said, more or less, what Raj had said, and interviewed several Chinese students. They predictably talked of learning about a new culture, and promoting international harmony, and all the usual parroted piffle that students from totalitarian dictatorships are prone to. But they also mentioned, with rare, even brave, honesty, that they were also coming to the UK because the degrees were easier to get than in China. They said they had specifically chosen British universities which gave the highest degree marks, that didn't fail anyone, that didn't expel anyone for plagiarism and that practically guaranteed them good grades.

That was why universities were obsessed with their place in the league tables – they had to make themselves attractive to foreign students, and thus they competed to give the highest marks they could get away with to every student. The race was on, ultimately, to see who could dumb down the most, and this was particularly urgent for the newer universities. These institutions didn't score well in the RAE which measured the value of research done by their staff, so didn't get the funding that such research would bring, so couldn't attract the best researchers and academics with higher salaries and perks and prestige, so utterly relied on overseas students for a great deal of their income. It was all so simple really – it was just the morality of it all that was hideously complex.

* * *

After finishing his lessons for the day, Crump decided to leave his paperwork and go and thank Miss Sharma in the library for the help she had given him after he'd been injured in the 'placard incident'.

Athena had told him that a couple of the veiled women had come over from outside the Abdullah centre and tried to help him. Apparently they hadn't stayed long. The bearded Muslim men, who had been inside the centre, soon came rushing out yelling, and pulled their women away from the fracas, even though they were just trying to help the injured Crump. Athena said one man even pushed one of the veiled women to the ground violently, but it was, of course, impossible to tell which one, as they were all dressed in black burqas and looked identical. If nothing else, thought Crump, burqas would make taking graduation photos or holiday snaps easier... Just one photo could be taken and distributed to everyone!

Crump entered the Stephen Lawrence Learning-Zone-which-everyone-called-a-library and looked around. He could see several students milling around by the bookshelves, but no Miss Sharma. There was a new section upstairs where there were computers as well as some more books and journals, so that is where he headed.

One thing that always annoyed Crump was when people were inappropriately and selfishly noisy. In libraries, in the cinema, in other quiet places – why couldn't people just keep quiet?

But keeping quiet was not what anyone was doing in the computer room. Despite the relatively serene atmosphere downstairs, where the occasional student browsed around the aisles and conversations were whispered, the upstairs appeared more like some kind of crèche, such was the noise coming from the students at the workstations. It was as though somebody had magically cast a spell to make toddlers grow into late adolescents who, despite the spots and the hair and the overpowering stench of deodorant, still had the brains of toddlers rattling around in their overgrown skulls. Arguing, shouting, laughing, yelling into mobile phones – it was like a wall of noise and no-one seemed to give a shit about it either.

Crump also noticed that, apart for a man in his twenties sitting at a workstation, and a young ginger-headed woman, he was the only white person in the room – not that that mattered, but Crump wondered if there may be some cultural reason for all the noise. He didn't think there was any festival this week – Diwali or Eid – but then again, he found it hard to keep up with the multicultural multi-faith calendar as there were just so many festivals these days.

No-one there seemed to have any manners or consideration for anyone else, and no-one was paying any heed whatsoever to the clip-art notices on the walls that asked for 'QUIET PLEASE'. It sounded as though no mobile phones had been turned off either – the occasional electronic bleeps and polyphonic ringtones made that clear. It looked like Lord of the Flies, Bangla-style, and with more gold jewellery.

There was also a group of slightly frightened-looking girls huddled together at a corner workstation – Crump recognised two of them as the Chinese girls he had seen being jostled while leaving the lift on his first day. They looked upset. Three young men were standing over them in the corner, probably trying to chat them up. Somehow, over the cacophony, Crump heard some kind of faint squeal. It was Miss Sharma's nervous and thin high-pitched voice, and it was imploring somebody to be quiet, rather unsuccessfully.

"Please... please...try to be quiet... this is a library," said the voice.

"No it ain't – it's a learning zone innit," came a mumbled reply, followed by nasty laughter.

"Oh yes...yes...this is a learning zone," repeated the voice, "...but...please be quiet...oh... please... please be quiet, please...oh..."

Crump looked around and saw Miss Sharma at a workstation in the far corner. He hadn't noticed her at first as she was only about five feet tall and was surrounded by several much taller students. He went over.

"Can I help you at all, Miss Sharma?" he asked. She looked at him blankly. "I was on the tour of the library you gave – I'm a member of staff – Crump – Kevin Crump."

A couple of the students sniggered and giggled at his name, repeating it under their breath – which was deeply ironic really, considering some of theirs.

"Oh yes, of course, no, I mean, yes, but, no..." said Miss Sharma. The young men she had being trying to shut up wandered off – one of them leered nastily at them both as he did so.

Miss Sharma looked rather flustered – it was clear that, for whatever reason, she was unable to keep order here and the students just ignored her.

"I just came to thank you," said Crump.

Suddenly, there was a high pitched scream, then a giggle rippled through the room. A loud polyphonic mobile phone rang, playing some rap tune or other, and several of the boys started singing out-of-tune ghetto gangsta patois along with it. It was all like some kind of zoo, but noisier and more animalistic.

"Oh...Thank me? Oh...I...oh..." said Miss Sharma, her cheeks flushed.

"Yes, for the other day – I was attacked..." Crump pointed at his head.

"Oh yes...oh...I see..."

Ms Sharma seemed nervous, even more so than usual. A student shrieked and laughed somewhere in the room and she jumped. Another mobile rang noisily.

"Are you...alright... now?"

"Yes, thank you," said Crump, "bit of a bruise but... the concussion's gone. Could've been worse."

Miss Sharma nodded. Crump continued:

"Case of mistaken identity, apparently."

"Oh...yes...um...that racist man..."

"That's right – but apparently he's not racist anymore," said Crump. Miss Sharma frowned. "He's changed, apparently. Born again."

"Once a racist always a racist," she said sternly, as another student screamed with manic laughter somewhere in the room.

"Anyway, I was thinking," Crump said, "perhaps I could, as an expression of thanks, take you out for, y'know, a coffee, or... something." A look of utter horror came over Miss Sharma's face and he thought for one awful moment she was going to faint or cry or scream, or all three at once.

"Oh... um... no... thank... er... you... um... now.. . if... you... er... don't... um... mind... I'm... um... very... er... busy..."

And with that she scuttled off quickly, turned a corner and was gone.

Crump stood baffled in the middle of the cacophony and chaos, not understanding at all what had happened. Maybe it's against her culture or religion or something, he thought, but surely politeness wasn't against her culture or religion too? Why did she just run off like that? He was only trying to say thank you, after all.

Then another sound registered in Crump's ears that was different from the shouting and screaming and mobile phone din of the computer suite. It was the sound of crying – whimpering really. Crump turned around and noticed it was coming from the corner of the room where he had seen the two Chinese girls.

Three young men, two Asian and one black, were standing over the girls, who were huddled together on one chair cowering in fear like mice cornered by cats. Crump pushed himself past students who were crowding around and then he saw that two of the students – a fat Asian guy and the tall black guy, both had their penises out and were waving them in the faces of the girls. Crump was so stunned by what he was seeing he didn't know what to say. All he could think, stupidly, was 'well, at least they're not erect,' and he just stood and stared as the students put away their flaccid members, buttoned up their low-slung jeans and, without a word, but with smug, invincible, satisfied looks on their faces, sauntered out of the room – in that dumb, mock-casual, vaguely threatening walk much loved of ghetto gangsters in America, and much copied amongst inner city youth in the UK.

The two girls looked petrified, so Crump crouched down and tried to speak to them. It wasn't helpful that these Chinese girls could hardly speak a word of English, but eventually, he persuaded them to leave the library with him. He took them to the student welfare office where he was sure someone could help, and left them in reception.

On his way back, he was going to go into the library to report the incident and also make a formal complaint about the students that had behaved so disgracefully – but then he thought about what that would mean. Firstly, he didn't know their names so how could he be sure they could be identified? Secondly, he had already got a first warning for supposed racism, so how would it look if he accused an Asian guy and a black guy of sexually inappropriate behaviour? It was, after all, his word against theirs and he knew where that had got him the last time, and he was sure they'd get all their mates to lie on their behalf too. And the Chinese girls barely had a handful of words of English between them, so would hardly be ideal witnesses.

As he walked back from the student welfare centre he could see the fat Asian guy and the black guy, and about seven or eight others, standing in front of the library and staring at him in a way that could only be called menacing. He looked at them, and the fat Asian and the black guy smiled – grinned, even. They knew he wasn't going to do anything. They knew it – he could tell. They knew their race made them untouchable.

Crump felt a dark sick pit of regret at the centre of his stomach – he was, both metaphorically and literally, passing by on the other side, but knew he just couldn't risk it. One little squeak of an accusation of racism from either of the students and he would be on a disciplinary, and that could even get him sacked – and utterly and completely destroy his academic career.

But then, it wasn't as though there'd been any physical assault – the students hadn't touched the girls, they had just been waving around their willies. But he also knew that he should have reported it – he should have, but he didn't. He couldn't. He just couldn't – for once, he had to think of himself. But he felt sick to his stomach for what he was doing – or, rather, what he was *not* doing. In fact, he hated himself for it and could almost feel his moral code being scrambled in his brain as he walked back to his office.

He made a mental note to monitor the situation, and he really wanted to report the noise and chaos of the first floor of the library to management too – but all that would happen would be that Miss Sharma would get into trouble. He would try and talk to her later and ask if she needed any help with enforcing rules in the library – a quiet word could often sort things out.

Crump also wanted to thank the burqa-wearing women for their concern and help when he was attacked, so made his way across the courtyard to the Abdullah building.

He was in luck – he could see a group of the veiled women standing outside, so he wouldn't have to actually go inside the unfamiliar building and negotiate with the security guards. They had all been told at the initial meeting that the Abdullah building was out of bounds for all not studying, researching or teaching there – something that puzzled Crump. Surely, a member of staff should have right of access to the main areas of any university building? How could a university ban its staff from a whole department – from a whole building? It was all very odd.

Making his way towards the group of veiled women, Crump felt not a little trepidation. Standing there dressed from head to foot in black burqas, they almost looked like some kind of alien creature as they huddled together – for some reason, Crump thought of Star Trek, and a blob creature that had been in the original series. He couldn't even see their hands, and when they moved, he couldn't see their legs move either. They glided, like nuns – with added value.

Did they believe their veil protected them from the gaze of lascivious men? Did they think men were so uncontrollable that if they glimpsed an ankle or a wrist – or, God help us, a face – they would have simply been unable to control their animal urges and would've ravaged them on the spot? Was wearing this garb their choice, or had it been imposed on them by their mosques or their men-folk? Or perhaps their women-folk, as women always seemed more religious and puritanical and right-wing than men in every society? And was it worn for mainly religious reasons – or were the reasons more cultural, or political? Crump had to admit to himself that he didn't really know.

How on earth could he thank these women if he couldn't see their faces? It would be like talking to a tent or a curtain – and how could one thank a fabric? And were they allowed to speak anyway, especially to a man? Crump knew quite a lot about religions, but he didn't know much about burqa decorum. Headscarves were obviously originally intended to keep women's long hair out of their eyes. After all, women wore headscarves in Europe too until fairly recently in history, because it was practical to do so. But wearing a full veil? That was the opposite of practical. Where could that tradition have come from? It seemed rather extreme by anyone's standards, although no doubt burqa-makers were delighted at the recent boost in trade.

Crump had no idea how to communicate with someone with a veil over their face, and whose eyes squinted through a little slit at the outside world – it was rather like talking to a tall, black, Muslim post box. Whenever Crump saw these women it always reminded him of post boxes – he couldn't help it – they just did.

Speaking to someone wearing sunglasses was slightly disconcerting, but speaking to someone wearing a full mask was downright weird, and Crump had only done so on the rare occasions he'd been to Halloween parties as a child. How do you speak to a mask? You can see no facial expression, no feelings, no humanity – just a mask, with small, flickering eyes trapped behind the plastic or the cloth. It was, in short, an enormous barrier to communication. Full stop. It was also just plain spooky. It gave him the creeps.

"Excuse me," said Crump, as he approached the burqa women.

They didn't respond and seemed to huddle a little closer together at his approach.

"Hi, I'm the man you helped the other day – who was hit – on the head..."

Crump pointed at his head, and two of the burqa women looked at him – he could see their eyes, dark and moist, through the little slits. He had no idea whether they could speak English or understand what he was saying. He also had no idea if they were smiling or frowning or happy or sad. He had no idea actually if they were women at all come to that, as there was really no way of telling the gender of the inhabitant of a burqa.

"I just wanted to thank you – for your help," he said, "I...I went to the hospital, but I'm better now, so...thank you all...er...very much..."

The burqa women's movements seemed to indicate they were a bit flustered, as though not knowing what to do. There was now only one woman looking at him through her eye-slit. The rest had turned their backs on him – at least he could tell back from front, which was a plus. He could see from the clear, dark, bright eyes of this young woman that she was young – early twenties maybe, or teenaged – and he could also see that her eyes were sad-looking, and moist. Was she crying? Her eyes looked worried and depressed, and yes, he could see as he peered closer – she *was* crying. Weeping quietly. He knew it.

Automatically and instinctively, Crump reached out and held her hand – her hand seemed to find his easily, as though she had reached out to him too.

"Are you alright?" he asked.

He could sense the tense fear coursing through the girl's hand like an electric current. Her eyes looked scared – really scared.

"You helped me – so I can help you, if you want..." he said quietly.

At that moment, an enormous force seemed to lift Crump off his feet and throw him to the ground. There was a lot of shouting in a foreign language – it sounded like Arabic, but he wasn't sure. A boot kicked him several times in the ribs, and then, in the testicles. He lay on the ground with his head to his knees for several moments. The pain was excruciating – it gnawed at his brain and body like rats. For a few numb moments he sank into a deep agony and simply could not move, but lay there with his eyes closed tight, breathing slowly and deeply and near-paralysed in a world of pain.

By the time Crump had come to and sat up, all the burqa women were gone and had been replaced by a group of bearded men in robes who were standing some way off. Two smart-suited security guards stood by them, looking over to him – one of them was talking into a walkie-talkie. Their posture made it clear that it wasn't a good idea to approach.

Regretfully, and feeling slightly dazed, and with a dull ache in his groin, Crump stood up and went back to his office, wondering what he should do. He felt that he should say something about this – but really didn't want to draw attention to himself, especially after his first warning. But why did no-one come to help him?

"You should report it," said Athena in the office. Raj nodded in agreement.

"I can't," said Crump, somewhat fumbling around for a reason why – his colleagues didn't know about his first warning yet.

"They must find these bloody hooligans, and other bloody hooligan fellows who were hitting you on head before also," said Raj, determinedly.

"Yes they should," added Athena.

Should, shouldn't, could, couldn't – it was all a great big headache. But he couldn't – just couldn't – risk any more trouble, even though he hadn't caused any of the trouble in the first place.

He'd only been at the university for a couple of weeks and he'd already been falsely accused of racism, been given a first warning, been hit on the head by a placard wielded by an angry mob, and been thrown to the floor and kicked in the balls by Arab security men. The beginning of term could, it was true, have gone better.

But it could have been worse, thought Crump, though he couldn't at that moment quite put his finger on exactly how.

* * *

Later, at the education department, Crump found himself standing in front of his class of trainee college teachers. He realised, when everyone eventually turned up, that he had forgotten to mention anything to his manager about the woman in his class who wore the burqa. She may even have been one of the women who had helped him after he had been attacked. He had no way of checking, and the woman within the burqa was extremely quiet and rarely spoke, so he felt awkward asking her outright.

He was certainly not happy trying to teach this student, or knowing that she would graduate from the teacher training course the next year ready to start teaching English in a college.

121

Would he like his children – if he had them – to be taught by someone wearing such garb? For them to be taught English by someone whose face they could not see?

Crump knew how the education system in all its forms was obsessed with diversity which had become, actually, some sort of quasi-religion itself. The great god of diversity – especially racial or religious diversity – could never ever be denied or challenged in any educational institution in Britain these days, not unless you wanted to cause yourself enormous problems and risk destroying your career.

After much thought, and feeling again that tight knot of regret in his stomach, Crump decided he couldn't risk making a complaint against the burqa-wearing woman in his class, or refuse to teach her, despite the fact that it went against all his principles and instincts. He really couldn't risk being accused of racism again. He would say nothing. He hated himself for it too.

The next week, the funeral of Freddie Finch took place. Of all the people in the department, only Sandy attended, and that was in a personal capacity, not as a representative of the university – they sent no-one and didn't even send any flowers or make any donation to the charity mentioned in the funeral notice. A small donation was made to the specified charity and flowers sent to the funeral thanks to a whip-round of lecturers at the department – and others from the university contributed too. But from the university itself – nothing.

Sandy explained that this had been their official policy for a few years – after taking legal advice, senior management had decided that the purchase of flowers or the gift of charitable donations on behalf of those who had taken their own lives could be perceived as an admission of guilt that the university had in some way been responsible for one of its employees taking that self-destructive decision. They had also, after the number of staff members who had taken their own lives had increased threefold over the previous fifteen years, added a clause to all permanent contracts stating that lump-sums paid out would be substantially reduced when paid out to the estates of those who had killed themselves. So, no flowers, no donations, no regrets – this was now university policy. Crump thought it was a disgusting policy, but what could he do?

He didn't attend the funeral, which was held in a crematorium near Bromley, but then he didn't even know the man, so it would have been awkward. Of course, Crump had filled Freddie Finch's shoes and, he later discovered, was even sitting at the late lecturer's desk, which made him feel slightly queasy when he thought of it, so he tried not to.

How must Freddie Finch's parents have felt – he had heard that they were both retired academics – when they realised that the university where their son was teaching hadn't even had the courtesy to send a bunch of flowers to his funeral, let alone send a representative? The head of department, Fiona Windrush should have gone, so should Wendy Webb, irrespective of how busy they were – they could even have gone in a personal capacity, if they had really wanted to make the legal situation clear. But no – Sandy was the only person from the university who'd attended the funeral. Apparently, Wendy Webb and all the other managers had deliberately scheduled an 'important' strategy meeting about access and widening participation at the same time, so they could always cite that as a reason for not attending the funeral if asked.

How convenient. How sad. How awful.

* * *

At West London College that Friday, Crump told Becky about his concerns. She, like him, was used to the kind of managerial nonsense that plagues every British educational institution these days, and she, like him, knew it was all bollocks – and nasty bollocks, at that.

"Just take it easy," she said in her usual laid-back way, "You're new there – you can't rock the boat."

"I know," said Crump, "but just think of it – they didn't

even send flowers to his funeral! Or make a donation to charity! Nothing!"

"I must admit, it is a bit shitty," said Becky, biting into a milk chocolate hobnob.

"A bit?"

"Well, OK, a lot – but you know what management fuckers are like," she said.

Crump always liked the way Becky was so direct.

"It's all legal bollocks – and they're all just cowards, to a man."

"And woman," added Crump.

"Oh especially woman – women managers are the worst! I'd always much rather have a boy boss. Not you of course..." she joked.

"Just so you could manipulate him?" said Crump.

Becky smiled.

"Why, of course, Mr Crump," she smiled, mock-fluttering her eye-lashes, "but a man would also be more consistent, less bitchy, and know how to delegate better – and also I'd have the opportunity to get off with him – not just to further my career, of course."

They both laughed. Crump liked Fridays at the college, not least because he could have a good chat with Becky who had a wonderful way of cheering him up, even when she was insulting him. She kept him sane. She was the only person he really trusted there too.

The next week went by pleasantly enough, with Crump constantly being startled at the low level of work he was getting from his university students. He was making good progress with his research too – he was now even thinking about extending it and doing a PhD.

Then, on Wednesday, there was an urgent email in his inbox, in amongst the usual plethora of irrelevant emails the department secretaries and university administrators insisted on constantly and incessantly spewing out to everyone, and the usual emailed essays from students. It was from Wendy Webb and requested a meeting with him as soon as possible – probably just about some dull administrative matter, he thought. She was supposed to be his mentor, after all.

There was also another urgent email, this time one from Fiona Windrush, that had been sent to everyone at the department, requesting – actually, more like demanding – everybody's attendance at an important meeting in the team room later that day. Crump had been meaning to go off straight after lessons and do some shopping – his cupboard at home was, literally, bare – but decided he most definitely could not, under any circumstances, miss this meeting. He very rarely saw Fiona Windrush anyway, so he certainly didn't want to make a bad impression – again – and the meeting sounded important too. He wondered what it could be about.

* * *

"You will not approach, talk to, or communicate with Miss Sharma in any way whatsoever. Is that understood?"

Wendy Webb was cross. In fact, she was so cross that her face had changed colour slightly and the tops of her ears had turned a bright tomato-y shade of red. Crump said that he understood – but he didn't really understand what he apparently should have understood.

He was amazed – stunned – when Wendy Webb had informed him that Miss Sharma had made a complaint of sexual harassment against him, simply for going up to her in the library and thanking her for helping him.

"But," said Crump, weakly, "I just went to thank her...for helping me...when I was attacked..."

"When you were attacked for being a racist," said Wendy Webb.

"Yes...I mean...no...I mean..." blustered Crump.

"You clearly don't know what you mean," Wendy said, "but I know what I mean when I warn you to stay away from this young woman and to stop pestering her."

"But I'm not... *'pestering'* her," he protested.

Crump had admitted approaching Miss Sharma and had been told that, according to university guidelines, this did, actually, amount to 'pestering' and could be considered sexual harassment if perceived to be such by the 'victim'. Perception was all, apparently. Reality didn't matter.

"We all need to be aware of the sensitivities of women, who for far too long have been oppressed by traditional patriarchal structures, and we also need to be sensitive to the needs of those from other cultures," said Wendy Webb.

"Yes, I know," said Crump, "and I am."

He had not considered Miss Sharma who, although Asian, had clearly been brought up in Britain and educated here, to be of another culture at all, really. She was a British Asian. It wasn't as though she were an asylum seeker who'd just fallen off the back of a lorry, or one of the international students in his classes.

"You are, perhaps, very lucky to be given a verbal warning for this," said Wendy Webb.

"Yes," said Crump, "I know," though he had to admit to himself that he now knew very little about anything at all if his thanking a colleague had somehow resulted in a complaint of sexual harassment.

Did Miss Sharma really perceive his thanking her as some kind of sexual approach, and, even if it had been, which it most certainly was not, was making someone know you fancied them now some sort of crime? Perhaps Miss Sharma's Asian culture was different in that way? Alternatively, perhaps Miss Sharma was completely and utterly bonkers and some kind of paranoid, feminist neurotic?

But then, she wasn't like Cecilia, refusing to speak to men – she quite happily spoke to men and had given them all a tour of the library, after all, and seemed perfectly normal, if a little nervy. Anyway, the only person in the whole university who could possibly complain about his attentions was Athena, and he hadn't even expressed his attraction to her directly yet.

Crump accepted a verbal warning from Wendy Webb as there was really nothing else he could do. To fight this would mean an investigation, possible suspension, a fitness to practise hearing and all the rest of it. He was like an innocent man in a police cell being given the option of accepting a caution for something he hadn't done and ending it there and then, or going to trial which might result in conviction and imprisonment – he just had to take the least worst option, especially as he had 'form'.

Quite simply, he couldn't afford a second written warning – because that was the very last stage before dismissal. You were allowed two verbal, and two written, warnings. He had now had one of each – quite an achievement for a new lecturer in the first few weeks of the first term of his first university teaching job.

In the afternoon, Crump went to the team room early to await the departmental meeting with Fiona Windrush. He got himself a coffee and read the education pages of the newspapers – the usual waffle about targets, outcomes and initiatives. Crump knew these educational statistics inside out – after all, he was doing research on representations of the British education in literature and film of the 19th and 20th centuries. He also knew that most people involved in education, especially managers, used statistics rather like a drunk uses a lamp post – for support rather than illumination. They were constantly trying to twist and invent and fake the statistics to show anything they wanted – and what they wanted, always, was a higher place in the league tables which would attract more 'customers' in the form of pupils and students, which would in turn mean more funding from government and create, to use a trite term much loved of managers, a 'virtuous circle', and 'add value' for everyone concerned.

It was really no different to running a factory, the way these people put it. They always talked of targets, production, productivity measures, and all of it – all of it – was complete and utter bollocks. What's more, everyone knew it was all complete and utter bollocks – from the principal of every college and the head teacher of every school, through the hierarchy of teachers top to bottom, from the managers to the support staff, to many, if not all, of the students and parents. But no-one had the guts to admit it.

Crump put the educational section of the newspaper down – it was all too depressing. He hadn't noticed others arriving, but when he looked up he could see that the room was now crammed with people waiting for the meeting to start. There weren't enough chairs for everyone so some staff sat on the carpet or stood leaning against the back wall. No-one was talking, which Crump found strange, not to mention rude – most were reading newspapers or journals, and some were marking essays.

Everyone looked annoyed to be there, except Crump who didn't really mind at all because it gave him a good opportunity to see some lecturers that he never saw from day to day. He recognised a few – but he hadn't seen some since the initial meeting at the beginning of term. Was that really less than a month ago? Crump felt about a decade older.

Why didn't the department try to facilitate some contact between department members? Apart from Athena, Raj and the ever-nodding Kwame, as well as Sandy, and Wendy – whose emails he now dreaded as they always seemed to herald complaints of racism and sexism – he didn't really know anyone at the department. There was Cecilia, of course, the mad man-phobic – Crump could see her standing by the window, willow-thin and her face pale as the belly of a dead fish. One thing he'd tried to do at West London College was to get staff actually talking to each other, getting them to get to know each other – even to socialise together if they wanted. It just made working life more pleasant somehow.

The door swung open and Fiona Windrush, handsomely authoritative – almost regal – swanned into the room, followed by one of the departmental secretaries.

"Right, if I could have your attention please," she said, and she smiled that smile that seemed to mean everything and nothing at the same time.

Crump was already confused and the meeting hadn't really started yet. Fiona surveyed the room and the staff members present. There was compete, pin-drop silence. She smiled smugly.

"Thank you for coming this afternoon," she said, "I have an urgent message to relay to all staff of this department – a complaint, you could say. But it's not just about us – this message has been circulated to all departments."

There was an audible sigh of relief in the room. Crump wouldn't have minded if it had been 'just them' – at least it wasn't 'just him', which had been the normal state of affairs until then.

"We have been reminded in the strongest possible terms that no member of staff is permitted to approach or enter the Abdullah building where the Department of Islamic Studies is located."

So that was it – Crump hoped that no-one had complained about him directly.

"Furthermore, a complaint was received about an individual who recently sexually harassed one of the women students from the Abdullah building, though his identity is not certain and the senior management of the Centre for Islamic Studies have very generously decided not to pursue the matter further," said Fiona Windrush, staring at Crump where he sat.

Shit! It was a complaint about him after all.

He could feel himself blushing so he looked down at the carpet in order to avoid Fiona's penetrating gaze. She was still staring at him though – he could sense it – and so he blushed even more. He wanted to leave but knew if he did then he would just draw attention to himself, so he closed his eyes and tried to breathe deeply, and hoped no-one would notice too much.

"I am sure I do not need to remind you of the importance of the generous donations to this university from benefactors in the Muslim world, nor of the importance of the presence of international students in our midst, from all corners of the globe, which enriches us all and helps to create a diverse and successful community that benefits each and every one of us," she said.

Why didn't she just say that the foreign students pay loads of cash to be here, that Arab and other donors pay millions to the university, and that we are just interested in them for their money, so everyone has to be extra nice to them at all times, do whatever they say, and pass them with flying colours even when they hand in work that would shame the average twelve year old?

A hand went up.

"Yes, er..."

"Athena," said Athena, "I was just wondering, does that mean we cannot even go into the Abdullah building to look around or talk to the women in the..."

She looked puzzled and fumbled for the word.

"Burqas..." said Crump, but immediately wished he hadn't as everyone turned round and looked at his reddened face, making him blush even more.

"Yes, burqas," said Athena.

"That is exactly what I mean," said Fiona Windrush, "we have to respect people's cultural differences as we all well know, and for these women, wearing a burqa..." she looked at Crump and smiled, somewhat haughtily, he thought,"...is a statement of their independence and female empowerment."

There were a couple of chortles in the room – one from Athena – and Cecilia stormed out of the room and slammed the door behind her. Crump, too, found it hard to understand how women wrapping themselves in cloth empowered them. He wondered if he would feel empowered if he wore a tent. No, he decided, he wouldn't – except, perhaps, at Glastonbury.

"No-one..." and Fiona looked at Crump again, "must ever – and I mean ever – approach or speak to any of the women who study at the Abdullah building, or speak to anyone in its immediate vicinity, male or female, or attempt to enter the building which, as you have been informed before, is out of bounds to all who do not work or study there. Is that understood?"

There were a few mumbled yeses and Fiona Windrush looked around like a stern headmistress telling off naughty eight-year-olds. Crump could see that Athena started to put her hand up but thought better of it. It was truly outrageous that staff should be banned from a whole building of the university like this. Crump was sure everyone was thinking the same thing too, but not one person – not one – dared to speak up or object to this order in any way.

"Good," Fiona Windrush said, and marched out of the team room, smiling a smile of victory.

Crump looked at Athena and shrugged, and she smiled weakly back. We all have to make compromises, he thought, especially when faced with enormous cheques. Money makes everyone's principles go out the window.

Whether you're a university manager accepting funding for students you know to be unfit to study, or a lecturer passing foreign students you know have cheated and should have failed because to do otherwise would get you reprimanded or lose you your career and salary, or someone who believes utterly in gender equality but who is prepared to turn a blind eye if people treat the genders unequally if it's done in the name of religion or ethnicity or culture – and especially, of course, if those people give you great piles of cash for the right to do so – we all have to make compromises, and we all have our price.

Crump felt guilty that his going up to thank the burqa women had led to all this – and he was sure it had. He almost felt like going and apologising to the be-suited Arab security guards who had thrown him to the floor and kicked him in his ribs and testicles – which, he pondered, was a very odd thing to feel indeed. But that's the way he felt.

Strange really that he had caused all these problems

because of his common courtesy and insistence on thanking the burqa women for their help.

Perhaps he should have just forgotten about the whole thing and stayed in his office – like Kwame, with his headphones on, nodding away to hip-hop all day long and seemingly completely unaware of anything going on in the world. Perhaps living under a tub was the best way to live – just keeping your head down and going along with whatever everyone else was going along with. Perhaps ignorance was bliss, after all.

But Crump couldn't stop thinking about the young woman in the burqa – the one with dark, worried eyes that were filled with tears.

CHAPTER SIX

Coming Out

Soon, the trees outside his office window lost their leaves, as autumn became winter and the nights drew in, and Crump settled into a pleasantly dull routine at Thames Metropolitan University.

Sometimes he enjoyed his job, sometimes he didn't, and sometimes he didn't know what to think. If not exactly the best of times, it certainly wasn't the worst; if not an age of wisdom exactly, it wasn't an age of complete and utter foolishness quite yet; and though it wasn't exactly a season of light or a spring of hope, at least it wasn't an age of darkness or a winter of despair either. Not yet, anyway.

As he reminded himself every day, it could have been better, but it could have been a hell of a lot worse too. Worse things happen at sea, as his mum always used to say. It was true. They did.

One week in November, all the senior staff were invited to hear the Vice-Chancellor speak in the grand lecture hall. Baroness Bloodstone had held the office for two years, which had been an exciting time for the university, what with the new Centre for Islamic Studies opening and the closure of the under-performing science departments. Rumour had it that she was only in the job because of the recommendation of her old friend Tony Blair, but she had been education secretary for over six months, and done all sorts of other important things too –

she was a member of so many committees she probably had a committee to organise the committees – so she obviously had the expertise and fully deserved her position and a place in the House of Lords.

Moreover, women were woefully under-represented at high levels of management, so it was about time that more universities had women in charge. Not that this had been a relevant factor in her appointment – she was there because she deserved to be there through merit, just like all the other women in management positions at the university, even if they had progressed through 'positive action' and possibly clandestine 'positive' discrimination.

The previous year she had received an award on behalf of the university from Prince Charles for the way Thames Metropolitan had attempted to tackle social exclusion and widen participation, and everyone had been delighted at this recognition of excellence and good practice.

The university was also proud that it was one of only three universities in the UK where a majority of senior managers were female, and it also had the largest proportion of ethnic minority staff in the country – it had received an award for each of these achievements too, presented by Prince Charles again, who was quite simply delighted, as usual. He had, after all, opened the Centre for Islamic Studies the previous year – a particular interest to him, as he was well known for his interest in the Islamic faith, and got on swimmingly with various despotic and corrupt Saudi princes – and he closely followed developments at Thames Metropolitan University, which he thought an excellent example to us all, though of course he'd never want anyone from his family or acquaintance to actually study there. Not even Prince Harry.

Baroness Bloodstone was enormously impressed by the gender and ethnicity positive action initiatives at Thames Metropolitan, and was especially pleased that the results of gender equality policies and 'positive action' had meant that women were now showing what they could do at senior management level. She tried to keep quiet the fact that she came from an upper-middle class family, with a wealthy surgeon father and a privileged non-working mother of aristocratic stock, and had gone to one of the most ancient and expensive girls' private schools in the country.

Hers was a belief in equality and fair treatment for all, and women and ethnic minorities deserved nothing less than full compensation for their terrible suffering and oppression through the centuries by having positive action in the workplace now. Conversely, white men deserved disadvantage at work because of their collective past behaviour in history and had to learn to make way for women and ethnic minorities, and celebrate diversity, and realise that equality of outcome was essential these days to redress the balance of power. They would of course be angry at losing their privileged position – but then they would, wouldn't they? Men always were.

Women had made wonderful progress at Thames Metropolitan University – progress that, due to patriarchal structures, they might not have made without positive action and mentoring programmes. Selection panels were fully aware of gender and diversity issues and the rewards the university would get if it appointed as many women and ethnic minority candidates as it could to management level. The happy evidence of the university's success could be seen in the fact that no department in the university had promoted a white man, or appointed one to senior management level, for over two years – a fact which made both the university, and Baroness Blackstone, justifiably proud. This was real equality in action.

No wonder the university had won so many awards for equality and diversity – proof, if any was needed, of the rightness of this focus on equality of outcome, and not the out-of-date, sexist, racist type of equality based on treating people equally on merit irrespective of race and gender. If they'd done that, then, at present rates, it would have taken over two hundred years to achieve the level of equality of outcome the university had achieved in a decade!

But Baroness Bloodstone was not Prince Charles. She had not been brought up to keep quiet in his vaguely inane and diplomatic manner, an upbringing evidenced by the fact she never seemed to shut up, especially in interviews. Usually, this was fine – she had deliberately 'working-classed' her accent from the prim, plummy tones she had learnt at her boarding school, to those of some kind of no-nonsense salt-of-the-earth northern housewife, watching the pennies and never living beyond her means. She emulated Mrs Thatcher shamelessly.

Of course, she did still eat in the poshest and priciest restaurants, especially as she was married to the multi-millionaire director of a media company, so money was no object – and, if she was truthful to herself, she really couldn't stand the working classes, especially in Manchester where she grew up. She, unfortunately, had to spend some time there when she was a local MP, going round and smiling at the obese, earring-ed, chavvy constituents, kissing their fat, ugly, retarded babies and eating their horrid and disgusting greasy food, if only for the photo-calls. The last time she went, she even had to eat a whole sausage in batter, and remembered that the toothless chip shop owner had asked her which sauce she wanted, red or brown. Red or brown? It was like they were speaking some strange alien language, but she smiled through it. Bit of both, she had said cheerfully, and he had smothered the greasy battered sausage with the vile gloop – disgustingly, it looked horribly like a severed cock sitting in a puddle of blood and shit on the chip paper. It had taken at least two days for her to stop feeling sick and to get rid of the taste and the smell, and she had sworn then and there that she'd never ever set foot in a chip shop again – and she hadn't.

It was always a great disappointment to her, amongst others on the political left, that the working classes were 1) constantly bloody ungrateful for the hard work she and others had done and were doing for them, especially when these working class voters promptly switched their vote to Conservative when they bought a house, and stopped being poor, and aspired to being middle-class, even though were still as common as muck and always would be... And 2) that they were so bloody awful in every single way imaginable – they were uncultured, ignorant, illiterate, innumerate, disgustingly obese, ugly, irresponsible, feckless, vulgar, drunken, sluttish, diseased, bigoted, racist, homophobic, Europhobic, work-o-phobic, lazy, idle, useless and thick – not glorious or proletarian or united at all, no matter what Lenin or Marx or even Tony Blair himself had said. *And* they had made her eat a battered sausage with red and brown sauce!

But that wasn't the point, she tried to convince herself – it's the principles that mattered, not whether or not she liked specific individuals. It was just bloody annoying that the working classes, the lower orders, or whatever one wanted to call them, couldn't be – well – couldn't be *exactly like her.*

Baroness Bloodstone had given a TV interview the previous week which had proved to be rather controversial.

"Naturally, it's not the kind of university *I* would want to go to," she had said, "it's not for *people like me*, but for many young people, especially those from families with no history of higher education, Thames Metropolitan University is a first-class place of study that is relevant to their needs and which will enable them to reach their potential and achieve their ambitions, and..."

The interviewer interrupted at this point: "Not for *people like you*? Could you clarify what you mean by that?"

She realised what she had said and desperately tried to backpedal:

"When I said '*not for people like me*', of course I didn't mean 'not for people like *me*'..."

"Oh," frowned the interviewer, "didn't you?"

"No, you see – that's a common mistake. When I said *me*, I meant not *just me*, but you too – or anyone – in an inclusive, accessible way, and when I said *people*, I meant me or you or anyone else as well... the point being that Thames Metropolitan University is an excellent university with wonderful staff and students and we should all be very proud, and stop knocking our achievements – we British always do that, don't we?"

"So you wouldn't want your children to go there then?"

"My children have already been to university."

"Oh? Where?"

"Oxford – and Cambridge – but I want to talk about the issues, not cartoon character personality politics, and that's why Thames Metropolitan is such an excellent university for the students who can benefit most from the first class education it offers, and..."

"But you wouldn't have wanted to go there yourself then?"

"Not at all," she lied, "I would've been proud to have gone to Thames Metropolitan University, but my talents lay elsewhere, so I chose a university which better suited me..."

"Where was that then?"

"Oxford – St Hilda's – and that's why we're supporting universities of all kinds and types so round pegs get put into round holes, and square pegs can get put into square holes..."

"And what about triangular-shaped pegs?"

"And triangular-shaped pegs can be put into..."

"And what about rhombuses, or hexagons – do they have holes?"

"Young man, everybody has a hole they can fit into, and I can assure you that anyone of any shape can find a happy hole in the excellent higher education system which our policies have expanded so that every young person can find their hole..."

The interviewer raised his eyebrows and smirked.

"...and that is why Thames Metropolitan is such an excellent university offering exciting opportunities to its diverse students."

The interviewer sneered in victory:

"So it's not just for thick people who can't get in anywhere else then?"

Baroness Bloodstone frowned in frustration – she knew she

had made a fool of herself. She made her excuses and ended the interview as politely and quickly as she could.

She knew that her blunder would have to be explained in some way in the speech she was due to give at the university, but she'd got out of worse scrapes – those with big gobs like her learn quickly how to do that. She also made a note of the interviewer's name. Because of her husband's connections she knew she could arrange it so that he would never be employed by any British media organisation ever again. And he wasn't.

Crump and the other junior lecturers weren't invited to Baroness Bloodstone's address, but Sandy was able to tell him all about it later. Apparently, all the bigwigs were there, including Alan Drakesford, the rather oleaginous and bibulous local Labour MP, as well as most of the senior management including Wendy Webb, Fiona Windrush and Edwin Wittering, all those in charge of university administration, representatives of the Centre for Islamic Studies, a representative of the Saudi government in full Arab garb, and various other foreign dignitaries including some sinister-looking men in suits, apparently from Russia, and several stony-faced Chinese too.

Baroness Bloodstone may have been a long-time sufferer from logorrhoea but, if she knew one thing, it was how to charm an audience and dig herself out of a hole of her own making. She was so good at this that she could even have an audience feeling sympathy for her for any mistake she had made, as though it were all someone else's fault and she was, in fact, the victim. No wonder she was good friends with Tony Blair.

One could see in her elegant features, too, how attractive she must have been when younger – she was still attractive, but in that handsome, managerial, unsexy way that many professional women aim for. When she was first fighting to get selected for a parliamentary seat, however, she was strikingly good-looking and she knew it. So did the all-male Labour selection panel, needless to say. As she had thought to herself more than once: who needs an all-woman short-list when you've got great tits?

She just instinctively knew how to manipulate – whether an audience, a selection panel, or the leader of a political party – and to use what she had to get what she wanted. She knew when to put herself forward as just one of the boys who wanted to be treated the same as the men, and when to put on the flirty act too and use her sex. She knew when to come over all mumsy and straight-talking, and also when to play the woman-as-victim card for all it was worth and claim special privilege for being an oppressed female. In short, she was a chameleon – either that, or a sociopath.

Perhaps her charm was why she had gone so far in politics. But whatever it was, it worked, because she managed to turn a roomful of sceptics, some of whom felt extremely insulted by her comments in the widely-publicised interview, into a roomful of believers in the utter rightness of everything she had said, was saying and would ever say again. She even got a standing ovation and a cheer, partly because she had made those sceptics feel guilty for doubting her, and partly perhaps because she managed to say a couple of gushing sycophantic greetings in Mandarin Chinese, Arabic and Russian to the VIP guests. Baroness Bloodstone could charm and manipulate in any language.

* * *

"Place was full of bloody ragheads and Chinks – and the damn Ruskies were there too – looked like the mafia," said Sandy, over morning whisky in his office, "I wonder why..."

"Perhaps they're interested in donating money, or starting joint ventures, or..."

"Well of course they bloody well are, old boy – remember, it's all just a business and there's money to be made."

Sandy knocked back his whisky and sighed.

"I know they're here for what they can get, but I don't know *exactly* what they're up to – but I know they're up to something – I can smell it."

All Crump could smell was the whisky on Sandy's breath,

but he sort of knew what Sandy meant. There *had* been a lot of suited men, and the occasional woman, looking around the university recently – some looked Chinese, some looked Arabic, and some looked Slavic. Crump had noticed them wandering around in groups or being shown round by some university administrator over the previous month or so, but didn't think this was at all unusual at a university. The fact that a long-term lecturer thought it was odd meant that it was. No doubt Sandy would find out more details later about their presence at the university and let him know all about it.

Later, over a sandwich in the canteen – a place Crump tended to avoid, partly due to the proximity to loud and rude students, and also because the food was predictably horrible and over-priced – Sandy was giving Crump some advice.

"You must get researching, my boy," said Sandy, "and you must start getting published too."

"I...I am working on my research on representations of the British education system in 19th and 20th century literature and film," stuttered Crump through a tasteless chicken sandwich. He had actually really wanted a ham sandwich but, out of respect for Muslim students and staff, the university no longer sold any pork products. All meat sold was halal too.

"Is it finished?" asked Sandy.

"Well...er...no, not yet – it should be, though, by the end of the academic year," said Crump.

"Oh no no no no no NO!" boomed Sandy, banging the table on the final 'No' so loudly that people stared. "You simply cannot think like that, old boy – you must get yourself published, as soon as possible and in as many places as possible."

"But...it's far from finished and..."

"Look, Crumpie, old chap," said Sandy, "your way of thinking would've been fine twenty or thirty years ago – but now..." he shrugged and looked Crump in the eye, "you need to get published because if you don't, the RAE will identify you as a poor performer and then you'll be up the Swannie, I should coco..."

The problem with the RAE was that, in common with all essentially American corporate business models which now ruled all institutions in the UK, assessing things against objectives meant counting them, and the *quantity* of research counted more – much more – than the *quality*. In other words, the more you wrote and got published, the better you were deemed to be as an academic.

So, after the RAE was introduced in the 1990s, lecturers began scribbling away with the frantic intensity of battery hens on speed, laying academic paper after paper to make long library shelves groan. These papers were read by very few, but journals in which to publish them flourished, as did conferences at which these academic battery hens could squawk their papers at other squawking battery hen academics. Playing this game was the only way to get a promotion and a pay rise in the modern British higher education system. Not playing the game meant trouble. Getting egg on one's face, even.

This may all seem fair enough, in a way – and would have been, perhaps, if the hundreds of academic papers these lecturers each produced were of a quality worth publishing or reading. But this was rarely, if ever, the case.

One trick that was common was evident when looking at the names of the academics who published such papers – they usually appeared with others and papers were often written by two or more academics. The collaborators were often PhD students who, as a reward for doing most of the work, got to get published as a co-author of a paper to which their lecturer supervisor had contributed very little, and thereby kick-start their academic careers.

Another common trick was republishing papers under different titles with only a few paragraphs changed, thereby magically creating further pieces of RAE-assessable research from one original – this was so common that practically every academic in the UK was guilty of upping their output this way. A little tweak here and there, a little rewriting – and, hey presto, you've created a whole new piece of research. It was called *being creative*.

A cynic may say that the vast majority of this research was utterly pointless, badly-written and a waste of good trees, but so long as it existed in paper form, it would count towards the RAE assessment of both individual academics and whole university departments, and so would allow an individual to carve out a career and a university to increase its funding. Quality counted for absolutely nothing – *quantity* was all. This was how modern universities in the UK, the US, and elsewhere operated. More *did* equal better, after all.

"Just knock something together old boy," continued Sandy, "get something published in some dullard journal or other – you could adapt it for more research later, or a PhD. Some lecturers have been writing the self same paper under different names for the past fifteen years, so don't feel guilty 'bout cutting a few corners eh?"

"But, I want to do good research – I know I can write an excellent paper, but I need time," said Crump.

"So then, don't write an excellent paper – write an *adequate* paper – get published, go to a few conferences – blah blah blah usual bollocks – and get a good RAE rating."

Sandy popped the final piece of sandwich into his mouth.

"I'll help you Crumpie – show your research to me, and I'll see what I can do."

"I'd appreciate that," said Crump.

He didn't know what he'd do without Sandy.

"You can write your masterwork later," said Sandy, "write a ground-breaking book or two – we all dream of that, or at least, used to..."

It was true – Crump *did* want his planned book on representations of the British education system in 19th and 20th century literature and film to become a widely admired set text – the authoritative text in the field – which is why he hadn't wanted to rush it.

"Course, 'twas always a delusion... I mean, who the hell reads tedious academic tomes anyway – apart from tedious academics? Fact of the matter is, dear boy, that most academics can't write very well at all, certainly not with any flair, and most of them aren't all that bright either. Regurgitate. Regurgitate. Regurgitate. That's what it's all about."

Sandy got up and Crump followed him out of the canteen. The sound of the word 'regurgitate' suddenly made Crump feel a bit sick and an acid reflux in his throat made him cough. Language did have power, after all.

"But for bloody hell's sake, get yourself published Crump – publish anything, it doesn't matter what, but get the blasted ball rolling or it'll roll back onto you, and then you'll be buggered."

Sandy could see the disappointed and subdued look in Crump's eyes.

"It's just the way it is, old boy – ideals and principles are all fine and dandy, but they do not a successful academic career make. You have to go with the flow – publish and be damned as't were. Drop your research round some time and I'll have a perusal, old boy."

Crump thanked Sandy again, before going off to attempt to teach Shakespeare to some near-illiterate students that afternoon. They should have come to the university the following year because then, due to an expanded coursework modular structure, it would actually be possible for a student to get a degree in English literature at Thames Metropolitan University without ever studying Shakespeare at all – or Chaucer, the romantic poets, or anything earlier than the 19th and 20th centuries. Students didn't want to study old and difficult stuff at all anymore – it was hardly relevant to their lives or the future world of work anyway. They just wanted to do their favourite books and films, so that was what they would soon be allowed to do. Thames Metropolitan was proud to be a customer-led organisation serving the needs of students successfully.

After leaving the class and having a good chat with Rajdeep and Athena in the office about everything and nothing – Kwame was at a conference again, this time on racism and rap – Crump made his way to the bus-stop to go home.

On the way, Crump could see some kind of protest outside the Stephen Lawrence Learning Zone, something that made Crump immediately nervous after the 'placard incident', and which made his buttocks tense in preparation for doing the proverbial runner in case he was mistaken for an ex-fascist again. Until, that is, he saw that the protesters were almost exclusively bearded and robed men and burqa women, presumably from the Abdullah building and the Centre for Islamic Studies. There were a few non-bearded and non-burqa-ed students too, who were supposedly 'socialist workers' according to their placards, though their absence from lectures seemed to suggest they were more socialist than worker. The placards this time did not display anti-fascist and anti-BNP designs. Instead they displayed anti-Israel slogans, including several accusing Israel of being a Nazi state with swastikas and stars of David intertwined, and lots of references to concentration camps and Israeli fascism against 'innocent' Palestinian Muslims.

From what Crump could see, some bordered on the anti-Semitic. In fact, some *were* anti-Semitic, but carefully used the word 'Zionist' instead of 'Jew' in their insults – (the latter would have broken the Race Relations Act and got the protestors arrested) – and they seemed to be accusing Israel of being the equivalent of Nazi Germany, or even worse. If he'd been Jewish, perhaps from a family whose members had been murdered in the camps, how would that have made him feel? Crump stood a while – at a safe distance – and listened to the angry chanting. Suddenly, a stench of sweat and rotting fish wafted into his nostrils and a thin, slimy voice seemed to creep up behind him like sick animal.

"Enjoying the show, are we, Kevin?"

It was Edwin Wittering, the head of the post-compulsory education department. He placed a hand on Crump's shoulder and rubbed it in what may have been an avuncular manner.

"Oh...errr...well...actually," said Crump, "I'm not exactly sure what..."

"Israel," interrupted Edwin Wittering, "and their Zionist plots – that's what it's all about."

"Oh?" said Crump.

"The governing body is deciding this evening whether or not to ban all Israeli academics from the university, and also whether to stop all co-operation with Israeli universities."

"Oh, do we co-operate much with Israeli universities?" asked Crump.

"Not to my knowledge, so we're lucky really," said Edwin Wittering, breathing his foul breath in Crump's face – a globule of spittle sat on the side of his lip, and there was what seemed to be a morsel of what looked like scrambled egg on his chin.

"But," said Crump, "surely Israel is a democracy, and the, y'know, Arab states aren't, are they?"

Edwin Wittering looked quite cross.

"Typical Zionist propaganda – you really shouldn't believe everything you read in the Zionist media, Kevin. And anyway, there's more to life than democracy..."

Crump wasn't sure what Edwin Wittering meant by this, but his hand rubbed Crump's shoulder again – a motion that made him shiver.

"The vote's practically a done deal – soon, Israeli academics and universities will be excluded from all scholarship at this university, and the policy will go national soon too."

Crump declined Edwin's kind offer of a lift home – the thought of being in a confined space with the man made him feel ill – and he continued to make his way to the bus stop.

It seemed strange to him that Israel was being singled out for exclusion like this. It was, after all, the only democracy in the Middle East, where freedom of worship was allowed, and which had a free press and freedom of speech, unlike the Muslim-ruled countries surrounding it, most of whom were rather brutal dictatorships which actively wanted to destroy Israel and rid the world of all Jews – this was, perhaps, the cause of occasional Israeli paranoia.

The Abdullah building and the Centre for Islamic Studies

had been funded by a Saudi Arabian regime that was fascist in all but name, which publicly beheaded people without trial – (often poor foreign nationals from Asia who hadn't even been given an interpreter in their show trials) – every Friday after prayers, and which had only outlawed slavery in the 1960s. And yet Arab academics or universities weren't banned, and neither were academics from other totalitarian states like China, or Russia, or the multifarious others in the Third World. It seemed to Crump, though he was no expert, that Israel was being picked on and unfairly singled out for criticism, and wondered if this was because of the traditional siding of many left-wingers with the Arab world, much as the Soviet Union had done with its traditional anti-Semitism, or perhaps because of the political influence of the large Muslim community in the UK.

He doubted the policy would affect Thames Met much, though, as there didn't seem to be any Israeli academics at the university anyway – at least, he knew of none. It would be a shame, however, for lecturers and their universities to be so excluded when they were not at all responsible for anything the Israeli government did or didn't do – just as the bearded men and burqa women were not responsible for what any Muslim country in the world did. Crump decided that, all in all, it would be better if he just didn't get involved – he had enough problems without getting drawn into arguments about politics in the Middle East which, he noticed, had been going on for thousands upon thousands of years without a solution being found. Perhaps they all just needed counselling – or free ice-cream, to cheer them up a bit.

* * *

"Always liked the Jew boys," said Mrs Glidewell as she served up bangers and mash with baked beans and fried onions to Crump in her downstairs flat, "I ain't never been one of them *anti-semenites*..."

Crump was getting into the habit of having his dinner – or 'his tea' – at Mrs Glidewell's ground floor flat about three times a week, for which he did her shopping as a thank you. In their age and background, they couldn't have been more different, yet in her kindly manner and the honest simplicity of her life, and in her complete lack of bitterness or malice despite the hardships of it, Mrs Glidewell had something that he didn't have and that he envied – he just wasn't sure what it was exactly. But it was good and solid and decent – and he knew it when he saw it.

"Them Jews was all over the East End when we was there, and we never had no problems – fancy some more mash, ducks?"

She always called him 'ducks' for some reason. Crump wondered whether, if he'd used that term of affection at the university, he'd have been accused of 'bird-ism', or 'poultry-ism', or 'beak-ism'...

Mrs Glidewell went to fetch the saucepan, returning to scoop yet more great mountains of buttery mash onto his plate. It wasn't haute cuisine but, to Crump, the food Mrs Glidewell had made was not only delicious, but also represented love and belonging too – he would have paid a lot for that.

"Course, all gawn now – when the Indians started coming in we moved out – most of the Jew boys went up north London an' all. Just ain't the same no more, the East End. But things change – can't stand still like a lemon, can we ducks?"

Crump agreed, and bit into the last of his sausages. He presumed by 'Indians' she meant perhaps the working class Pakistanis and Bangladeshis who now comprised a large proportion of inhabitants of the East End, rather than the immigrants from India who tended to be wealthier middle class professionals living in the home counties – but he certainly wasn't going to argue.

"'Ere, I got some jam roly-poly for afters, ducks."

Crump nodded and smiled. He hadn't tasted jam roly-poly since... well, since when exactly? Perhaps since school – he didn't tend to eat puddings these days anyway. But jam roly-poly – even the name seemed to taste good on the tongue.

Why was it, these days, that everyone tried to prove how sophisticated they were by constantly eating foreign or imported or complicated food, rejecting what were great British classics? Did they think they'd be thought less of for eating them? Crump couldn't afford to eat out much – but the number of times he'd eaten fashionably awful food in restaurants and longed for a good roast dinner, or a steak and kidney pudding, or bangers and mash and jam roly-poly! Good, proper food – that's what it was. The food that built the greatest empire the world has ever seen, an empire that spread democracy, liberty, opportunity, the rule of law, the English language, *civilisation itself*, to the whole wide world. And it was just jam roly-poly!

It was great to have choice and variation, but enjoying that surely didn't mean you had to disparage and demean good British cooking? Unless, of course, you were a bit racist or anti-British perhaps, or were painfully insecure about your social class.

Crump tucked into his jam roly-poly with custardy glee. Life didn't get any better than this.

* * *

The term continued, as did the lessons and lectures, with Crump becoming increasingly attuned to the low level of the students he was expected to teach. He wasn't even surprised now when a student clearly couldn't understand anything he was saying or when he was handed an essay downloaded from the internet. He was, as Sandy would say, *playing the game*.

Sandy was very helpful with hints about getting his research published. On his advice, Crump applied for and accepted a place at a couple of conferences for the following Easter when he would present his paper. Also on Sandy's advice, he had decided to make the research shorter and less in-depth, for now anyway. The ground-breaking book could wait.

Happily, he wasn't called into Wendy Webb's office again that term. They smiled at each other in the corridor, but apart from that he had little contact with her, even though she was supposedly his mentor – for which she got paid extra, he now realised.

He was, however, called in to see Elizabeth Clint, head of the English department at West London College, one Friday in early December. She was a grumpy-looking woman in her fifties with greying hair and a permanent snooty and supercilious expression on her face as she looked down her long nose at whoever she was talking to.

"Kevin, I just wanted to ask if there is anything you wish to tell me," she said, mysteriously.

It was really amazing that after over five years this woman couldn't even get his name right and call him 'Crump' like everyone else. Or perhaps she called him Kevin because she knew he hated it?

"Errr...no?" Crump asked, or maybe told, her – he wasn't sure.

Elizabeth Clint rolled her eyes at him, then raised her eyebrows.

"Should there be?" asked Crump.

She sighed wearily.

"When you first started working for West London college, you signed a contract."

Crump had vague memories of doing so, so said: "Yes."

"In that contract it clearly states that should a teacher be accused of a criminal offence or be subject to a disciplinary procedure at *any* institution, then management here must be informed."

"Yes," said Crump, even though he hadn't known about that rule.

"So why, Kevin, did you not inform us that you had been accused of both sexism and racism, and had received a first verbal warning and a first written warning from Thames Metropolitan University?"

So that was it. She was angry because she hadn't been informed. What a petty, dull, jobsworth she was to doubt a teacher who had worked at the college for years and put in countless hours of unpaid time to make the department run more effectively. And wasn't what happened at his university supposed to be confidential anyway? Crump was annoyed.

"It must have slipped my mind," he said grumpily, "I am rather busy, you know, what with doing two jobs and putting in lots of *unpaid* overtime here."

Elizabeth Clint looked at him as though he were a peasant who had dared speak to a duchess.

"There's no need to be rude," she said, "actually, I have known about this for quite some time."

"Oh?" asked Crump.

"Yes," she smiled – or was it 'sneered'? – "I actually did my initial teacher training at the university too."

"Surely it was a polytechnic then," said Crump, relishing his feigned innocence and the joy of putting her down a peg or two.

"That's right," said Elizabeth Clint, through gritted teeth, "and my tutor happened to be Edwin."

"Edwin Wittering?" asked Crump.

"That's right," smiled Elizabeth, "so I get to know all that goes on at the university, including the warnings you have received for being racist and sexist."

"I am not racist or sexist," said Crump, "it was all a misunderstanding...It's a long story."

"I'm sure," Elizabeth smiled, "it usually is – but because you chose not to report those warnings to us officially and voluntarily, and because we have a duty of care to protect the vulnerable young people at the college from the influence of those who may be unfit to teach, I am hereby suspending you pending a fitness to practise hearing."

Elizabeth Clint smiled. Crump didn't.

"What?" he said, stunned.

"You are now suspended, so you should collect your things

and leave college premises please. You have ten minutes."

"But...but...I'm on an hourly rate contract, so I won't get paid if I'm suspended."

"It was your choice to go and work at the university, Kevin, and cause us all so much disruption here."

"So... when will the fitness to practise hearing be?" Crump asked.

"Probably before Easter – March if you're lucky..."

"But...I've already been through all this at the university – it's all been sorted out..."

Crump didn't know what else to say.

"*We* are not the university Kevin – we do things in our own way here – and all accusations of racism and sexism must go to a fitness to practise hearing – they are the rules."

"But has anyone made any complaint about me in college – *ever* – for racism or sexism?" asked Crump.

"That is not the point," said Elizabeth Clint, smiling just a little too widely for Crump's liking – she was clearly enjoying this. "We have a duty of care and you have been accused of being a racist and a sexist, so you must answer for that here, in front of a tribunal. If I were you, I'd contact your union. Now if you don't mind, I'm a very busy woman."

And with that, she stood up and gestured towards the door.

"You've got ten minutes," she said to him before he left, "and then security will escort you off the premises."

* * *

"Oh she's always been a stuck-up bitch," said Becky over drinks in the pub later.

"But I had no idea she could do that – suspend me, I mean – or that she was being informed of anything that happened at the university. It's like she's been spying on me."

He had told Becky all about the absurd accusations of racism and sexism. She was mixed race herself and knew that the accusations couldn't be true – she certainly didn't buy the guilty-until-proven-innocent, all-white-people-are-racist attitudes of some of those working in the education system, both black and white.

"Reckon she's doing it to look good – y'know, the more people you accuse of racism and sexism and formally investigate, the more you as a manager will be seen to be taking it seriously – taking action. I think the old bag wants a promotion – prob'ly deputy principal or something."

"I've just lost almost a fifth of my salary overnight," said Crump.

This wouldn't have happened if he'd been full-time at the college, or even if he'd had a contract directly with them, but all part-time staff now had 'associate lecturer' contracts with outside agencies whether they liked it or not, which paid for the hours taught and nothing else – so no sick or holiday pay, no pay for cancelled classes and certainly no job security or pay whilst suspended. 'Exploited casual worker' would have been a more accurate job title. Bizarrely, and almost unbelievably, even part-time burger-flippers in McDonalds had better employment rights that 'associate lecturers'.

"I know," said Becky, "come round to my gran's on Sunday – you know we do *de old Jamaican ting wid plenty rice and peas!*"

Her Jamaican accent was spot-on.

"Racist," said Crump, teasing her, and they giggled, clinked their glasses and downed their beers in one.

Crump spent the weekend quietly, sorting stuff out in his flat and doing some research for his paper. Happily, much of that involved sipping a glass of wine while watching several videos and DVDs, from 'Goodbye Mr Chips' (1939 version) to Laurie Anderson's 'If', and several other British films in which schools and the education system were represented. He didn't think they'd ever got it right really, not unless things had changed even more than he realised since those days. That the image portrayed was a fantasy and a construct – a projection of the education people would have liked to have had – was going to be the thrust of his research paper, he decided. He quite simply didn't believe any novel or film could ever be a true representation – perhaps because the process of education was so inherently undramatic, or perhaps because the process of film-making and storytelling was inherently manipulative in its need for drama and action.

On Sunday morning Crump was picked up by Becky in her rusty old VW beetle and taken to a block of flats near Brixton. There, Becky's gran fed them all – and there were over ten present, all Becky's brothers, her mum, and some cousins, and friends – a wonderful Jamaican-style Sunday lunch.

Crump realised, as he sat there chatting with his fellow guests and enjoying the happy and warm atmosphere, just how odd so many of the people working in the education system really were, and what a bubble they lived in. There were no agendas here, no snide backbiting and nonsense policies, no box-ticking and endlessly pretending everything was wonderful when it was quite obviously shot to shit. No, on that Sunday, Crump just ate and drank and talked, and enjoyed himself with several normal, everyday, ordinary people of different ages and colours and backgrounds, all united in their enjoyment of the moment and the food and the company, and not a single diversity policy document in sight, either.

How stuck in his rut of academic life he'd become, he realised, and he was only about to finish his first term at the university! What would he be like in five years? Or ten? He shuddered to think.

He felt the same way as he did when he had tea with Mrs Glidewell. This was real life, and these were real people, and this – not stupid targets and outcomes, not ridiculous plans and policies – was what he had to keep in touch with if he wasn't to go completely and utterly insane.

He liked every single one of the strangers around the table that day far more than the vast majority of his colleagues at the university. Apart from Athena, Raj and Sandy, he couldn't have cared less if he were never to see any of the others ever again. But it was bound to get better the more he progressed in the higher education system, and eventually it wouldn't just seem so...so...so what? He couldn't even think of the right word – and he was an English teacher! But he couldn't leave – this was his career – his life. What choice did he have anyway? He couldn't do anything else.

And he did, it was true, enjoy it – at least, sometimes. He enjoyed teaching – though he would have preferred able and intelligent students to teach – and also enjoyed using his brain, thinking, doing research. But it was the rest that did his head in – everything else that the job involved, and this 'everything else' seemed to take up most of his time too. That was not *education*, and he knew it.

They had all been informed at a departmental meeting that there would be a 'do' in the department in the last week of term. It was not called a 'Christmas party' – the diversity policy at the university forbade the use of the 'C' word for fear of offending those of other faiths, especially the Muslims, and especially the Saudis – so it was called 'Winter Break' instead of the 'Christmas Holidays', and the 'Christmas party' was called an 'End of Term Do'. Crump was just glad they hadn't called it 'Winterval', though some staff did wish each other season's greetings using the gruesomely banal Americanism 'Happy Holidays' instead of 'Merry Christmas'. All very strange really, because the same politically correct staff who were so keen *not* to offend anyone by using the word 'Christmas' seemed to insist on wishing people a Happy Eid, or a Happy Diwali, or a Happy International Women's Day, without a moment's thought for all those they were thereby excluding and offending.

At the departmental meeting, Crump had noticed two new faces. One, a young Chinese-looking man, introduced himself as Johnny Wong and was an expert in the film industry in Hong Kong, especially Ang Lee. The other – a rather scruffy-looking, forty-something woman – had long, tangled, ginger hair, and wore a dress the colour of snot. She was dripping with snot-coloured jewellery too. Apparently, she was an expert in women's writing, especially Jeanette Winterton, and looked quite like her too. Athena later told Raj and Crump – and even Kwame had his headphones off and was joining in the conversation – that her name was 'Margaret'.

"Margaret who?" Raj had, quite understandably, asked.

"Just Margaret," said Athena, "she refuses to have a surname – she believes it's a relic of patriarchal oppression."

Oh God, not another one, thought Crump, but said nothing.

"Blimey muss get like complicate an stuff innit man," said Kwame, rocking back and forth on his chair in hysterics, "Even I got surname and ting wiv my name like innit yeah!"

"So she's got no other name at all?" asked Crump.

"No, just...Margaret," said Athena, and they all looked at each other and shrugged.

Raj looked perplexed.

"But what she will be doing when she is getting married?" he said.

"I don't think," said Crump, wondering simultaneously how she managed to get paid without a surname to identify her bank account, "that we should assume that she's...the marrying kind..."

Athena nodded and smiled sheepishly in agreement. Raj looked blank, then all of a sudden became acutely embarrassed as the truth dawned on him. Kwame sucked the air through his teeth and put on his headphones as if retreating back into a safe, solitary world.

Crump sometimes wished he could do the same.

* * *

The last week before Christmas flew by. Apart from a counselling session with Mandy Pandy, where she actually seemed rather cheerful for once – (Crump thought she may have been at the happy pills) – life plodded on uneventfully.

It was sad that the university diversity policy didn't allow Christmas trees or decorations – Crump always liked seeing them go up as the winter evenings darkened, and they certainly always seemed to cheer everyone up – but he certainly wasn't going to share his views with anyone for fear of being labelled racist again.

The midwinter festival now known as Christmas was only as religious as you wanted to make it anyway – it was nice and vague and could be enjoyed by Christians and non-Christians alike, as was the happy and vague British tradition. It would surely have been better to put up lots of decorations and trees and make Christmas at the university an inclusive, cultural festival for everyone, rather than effectively banning it and all the imagery around it. No people of other faiths or cultures or races seemed to mind much anyway – it always seemed to be the white, non-religious, self-righteous, politically correct middle-classes who protested about such things and demanded that they be banned – for the possible offence that may be caused to others.

Crump intended to spend that Friday going up to Trafalgar Square and enjoying the carols and the tree from Norway and the atmosphere his university found so intolerant and unacceptable. At least the great cults of diversity and multiculturalism hadn't managed to ban Christmas in the UK completely. Yet.

On Crump's last day that term he noticed a new teacher training student already sitting in the class when he arrived – this was most unusual as most of his trainee teachers were reliably late, but then, so were many of the teacher training staff. The student was instantly recognisable – it was Nick Craven, the former NF/BNP activist who had now found God and repented. Crump wondered whether he'd repented for being the cause of a demonstration against him during which a placard had cut Crump's head open, but supposed that not even God could blame this man for a case of mistaken identity and the violence of others.

According to Athena, there had been a meeting during which Nick Craven had convinced the university and the demonstrators that he was now a changed man. Some deal was done, apparently, and he was allowed to stay on at the university, especially as he had been supported by other faith groups, and especially as the university had received legal advice that they would be liable to get sued for massive damages if they banned an individual solely for his present or former beliefs. He had been advised to keep a low profile and had agreed.

"I've been moved to your class because Camilla Cox said I'd prefer it here," he said.

"Oh does she?" said Crump.

Camilla Cox was a fussy and annoying fellow teacher trainer Crump tried hard to avoid. He actually tried to avoid most teacher trainers, finding them irritating in their conformity to fashionable PC educational opinion, obsessed with institutional hierarchy politics, often really rather badly educated, and, quite frankly, a bore to be around.

"Yes, she said I'd be happier here, so... here I am."

Typical, thought Crump, adding students to a class – in the last week of term as well – and not even informing the teacher. Simply bad manners, bad management, bad everything – but not untypical of the way things are usually done in the education system.

And why did Camilla Cox not want Nick Craven in her class? Was he disruptive? Did he state extreme opinions or make others uncomfortable? What, in other words, was this all about?

At the end of the lesson Crump was no wiser than at the beginning. Nick Craven was a keen student – perhaps even the best in the class – highly educated, polite and dedicated to devoting his life to teaching, all be it in a 'giving-my-life-to-Jesus' kind of way. Crump was sure there'd be some missionary hellhole of an outpost in one of the darker corners of the world eager to have him indoctrinate all the natives in the wondrous ways of two thousand years of the Christian traditions of conflict and slaughter.

Nick Craven wished Crump a very Merry Christmas as he left, and explained how seriously he took the birth of 'Our Lord'. He said he'd be spending Christmas Day helping the poor in a soup kitchen, which made Crump feel like some kind of ungrateful, selfish, greedy evil pig for not doing the same – which, perhaps, was just the intention.

* * *

The End of Term Do was held in the restaurant area of the Mandela Building which was usually rented out for functions, so it was the first time Crump had actually been in there.

It was a rather dour occasion, perhaps due to the lack of any tinselly Christmas decorations or lights or carols, or perhaps because of the buffet, which consisted of plates of stale crisps and a few limp sandwiches – pork-free and halal, as usual – or maybe just because most of the people there, all from the humanities departments, were talking about nothing else but teaching and university business. Teachers really were the worst for talking shop, as Crump well knew – put a couple of teachers in a prison cell waiting for their own executions and they'd spend their final moments discussing lesson plans, the finer points of educational policy and what was currently considered 'best practice'.

There was, however, one good thing – the traditionalist Muslim presence at the university had not, happily, managed to stop the booze flowing. Apparently, some representatives of the Centre for Islamic Studies had put in a complaint about this, which was still pending, and Crump noticed that at least some Muslim staff had not turned up, presumably in protest. For now, however, alcohol was allowed, and even though it mainly consisted of cheap plonk and beer, there was plenty of it, so Crump decided the best thing to do was to get completely and utterly, stonkingly pissed. Binge drinking had its place, he thought to himself.

Everyone was knocking back the booze impressively –

which perhaps they wouldn't have been doing if they'd known that it had been bought for a very reasonable price from an East European who worked in the kitchens, and who had himself bought it from 'contacts' he had in London – 'contacts' whose day jobs mainly consisted of stealing credit cards, people trafficking and smuggling hard drugs. Still, a bargain was a bargain.

"Utterly vile," spluttered Sandy, spitting his wine back into the glass, "remind me never to go to bloody Bulgaria!"

"There's cans of lager there," said Crump, handing him one.

"Where from this time? Albania? Montenegro? The former Yugoslav Republic of Pissadonia" he scoffed, squinting at the Slavic text on the can, "Still, who gives a proverbial, so long as it does the job, eh, Crumpie?" and he took a long swig from the can, then burped loudly.

Crump spent a happy half hour or so drinking and chatting with Sandy – but mostly drinking – then he saw Athena arrive with Raj. He'd been meaning to invite her for a drink at the weekend, so they could at least go out once before he went back to his mum's for Christmas, but for some stupid reason he just couldn't ask her. At his age, that was embarrassing – he wasn't some tongue-tied, timid teenager after all. No, he was a tongue-tied, timid twenty-nine year old who had been worrying about asking Athena out for a Christmas drink for a month or more. But now he'd had a few drinks and was well-oiled to the point of eloquent fluency, and there was nothing like alcohol-induced courage to instigate courtship rituals.

"Hi... you're here," said Crump to Athena, stupidly.

"I'm...here, yes," said Athena.

"Yes," he said, and blushed.

Crump thought she looked gorgeous in her dress. But she would've looked beautiful in anything – or nothing. Raj, for some reason, was wearing a gold lamé jacket, giving him the slight look of a short, plump, Indian cousin of Elvis Presley.

"Jolly nice restaurant eh?" said Rajdeep, "now where they

are putting the food – they were saying there would be buffet?"

"Not up to much, I'm afraid," said Crump.

"What, exactly, is the phrase 'not up to much' meaning when translated from native British dialect of understatement?"

"Pretty awful, if you must know, so... frankly, I wouldn't bother – but there's plenty of booze, just over there," said Crump, and Raj went off to explore.

He looked at Athena.

"Shall I... er... I mean... would you... er... like... er... um... another... er... um..."

"Drink?" she asked, and Crump nodded in relief, "A glass of wine would be nice. Red."

Crump went off to get it for her and saw Raj hovering over the food.

"And *this* is being considered fit for the human consumption at this university?" he bellowed, holding up a limp, sad-looking sandwich. "No wonder everybody is getting drunk as a lord."

"We could have something better later – maybe a takeaway," said Crump.

"Do you know what those bloody bastard Bengalis are putting in your beloved takeaways?" asked Raj, "because I can assure you, old fellow, that you are not wanting to know gastronomic details of ingredients of UK Indian take-away!"

Crump took the glass of wine back to Athena, and stood silently by her while they each took simultaneous sips of wine, wincing in unison at its bitterness. He was just about to ask her out for a Christmas drink when Raj returned.

Two hours later, Crump still hadn't asked Athena if she'd like to go for a Christmas drink the following evening, and by now he was getting more than a little tipsy. He was starting to see double and he knew he was slurring his words a bit.

Why didn't he just ask? Why? Why couldn't he say it? What was the worst that could happen, after all? Well, Athena could reject him, laugh at him, rip his heart out and squeeze it into a tiny ball of misery and despair, and throw it back into his sobbing, desperate face – but apart from that, what was the worst that could happen?

Crump decided to go to the toilet to steel himself for the challenge of popping the question. It was only asking her out for a Christmas drink – so why couldn't he do it? Why? He staggered off to the gents feeling angry and frustrated with himself, wondering if he would ever be any better at this kind of thing. Would he still be the same at fifty, or sixty, or seventy? Would he still feel anxious about meeting new people, or asking someone for a Christmas drink? And when it was his day to die, would he be too worried about the reaction of the doctors or nurses to ask them to give him a sip of water or tuck him up warm or call his family? Why? Why did he feel like this? Why was he so anxious all the time? It was enough to drive anyone to drink, which was appropriate, really, considering he was now as pissed as a fart.

Crump stood at the urinal in the toilets and weed gallons of wee onto the stained stainless steel. Usually, he only stood at the urinal when there was nobody else there when he entered, otherwise he used a cubicle – another disorder caused by childhood trauma no doubt. But then, women weren't expected to spread their legs in the full view of others while weeing, so why should men *not* be shy about such things?

Crump heard somebody come into the gents. This was fine – once he was in full flow he didn't really mind if he had an audience watching. It was just the start that mattered – that agonising inability to get the juices flowing before the judgmental eyes of others. Somebody had probably done a PhD on it, thought Crump – somebody had done a PhD on most things, after all. It was only when Crump turned to look at the person next to him – and looked down to see a large fleshy cock dispensing urine into the bowl – that he jumped out of his skin, peeing all over his trousers and falling backwards onto the toilet floor. He was drunk and confused and now felt sick too. Was this, perchance, all a dream?

"Are... you alright?" asked Wendy Webb, looking over her shoulder – or was it *his* shoulder – at where Crump lay on the floor, while still peeing into the urinal.

It certainly wasn't a dream. Wendy Webb, his head of department – his *female* head of department – had a penis! And it was a real penis! At least, it looked real. And Crump had even seen more than just the penis – he'd seen the balls too, and the dark thatch of pubic hair – due to Wendy's hitching up her dress and dropping her knickers to wee, exposing the lot. So it couldn't be a fake penis – not with all that – and it looked absolutely normal and real and male. And rather large, actually, he noticed. Crump struggled to his feet. Wendy was still peeing. He rushed out of the toilet.

What had he just seen? *What!?* And shouldn't Wendy Webb have been using the female toilets anyway? *What on earth was going on?!*

"Are you OK?" asked Athena, as she watched Crump knocked back his glass of wine in one, "You look as white as a ghost."

"Y...yes...I'm f...fine..."

But even Crump knew that he looked terrified – traumatised even. Perhaps that was why, now, after having such a shock, he could do it. He took a deep breath.

"Would-you-like-to-come-for-a-Christmas-drink-tomorrow?" he said, slurring all the word together into one long one.

There, that wasn't that bad, was it? Athena laughed – the cheerful giggle he loved.

"That's funny," she said.

Funny? thought Crump. Why? What was funny?

"I was just about to ask you – I have a friend in Lewisham, quite near your house I think, so we're all going out for drinks tomorrow."

"Oh, so... yes... let's... um... go out... er... tomorrow... in... er... um... Lewisham," said Crump.

"Yes," said Athena.

She had said yes! He almost yelped with pleasure! Yes!

It was a shame her friend would be there, but at least he had asked her – it had only taken several weeks for him to do so – and now they were definitely going to go out together. He felt great and went to get more drinks to celebrate.

Memories after this were all a bit vague. All Crump could remember was his having another drink, then going up to his office to get something – though he couldn't remember what – and then...and then...something happened. Something. But he didn't know what. And there was someone else there, but who? He couldn't remember. It was all, somehow, strangely, vague and woolly, and as thin as mist in his memory.

He woke up the next day, aching and stiff, in his bed at home, and learnt from a phone call from Athena that she and Raj had put him in a taxi. She said he'd been acting strangely, very disorientated and confused, babbling about a ghost, and having sex, and strange things she couldn't understand. Try as he might, Crump couldn't remember a thing, which was very worrying, actually.

Had he said anything bad to Wendy Webb or anyone else? Had he offended anyone? A knot of worry tightened in his gut. He lifted up the bedclothes and looked at his penis. He rolled it around in his fingers. It did feel rather tender – sore even. But surely, he couldn't have had sex? Wouldn't he remember that? After all, it happened rarely enough. And if he'd had sex, then who had he had sex with? Athena? No, she would've mentioned it – and he would've remembered. Surely?

And why couldn't he remember anything? He'd drunk that much before easily and been fine – so why had he forgotten it all, unless... Shit, there was only one explanation – shit and bloody fucking hell, he thought – I was drugged!

Crump had read once about how the ancient Egyptians used to scrape the Pharaoh's brains out through his nostrils with a hook. He felt as though something similar might have happened to him during the night, and he had what was probably the worst hangover he'd ever had – and that was against some rather stiff competition too.

He spent the day in bed, recovering – though Mrs Glidewell, bless her, brought him cups of tea from time to time, and also made him the most enormous English breakfast – the Full Monty with eggs, bacon, beans, sausages, fried bread, the lot. He forced himself to eat it – he knew full well the restorative powers of a good fry-up.

'My Stanley had this every mornin' of his life – it'll warm your cockles, ducks, you take my word' she had said.

Crump wondered how her husband had managed to avoid a heart attack long enough to die from *prostrate* cancer if he'd eaten this every day of his life. Or perhaps all the healthy eating advice we're bombarded with these days was actually wrong, and you could eat a fried breakfast every day and still have a healthy heart? Perhaps it was all in the genes? Who knew? Mrs Glidewell also gave him a large tot of whisky, the hair of the dog that bit him – or perhaps of the woman who'd shagged – and possibly raped – him?

Later, he had a bath, shaved and got ready. He spent two nervous hours deciding what to wear, which was odd as he only had two decent shirts for going out in, and only one decent pair of shoes. He looked, he thought, pretty good as he admired himself in the full-length mirror. Perhaps he'd have more luck with the opposite sex if he'd make this effort all the time?

It was a mild, December evening and he felt on top of the world as he got the bus to Lewisham where he was due to meet Athena by the clock tower at 8pm.

He knew she would be late – the Greeks always are. But then, he thought, so were all of the nationalities at Thames Metropolitan, students and teachers. But he knew how Mediterranean people lived on a different timescale, what with their sleeping in the afternoons, eating dinner at ten and staying up half the night. His friend Otis in Greece had written to him about that, so Athena was doing rather well, he thought, to arrive at 8.20.

Unfortunately, she arrived soon after some local inner-city kids in hoodies had begun pestering him, calling him names as he stood at the clock tower – 'faggot', 'batty boy' and 'white cunt' amongst them – and all because he refused to give them a pound each. If he'd had any change he might have done – but he certainly wasn't going to trust them to break a twenty.

Crump had felt the tight knot of anxiety in his stomach – already tight enough to snap – tightening even further as he stood there, being mocked and taunted by four boys who must have been no older than thirteen or fourteen. When Athena arrived, she shouted and screamed at them and they cycled off, rather subdued. He was glad really, as he thought they would soon threaten him with a knife or hit him or mug him. It was dark now and, even though there were people around, he doubted anyone would bother to come to his aid should the worst happen. He could see images of his bleeding face lying in the gutter as the locals rushed past, unwilling or unable to help as a Nike trainer crunched down on his...

"That's what their mums are like," said Athena, "they're just insecure little boys really..."

Perhaps she was right, but whatever the case, Crump was annoyed that the first event of the evening was being rescued by a woman he quite possibly loved and wanted to impress from a gang of teenagers less than half his age. It wasn't very, well, brave or macho – and made him seem rather wimpish.

Despite everything, men and women were just monkeys, and a man needed status to be respected by a woman. Not to mention himself. No-one liked a wimp, no matter what they said. If you were a man you were either a hero or a zero in others' eyes – there was no middle ground. And women thought they had it hard...

They walked together down the high street. He tried to put the incident behind him and was in a good mood now, and Athena seemed to be in one too. She was dressed in a dark ocean-blue dress and was wearing beautiful earrings. He smiled at her – she smiled at him – they smiled at each other.

Perhaps she felt the same way about him as he felt about her? Perhaps he'd be able to make it clear tonight that he was really attracted to her – perhaps not directly (well it had taken him weeks to ask her out for a drink, and not even a date really) but in a roundabout, vague, *hinting* way. Perhaps.

They walked past the Christmas party crowds, though as this was a Saturday there were thankfully no noisy office party herds roaming the streets. And Crump was happy to see a Christmas tree and some decorations in Lewisham, even though they were tatty and looked like they'd been taken out of last year's – or even last century's – box.

Athena turned and smiled at him again and his heart fluttered.

"You're wearing perfume!" she said, sniffing his face.

"Oh...um...er...yes...er... aftershave..." He blushed.

"I like it – it smells like..."

Athena furrowed her brow in thought. Smells like what, he thought – like flowers, summer, marzipan – like the sea, like sweat, like sex, what?

"It smells like *you*", she smiled.

Well, he thought, it could've been worse.

"Thanks, I think," he said.

Athena laughed and held his hand. She *held his hand!* Crump could scarcely believe it – she did fancy him, after all. This night was going to be one of the best in his life – maybe *the* best. He could just feel it.

They reached the pub – it was called the Royal Oak, even though there probably wasn't an oak tree for miles, or a Royal for that matter. Athena led him inside. It was hot and noisy and crowded – but then, it was a Saturday before Christmas. Athena offered to buy him a drink, but he refused and instead went to the bar himself. He bought them a lager each and returned to Athena who had found a free table.

"This," she said, "is Diane."

Crump smiled at the blonde woman sitting next to Athena – she looked like a young Jodie Foster.

"And this is another friend, Jean."

Crump also smiled at the older woman with short cropped hair and red-rimmed glasses who smiled weakly back. And then it happened. The room seemed to collapse in on itself – space contracting and time expanding, like in a car crash.

"Diane's my girlfriend," said Athena, and then Diane gave her a long, sexual kiss and rubbed her hand between Athena's thighs.

Crump's jaw fell open as his eyes took in what he was seeing – the scene around him was swimming and swirling in a maelstrom of shock and confusion. It was as though a lightning bolt had pierced his skull and left his brain blackened and burning in the thick acrid smoke of hopelessness and despair.

"I think I should have told you earlier," said Athena, looking sympathetic, with Diane looking smug and Jean looking gleeful in an old man-hating lesbian kind of a way.

I think I should have told you earlier!!! Is that what she had said? Crump could hardly take in any words spoken to him now. He saw mouths move but...it was all a wall of noise. No words any more. Just noise. Without meaning. Like life.

The rest of the evening was a blur – again. Crump didn't mind at all being in a gay pub so just sat and drank, and drank, and drank, while Athena was touched up and snogged by her girlfriend. Things could not really get any worse than this, he thought – the woman he quite probably loved was very much not interested in his affections, nor those of any man. She was a lesbian – a dyke – of the Sapphic tendency! She was a muff-muncher, a tit-tickler – she supped from the furry cup! *Fucking hell!!!*

For a mad, drunken, evil little minute, he started to plan ways of turning Athena straight somehow, before realising in despair that the situation was completely and utterly hopeless. The best he could hope for that she was bisexual, or perhaps that he'd get a drunken sympathy shag from her on some future unspecific occasion – and he was then disgusted that the thought had even appeared in his head. He didn't want a one-night-stand with Athena – he wanted far more than that.

This was not, it had to be said, the best Christmas present he'd ever had. Why hadn't she told him earlier? *Why?* Was taking him to a gay pub and kissing her girlfriend in front of him really the best way of coming out to him? Did she do it on purpose? Was Athena really that nasty? Did she hate him in some way? Had he got her so wrong? Was he a complete and utter fucking idiot of the first order? He certainly felt like one.

At about ten o'clock, when he was suitably drunk, he decided to leave. He felt dreadful – drunk, sad, downcast, disillusioned, numb, weary – and just wanted to go home to bed. It was as though he'd been gutted like a fish, so empty was the cavity where his heart had once been. He wished Athena and the others goodnight in a mumble, and made his way to the exit.

After buying a kebab from a takeaway van, he made his way back to the bus stop, robotically stuffing the tasteless slivers of greasy meat into his mouth. He walked slowly, thinking, just thinking, wishing he could just cry – but he only felt blank, as though every emotion and feeling inside him had been wiped. Deleted. Erased. Gone for good.

Suddenly, he heard several quickly-approaching footsteps behind him. He turned, and as he did so the first fist hit him square in the face. His kebab went flying and splatted in the road.

"You fuckin' faggot," came a barely-broken voice as several fists hit him to the ground.

He recognised the voice – it was one of the kids who'd been hassling him earlier by the clock tower. He looked up at their grinning teenage faces and they laughed at him as they hit and kicked him on the pavement. Crump couldn't remember anything much after that.

He woke drowsily a few hours later in Lewisham hospital, in the same ward as before, and the same female doctor he had seen before was standing over him too. She examined him and said he could go home as he just had lots of bruising and a few small cuts, but told him to come back if he felt dizzy or sick, and to be more careful in future.

She also wanted him to report this as a homophobic attack to the police. Apparently, an ambulance had been passing, and the paramedics had chased the boys off and taken him to hospital, so they had heard the homophobic insults. The police arrived later but, obviously, the attackers had scarpered by then.

"But I'm not gay," groaned Crump.

The doctor nodded and smiled sympathetically at him. She held his arm reassuringly.

"It's OK you know, my younger brother's gay – it's all about accepting yourself," she said.

"But, really..." Crump started, but couldn't be bothered to finish the sentence – he was too weary.

"If you don't want to report this to the police as a homophobic attack then, well, that's your choice," she said, "but remember, silence can sometimes be a betrayal."

The paramedics had automatically called the police the evening he'd been attacked, and an officer came later that morning to take a statement. He looked about fourteen, and said in what seemed like a newly-broken voice that, because of the insulting and offensive language used by Crump's attackers, he was going to report the attack as a homophobic incident. The only description of his attackers Crump could give was that they were teenage boys, black, wearing hoodies and trainers – which he supposed narrowed it down to about twenty thousand individuals in inner London. He didn't expect the police to have caught his attackers or arrested anyone, and they hadn't. He knew they never would, either.

After speaking to the police, Crump discharged himself from hospital. He went back home and slept for hours – he needed to retreat into himself for a while. His body felt sore, as did his head, and he was covered in bruises. Still, he was lucky he hadn't been seriously hurt – he could have been stabbed, or shot, or anything. How on earth had London got so violent, he wondered. He had no idea.

The next day, he picked up the cheap hire car he'd booked earlier and drove the entire length of the M4 back to South Wales to be with his mum for Christmas. He felt tired, and ill, and completely and utterly sick and tired of everything, and he knew he needed a rest. He also had a monster of a headache, though he wasn't sure if that was the result of the attack or the swarms of thoughts gnawing away in his skull.

Perhaps he would feel better after a couple of weeks away from it all? He could hardly feel any worse.

It had been an interesting first term in academia, all in all.

And it had felt like a thousand years.

CHAPTER SEVEN

Moving On

January – a new year, a new start. A time to put the past behind you and, as psychobabble therapists regularly advise gormless guests on mind-rotting daytime TV shows, to seek *closure* and *move on*.

Looking forward and not back; out with the old and in with the new; a smile on the face and a song in the heart, and the turning over of new leaves throughout the happy land. A time for new beginnings, can-do optimism, possibility and hopefulness.

No wonder so many people always died in January – the stress and despair caused by all that hope must have been the final straw.

That was what his mum always said anyway, and she said it was what her own mother had said too. Perhaps it was just the dour, glass-half-empty, Welsh chapel doom-mongering talking again. But it was true, if the TV news was anything to go by anyway – a lot of famous people *did* tend to peg out in January, perhaps the result of all the Christmas excess, perhaps not.

Crump had spent a quiet, relaxing Christmas in Swansea with his mum and felt refreshed – not to mention well-fed – for it too. He knew that he'd lost a bit of weight recently, but his mum seemed to think he was practically anorexic, so proceeded to feed him up in a way perhaps only Welsh mothers knew how. Nothing like a bit of home cooking to perk things up – nothing like a break from the old routine to add a spring in the step either.

"I'm so proud of you," his mum had said more often then he'd liked, "just think, you're a lecturer at a university – your dad would've been so proud!"

He had felt an awful groaning twisting pain in his stomach – it could have been anxiety or guilt or shame. Maybe it was just indigestion.

"Never forget, your granddad was a miner who left school at twelve years of age..."

Crump hadn't forgotten that, nor that both of his parents had left school young too, his father to work on the railway, his mother to train as a nurse. He loved to see his mum enjoying her retirement and wished his dad could be there too – it always seemed so unfair when men worked hard all their lives only to drop dead before retirement. But then, his father had to work his guts out to lift himself out of the poverty into which he'd been born, so could never really relax, not really, could never really stop working working working – and it killed him in the end. At least his mum could enjoy her retirement years, but it would have been so much better if his dad had still been around to share them. It had been nearly fifteen years since he had dropped dead from a heart attack and, although it was a cliché, it was true – it really did just seem like yesterday. Crump missed him. Every day.

How could he tell his mum about the trouble he had got into at university? How could he even tell her about the low standards and the cheating and all the rest? How could he tell her how unhappy he had become or how the whole university education system was nothing more than a business – and a scam business at that? How could he? She was so proud of him. It would break her heart.

In common with many from her generation, especially from Wales, his mum had an overriding belief – almost a religious faith – in the utter rightness and goodness and transformative

173

powers of education. It had, after all, allowed her to become a nurse – rather than the skivvy in service she might have been in a previous age – and had allowed Crump's father to become educated enough as an adult to become a union official, rather than the poverty-stricken and exploited worker he would have been just a few decades before. Education had transformed untold millions of lives for the better, and, apart from material advantages, it also meant that both his parents were also thinking people who engaged with the world, read books and had *culture*. They had both been brought up in modest circumstances, or grinding poverty in the case of his father, but they had always had that intellectual and cultural curiosity long before they had improved their lives financially. In a way, money wasn't really the issue – attitude was – and they had always had an unswerving faith in the education system, the power of knowledge and the benefits of culture. Crump used to have faith in the education system too, but he had lost his faith and he knew it – and he felt ashamed of himself, somehow, for losing it.

It was disappointing – in fact, it was rather disgusting – that so many people these days had far more money than either his mother or his father could ever have dreamed of, yet had absolutely no real education, no interest in anything other than themselves, and the clothes they wore, and TV reality shows, and becoming 'famous', and simply 'lived under a tub' as his mum always said. Perhaps they didn't deserve the opportunities they'd been given, Crump thought – perhaps these morons deserved to go down a coal mine twelve hours a day to get exploited by the ruling class until they dropped dead from lung disease by the age of forty.

People had fought – fought hard and long, and suffered – for opportunities that everybody now had, opportunities that many casually rejected in favour of living stupid, shallow, ignorant, culture-less and uneducated lives in a 'culture' where supposed role models such as cretinous, foul-mouthed TV chefs and stick-thin, bimbo models actually boasted about never having read a single book in their whole lives. He sometimes wondered why principled people like his father had bothered – people would always disappoint, no matter what anyone did.

"It's a growing university, so there'll be lots of opportunities in future..."

Crump forced a smile and tried to sound as optimistic as he could.

"I knew you'd fall on your feet – you were always the brains in the family, always reading..."

"You and dad were always reading too," said Crump.

"I know but...we were always catching up really, but you Kevin – you were always at the top of the class."

"Maybe one day I'll even be a head of department...and do my PhD and publish my book too...next year maybe..."

"Publish a book? Oh Kevin, your dad would be so proud of you – so proud."

Would he? Would his father have wanted his son to accept what was happening in the education system, to turn a blind eye to its decline, to just go along with the status quo for a quiet life like everybody else?

No. Crump knew that. No he wouldn't – he was a fighter, a brave man – a man who would stand up to injustice even if he was a lone voice in the wilderness, even if the world were against him. He would never just follow everyone else like a sheep if he knew something was wrong – he would stand up and be counted and have the guts to try and change things for the better. And he wouldn't live a lie. Nor would his mum for that matter. But he couldn't tell his mum about how he felt about everything – he just couldn't. Maybe he was a coward, or maybe he just wanted to spare her feelings, not upset her. But he just couldn't tell her and he felt ashamed of that. He was living a lie and he knew it. He was half the man his father was.

That Christmas there were quite a few bright and sunny days, so Crump drove out in his hire car to the glorious beaches of the Gower Peninsula a few miles from where his mother lived. There was really no better way to clear one's head than a solitary walk on a sandy beach with only the wind and the waves for company, and Crump always felt better for it. His drives also allowed him the opportunity to visit one of the local off-licences and stock up on bottles – he didn't want his mum to know how much he was drinking, though he wasn't overdoing it really, not compared to many men his age. He could keep it all in the car too, which was handy.

All in all he felt healthier and happier and more optimistic for the Christmas break and felt ready – just about – to face whatever the new term could throw at him. Or at least he thought so.

* * *

Crump was standing by his old school in the small suburban town of Durnford, fifteen miles from London, where he had grown up. It was a beautifully sunny, if slightly chilly, Sunday afternoon in early January and he was on his way back from Swansea to London in his hire car. He had decided, on a whim, to turn off the motorway and have a look round what was his home town.

Since he'd gone off to university at nineteen he'd never been back – his mother had retired and moved back to South Wales the same year. They had no family in the town or immediate area, and Crump was never one for having a gang of friends at school and hadn't seen anyone at all from his home town since he'd left, so there had never been any reason to go back before. There wasn't any reason to go back now either, but as he was passing, curiosity got the better of him when he saw the town's name on a road sign. It all seemed so long ago, but just like yesterday too, as one's youth always does – and the town seemed the same, but different, too. Just like him.

His old grammar school looked much the same. There were some new buildings, and it looked a bit more modern somehow – when he was there the paint was peeling off the walls and the textbooks and facilities seemingly hadn't been updated in decades. Not that that meant he hadn't got a good education – (as if having expensive, shiny new equipment made pupils brainier or better able to be educated anyway!) – because he certainly had, despite some pretty ropey teaching and a few sadistic teachers.

He noticed that the old entrance had new security gates, as did the drive that led to the playing fields, and there seemed to be CCTV cameras watching everything too, probably because the school now had equipment worth nicking. When he was there the only break-in was just kids who vandalised the art room – they hadn't nicked anything, probably as there wasn't much call for poster paint amongst the criminal fraternity. Now, any intruder could steal computers and state-of-the art technology worth thousands.

Feeling self-conscious, as though someone were watching him and possibly getting the wrong idea, he started walking along the street – watched, as it happens, via CCTV, by Barry Bird, aged 38, CCTV monitoring manager, paralysed from the waist down since a motorbike crash at the age of 19, who hated his job more than he could say, but was following every move of the shifty man of average build and height who was loitering outside the grammar school because that was what he was paid to do. Barry Bird hated it whenever a motorbike passed by on the screen.

Crump walked past the windows of the classroom he'd first entered as a bright-eyed twelve year old on his first day of school, and then walked down the short distance down the road to his old primary school. It was a late Victorian building – one with the obsolete 'BOYS' and 'GIRLS' carved into the brick above separate entrances – and looked almost exactly the same as he had remembered it too. He had spent seven years at the secondary school, and before that four at the primary school and three at the infants next door too, from the age of five. Fourteen years. Fourteen years of his life – the formative ones too – had been spent in this small geographical area, so it was odd that he didn't feel any real attachment to it at all. None. They were just buildings, and that was all – and now they were part of other children's day-to-day lives. Funny, though, how old schools and buildings, despite a few cosmetic changes, never really seemed to change that much at all; it was people who changed really, not things. He was sure if he'd entered his old classrooms that they would have looked almost exactly the same as he remembered. They probably would have even smelt the same too – they would have smelt of *boy*.

He stood looking at the empty primary school playground. A feeling of nostalgia and sadness filled him – perhaps it was just an *awareness* of sadness, of time passing and growing up. Growing old. Sundays always seemed sad, for some reason. Perhaps it was the effect of all that praying going on in churches up and down the country.

Surprisingly, he also felt anger, but not due to any specific memory, though there were some bad swirling with the good in his psyche's vortex of recollections. No, he was angry because of what he could see in the primary school playground. This was where, twenty years previously, he had played conkers and Top Trumps, where he had run with the pack in British Bulldog and crept up to the wall in Hello Mister Wolf, where he had waited eagerly to be picked for the football team at lunchtimes – (though he was always one of the last to be picked) – and where the girls had pinched his legs and poked their tongues out at the boys.

But now, where there used to be hopscotch grids painted on the tarmac, and where lunchtime football matches – about twenty-five a side, he remembered – used to take place, there were three smallish climbing frames. But, more than that, Crump could see the tarmac was no longer tarmac – it was some kind of soft-looking black synthetic material which a sign on one of the frames advertised as 'SAFE-PLAY'. There was also a large notice on the fence that read 'NO BALL GAMES' with a picture of a ball with a red line through it, and another that said, simply, 'RESPECT'. The signs were sponsored by one of the larger supermarkets whose logo adorned everything.

He knew all about health and safety hysteria – he had to put up with it when teaching in the college – and knew it was all caused, ultimately, by the gold-digging litigiousness of the great compensation-craving British public and an irrational perception of risk. But all individuals and institutions had to cover their backs through health and safety procedures and risk-assessment policies, and the corresponding copious paperwork, for fear of falling foul of some regulation or other and getting sued for an oversight.

Crump had even heard that, perhaps due to the education system seemingly becoming so feminised, and parents becoming so irrationally paranoid and hysterical, men in teaching at secondary and especially primary level were constantly made to feel as though they were all potentially predatory paedophiles. For example, many were not even allowed to be in a classroom alone with younger children without another adult, preferably a 'safe' woman, present – and doors always had to be kept open when male teachers were with classes. Just in case...

Paranoid parents and the media were now engaged in a competition to see who could be the most hysterical – so much so that all men who wanted to work with children were seen as highly suspect and a potential danger, so had to be watched and monitored closely at all times. And then people wondered why men weren't going into teaching... It was all very silly and it was all very sad, not to mention sexist. *Misandrist* was the word. But it was 'good practice', and was what parents apparently wanted – ironic, really, as it was parents, statistically, who posed the biggest threat by far to their own children and who were most likely to physically, emotionally or sexually abuse them. Crump wondered whether women in teaching would put up with such a state of affairs, and wondered why the teaching unions didn't seem to be doing anything at all to defend male teachers against the constant atmosphere of suspicion they had to face every day.

He remembered that Becky had once told him that a lot of games he remembered playing, such as British Bulldog, were now routinely banned in primary school playgrounds for being too 'rough', as were all games that might ever make children feel excluded and supposedly would 'lower their self esteem' – in other words, any playground game in which there were winners and losers. Every child had to be a winner in everything these days and failure was not an option.

Also, playgrounds these days were not longer called playgrounds – they were, officially, 'socialisation spaces', a concept that has very conveniently and 'enrichingly' allowed schools to sell off playgrounds and playing fields to developers if there were enough 'socialisation spaces' inside the school in the form of corridors and canteens to meet legal requirements. Newly built schools usually had no playground at all.

These days, all children at this and other primary schools were clearly expected to stand around playing hand-clap games and chatting and 'engaging in socialisation', or perhaps playing on the safe climbing frame, under constant supervision from the fully CRB-checked, and female, playground wardens – or 'child welfare managers' as they liked to be called. Sadly, a lot of children were now so obese that they couldn't haul their adipose bodies onto a climbing frame at all, so it got used much less than it should have been – which further minimised the danger of injury, of course, as that meant there was no possibility of their ever falling off, so everyone was happy.

Crump also knew that, these days, for whatever reason, kids didn't even play conkers, and not just because it had been banned in playgrounds for being too dangerous – because of course a piece of conker *could* fly off and hurt a child, and then the parents could sue the school, so best to be on the safe side and just completely ban it, and so they did. He had seen, every September in London, unopened conkers lying on the ground in parks and on streets, un-picked-up and neglected, and wistfully remembered his excitement as a boy when he found freshly-fallen conkers, and the sheer joy of stamping open the green fleshy shell to reveal the gorgeously shiny horse chestnut nestling within like some woody jewel. Now they were left on the ground to rot – something that would have been seen as heresy by all small boys not so many years previously.

These days, he thought, boys were just not allowed to be boys, and all children were cooped up at home on their computers, getting fat through their inactivity, not learning how to take risks or develop resilience or learn about the natural world, and all because of a perceived threat of the dreaded lurking 'paedophiles' that does not really even exist in any significant way, or in any greater way than it did in the past. Most people clearly didn't realise the damage, both mental and physical, they were doing to children by this fearfulness and enforced caution and suspicion, or the fact that children, these days, were safer than at any other time in human history.

"Everything alright, sir?" a voice came from behind.

Crump was still looking through the wire fence at the playground and had become so lost in his thoughts and reminiscences that he hadn't noticed that a police car had parked on the road behind him or that two officers had got out. He turned round.

"Oh," said Crump, startled – he couldn't help feeling guilty whenever he saw policemen but never understood why, "Yes...er...fine," he said, not knowing what else to say.

The two police officers, both younger than him, peered at him closely. He blushed and looked away, somewhat shiftily he knew, but he really couldn't help it.

"Do you mind telling us what you're doing, sir?" said the same police officer while the other wrote in his notebook. They reminded him of prefects at school – the same matter-of-fact emotionless statements, the same enjoyment of authority and rules.

"Well...er...I'm...er...just...er...looking," said Crump, stupidly, but honestly – he *was* 'just looking' at his old school playground on a Sunday afternoon.

"Looking at what, exactly, sir?"

"Looking...er...at...er...the playground," he said, gesturing to it.

"Like looking at playgrounds do we, sir," asked the police officer, narrowing his eyes.

His colleague frowned and scribbled frantically in his notebook.

Crump suddenly realised that, despite there being no children at all in the playground, the police officers seemed to be suspecting him of being a paedophile.

"Oh...no...oh...er...um..." he said, "I mean, you see, this is my old school, so I thought I'd stop and, y'know, have a...look...at..."

"Disappointed are we, sir?" the policeman interrupted, "Expected to see lots of pretty little kiddies running around, did we?"

My God, thought Crump, they really *do* think I'm a kiddie-fiddler! But what kind of paedophile would think schools were open on a Sunday? A very stupid one, probably.

"God, no, I...I'm just on my way back to London and...thought I'd...stop and look at the old school...that's all," said Crump, smiling slightly.

This was a big mistake. A smile could mean he was a shifty paedophile, after all, in this day and age – it could be seen as a leery, pervy smile of sexually suspect 'strange man'. Best not to smile – smiling always meant trouble.

The police officers looked at Crump, then at each other. He thought they didn't believe him, and they didn't. They asked him to empty his pockets and took his details, checking them via walkie-talkie against their records. Eventually, after convincing themselves that Crump wasn't a monstrous predatory paedophile after all, they left.

"Can't be too careful these days, sir," one of the police officers said as he was leaving.

He was right – you can't.

"Oi Crumpet!" a voice shouted as he unlocked his car later

with a beep. It was a voice he recognised – a voice which had hardly changed at all in the intervening fifteen years.

"Thought it was you," said a fat man in a shiny suit, "I ain't see ya for donkey's years!"

Oh God, thought Crump, it's him – I come back to my old town and the only person I bump into is the class bully, McHuffer.

Mark McHuffer, the boy who thought how amusing it would be to – repeatedly – put a drawing pin on his chair before he sat down, to put salt in his pudding, to steal his underpants from the changing room in PE and put them in the teacher's desk drawer – Mark McHuffer, who had left school at sixteen and whom Crump hadn't seen since. Life was always a 'laugh' with Mark McHuffer – for him anyway. It could have been anyone – *anyone* – that he'd bump into on his return to his home town. Why did it have to be him? Why?

"Oh...er...hi...it's..."

"Mark," said McHuffer, "Old Huffy – you remember!"

Unfortunately, yes, he did.

"Mark, yes, well, how...are you...these days?"

McHuffer had always been a stockily built kid, but now he was, quite simply, obese. A real porker – at least twenty stone. More, probably. A bovver-boy Buddha. He looked forty five – fifty even – and had completely shaved his head too. It turned out he was now married with two kids and, somewhat scarily, ran and owned a nursery with his wife, looking after little children all day long, which seemed to Crump about as likely as Hitler running a company that organised Bar Mitzvahs.

When McHuffer said what he did, Crump almost laughed out loud. He remembered the way McHuffer had seemed like a psychopath at school, had no feelings for anybody else and liked – really, *really* enjoyed – inflicting pain on other pupils. Hurting others had been his hobby – perhaps, even, his reason to be. And now he was looking after toddlers?

He told McHuffer that he was now a senior university lecturer – (well, how was he to know any different?) – and turned down his offer of a pint because of the time. They exchanged phone numbers – Crump gave a false one, from his local Chinese takeaway actually – and they said they'd call each other soon.

Crump had deliberately not joined social networking websites so he could avoid all this rose-coloured-spectacles bullshit schooldays nostalgia, but here it was in the shape McHuffer and his pally back-slapping 'oh-what-fun-we-had' bonhomie. He so wanted to break McHuffer's nose – smack him in his jaw so hard he'd fly back through the air in slow motion and be knocked out cold – and fantasised about doing just that as he smiled at McHuffer's fat, grinning face. It wouldn't have been any good though – Crump knew that he was to fighting what the average boxer was to intellectual curiosity – so, as always, he just enjoyed the fantasy for what it was whilst he suffered the reality. It was safer that way.

It was with not a little relief that Crump got into his hire car and drove away. Never coming back here again, he thought, and he meant it. This place was no longer his home in any way whatsoever.

As a sort of last halloo Crump thought he'd drive round the town centre one-way system to see how the place had changed. It was much the same – the same park and library, the same Norman church tower next to the River Durn, the same car parks. He could see that the bank on the corner where his mum used to go when she took him to town as a little boy was now a bar offering cheap shots and meal deals, and there also seemed to be countless charity shops, pound shops and takeaways where previously there had been 'real' shops, such as butchers, bakers and greengrocers. Several shops were boarded up.

In general, the town centre seemed much more down-at-heel and shabby than when Crump had lived there, no doubt partly caused by the opening of a vast out-of-town shopping centre. It was a shame, but then the town was still relatively prosperous as a dormitory suburb of London, and Crump supposed that, despite being an utterly dull place to live, there were certainly worse places to bring up kids – anywhere in inner London for a start. At least there were good schools in the area, green spaces and a relative lack of street crime.

Crump drove past all the same streets and houses he remembered from childhood and it all looked much the same, but there did seem to be a lot of new houses built on what had been waste ground, or people's gardens, when he had lived there. It all seemed more overcrowded now – more cramped somehow – even though there were hardly any people about on a Sunday evening. It was just that every available space had been built on, with new-build houses everywhere, mostly executive-style homes. Where on earth were they going to build new homes when all that spare land was gone? The countryside?

It was such a paradox, thought Crump, as he rejoined the motorway bound for London – everyone now seemed richer than they were twenty or thirty years ago, but everyone seemed so much poorer in terms of their quality of life. People were more stressed, for a start. Perhaps because just affording to buy somewhere to live, even for those with reasonable jobs, was near impossible, or perhaps because they just had higher expectations than they could possibly achieve. Or maybe it was something deeper and more profound, and caused by so much family breakdown and divorce in Britain – children certainly seemed unhappier than when he was a scruffy kid riding around on his bike, exploring his surroundings and living largely out-of-doors, and only going home for his tea or when it got dark. He was happy then – probably the happiest he'd ever been actually, except on the numerous occasions when he'd fallen off his bike and hurt himself. Balance was never his strong point.

Crump had noticed this change in society, especially after returning from travelling round Europe on his inter-rail trip after university – unlike in mainland Europe, there were simply no children playing in the streets any more in Britain. None. It was as though the Chitty-Chitty Bang-Bang child-catcher had crawled through every street and lane, through every road and avenue, snatching the children away to lock in a dungeon somewhere. And, thought Crump, what is a child's bedroom but a dungeon, if they are trapped in there in captivity and unable to escape because of parental paranoia and enforced anxiety, tip-tap-tapping on their computer keyboards, playing computer games and surfing the internet all day long? How had this happened, all in the space of a couple of decades? It was terribly, and awfully, and absurdly, sad.

Maybe it was just nostalgia, that trick of the memory, that made Crump think it had been much better to be a child when he was young. Maybe not. Maybe it was just different, not worse, anyway. But it seemed worse, for sure.

* * *

Crump arrived back in Eltham later than expected. He had really wanted to have more time to get organised and sort out his stuff for work that evening, but what with the traffic and his troubled trip down memory lane, it was after 8pm by the time he arrived. His mum had given him a present to give to Mrs Glidewell – some homemade marmalade and jam that a friend of hers had made the previous summer – she'd like that.

He parked the car a short distance down the street – (he'd return it the following evening) – and got out into the cold, clear-skied winter night. The harshness of the winter air hurt his lungs as he inhaled, and he coughed at the cold.

As he approached the house, he could see that the lights weren't on. That was unusual – Mrs Glidewell never went anywhere in the evenings, and didn't usually go to bed until about ten o'clock. Crump opened the front door that he shared with his landlady – the house felt cold, as though it hadn't been heated for days. Perhaps Mrs Glidewell had gone away for the New Year? But she had no children, and had never gone away before. Crump was sure she would have said something.

After going upstairs to his flat and putting his bags in his room, he returned downstairs to check the heating and, more importantly, to see if Mrs Glidewell was in.

He called out, but there was no reply. He called again – nothing – so he went through into the living room and turned on the light. Mrs Glidewell was sitting in her armchair, a dressing gown on and a blanket on her knees. Her eyes were closed. Was she asleep? Unconscious? Dead?

A tight knot of anxiety twisted in Crump's stomach and his legs felt weak. He touched her arm – it was cold, yes, but there was warmth with it – and she was definitely breathing. Crump tried to gently shake the old lady awake a couple of times and called out her name – he realised only then that he didn't know her first name. He dialled 999 from her phone.

The paramedic arrived quickly and listened for vital signs, preparing her for the trip to hospital. The ambulance got there a few minutes later. It looked like hypothermia, they said. Why hadn't she put on the heating? She had enough money to keep warm in winter, surely?

Crump travelled in the ambulance and took a seat in the hospital waiting room. Eventually, they told him that Mrs Glidewell had been admitted for one night, and probably longer. He gave his name and number to the hospital, but told them he didn't know her next of kin, or even if she had any family at all. Then he got a taxi home. He hadn't even unpacked his bags yet and it was now nearly eleven. He'd just have to organise his stuff in the morning – he was well and truly exhausted, and needed to get some sleep.

After eating one of the worst Chinese takeaways he'd ever tasted, he set his alarm for early the next morning and went to bed. He was asleep seconds after his head hit the pillow.

* * *

"Thank golly we are not having to do teaching until next week – I am quite unprepared," said Rajdeep.

Crump was in the same boat. Thankfully, the students

wouldn't be back at lectures until the following Monday but staff were expected back a week earlier.

He was sitting with Raj in the department office. Kwame was still away in the States, having been invited to a conference on black history by one of the all-black universities.

Athena was there too. Athena – the goddess he worshipped – the woman he had loved, or at least thought he had loved. The woman he still loved. Perhaps.

How could she do that to him? How could she not let him know that she was a lesbian? How could she come out *like that*? It was cruel and it had utterly crushed him. Surely she realised how he felt about her? Can't women tell when men fancy them? Weren't women supposed to be good at *that sort of thing*? Where was the 'female intuition' in what Athena had done? Where was the famous female 'multi-tasking' come to that – couldn't she have told him about her being a lesbian *and* gone out for a drink with him? Where was the *humanity* in the way she had chosen to come out to him? His head was swirling with questions.

"Are you OK?" Athena asked Crump after Raj had gone out for a break.

"Yes," he said, lying.

"I'm sorry about...well...y'know," said Athena, "I didn't mean to..."

Crump nodded sadly.

"I really didn't mean to hurt you," she said.

He said nothing, but he was grateful to Athena for that. He knew she meant it – and that meant more than she could possibly know.

His heart was still broken, and it would take a long time for him to come to terms with what had happened, but he knew he would just have to accept it – or try to be stoical, at least. They'd have to work together anyway, so for practical reasons alone it would be better if he managed to stay friends with Athena. What had happened was just *one of those things* – nobody's fault, even though he had been terribly hurt by it. 'Life is real, life is earnest', as his mum had always said. And it was. So he just had to get on with it. Nose to the grindstone. Keep calm and carry on. That sort of thing...

"I meant to do some planning over Christmas but...well...you know the way it goes..." Crump said, when Raj came back into the room.

"Oh gosh, I do," said Rajdeep, shaking his head.

"Suppose we all had a good rest though, so it's not time wasted."

"Yes yes," said Raj, "having the rest is also the preparation." And they nodded at each other at this half truth.

"Well I'm totally prepared," said Athena, tongue-in-cheek, "for the first three weeks of this term's lessons too."

"Well you are woman," said Rajdeep, looking cheeky, "you are used to the multi-tasking. We men are having more stress in our lives, which is why we are dying younger..."

"Which is why we've been so deep in intellectual thought over the holidays that we have failed to prepare..." said Crump, smiling.

"So you will prepare to fail, because you have failed to prepare" said Athena jokingly, mocking the trite corporate management mantra parroted by so many teachers.

"Have you really prepared everything?" asked Crump.

She smiled at him – somewhat warmly, he thought.

"Course not!" she giggled, "just winding you up, boys!"

"You know," said Rajdeep with a grin on his face, "multi-tasking is scientifically proven not to be working anyway – which is why men are achieving so much. Women are always getting so distracted – y'know, losing the focus – with brain like the butterfly."

They all laughed and Athena gave Raj a mock smack on his arm.

"Anyway, we are having so many bloody meetings this week there will be no time for preparing for the teaching," said Rajdeep.

It was true. There were meetings every day, ranging from

diversity meetings, to policy meetings, to staff training of various kinds – and they would all have to be endured. Absence was not an option, as the copious emails that had been sent out by the office made clear.

Crump was hoping that it would be an easy week – he had to get some lessons planned and do mounds of paperwork, not to mention his ongoing research. As a contractual obligation, he also had to add his lesson plans and PowerPoint slides to the university intranet so other staff and students could access them, which took even more time.

One thing that had changed in recent years was the idea that, in order to teach effectively, one had to use that corporate business favourite PowerPoint to give a good lecture, or even a lesson. Sandy referred to it as 'PowerPointlessness' and never used it – but then he was a senior lecturer and more or less untouchable. Crump, on the other hand, was on the lowest rung of the lowest ladder, so had to do exactly what he was told to do, even if he knew that to be pointless, stupid and wrong – that was just how institutional hierarchies worked.

A good lecture or lesson certainly did not *need* PowerPoint – in fact, its very use would mean not only that the lecturer would be forced to think and lecture in a simplistic, bullet-pointed way, but also that the audience would not be listening to the speaker at all but would just be gawping at the inane graphics and bullet points on the screen. And everything had to be written in the Comic Sans font, because, supposedly, this made it easier to read for dyslexics and others. It was a comic-book, infantile font for a comic, infantile age – but use any other font and you'd be criticised for not being sensitive to the needs of your students with learning difficulties and not embedding differentiation in your teaching.

No-one seemed to appreciate any more that what you really needed for a good lecture or lesson was an intelligent, educated and knowledgeable teacher who knew and loved their subject and wished to communicate that to an audience. It was all superficial now, all surface and no substance, all used-car-salesperson spiel – and no-one seemed to care if some badly educated mediocrity taught lessons or gave lectures, so long as they wrote lesson plans according to the latest fashionable fake theories of education, and presented the lesson using PowerPoint like some corporate clone selling consumers a product – which was precisely what education had become, actually. No-one seemed to realise that presentation wasn't everything, or even that speaking well was not necessarily the same thing as having something worth saying or listening to, and was often, in fact, the exact opposite.

Fiona Windrush herself was giving a lecture that afternoon to all staff of the Department of Cultural, Creative and Communicative Studies. Everyone assembled in the lecture hall in the Mandela building after lunch, and Crump sat with Raj and Athena towards the back. Sandy was there, at the front with the other senior lecturers, and he could see Margaret No-name and Johnny Wong, the new members of staff, in front of him to the left. Cecilia was there too, ghostly pale in a small group of silent women.

Wendy Webb entered the lecture hall and found a seat. Crump had told no-one of what he had seen in the toilet at the Christmas Do, but would definitely have to ask Sandy later. He was already worrying about what he would say to Wendy when they first talked that term. Should he just try to forget what he'd seen – or would Wendy raise it, so to speak?

Fiona Windrush swanned into the room and, as if by magic, everybody stopped chatting and was silent – such was the power of a head of department and the fear that such managers could instil in the hearts of subordinates. The silence was briefly disturbed by the elephant's trumpet sound of somebody blowing their nose. Crump knew it was Sandy – he was the only lecturer who would dare. Fiona looked at him hard, and Sandy put away his hanky.

Crump thought how pale Fiona looked from a distance for someone who identified herself as black – Becky was darker, and she was mixed race, and pale mixed race at that. But then a lot of white girls from southern Europe were darker than some people who considered themselves to be non-white too, so what was 'black' or 'white' or any other skin colour really but a simplistic identity and label one gave to oneself? But surely skin colour, if not 'race', was more than just a construct? It was a visual thing, surely?

Fiona's eyes scanned the lecture hall. She smiled.

"Welcome back, everyone, to our *award-winning* university and department. I hope you all had a good winter break," she said

There were mumbles of 'yes' and chirpy 'yes, thank yous' from the usual sycophants, who always sat towards the front, but Crump said nothing.

"Good," said Fiona Windrush, "and I sincerely hope we shall all have a Happy New Year."

She paused and looked around the room until she saw Crump, stared at him briefly, smiled, nodded and then took a deep breath.

"Unfortunately," she went on, "there were several events last term which I certainly hope not to see repeated."

Crump started to blush as Fiona met his eye. He looked away.

"That's why we are introducing a regular diversity training programme, in addition to expanded and enhanced CPD, which all lecturers will have to attend without fail."

"Why they are using all these bloody acronyms in education system!" said Raj later.

They were sitting in the staff section of the cafeteria drinking what was alleged to be tea.

"CPD's an abbreviation, or an 'initialism' – it's not an acronym," said Crump, "because you can't pronounce it as a single word, like NATO."

Crump was teasing Raj and he knew it.

"Yes thank you, Mr Crump, your pedantic contribution has duly been noted," said Raj, deliberately thickening his accent, "Thank you sir for educating poor ignorant Indian peasant boy fool such as I into intricacies of your jolly bloody wonderful English language, oh goodness gracious me yes indeed isn't it?!"

They all laughed. Crump was so glad that Raj and Athena were friendly and easy-going enough to share a joke. It would have been hell working at Thames Met without their company.

"It is just jolly bloody shame that no-one at this university seems to be knowing what English word 'tea' is meaning."

Rajdeep wrinkled his nose at the tepid grey water in his polystyrene cup.

They had just one more lecture to go and then they could all go home. It was a lecture on gender, race, diversity and language, and was also to be given by Fiona Windrush.

As usual, on days like this, they were all weighed down with paperwork that had been handed out at lectures – there was a programme for the CPD, and a diversity training timetable, as well as details of other new regulations and guidelines, which were almost certainly all completely pointless and unnecessary, the result of the usual paper-shuffling paperwork-generating pen-pushing bureaucrats. Did these people not realise that nobody – *nobody* – actually read what they churned out, that the usual endless copies of this or that were usually simply glanced at by everyone with a look of disdain before being filed in a drawer somewhere never to be seen again? Would the running of the education system be harmed in any real way if a great big bonfire were made of all of it, and the pen-pushing pompous jobsworths responsible for it put on top of those bonfires and burnt to a crisp in the inferno? Such were the thoughts sizzling in Crump's brain as he sat down wearily at the back of the lecture hall in readiness of Fiona Windrush's lecture. He knew he wasn't going to like it, and he didn't.

"All white people are racist and all men are sexist – they just don't know it and are in a state of denial," said Fiona Windrush to the lecture hall audience. "A great deal of research has been done, including some at this university, proving that very fact.

Therefore, we all have to be self-aware, and realise that we must constantly be on our guard against sexist, racist and other discriminatory forms of language."

A handout was passed round the lecture hall. The handout – the comfort blanket of every modern teacher. Strange to think that there was a time before photocopiers were invented when people got a first class education without the use of handouts. Instead they used things called 'books' and teachers wrote things on blackboards in chalk.

Of course, the very word 'blackboard' was an example of institutional racism – it had been changed to 'chalkboard' many years before by national decree – and every phrase using the word 'black' was now frowned upon throughout the education system. There were to be no more blackboards, blacklegs, black markets or blackmail – which was rather appropriate really as the whole thing was an exercise in emotional blackmail, or 'emotional extortion' to use non-discriminatory language.

As the document they had each been handed stated:

"Language defines our attitudes and is unfortunately riddled with terms which demean, belittle, ignore or insult sections of our diverse society. We have a duty, therefore, to use words and expressions that do not perpetuate or reinforce discriminatory or offensive attitudes. The eradication of such offensive and inappropriate language will help to alter attitudes and change behaviours. In line with a number of other policies, the University is committed to the elimination of practices and the challenging of attitudes which are considered to be offensive and discriminatory."

Which, in theory, thought Crump, sounded fine.

But the question was – who was deciding what was offensive and inappropriate? The word 'inappropriate' was usually used by people to stop others saying what they didn't like to hear, for a start, and was one of the trite, weasel words much loved by bullying managers everywhere to stop anything they didn't like. The phrase 'are considered to be offensive' was fine as far as it went, but who was doing the considering? It seemed to be allowing perception to replace an evidence-based approach – which was a very dangerous development indeed, bearing in mind that one person's perception of what was racist or sexist could differ substantially from another's and always would, because the definitions of those words and concepts were fluid and based on opinion, not fact.

For example, Crump didn't think it was offensive or inappropriate to use the word 'black', as its everyday usage was usually nothing whatever to do with race or skin colour, and was obviously only used in negative phrases due to the night (dangerous and frightening) being vaguely black, and the day (safe and peaceful) being vaguely white. It was also true that white was a colour sometimes used to represent death – for example, funeral flowers were traditionally white and it was an unlucky colour in China and other cultures, due to the bones of the dead being white – but no-one had suggested banning negative phrases using the word 'white', such as 'white lies' or 'white elephant'. Though he would never wish to deliberately offend anyone, he didn't see why he or anyone else should stop using the word 'black' in everyday phrases. It was all just too silly for words.

For the sake of a quiet life, however, he was prepared to use up-to-date words and phrases about race, so didn't mind saying Black and Minority Ethnic (or BME) which was now the preferred expression for all ethnic minorities. It was a silly phrase as it implied that ethnic minorities weren't black – though the intention to include some white 'ethnic' minorities, such as Irish or Polish people, was apparently one of the motivations for the name change. The phrase 'ethnic minority' had been changed to 'minority ethnic', supposedly because the first word was the most important, so the minority status, not the ethnicity, was the concept to be emphasised. Crump wondered if people had 'coffee cups' these days rather than cups of coffee, and went on 'holiday summers' too, as the holiday was obviously more important than the season. The only thing these policies actually seemed to show – beyond doubt – was that there was a huge diversity and race relations industry in the UK which kept vast armies of self-righteous busy-bodies in careers which almost certainly paid them massively inflated salaries from taxpayers' money for thinking up such pointless drivel – or, more precisely, for just copying whatever drivel they'd thought up in America.

Crump was familiar with the anti-sexist language guidelines already. There was to be no use of the word 'he' without the word 'she', even if it mangled the English language and destroyed its form. So *'every man gets what he deserves'* would become *'every man or woman gets what he or she deserves'*, thereby ruining utterly the balance and beauty of the sentence. This linguistic political correctness was like some 'vowel cancer' eating away at the beauty and elegance of the English language, but the disease had not started in England or even Britain – a lot of these ideas originated in the 1960s and 70s in influential American universities, and had spread like a brain-eating virus around the world. Hippies had a lot to answer for.

There was to be no mention of men without women, even if a certain event or historical episode was male only. Crump had even seen a description of the 1944 Normandy landings in a university journal where soldiers were referred to 'he or she' throughout. He hadn't remembered seeing any women in 'Saving Private Ryan'; to his knowledge, the soldiers involved in the Normandy Landings, and those soldiers trying to kill them, were completely, and irredeemably, male. He wondered if the same linguistic gender equality rule applied when women were in the majority: would midwives now be referred to as 'he or she' or 'she or he' from now on, for example, even though most, if not all, were female – though he well knew that the word merely meant 'with the wife' and had never actually referred to the gender of the person performing the role?

In general, Crump agreed with acknowledging racial or

gender issues, and avoiding unnecessary offence, but certainly did not think it was anywhere near as important as other factors, and he was dead-set against the English language being censored in such a way – it was, really, a Stalinist method of thought-control, and certainly not about liberty or equality – or common sense – at all.

One thing Crump absolutely hated was the idea that the words Man or Mankind should be disposed of. He knew that these words referred to both men and women (when the capital M was used) and always had – a meaning English shared with German. He also knew that male pronouns had, since the Middle Ages, referred to both men and women ('wyf-men' in Anglo-Saxon), and were not necessarily male-specific.

He had noticed how teacher trainers – 80% of whom were female and often rather left-wing and feministic – deliberately *excluded* males in their writing by only using the pronoun 'she' or 'her', and not even saying 'she and he' or 'her and him'. He also noticed how feminists were not very keen to make phrases such as 'con man', 'tax man', 'dirty old man' gender neutral or put pressure of anyone to stop automatically referring to criminals as male – it was only the good, high-status jobs and positive roles where gender neutrality and female presence were demanded, a selective cherry-picked equality that was, by definition, unequal and sexist.

But no matter how he felt, Crump really could not risk challenging any university policy, not after the events of the previous term. He would just keep quiet and not make a fuss. What really mattered was that *he* knew it was all daft – all just part of an absurd game which in no way at all tackled or minimised racism or sexism in any real sense. Anyway, it all depended on what one defined as racism or sexism – both words were abstract nouns so could mean anything one wanted them to mean really, which was the beauty and danger of abstract nouns. But it was better to keep shtum, all in all – you never knew who could be listening.

One handout Crump received in the lecture was a list of

outlawed words and phrases and the acceptably inoffensive words and phrases that should be used instead. Many of the preferred descriptions of race and gender used the word 'person' or 'human' and thus sounded utterly artificial, as these were essentially Latinate words to be used in written, not spoken, English. Seventy per cent of everyday English language was derived from shorter-syllabled, short-vowelled Anglo-Saxon words, and not the softer, longer Latinate written words such as 'person' or 'human' which should really be avoided in speech if a clumsy, artificial note was not to be sounded.

The handouts and guidelines they'd been given also stressed over and over again the relativistic view of the universe. No culture or political system was better or worse – that was all just Eurocentric racism and imperialism – and no artistic endeavour was superior or inferior to any other either. So the complete works of Beethoven were in no way better or superior to an Aborigine banging two sticks together in the Outback, and European-style liberal pluralistic democracy was in no way better or superior to any other system, such as that in brutal Islamic or communist dictatorships . Everything was relative, even morality.

No-one had stopped to think that this relativism could easily have been used to justify the actions of Hitler and Stalin, not to mention practices such as cannibalism, paedophilia and bestiality. That was the danger of relativism – there was no right or wrong, no better or worse, nothing beyond the subjective and the perceived, and anything and everything was as equally as valid and acceptable and worthwhile as everything else.

There was also a passage on the handout in bold which stated that all religions and cultures must be respected, and that teachers and lecturers should be aware of the sensitivities of those of other cultures, especially in our multi-faith society – which Crump knew meant that criticism of religion at the university had now been banned. It seemed extraordinary that, in a university of all places, people were being discouraged from challenging others' opinions or thinking in a rational, evidence-based way – especially as there was no evidence whatsoever for the existence of God and plenty for the scientific discoveries such as evolution which contradicted many religious texts. Surely that was the whole point of faith – that there was no evidence for it and you had to make a 'leap of faith' to believe in it?

On the way home on the bus Crump re-read the list of banned words that Fiona had handed out in the lecture. Occasionally, he laughed out loud, which made a couple of fellow passengers look round at him – but London was full of the sad and the mad, many of them on buses babbling and laughing to themselves, so no-one cared that much. Crump was too lost in thought as he read the absurd and risible list to notice any strange looks anyway.

It was the first word on the list that made him laugh the loudest. The words 'fail' and 'failure' were no longer to be used in the department, or anywhere in the university – they 'reinforced negative perceptions' apparently. Instead, the terms 'deferred success' or 'achieve a deficiency' were to be used – all phrases with positive connotations, but utterly absurd – quite apart from the fact that failure was a good thing, because without it success meant nothing. If everyone won a gold medal, then gold medals would be worthless, which was one obvious problem with the grade inflation and A-grades-and-degrees-for-everyone, all-must-have-prizes orthodoxy of the present British education system. Failure also inculcated resilience and hard work in those who encountered it – no success was ever achieved without facing a great deal of failure on the way, after all – and it also allowed people to discover where their talents lay. Failure was, in a nutshell, a good thing. But not according to the handout – the word was now, officially, banned.

There were other phrases on the list too – 'wrong' should now be 'differently logical'; an 'ignorant student' should now be called a 'knowledge-based non-possessing' student; 'lazy' would be 'motivationally deficient', and 'disruptive' would become 'abundantly verbal'. Crump would actually have to use these ridiculous phrases in his reports. He wondered which phrase the university would use to mean 'dead' – 'metabolically differently-abled' perhaps? Would gossip be rechristened 'speedy transmission of near-factual information'? And would body odour be renamed 'non-discretionary fragrance'? Perhaps as a 'learning facilitator' it was not his place to ask such questions.

* * *

Later that week, they all went to the pub and, after a couple of drinks, most people went home leaving Crump alone with Sandy. It was the chance he'd been waiting for.

"He's been that way for almost ten years now, old boy," said Sandy, taking a gulp of his pint, "though he hasn't gone all the way, as't were..."

"But," asked Crump, "why didn't anyone say anything?"

"Why should they Crumpie?" said Sandy.

Crump wished he wouldn't call him that.

"Wendy now wants to be a 'she', so that's what 'he' is – except on official documents – passports and the all that malarkey – for that you need the full op."

"So what... I mean... who... is he... I mean... she... now... exactly?" asked Crump.

"After I'd been teaching here for about six or seven years, back in the early eighties, a man called William Webb got a job here as a junior lecturer – like you."

Crump nodded.

"Course," said Sandy, "he looked a bit different then – long hippy hair, radical badges on the lapel, copy of Das Kapital on the shelf, bust of Lenin on the desk – the usual, really, for the time at the polytechnic. We called him Willy – which, looking back, was quite marvellously ironic..."

"So... when did he....?"

"Start dressing as a woman?" Crump nodded. "'About ten years ago, old boy. Before that, well – he was one of the most macho members of the department – played footie on a Sunday, liked his pint with the lads, that kind of thing – and you had to like *that kind of thing* back then if you were 'working class' or at least pretending to be..."

Crump knew what he meant. He'd known quite a few teachers who'd had privileged backgrounds and they usually kept it very quiet indeed, especially if, as was often the case, they held left-wing political views.

"And he was quite a stud really, in his day," Sandy said, as images of Wendy Webb's penis poked into Crump's brain, "Oh yes, my boy – we didn't call him Slick Willy for nothing!"

Crump wondered why he hadn't suspected before – after all Wendy Webb was rather masculine in her features and she wore an obvious wig. Having said that, quite a fair number of women in teaching were rather masculine in their features, so he couldn't go round assuming they were actually male or expecting them all to be part of the male to female transsexual and/or transgendered community.

"Then he just came into the staff room one day about ten years ago dressed like a girl – and in those days he looked pretty hideous too – makeup everywhere, like a toddler let loose in the dressing up box – and announced that from that moment on he wanted to be known as Wendy and live his life as a woman."

Crump took a great big gulp of his lager. He needed it.

"So he lived like a woman from then on, old boy – took all the hormone pills – had the breast implants – and came to look rather more like a woman and rather less like a man in a dress."

"But..."

"He hasn't had the operation? No, but when – or if – he does, 'he' can become a 'she' on the passport, and on the old gravestone when the time comes."

"So Wendy's been living like that for ten years and still has a..."

"Todger? I should coco, and a whopper from what I've heard. Lives with a former student, apparently – female – a looker too. P'raps that's why he's rather keen not to get his plonker turned inside out to make a fake fanny eh! Cheers!"

Crump felt that he was still ever so slightly traumatised by the sight he'd had of Wendy Webb's cock at the end-of-term do. But it was the events that may have happened afterwards that were beginning to trouble him. He had noticed some soreness on his penis and was having difficulty in peeing too, and was pretty sure he had some kind of infection or sexually transmitted disease. Perhaps someone did have sex with him at the party. But who? He obviously looked a bit worried, because Sandy said:

"Cheer up Crumpie – may never happen y'know! Probably will, of course..."

Crump smiled at this *because it was true.*

"The thing you've got to remember is that these days it's almost impossible for a man – 'specially a white man – to get promotion in the higher education system and become a head of department," Sandy said, "Positive action and discrimination are what it's all about now, so sometimes Crumpie old boy, people need to play the game... in whichever way they can..."

Sandy's red face grinned and he winked at Crump before downing his pint in one. Crump thought about what Sandy had just said. Did Sandy really say what he thought he'd said? Could it really be true that Wendy Webb – or Willy Webb as he was previously – had decided to live and dress as a woman specifically in order to take advantage of the promotional opportunities it would offer?

"I remember talking to Willy about the lack of opportunities available to men like him and how much faster and further his career would go if he could change his sex and/or colour – we were in a pub just round the corner from here actually. Well, I thought nothing of it...until..."

Sandy smiled at Crump. Surely Willy hadn't changed his

sex to take advantage of the improved opportunities available to women? Or had he?

"Changing colour was a bit tricky, so now, old Slick Willy in the form of Wendy Webb is in a nice plum management position and likely to become the next head of department when our great leader Fiona moves on to better things."

"But, that's absurd – people changing their sex to get promotion? I mean..."

Crump didn't know what he meant, but it was profound.

"What about their lives, their partners, their children?"

"The old boy's still got a todger – he's just got a nice pair o' tits too and no nasty stubble either..."

"But people aren't prepared to change sex just for promotion, surely?"

Sandy leaned forward and looked into Crump's eyes.

"It's all just a game Crumpie, my boy – just a game. And people will do whatever they can to achieve the status they desire – and if that means changing sex or race, then so be it! And Willy's not the only one to have played the game either," said Sandy, "Pint?"

Crump nodded, and Sandy went to the bar, leaving him deep in thought. So people were changing their sex and race for the sake of their careers? He simply couldn't believe it. Not the only one, Sandy had said – *not the only one*. Who else? Who else had changed their sex? Or even their race? It was all almost unbelievable – almost, but not completely. It was true, after all, that Wendy Webb was now in a powerful and well-paid position in the department. Would she be there if *she* were still a *he*?

It was all utterly mind-blowing, so Crump decided to do what he always did when he was confused – he got completely and utterly pissed as a fart.

* * *

The next day – a Friday – was given over to diversity training. It had been scheduled for Friday afternoons, which was an unpopular time for most staff who tended to knock off early then. Crump's head was thumping with a monster of a hangover so he was hoping he could just doze off while the diversity person droned on. He was to have no such luck.

The trainer was a middle-aged white woman called Barbra, with wild frizzy hair, goofy teeth and a voice so grating it sounded like the vocal equivalent of breaking glass. As soon as she came into the room Crump knew this was *not* going to be a day whose events would be conducive to his hangover-management strategy.

"You," said Barbra, pointing at Crump, "are a racist."

She glared at him. Crump was in a class with fifteen others, including Raj and Athena. He looked over at them – they shrugged and smiled back.

"You nasty, disgusting white male pig – you think you're superior to me don't you, because I'm female, and you think these people of colour are niggers, wogs, Pakis and coons and that you *whitie* are the best – don't you?"

Crump was shocked by her language, as was the rest of the class judging by their stunned silence – he almost heard some jaws fall open. Barbra had a slight American – (or was it Canadian?) – accent, or perhaps she *was* British but speaking in diversity-speak, so just sounded American.

Then Barbra let out the most enormous, shrieking scream: "DON'T YOU!?"

"Er..." said Crump eventually, his head throbbing, "No."

"Shhh!" said Barbra leaning into Crump's face, "Don't you dare speak when I'm speaking!"

Crump looked at her wild eyes and her huge teeth sticking out at him, like fangs.

"How *dare* you think you are superior to women or people of colour just because of your gender and race!"

She looked distraught and on the verge of tears, her anger melting into a teary self-pity which may have been real or fake – he couldn't tell.

"Your kind enslaved the ancestors of people of colour – you

have oppressed those not like you with your pretty, pretty white skin – haven't you!?"

She squealed a mocking laugh and was again staring at him with those wild raging eyes. Crump's head thumped. He wished he were still in bed, far away from this mad woman and her strange and diverse brain.

"No..." he said, wearily, "No, I haven't."

"Liar!" she screamed, "You deny the pain of all the peoples you enslaved and oppressed – and you deny all those women you possessed and tortured and raped – you disgusting and vile, evil white monster!"

And with that Barbra started weeping and tearing at her hair.

"You are the very devil himself! You evil white man!"

And she broke down and crouched on the floor sobbing, her wild hair falling over her face.

Crump looked around at the class. He could see that Raj and Athena were having to stop themselves laughing out loud by biting their lips, as was the new lecturer Johnny Wong. Most of the other lecturers present seemed confused and stunned. Kwame was nodding with his eyes closed – he had missed the whole thing while he was listening to music through ear plugs. Not for the first time, Crump wished he were Kwame.

Of the others in the class, most just seemed baffled, and looked at Barbra weeping on the floor, wondering what to do. Crump also actually suspected that a couple of the foreign lecturers probably hadn't understood much of what Barbra had said anyway.

But Cecilia and Margaret No-name, who were sitting together, were staring at Crump with looks of pure hatred on their faces, their eyes piercing him with rage. A couple of the black and brown faces in the class were also looking at him reproachfully. He couldn't tell what his colleague in the black burqa was thinking, but then she did have a piece of cloth covering her face, so communication was somewhat hampered. Crump looked at her eye-slit – were her eyes angry, sad, or just normal? It was impossible to tell. Her eyes just looked very 'eye-y'.

Bloody hell, thought Crump, his hangover gnawing at the inside of his skull like rats. But this was only the beginning. When Barbra eventually stood up, she just looked upset and teary, her volcanic anger having blown itself out to be replaced by the emotional blackmail of her sadness and suffering.

Someone in the class asked if she was alright. She nodded and sighed deeply, and held her hand on her chest.

"It's just," she said in an affected and weak, verge-of-tears, child-like voice, "it just hurts me so much to feel the pain of all those people... who have suffered... suffered so much... at the hands of white male oppressors!"

She pointed at Crump and stared at him with her scary mad eyes again.

As far as he was concerned, she was clearly *not* 'alright' – she was clearly completely and utterly off her rocker and probably suffering some kind of identifiable mental illness. Crump knew that as a diversity trainer and consultant she'd be paid in the range of six hundred to a thousand pounds for this training session alone. Incredible, he thought, utterly incredible – and he wondered what other job such a mad old harpy could possible do in real society, there not being much call for hysterical lunatics in most careers – though he supposed there'd probably be some kind of job at the council for her, as a lunatic inclusion office maybe. Or else in politics. Or a job in TV, perhaps...

Crump doubted very much the efficacy of diversity training anyway. He thought it bizarre, to say the least, that in order to make people realise how similar they were to each other, their differences were constantly being emphasised – yet this was the basis of diversity training sessions like the one he was enduring. The ethos seemed to be: don't think about how alike you are to others, think how different you are, and never stop focusing on those differences or elevating them to be a central part of your identity – and perhaps even use those differences as a reason and/or excuse for failure in any sphere, and to claim special treatment and 'positive action'. Enjoy being a victim and seek out offence wherever you can, and remember that your feelings are the most important thing in the universe and should never ever be hurt by others' opinions – diversity of opinion or debate were most certainly not to be encouraged.

But surely, this was all divisive – encouraging people to see themselves as victims, to be over-sensitive and to see their race or gender as their main identifying feature and something that could disadvantage them in their lives?

Crump had made it a point for years to tell every class he taught, in the first lesson, that every person in his class was an individual, not a representative of a race or gender or anything else, and that's how they should see themselves – as students, first and foremost. It was a radical approach that went against all current educational guidelines and best practice.

But then, everyone wanted to be a victim, to claim victim status – that prerequisite to claiming special treatment, unfair advantage and targeted funding. It was just as Sandy said – all just a business and all just a game. And that was what it was all about.

As a white male oppressor – the only white male oppressor in the diversity class, he noticed – Crump was singled out by Barbra as a racist and a sexist because of his race and sex, though Barbra seemed utterly unaware of the irony. Perhaps she was American, after all.

They then did a classic activity that Crump had read about and which was fashionable amongst those involved in diversity education. It was called 'blue eyes, brown eyes', and the idea was to select the blue-eyed individuals and make them the inferiors of their masters, the brown-eyed people. As there were only four white people in the class, only two of whom had blue eyes, this wouldn't be possible, so it was decided by Barbra that, for training purposes, some ethnic minority students had to be honorary white blue-eyed oppressors to make up numbers.

She divided the class into two groups. One group – the blue-eyed slaves – consisted of Crump, Athena, Cecilia and Margaret No-name, plus three ethnic minority lecturers. The other group – the masters – comprised only Afro-Caribbean and Asian lecturers. They were given instructions to do tasks, and Crump and the other white oppressors would have to take orders from their masters.

The idea behind this, Crump knew, was the typical role-playing empathy-awareness that was much-loved by teachers everywhere. It was designed so white people would empathise with 'people of colour' and 'feel their pain' for being so oppressed throughout history and for being enslaved by their white masters. No mention was made of the role of slavery in *all* countries and cultures until relatively recently, or the fact that almost all African slaves were actually enslaved by black Africans settling tribal scores and raping and pillaging their lands for personal gain, and were most usually traded by Africans and Arabs. And no mention, of course, was made of the fact that, as a white man born in the late 20th century, neither Crump nor any other white person bore any responsibility at all for the African slave trade of over 200 years ago, and no man bore responsibility for historical discrimination against women – or men – either.

He could have reminded Barbra that, actually, Britain abolished slavery in 1807 – a full 60 years before the United States – and a third of the British navy then died trying to stop countries like Spain and Portugal continuing the slave trade after that. He could also have reminded her that Britain had never had the segregationist anti-black policies current in the US until the 1960s. And, moreover, he could have reminded her that there were, and always had been, very many ethnic minorities and women who were far more privileged than most white men, a fact that was still true today. But Crump just accepted that it would all be much better if he just went along with the mad, hysterical woman and then he'd be able to go home and get some much-needed sleep.

As an oppressed blue-eyed slave, Crump went along with being ordered about by members of the other group. He could see what Barbra was doing – she was trying to get everyone in the class who was not white or male to identify with being oppressed – to make them angry and mould them into victims, and specifically victims of white, male society. It was a self-obsessed, self-pitying false victimhood that encouraged people to see offence in everything and everyone and to see themselves as victim first and foremost – it was, essentially, anti-resilience training.

Crump much preferred a colour-blind and gender-blind way of seeing and tended to agree with the attitude that said 'nobody can make you feel bad about yourself without your permission.' The irony was that he, as a white man, had come from a far more modest background than very many ethnic minorities and women he encountered anyway.

Barbra encouraged them to insult and abuse him and the other blue-eyed slaves – but especially him. She was, quite simply, encouraging them to bully him. As Crump had expected, in some of the discussions the diversity drummed into people's heads meant that they started to get angry and emotional and to see themselves as victims. One woman cried for her slave ancestors in Africa (even though her ancestors could well have been slave-catchers and traders); another remembered how she wasn't given a bike by her mum as a child unlike her brother – a typical example of stereotyping and social conditioning by the patriarchy, said Barbra; a third got emotional when she thought back to how she hadn't been allowed to join the army in her home country, and how sexist this was – though perhaps most women would have considered not being given the right to get shot at and blown to pieces in a war one of the more positive benefits of global gender inequalities.

Even Raj got emotional when he remembered the Indian caste system, though he defended the British influence in India – something Barbra was disgusted by. She told him he was a traitor who had been brainwashed into self-hatred by the white man. Raj protested, but it was no good – and as a traitor to his race he was made to join the blue-eyed slave group as punishment, as was a black lecturer who wouldn't accept Barbra's point of view. There was obviously no diversity of opinion allowed in this diversity lesson. Cecilia and Margaret No-name were transferred to the master brown-eyed oppressor group, something that clearly delighted them.

Before long, the whole room was full of a great wailing and gnashing of teeth as everybody began relating all the episodes of their life when they had been victims of men or white people or both. Barbra said that if they'd been victims of women or black people that also counted as oppression by white men, as it was white men who had created the structures of oppression in society within which women and black people had to operate. So no woman or black person in prison was ever truly guilty of anything, she said – it was the white man who was always guilty in a society he had made. It was, quite possibly, the best piece of false reasoning and twisted logic Crump had ever heard.

"If the world was ruled by women," said Margaret No-name in her estuary English accent, and obviously incapable of using a proper subjunctive, "then none of these bad things like war or suffering would happen and we'd all live in peace", at which, Crump couldn't help letting out a loud and cynical guffaw.

The whole idea was ridiculous, sexist, unrealistic and just totally phoney – did anyone really think that if women were directly in charge anything would be different? It was *people* who caused wars and suffering! *People* – men and women both, though the former was often the active part and the latter often the force and encouragement and motivation behind the male hand on the trigger. Also, he knew that plenty of research had shown that women tended to be more right-wing and religious and war-mongering than men, not the other way round. He looked up to see Barbra staring at him with a look of utter hatred on her face.

"What did you say you dirty little nigger!"

She almost spat the words out.

Crump thought they had finished the 'blue eyes, brown eyes' master/slave game, but obviously not as she was still in role.

"I didn't say anything," said Crump, honestly, "I just laughed at the idea that a world run by women would be like some kind of utopia...full of peace and love...like some Coca-Cola advert or some Miss World speech circa 1976."

"And how do you know, you disgusting and vile male oppressor, that the world would not be like that if women and people of colour were in charge?" she said.

Crump laughed cynically again, but noticed now that no-one else was laughing.

"Because it's just not realistic," he said, "It's human nature you're complaining about, not men or white people."

Barbra looked as though she would burst in anger, as though some unknown force were pumping her up with rage. The class fell utterly silent – the lull before the storm.

"Aaaaarrrrrrrgggggghhhhhh!"

The scream seemed to last for minutes.

"Not realistic? *Not realistic!!!* How dare you!" shrieked Barbra like a banshee in her high-pitched voice as she stood over him, "How dare a nasty, evil, racist, sexist, rapist of a man like you accuse me of being wrong. You are so sexist and racist that you cannot see your own sexism and racism!"

Then Barbra fell to the floor and started sobbing and wailing uncontrollably. She waved her hand at the class and everyone understood that this would be the right moment to break for lunch. Gingerly, everyone left the class as Barbra sobbed away histrionically on the floor.

Crump decided that he'd have to sort this out with her – he couldn't let her accuse him of things like that without some kind of explanation. If she didn't want him in her class, then fine – he didn't want to be there anyway, and he couldn't see how anyone was learning anything at all about diversity or tolerance either.

He told Raj and Athena that he would catch up with them later, then waited for the room to empty. He closed the door.

"Barbra," he said, "I think it's best if I go home..."

There was no reply – Barbra sat on the carpet sobbing with her face in her hands.

"It's just, there doesn't seem any point in me being here...just to be insulted..."

Again, no reply. Crump crouched down and touched Barbra's shoulder.

"Barbra," he said, and then it happened.

Barbra let out a mad, wild screaming shriek at the top of her voice and went for him, like a cat with its claws bared. He toppled over and onto the floor and Barbra was now on top of him. She was scratching at his face with her sharp nails and pulling his hair.

Crump was taken utterly by surprise – he was expecting insults, but not violence. After managing to grab Barbra by her wild hair and pull her head back, he managed to manoeuvre her onto the floor with him on top, thereby avoiding her scratching fingernails which, he could tell, had drawn blood on his face.

Then Barbra started wailing and crying:

'Rape!' she shrieked, "Rape!"

The screams pierced his brain like knives.

There was nothing else for it. Crump slapped her around the face – hard, but not too hard – and the screeching and screaming stopped. Barbra now lay on the floor breathing deeply. Crump stood up.

Then he walked out of the room, stunned by what had happened but happy to get away from his mad attacker. He'd had enough of this. All he wanted was to go home.

He knew he could quite easily make a formal complaint of assault against Barbra if he so wished, but it was just his word against hers, and he knew he risked getting into trouble for doing so. It was a shame there were no witnesses really. He'd have to think about whether he wanted the hassle, what with everything that had happened the previous term.

And anyway, he had more important things to do than worry about the diversity trainer from hell. He was a lecturer for goodness sake – he had more than enough to do as it was.

At home, he put the answer phone on, had a bath, ordered a pizza, drank more whisky than was good for him, and went to bed.

His sleep was deep and dreamless, and the best he'd had for ages.

CHAPTER EIGHT

Getting Hurt

"Chlamydia!" said the doctor, cheerfully.

It was Saturday morning and Crump was sitting at the local hospital's department of genito-urinary medicine. He had been having difficulty peeing, and there was slight pain when he did so, plus some unusual discharge, so he had concluded that something must be wrong *down there*.

He wasn't all that nervous about going for a test, probably because he'd been to a clap clinic before whilst at university. It was terribly bad luck, but he had managed to catch VD and lose his virginity at the same time, which said an awful lot about the general drunken awfulness of the experience. He'd been terrified of going to a clap clinic back then, what with hearing accounts about how they shove little metal umbrellas down penises to scrape out the gunge, and other horror stories. But no – just a little prick, so to speak, and it was all over.

The worst thing, both then and now, was the waiting room. Back then he'd had to sit opposite a girl who was on his course, as well as a junior lecturer who had taught him a module on Sylvia Plath and Virginia Woolf – which was bad enough in itself – and they couldn't bear to look at each other, so looked at the floor, just like everyone else did.

This time, there was only one other guy in the waiting room, and Crump didn't know him either, thank goodness – seeing one of his students there would have been toe-curlingly embarrassing. At university, he'd been diagnosed with an NSU – non-specific urethritis. On this occasion he had the same thing, but now they called it:

"Chlamydia!" said the doctor, somewhat triumphantly as if in celebration, before assuring Crump that a dose of antibiotics would soon clear it up.

Chlamydia – it was such a nice word, in its way. From the Greek *khlamus* meaning 'mantle', referring to the cloak-like shape of the micro-organism, but sounding frighteningly like one of those names social climbing middle-class parents give their kids. No doubt someone somewhere had a son or a daughter at one of the lesser private schools called Chlamydia. Someone somewhere probably also had children called Fallopia, Colostoma and Spudulika too.

People called their kids the strangest things these days, Crump thought, like celebrities calling their kids after fruit – Apple or Peaches – or people trying to be posh by calling their kids after exotic countries like India, or seasons like Summer or Autumn. There were not, to his knowledge, any children called Satsuma or Banana, Afghanistan or Pakistan, or Spring or Winter – though, of course, he could be wrong.

The doctor asked him if he wanted to have an HIV test – Crump said he would have to think about that. He already had to deal with the fact that someone – (but who?) – had apparently, without his knowledge or consent, had sex with him, (though he may have given consent and forgotten of course – he couldn't remember a single thing about it), and that he had caught an STD from that sexual encounter. To find out he was HIV positive too – though highly unlikely – would be a stressful step too far.

Crump was actually more embarrassed that he had to admit to the doctor that, apart from that one mysterious occasion at Christmas, he hadn't had sex for a very long time and that he didn't have 'multiple partners' – which seemed quite the thing, especially in south London – and also that he couldn't actually remember who he had caught the STD from.

He didn't even have a girlfriend, and there wasn't anyone on the horizon either.

There were plenty of people who laid themselves open, as it were, to getting STDs with their promiscuous and irresponsible behaviour – but Crump was almost monastic in his enforced abstinence, and that didn't look like changing soon. He didn't want it to change either – not if he couldn't be with Athena.

He collected the tablets, said he'd think about the HIV test and walked out into the waiting room. It was the smell that hit him first.

"Hello there," said a slimy thin voice.

It was Edwin Wittering. The vile, putrid breath hit him in the face, even though he was standing some feet away.

"Fancy seeing you here!"

Crump didn't know where to look and was aware he was blushing, but Edwin seemed to have no such hang-ups about being in a clap clinic.

"Oh don't be embarrassed," he said, rubbing Crump's arm in what was presumably an affectionate 'we're all in this thing together' way, "We all do it, you know!"

And then he smiled to bare his yellowing teeth, and laughed an irritating nasal laugh that turned Crump's stomach.

"Yes...er...well...I..."

"We should meet up some time," said Edwin, "go for a coffee – or something stronger – have a little chat. I know what it's like..."

Now Edwin's hand had crept round to Crump's lower back and was rubbing it.

"Well...err...thanks...maybe...yes...bye," said Crump, and walked quickly through the swing doors out into the corridor.

He didn't stop walking – or, rather, marching – until he got to the bus stop.

What the hell was that, thought Crump to himself, and what did he mean 'I know what it's like'? He knows what *what's* like? Being a new lecturer? Having an STD? Crump could still smell the foetid stench of Edwin in the air, though he was standing at the bus stop in the cold bright morning of a windy day. What, thought Crump, was going on?

Crump arrived home to see an ambulance outside the house – he could see Mrs Glidewell being slowly walked inside.

"Hello ducks," she said when she saw him, and Crump immediately felt better.

He assured the ambulance staff that he'd keep an eye on Edna – Mrs Glidewell – and that he'd make sure she was eating properly and keeping the house warm enough, and that he'd call them if she was feeling ill. They went inside and he made them both a nice cup of tea.

"Can't be doin' with hospitals, ducks, but ta for calling the ambulance and gettin' me there an' all," she said, crunching on a custard cream.

"No problem," said Crump, "it's great to have you back," and he meant it.

"Oh the grub in hospital was shockin' it was," said Mrs Glidewell, "no good British grub no more – just fancy stuff – an' see, I don't like fancy stuff. All them...oil and spices...For dinner today we had *laminated* chicken and *desecrated* coconut – together! I just ain't used to it, I ain't!"

"You can eat whatever you want now though – now you're at home," said Crump, smiling warmly at the malapropisms.

"Oh an' I intend to eat good and proper, ducks," she said, "and the veg down the hospital – they don't even half cook 'em proper or nothing, they don't, but I don't like 'em *Ali-canti* – I can't chew 'em like that!"

Crump decided not to tell Mrs Glidewell that what she meant was *Al dente* – or *undercooked* was often the case – but agreed with her sentiments. Since when had it become standard in Britain for people to undercook food so much? Either you cook it properly, or you don't cook it at all and have it raw – but to half cook it seems so... *indecisive* somehow.

It was clear that Mrs Glidewell needed a good rest and he'd

check on her every day from now on to see she was keeping the place warm enough and ask if she wanted any shopping done.

"What's all them scratches on your face?" she asked.

"Oh," said Crump, feeling the marks, "they're nothing – just an accident."

He didn't want to worry her with an account of how he'd been attacked by a shrieking banshee lunatic of a diversity trainer. It was lucky really that the scratches weren't deep and would soon be gone, but it was surprising the damage finger nails could do. Perhaps that's what they were for, in evolutionary terms – like human claws.

"And noise!" Mrs Glidewell said, "the hospital was noisier than Piccadilly Circus! Bedlam it was! Too many *cooks* and not enough *Indians* making the *broth*, that's the trouble with them places..."

Crump knew what she meant – sort of. The health service, just like the education service, had been taken over by the suits – those management-speak-spouting, bean-counting, target-setting twits who controlled the lives of everybody in every institution despite knowing nothing about what it was to be a nurse, a doctor, a teacher, or anyone actually doing a useful job instead of just assessing and judging those who were actually doing them.

Crump had long thought, from his experiences at West London College, that well over half of these management clones could be sacked with no harmful effect whatsoever on the day-to-day running of the place. The money and time freed up could have been spent on far better things – education, for example.

But the problem was, the more management clones there were, the more targets they set, so the more management clones were needed to be employed to assess whether those targets had been met, and so it went round and round in a surreal spiral of insanity with which everyone was happy because it looked very pretty and professional indeed – despite being nothing of the sort.

Weighing the pig had become much more important than checking it was still breathing – or whether it had starved to death – and it was all about weighing the pig these days.

* * *

The teaching for the new term began, taking off where it had left off, and Crump duly bit his lip at the sheer ignorance and low ability of the students in his classes – and the fact that some couldn't actually speak more than pidgin English which, shockingly, included some of the prospective English teachers he taught every Thursday in the education department.

A common trick he had learnt at the college was to give 'FOFO' lessons. 'FOFO' stood for *'Fuck Off and Find Out'*, and they were a great way of getting rid of a class by sending them to the library to do research and then report back to class in the last minutes of the lesson. Happily, these lessons were welcomed by the currently fashionable, anti-didactic, teacher-as-learning-facilitator, best practice teaching theories because they promoted 'active learning' – he was facilitating his students to discover knowledge for themselves rather than teaching them anything at all. They also allowed Crump what was essentially a free lesson to catch up on marking and planning instead of actually doing any teaching, and the students loved dossing around in the library for a couple of hours instead of doing any real work or thinking. So everyone was happy with 'FOFO' lessons, all in all.

Crump had been pleased to receive confirmation of two conferences at Easter – at the universities of Colchester and East Sussex – where he could present his paper on the portrayal of the British education system in 19th and 20th century literature and film. Sandy was being very helpful with the comments he was making about his research too.

He was less pleased to see an email in his inbox from Wendy Webb requesting that he go to see her at an appointed time that week. It could only mean one thing – there had been another complaint. And Crump just knew it was from Barbra. He realised now that he should have gone to Wendy before and told her what had happened – that he had been attacked – though he probably would have been accused of sexism or worse if he had. He had rather hoped it would just 'go away' if he did nothing. He hated himself for his stupidity and cowardice.

"You *hit* her?" said Wendy Webb, sounding shocked.

"I slapped her face to calm her down – in self defence," said Crump, "she attacked me!"

Wendy Webb, who, if she felt any embarrassment at Crump seeing her penis certainly wasn't showing it and was behaving as though nothing at all had happened, looked tense and annoyed.

"That," she said, "is your counter-argument."

"No it's not – I'm saying she went...nuts...and attacked me, so I defended myself."

"So you say – so why didn't you report this violent attack?" Wendy raised her eyebrows at him.

It was a good question. The problem now was that because Barbra had made a complaint against him, everything he said would be considered a response to it – the counter-argument of an accused man trying to wriggle off the hook. That way of doing things was one reason why everyone these days reported everyone for everything, and why everyone was so sensitive and easy to offend all the time – so they could put their complaint in first and get automatic victim status, thereby ensuring that they wouldn't find themselves in his current predicament.

Crump was now in the absurd position of having to defend himself against accusations from the woman who had attacked him as though *she* were the victim and he were the perpetrator. This matter was not helped by the fact that he was male and his accuser female, so automatically deserving of sympathy. She'd probably planned the whole thing, Crump thought, the evil, nasty, malicious, manipulative, devious bitch! Sometimes, he thought, insulting sexist language was the only true way to describe reality – probably the reason it had come into existence in the first place.

"I..." he mumbled, "I just thought it better not to..."

It sounded like a weak attempt to cover up his misdemeanours, though it was absolutely true. If he had lied, Wendy probably would have believed him. He didn't mention the fact that he was frightened that he'd be accused of sexism and/or racism again if he had complained. But at least it seemed that Barbra hadn't actually accused him of rape, which was a plus – though he could prove his innocence with DNA tests there if necessary.

Wendy Webb looked at him, somewhat sympathetically he thought, and sighed.

"Well you thought wrongly, I'm afraid," she said sadly, "Every case of this nature must always be reported – we have systems and procedures for just this sort of thing. Unfortunately, because you failed to report the attack you allege took place..."

"It did take place – look at the scratches on my face," he said, touching the red marks, "where do you think they came from?"

Wendy Webb thought for a moment.

"Have you... got a cat?"

Crump was stunned.

"No I haven't got a cat," he said, annoyed, adding crossly: "though that doesn't necessarily mean I'm 'cattist'."

"No need for that," said Wendy, frowning.

She sighed sadly and shook her head.

"You could have made those scratches yourself, you see..."

"But I didn't," said Crump.

"Now if you'd come to see me sooner..."

They looked at each other like cats on a wall, each wary of the other's intentions.

"Look – it doesn't matter if it took place or not, really," said Wendy, "the fact is that Barbra has lodged an official complaint about your behaviour in the diversity training session – she said you were very rude and aggressive, and also that you did not accept the fact that you are racist and sexist..."

"But I'm not racist and sexist," said Crump.

"You do have two warnings for being racist and sexist – one written and one verbal – warnings, which I have to remind you, you willingly accepted."

"Only because I had no other choice!" said Crump, realising that he was now well and truly stuffed; he deeply regretted accepting the warnings in the first place.

Wendy Webb was clearly offended.

"Mr Crump, I have done everything I can to make your time with us as productive as possible, and I deeply resent the insinuation that you were somehow pressured into admitting to racism and sexism by me, " said Wendy, sounding cross, "You have actually been treated more than generously."

Crump knew he was expected to apologise.

"I'm sorry if I offended you," he said, "of course, I didn't mean that at all, and I accept fully the warnings given to me...it's just that..."

She looked at him and raised her bushy eyebrows. He noticed her blond wig was slightly wonky.

"...just that I defended myself against a woman who attacked me, and now I'm the one assumed to be to blame, somehow..."

Wendy Webb nodded, again perhaps more sympathetically then she previously ever had. Perhaps she was on his side after all.

"Having seen life from both sides of the fence, as it were, I can say that, yes, it is rather usual for people to automatically assume the man is guilty and the woman is innocent in most situations, and that a man who hits a woman is always in the wrong in many people's eyes, even if he is defending himself..."

Crump looked at her. Was she going to let him off? Could she see that he was the victim here? Was Barbra going to be called in to be told that her diversity training services would no longer be needed by the university? Had the world gone sane at last? Of course it hadn't.

"I have to inform you, however, that Barbra is one of the best diversity trainers in the business, and she complained about you – and not the other way round. If only you'd come to me sooner," she said, "Still, what's done is done, and..."

"And?" said Crump, not knowing really what she was going to do.

"And so, I shall give you a choice."

Wendy Webb looked him straight in the eye.

"Either, you accept that you assaulted Barbra, in which case you will be given a second and final written warning, as well as having to write a letter of apology to her and the university, admitting all liability and exonerating the university of all responsibility...."

"Or?" asked Crump, wearily.

"Or, you choose to deny the allegation made against you – in which case you'll be immediately suspended from your position pending a fitness to practice tribunal – which would take place in about six months' time – and proceedings may well be brought against you for compensation for the assault you perpetrated on university premises."

Crump sighed – he was stuck in an impossible position again.

"Moreover, it is possible that the police would need to be informed of the assault that took place which *could* lead to you being arrested for common assault, if not grievous bodily harm. A conviction for common assault is serious, and would probably make finding any teaching position difficult in future."

That would be a very real and serious development, he knew.

"And I do not need to remind you that grievous bodily harm is one of the offences that no teacher is permitted to have on their CRB record, and so you would be effectively banned from teaching for life if convicted."

Crump put his hands to his head. How could this happen? How? He was attacked by some mad harpy and now he was the one getting punished! His head was spinning.

"So," said Wendy, "what is your choice? I'm being very generous actually, in offering you a choice. Many wouldn't."

Crump actually had no 'choice', as they both knew full well. He accepted the second written warning.

Wendy said the letter would be in the post that day and reminded him that he now had two written warnings, and one verbal, so one more verbal warning would mean the end of his lecturing job at Thames Metropolitan University.

Crump nodded, amazed and disturbed at how all this had happened – and so quickly. And it was only the beginning of the second term of his university career. He resolved to keep as quiet as possible for the rest of the year, to just get on with his teaching and research – to just try and *fit in*.

While wandering around the campus to clear his head, Crump saw the burqa girl again. He somehow knew it was her, despite the fact that she was standing with the other identically veiled women outside the Abdullah Building. She looked straight at Crump as he walked by and he knew it was her from her eyes. He could see that she recognised him, just through the expression in them, and saw again that same fear – even terror – in those sad, dark eyes, as though she were pleading for help.

But it was no good – Crump could in no way go up to her and ask if anything was wrong, after being explicitly told not to approach anyone from the Abdullah building. He would just have to keep himself to himself from now on.

He was even starting to wonder if he could trust Athena and Rajdeep. The way Wendy Webb had behaved, the way she seemed to know his opinions, in this meeting and at other times, had puzzled him. It was as though she knew what he'd said in private conversations with his colleagues – nothing explicit, nothing word-for-word – but just an inkling that maybe, just maybe, whatever he said in confidence to Athena or Raj didn't stay with them and them alone. Crump wasn't sure how he'd cope with Athena or Rajdeep betraying him – apart from Sandy, they were the only people he really trusted at the university. To lose their trust would be devastating.

Or perhaps he was just getting paranoid, seeing shadows where there were none. He decided to banish these thoughts of betrayal from his brain as much as possible – he was sure that Athena and Rajdeep would never spy on him anyway.

The term plodded on and Crump almost switched to autopilot in his teaching. Depressingly, it was what the students liked – they hated being made to think or engaging in intellectual debate. What they wanted was to be spoon-fed information – to be told exactly what to write and say – so they could regurgitate it and get good marks for their coursework essays.

Most of any degree comprised dissertations and essays like this, so a student on a humanities course may only ever have to do one or two exams in two years. On Master's courses, there were no exams at all anyway, just submitted dissertations, so the potential for cheating was huge.

Moreover, as no-one ever bothered – or even wanted – to check the qualifications of any lucrative international students, and it was rumoured that a sizeable number of overseas students actually used forged certificates to get onto their courses, especially postgraduates. Some simply changed their name to that of a legitimate graduate from a foreign university too. There were, allegedly, some one hundred and thirty two Chinese students called Chung Fai Fung studying for Master's degrees at British universities at present – the real Mr Chung Fai Fung had emigrated to Ottawa, Canada from Hong Kong in 1996 where he worked in IT, completely unaware that he'd effectively been 'academically cloned'.

For the remainder of the term, Crump did what he was meant to do – he gave pretty, dumbed-down PowerPoint lessons and lectures, never expressed an individual or controversial opinion, and talked through every single point as though to a class of ignoramuses, which was not actually too far from the truth in most classes. Every little thing needed to be explained several times – he could not assume students had any prior knowledge whatsoever.

He taught to the test and explained to the students exactly how to answer the essay questions that they would have to complete over the Easter vacation. All department members had been told what the options were and to go through each question step by step, listing the points that every student should make in their answers to any given question, telling them which sources and texts to use, and even outlining what conclusion to draw from the points they had made in the essay. It reminded Crump of the colouring-in books he had had as a small child, or perhaps the join-the-dots puzzles he'd done on rainy Sunday afternoons aged about eight. These puzzles involved very little real thinking, but were soothingly repetitive, a kind of mental masturbation of the type he was now involved in too – pointless, messy, and really rather sad.

The work he was setting was at a level he was sure he would have been able to reach in the second or third year of secondary school at age fourteen – because, apart from the top fifteen or twenty per cent, the students in his classes had a low secondary school level of intelligence, knowledge and ability, and would certainly not have passed old-style O-levels. Of course, they would all pass with distinction and be awarded top degrees and Master's from a British university, and no doubt go on to use their incompetence and ignorance to go on to great and terrible things in future all over the world.

Crump was getting to know some of the students better, but the truth was that most saw him as nothing more than the key to getting good marks. It was the marks they wanted, not the education.

A couple of students had even tried to bribe him – a Chinese girl, and a young Russian man who had hardly ever been to class, had waved wads of cash at him after class – about £500 or so, each. Crump had refused, but wondered if any lecturers took the cash. He had merely explained to the students that, although he'd mark some of the assessed essays, they were all checked and given a final mark by the senior lecturers and not him. The students went away crestfallen, and looked at him as though 1) he had committed some awful misdemeanour by refusing their bribes, and 2) he was even less deserving of respect than a 'normal' lecturer because *he didn't even have the power to give final marks to essays!* Crump decided not to report the attempt to bribe – there hardly seemed any point really seeing as so much assessed work was obviously ripped off anyway.

And he had to keep his nose clean too and he knew it. To accuse international students of something as heinous as attempted bribery could lead to a charge of racism or similar, and he just couldn't face having to cope with another false accusation. He suspected strongly, however, that some of their other teachers could be accepting 'bribes' though, possibly as fees for 'private tuition' or 'consultation'. Such methods were apparently standard in many countries in Europe and elsewhere, and now seem to have spread to the UK.

He got to know his class of trainee teachers especially well, and often had chats every Thursday morning with Nick Craven, the former fascist, born-again Christian who looked a bit like him, as well as the veiled woman in his class who was, he discovered, a convert to Islam called Sandra. They were always early and arrived well before the other students, so they often had interesting chats before the tedium of formal education started and he would have to stick to spoon-feeding the class the prescribed curriculum.

Crump explained to them that he was an atheist, but was tolerant of anybody's religious or political beliefs, and they all had very civil and interesting discussions about faith and belief and ethics in those minutes before the class started. Actually, Crump was surprised at the two students' openness and willingness to discuss such an incendiary subject as religion and the issues around it – (he had known before from his years at the college how angry some religious people could get when challenged about their faith) – but their discussions were always civil and friendly, despite the huge difference between his atheistic, evidence-hungry, rationalist beliefs and the spiritual ones of an evangelical born-again Christian and a devout burqa-clad Muslim convert.

And he was happy, too, to learn more about these students' interpretations of their religions – in fact, he felt a distinct and empathetic agreement with Aristotle who, over two thousand years ago put some of his vast wisdom in a nutshell when he said: 'I learn as I teach'.

It was, Crump realised, the only time of the week when he felt his brain was actually engaged in any intellectual dialogue with students – the irony being that it wasn't actually part of the lesson at all. He didn't agree with Nick's evangelical Christian views, but the man had obviously changed for the better if he'd gone from being a racist fascist who believed in violence, to a born-again Christian committed to love and peace and missionary work: no matter what Crump thought of religion, that was surely a positive development.

He liked discovering from Sandra how and why she had converted to Islam – (it was, as expected, through marriage) – and why she wore the veil. It was supposedly all to do with 'modesty', but perhaps more to do with the village peasant culture of her Pakistani husband and conservative tradition – Crump knew there was actually no explicit instruction in the Koran to wear a veil, nor to refrain from alcohol for that matter. It was all a matter of interpretation. He was also just trying to get inside the head of the burqa-wearing girl, to try and understand why she chose to wear the burqa and if it was her choice at all, or if it was imposed on her. He still wasn't sure.

Crump continued to attend department training sessions every Friday, except when Barbra was taking them, and also wrote, as instructed, a letter of apology to both her and the university. He kept it short, simply apologising for his behaviour – he thought that was best.

The second warning letter, signed by Fiona Windrush,

duly arrived. It sounded stern and vaguely threatening, and detailed every single point that Wendy Webb had outlined to him earlier.

Becky told him not to worry about it when they met up for their fortnightly chat over drinks near the college, but of course he did. One more misdemeanour and that would be it – the end of his lecturing at Thames Met, and the end of his whole career. And he so wanted an academic career – a proper one – not just the peddling of a scam to students who thought that because they had paid for their university education they should pass with distinction. He wanted to engage in intellectual debate and to express his love of his subject to equally passionate students – he didn't want this awful grind. But he knew he had to play the game if he were to climb the ladder to where he wanted to be. He just had to, so he did – though he was more than a little ashamed at his craven acquiescence.

A letter also arrived from West London College informing him that the fitness to practise meeting would be at the end of March. He supposed that now Elizabeth Clint would want thanking for making sure the hearing would happen before Easter as he'd requested.

What on earth was wrong with these people? They had almost wrecked his life with their stupid idiotic rules and regulations, and then they expected him to thank them for it! Wendy Webb was the same – expecting to be thanked for giving him a choice between disgrace on the one hand, and complete and utter disgrace on the other. It was like an executioner expecting to be thanked by an innocent condemned man for sharpening his axe.

There were only two things that Crump was looking forward to in the Spring term. Firstly, his thirtieth birthday on 9th March, an event which he knew would fill most people with apprehension – depression even. All that awful tallying of how much hadn't been achieved in one's twenties and how much could have been, not to mention the thinning hairline and paunch, and the watching your dreams fade out of view that awaits all those entering their thirties, especially in a youth-obsessed age. Crump was looking forward to it immensely.

No longer would he be expected to be a hip and sexy twenty-something, and to do the things young people were supposed to like doing, which he usually hated. When he reached his thirties he could do whatever he liked and no-one would think it odd that he wasn't going out to nightclubs, or listening to rap, or taking drugs or shagging drunken 'slappers' like an alley cat every Friday night. It would all be a great big relief to be able to act middle-aged at last because that, he knew, is what he'd always been in his tastes, probably since birth.

Secondly, the university was having a visit. Not a royal visit, thank goodness, or even a visit from one of the bigwigs of university administration. No – this visit was something special, so much so that Crump let out a little squeal of delight when Raj told him. Apparently, it had all been arranged by a senior lecturer in the department of politics without prior approval – university managers were in a spitting rage about it but could do nothing to prevent the visit at this late stage. The lecturer was retiring this year so didn't give a fig about any consequences they could threaten him with anyway. Luckily, he was also dying of cancer, so didn't even care if they took away his pension – he apparently had about six months. Crump and Raj each had a ticket to the lecture too, thanks to Sandy pulling a few strings.

It was going to be the most controversial visit to Thames Metropolitan since Tony Blair gave a speech about the war in Iraq whilst on a visit to praise its ethnic minority widening participation successes – (despite of course the fact that he would never ever dream of sending any of his children to such an academic shit-hole) – which was good for getting a few extra black votes even if it lost a few Muslim ones.

And it would turn out to be the most controversial visit to a British university since the 1990s, when the geneticist and author Chaim Goldstein had given a lecture at Oxford

University about his theories of the innate average IQ differences between the races – or at least between populations whose skin colours were different – because that is what his thirty years of research had revealed. Or perhaps since Noam Moochy, the well-known American academic, had given a lecture at the University of Sheffield about how the sexes had innate brain differences, with males having a higher IQ on average and dominating the higher levels. Despite many years of his and others' intensive research, Moochy was now banned from most UK universities and had been sacked from his American university too for publishing his research results which, he reminded everyone in vain, were not his opinions but the results of his extensive brain research. They were, he insisted, free to do further research.

Sadly, these days, universities were no longer places for free thought. If any research went against the prevailing orthodoxy of political correctness, especially on race and gender, then you'd be a very brave man (or woman) indeed to publish it, or even do it in the first place – but then you probably wouldn't get funding anyway, so original research wasn't done very often at British universities any more, at least not if it touched on sensitive and controversial issues and came to the 'wrong' conclusions about them.

The momentous visit was going to happen on Crump's thirtieth birthday too, and on that day, Rudyard Perkins, the much-admired – but also much-derided – academic, scientist, rationalist, resolute atheist and best-selling author, was coming to Thames Metropolitan University to give a lecture entitled 'The Lie of Religion'.

The Muslims, especially from the Abdullah building, and especially the Saudi funders of the Centre for Islamic Studies, had made an almighty fuss, as had the Christians, the Hindus, the Sikhs, and every other religious grouping in the diverse and vibrant international community at Thames Met – even a few of the tiny number of Jews at the university were in agreement that the visit should not go ahead. It was perhaps the only time in his life that Crump had seen people of all religions united, even if it was in their opposition towards a man whose professed atheism and rationalism had made him a hate figure – especially amongst all the members of the multi-faith community who sought to stifle free thought and speech, and drag Britain back into the dark ages of religious compulsion and blind devotion.

But it was the Muslims who were the most vocal, perhaps because Rudyard Perkins' mother was Jewish. She had luckily escaped Nazi Germany on the Kinder-transport in 1939, but almost all of the rest of her family died in the death camps at Belsen and Auschwitz. And even though his father had been an English schoolmaster, and despite the fact that Rudyard Perkins was a determined atheist so not even a practising Jew, even if he did acknowledge that part of his heritage, many Muslims seemed to think that he was not only a Jew, but also a Zionist, an 'Islamophobe', a bigot, a racist, a rabid supporter of every single Israeli policy in history, and that he should not, bearing in mind the university's anti-Israel policy, be allowed to come and give a lecture at Thames Metropolitan.

The Muslim protectors were told by the university that their new policy only affected Israelis, not Jews, so they could not stop Rudyard Perkins' visit because he was a British citizen with a readership at Oxford. This predictably led to accusations of 'Islamophobia' from the Muslim representatives. Protests were planned.

Crump had decided that he wouldn't do anything specific to celebrate his birthday. He was not much of a one for get-togethers anyway and always hated New Year celebrations, other people's birthday parties, wedding receptions, that kind of thing. A couple of drinks in a quiet pub and a nice meal was more his kind of style, especially as birthday parties seemed so utterly childish – it's fine if you're eight years old, but why on earth do people continue the habit into adulthood? He just didn't get it – or perhaps it was just another sign of people's self-obsession and the infantilisation of the modern age? He knew, of course, that he'd get a card from his mum, but they didn't bother with expensive presents these days, for birthdays or Christmas – it was all just a consumerist con, and something best left behind with childhood. He neither wanted, nor expected, anything.

Besides, he had the best present he could ever wish for – a chance to hear a lecture from one of the most significant academic figures in the world, and that was enough for him. And anyway, birthdays in themselves had been scientifically proven to be good for you – those who had the most tended to live the longest, after all.

On his birthday – a Thursday – he arrived at work early. The lecture was due to take place at three, and thankfully he had no teaching that afternoon. He just had to do some paperwork and some teaching in the morning, and then he'd be free to attend the lecture, and, with any luck, meet the great man afterwards.

He also had no teaching the following day, now that he'd been suspended from the college, and had not even been expected to attend the training sessions – on both Thursday and Friday that week Barbra was going to be taking sessions on 'disablist' language and attitudes. He wondered what she would do this time as part of her training strategy – chain people to wheelchairs? Break the legs of half the class perhaps? Stick pencils in people's eyes to force them to empathise with the blind?

Sometimes, he thought, getting into trouble had positive repercussions – he now had to attend only about half as many diversity and training and CPD sessions as everyone else. Raj, however, was expected to attend them all, but decided that there was no way he was going to miss Perkins' lecture – not when he was one of the lucky few who had a ticket. He decided to phone in sick.

At about ten in the morning, some protestors started arriving and congregating at various points around the campus. Some were Muslims, but there were also Evangelicals, Catholics, and several other Christian denominations, as well as various assorted Hindus, Sikhs, Jews and Buddhists. There was also a handful of supporters of Perkins from the student humanist and secular societies – but most student societies had sided with those protesting the visit, on the grounds that Rudyard Perkins' presence would cause offence to ethnic and religious minorities. So the socialist workers and various left-wing 'liberal' groupings were chanting anti-Zionist slogans with the Muslims, apparently unaware that any Islamic state would have imprisoned and perhaps beheaded the lot of them for their views. But they looked a peaceful lot in general, and all their noisiness seemed good-natured.

The lecture was to take place in the Mandela building, and Rudyard Perkins was to arrive by car and to be led to a hospitality room where he could get prepared for his lecture. The police had been informed but didn't expect anything more than the usual jeering and booing, so had provided a modest number of officers to manage the small crowd expected. Rudyard Perkins had given lectures at universities all over the world without any real trouble – he was, after all, a reader at Oxford university, and there had never been any real problems there either. It was not as though he were some kind of a Nazi or racist or bigoted extremist; he was simply a rationalist who demanded scientific evidence for his beliefs, which is why he was an atheist – albeit a high profile one – and that was it. He, of course, hoped others would also see how religion was illogical and irrational and caused no end of trouble in the world, but he debated his points of view in a pleasant, civil, though robust, manner. What people really hated about him was that he challenged them and exposed them for what they were – which was more often than not people who used religion to prop up their own authority and power, to silence criticism and to make money.

'The Lie of Religion' was, it's true, a provocative title for the lecture. But then, in stark empirical terms, any religion *was*, literally, a 'lie' because there was absolutely no real evidence for religious beliefs at all – because they were about faith which, by definition, required a leap of faith, and so evidence didn't really matter in those terms. That was why it was called *Faith*, and not merely *belief* – they were essentially two different sports played on different pitches with different goalposts. In the face of Evangelicals and others who believed the earth was only six thousand years old and that evolution was a lie, and that fossils were put in the ground by God to test people's faith, Perkins' voice was a voice of Reason and reasonableness. And his voice refused to be silenced by those who believed in surrendering civilised values to misplaced multiculturalism and absurd over-sensitivity to people's religious feelings, and who promoted a dangerous relativism between evidence-based knowledge such as evolutionary theory, and the faith-based learned imagination of all literalist religious beliefs such as Creationism.

Perkins promoted the view that a reluctance to offend was a very dangerous thing and had been used as emotional blackmail for years in the UK to allow the religious to claim special treatment and immunity from criticism – something which concerned many. Far too many teachers these days were guilty of pandering to religious groups in their cowardly eagerness never to offend students or parents – all in order, ultimately, to help their own careers. Even science teachers in Britain – apparently, up to half of them – were now, shamefully, teaching Creationism or 'Intelligent Design' as an equal and equivalent, but different, theory to the scientific fact of evolution for which vast quantities of evidence existed. This was like teaching students that the theory that the sun went round the earth, as stated in the Bible, was an equivalent theory to the one that told the truth – that the earth went round the sun.

Rudyard Perkins was keen on quoting Mark Twain, who said: "Faith is believing what you know isn't true" and much of what was in the Bible and the Koran could be proven, by science, to be completely and utterly factually wrong.

It was as if, in order not to offend any ethnic or religious community, some teachers were prepared to prostitute themselves to a lie and betray the sound principles of the science they were teaching. But then, if these teachers told the truth and rejected superstitious unscientific nonsense, some students or their parents would almost certainly complain, and inspectors would probably criticise them as well for not promoting diversity or being sensitive to students' cultural needs. In this climate of muddled multiculturalism and the surrender of science to make-believe, Rudyard Perkins' clear and rational logic had made him a hero tomany, but an enemy to others too, especially in the United States.

By the time of Perkins' expected arrival, there were hundreds of people standing behind barriers next to the road and the Mandela building, waving placards and chanting slogans. Some had loud hailers and were leading chants in both Arabic and English. In general, it was good humoured, but one group of Muslims in particular seemed extremely angry – a bearded man in a robe was leading the chanting – and the other bearded men, and women in burqas, as well as the leftwing protestors, were chanting their slogans too – the usual 'Death to America', as well as something that sounded like 'lions are purrers' which turned out, on closer listening, to actually be 'Zionists are murderers' – and other equally unintelligible chants. Their placards stated much the same thing, with the Star of David twisted into a swastika, and other anti-Israel slogans accusing Perkins of being a puppet of the Zionists – i.e. the Jews. It was very clever really – if they said 'Zionists', they could get away with saying anything which, if they had used the word 'Jews', would be breaking the Race Relations Act and would lead to their being arrested. The small group of atheists and humanists opposite them couldn't hope to out-chant them.

On the opposition to evolution, if nothing else, most of the religious groups seemed united. The Christian Evangelicals were also loud, chanting about Jesus and singing hymns – and for some reason a lot of their placards referred to abortion and gays. The turbaned Sikhs were chanting something too, as were a handful of Hindus, but the group from the student Buddhist society were as quiet as mice as they stood limply holding placards calling for world peace. No-one was listening to their smiling silence either.

"Perhaps they are meditating," said Raj.

It was hard to tell really: they seemed unanimated and serene-looking all of the time no matter what they were doing – or not, as the case may be. Not for the first time, Crump wondered how anyone ever got anything done in Buddhist monasteries, what with all the tranquil meditating and being at peace etc.

As he approached the Mandela building, Crump could see that there were quite a few Arab-looking men in suits standing in the background, some with shades and all looking like they were from some secret service or other. There were also a few Chinese and Russian-looking men in suits observing the crowd from a distance – these were now seemingly a permanent feature on campus. There were some photographers and camcorder-operators too, presumably from the British press, though there were some from the foreign media too, and probably some from pressure groups and other monitors.

Both Crump and Raj decided to wait for Rudyard Perkins' arrival outside instead of going into the Mandela building early, so they stood listening to the competing chants of the religious groupings and waited for his arrival.

"I simply do not understand why people are wanting belief in the God," said Raj, "or gods, as Hindus are doing."

"S'pose it's just comforting," said Crump.

"But there is no evidence for existence of the God," said Raj, crossly, "so why anyone is believing? And as for all these jolly silly fellows who are not believing in the evolution in face of overwhelming evidence..."

He shook his head, sadly.

"I suppose faith is just one part of religion," said Crump,

"there's tradition, family structures, identity, art and music, and the evolutionary instinct to conform and to belong..."

"But there is no evidence," said Raj, crossly, "so why people are believing? It is fairytale! I am having no faith in human race sometimes – I am thinking there is existing too much potential in every human being to be completely and utterly stupid."

"Just human nature, I suppose," said Crump, "perhaps the group identity and shared belief of religion is part of human evolution itself – sort of, tribal..."

"Look at India," interrupted Raj, "look at all problems the religion has been causing there over centuries." He shook his head, sadly. "You know, when my father was dying – he had the cancer in the throat – he was smoking strong cigarettes all life – I was visiting when he was close to the death, and I was asking him if I should be praying for him – my father was the long-life communist – and you know what he was saying?"

Crump shrugged and Rajdeep grinned, a glint in his eye.

"He was barely speaking – but he said, 'pray for me, but only if you are intending to sacrifice goat or virgin too!'"

They both chuckled at Raj's father's wit.

"And my father and I, we were laughing so much at absurdity of all the religion and believing in the silly gods. So I was not praying or sacrificing goat or virgin – and my father was living six weeks more and was dying with smile on face! That is why I am supporting IRA."

Crump frowned. He didn't realise that Rajdeep had Irish blood.

"No not that IRA!" said Raj, shaking his head, "Indian Rationalist Association – my father was big supporter – they are visiting village and exposing spiritual conmen gurus who are stealing money from ignorant peasants with magic tricks and hocus pocus mumbo jumbo."

"Good for them," said Crump – he always hated to see people exploited and enjoyed it when those who would do so were exposed for the charlatans they were.

"My father used to be saying – a religious person is blind man in dark room looking for black cat who is not there."

Crump was just about to ask Raj about the origin of that quote when, suddenly, the noise level increased and a car could be seen turning into the main university entrance and making its way towards the Mandela building. The chanting of the protestors got louder as they realised Rudyard Perkins was arriving, and pretty soon some were shouting and screaming slogans in the direction of the car.

A couple of people jostled Crump and Raj to get closer to the barrier. Rudyard Perkins got out of the car, smiled defiantly, waved at the religious protestors and the small group of supporters, and entered the Mandela building. He is actually here at last, thought Crump, a great big birthday smile on his face.

A few minutes later, Crump and Rajdeep were sitting in the lecture hall – at the back, as usual. They were both surprised by the number of obviously religious people in the audience – at least Perkins wouldn't be preaching to the converted. There were several Muslim men with beards and robes, and women in burqas and headscarves; there were a couple of Jews and a small group of Sikhs; and there seemed to be a rather large group of smartly-dressed Evangelical Christians, some of whom, Crump could hear, were definitely American – it was in the puritan-seeded USA that opposition to the 'atheist fundamentalist' Rudyard Perkins was at its most extreme. Crump could also see Fiona Windrush, Wendy Webb and Edwin Wittering at the front and was glad he was sitting away from them. He just knew that senior managers would be present at a lecture like this – it was one of the perks of any educational manager's job to rub shoulders with visitors who were massively more significant than they could ever hope to be.

The university, despite trying desperately to stop the lecture and apologising profusely to the department of Islamic studies for their inability to do so, did not seem to mind any publicity that would come its way because of it – Thames Metropolitan getting a mention in any news item anywhere was just another advertising opportunity and a chance to drum up business. 'Brand awareness' was what they called it – others would have called it 'putting yourself about a bit'. Either way, the more the name was mentioned the better, according to the marketing department, and they also loved the fact that the splendid university buildings were so often used in adverts and TV programmes, especially BBC historical costume dramas which were shown internationally.

At Easter there would be a charity event on the site where a great number of extremely important people, including dignitaries from China, Russia and the Arab world, would pay £10,000 a head for dinner and the opportunity to bid at a charity auction in the presence of people such as Tony Blair and Bill Clinton, as well as the rich and famous from all over the world. The Perkins lecture was small fry compared to that very big fish, so even though it would have been better, according to the university managers, if the lecture had been cancelled on the grounds of being sensitive to the diverse needs of students, its going ahead was not such a disaster after all, especially as so many religious students seemed to be enjoying their chanting and heckling very much indeed.

The lecture was, quite simply, brilliant. There had been both tense excitement and some booing when Rudyard Perkins had entered the hall, but everybody's attention was soon rapt by the civil eloquence with which the lecture was delivered. There was no ranting or shouting, but instead a calm and rational exposition of the 'Lie of Religion' which took in history, theology, philosophy, genetics and the theory of evolution. And unlike so many lecturers, especially the more intellectually mediocre amongst them, Rudyard Perkins did not use PowerPoint.

But Perkins was not a *good* lecturer, he was a *great* lecturer – an inspiring, highly-educated and groundbreaking academic and a much-admired, best-selling author. Crump sat spellbound by his words and his elegant and thorough annihilation of the arguments of those who rejected the theory of evolution and the vast quantities of empirical evidence to back it up, and believed instead that the beautiful and poetic metaphors in ancient religious texts were stark and unquestionable fact. And because his arguments were so sound, and he was so civil and logical, the religious people at the lecture also seemed to be agreeing with what he was saying – or, at least, not assuming that this learned man, who was prepared to state that their religions were just man-made fairytales that involved worshipping an invisible sky pixie, was some kind of ogre who wanted to refuse them the right to hold their beliefs.

Particularly impressive and elegant was his rejection of the idea that somehow a belief in Darwin's theory of natural selection legitimised belief in fascism, racism or any other brutal ideology – (he actually showed convincingly that fascism and communism were, essentially, types of religions themselves) – or that it made the world a bleak, selfish and meaningless place to live one's life. All these 'graven images' were well and truly shattered by the lecture, and at the end every single person in the hall – except a small number of the Muslims and Evangelicals – stood up and applauded.

For the first time in very many months, Crump felt that he had faith in education. Because this is what education could do – it could excite and inspire in a beautiful and intense way which was absolutely and completely good, and which enriched everybody's life for the better. It was such a shame that there was so very little education in the education system any more, he thought, as he and Raj stood and applauded wildly like excited little boys at a man who was, or should have been, a hero to everyone who values education, and the values and benefits it should stand for.

After the lecture, Rudyard Perkins explained that he was unable to stay and answer any further questions or meet people because the police had advised him to leave as soon as possible. Crump and Raj looked at each other quizzically, but filed out of the building like everyone else, delighted, despite being unable to meet the great man, that they had been present at a lecture given by a true master. Why would the police advise him to leave straight away? There hadn't seemed to be any problems when they had watched him arrive earlier.

When they exited the Mandela building the reason became clear – there seemed to be three, or maybe four, or perhaps even five times the number of protesters than had been present when they'd entered the building, and the shouting and chanting of slogans was so loud as to be deafening. The entire campus was crammed with people, and there seemed to be a huge number of women in burqas and bearded, robed Muslim men in the crowd. The police presence seemed far too small, despite a few riot police in headgear. Crump could see an officer speaking into his walkie-talkie looking somewhat flustered.

"Bloody hell," said Raj, which described Crump's thoughts exactly.

They decided not to try and regain their former positions, or to try and leave the campus, but to go and stand by the iron railings next to the main road, well away from the noisiest and densest mass of protestors.

"Where they are all coming from?" said Raj, as they pushed through the crowds.

"God knows," said Crump, with accidental irony.

Just then, the noise seemed to get louder and louder, and people by the campus road started screaming and shouting and yelling, though Crump couldn't identify specific words or slogans any more. It seemed that Rudyard Perkins had left the building.

Why weren't the police doing anything more to control this, he thought, and why weren't there more officers present? They got lots of police to football matches and pop concerts and demonstrations in Trafalgar Square, so they could easily mobilise officers if they wanted, surely? There just didn't seem to be enough police there, somehow. Surely, they weren't deliberately being low-key because of some kind of pandering to the sensibilities of the religious? Or were they? Perhaps the police were just so terrified of being called racist these days that they deliberately were refusing to intervene too much in a protest like this one, where well over half of the protestors were from an ethnic minority. But surely that couldn't be the case, could it?

From where they stood some distance away, Crump and Raj could see the car containing Rudyard Perkins being driven slowly down the road in the middle of the campus. But there were protestors everywhere and there didn't seem to be crash barriers – if there had been any, they'd all been knocked down or removed.

Then people started to throw things – fruit at first, Crump could see – what looked like rotten tomatoes, some of which splattered on the car like blood. Then coins and bottles and stones – and then bricks, one of which shattered the car's windscreen. A huge roar went up in the crowd at this point and it seemed to surge forward. Crump and Raj clung to the fence they were standing by in order to avoid being dragged into the heaving mass of people.

"I really am thinking it is jolly well true," shouted Raj into Crump's ear, "that the larger the crowd, the lower the IQ of every individual in the crowd is becoming..."

But Crump couldn't hear a word he said. Over the piercing screams and shouts and yells he could see that the protestors had managed to smash the car's windscreen, and now surrounded it. The police had been forced back and kept back from the car by the mob.

Crump looked in horror as they then roughly manhandled first the driver, then Rudyard Perkins, out of the vehicle. He could see that many of those who were now dragging them from the car were wearing balaclavas and were dressed in military garb. But Rudyard Perkins looked calm – almost serene.

Crump was certain Perkins looked at him and met his eye

at that moment. He didn't seem to struggle at all and seemed to have an aura of total equanimity about him as the fists began to fly – he even seemed to be smiling slightly, stoically accepting the chaos all around. Then Crump saw Perkins disappear from view and get swallowed by the heaving crowd.

He could stand it no longer – he lunged into the crowd, pushing his way forward. Rajdeep screamed at him but he was determined to try and stop this. He pushed through the crowd as another huge cheer went up. Cries of Allah uh Akbar – God is Great – pulsed through the mass of people around him.

Crump was screaming by now – yelling with all his might. But the noise of the protesters was so loud that he couldn't even hear himself scream. The crowd seemed to erupt into a riot of flying fists as Muslims, Christians, Hindus, Sikhs, atheists – and even Buddhists – began fighting each other all around.

There were sirens now – some near – and the occasional missile started falling from the sky. The crowd immediately seemed to disperse and people began running in all directions. Bricks and rocks were raining down now, and a short way off a Molotov cocktail exploded in flame. Crump was knocked to the ground and could feel feet trampling over his body. To his amazement, he felt no fear.

Suddenly, a hand grabbed Crump's arm and pulled him up from the ground and out of the crowd. It was a woman in a burqa. No, it was *the* woman in the burqa he had seen before – he could tell from the eyes. But now they didn't look frightened and sad – they were calm and warm and smiling. And there were other women in burqas around too. They all helped in leading Crump away from the screaming, chaotic crowd, and the wailing sirens, and the bricks and rocks raining down around them. Crump allowed himself to be led by the burqa-clad women. He trusted them. He didn't know why, after what he had just witnessed, he should trust these devout – even fanatical – Muslims so much, but he just did. He couldn't explain it.

And then Crump woke up.

He was lying in bed in a windowless ward in a hospital. His head hurt and his lips were dry and parched. He struggled to sit up and reached out for the polystyrene cup on the table next to his bed and sipped some tepid water from it. He had no idea what time it was or whether it was day or night, but was glad to see his glasses folded up on the bedside table. Every bed in the ward was occupied and most people were resting quietly. Nurses were walking around with the usual noise and chatter. Crump's head throbbed. He reached to his scalp and felt a bandage on his head. What had happened?

"Mornin' sweetheart!" said a cheerful voice.

Morning? thought Crump. Had he been asleep since yesterday afternoon? And how had he got to hospital? The last thing he remembered was... what exactly? Lying on the ground and bricks raining down and people rushing around him – and then...then... Then he was rescued by the burqa girl – but what had happened after that? Who had taken him to hospital? Who had rescued him?

"You got bad knock – but you feelin' better yah?" asked the smiling black nurse standing over him.

She had a heavy African accent – (though he couldn't identify the country) – which reminded Crump of some of his students.

"What... happened? What time..." asked Crump.

"You just lie down and restin' – doctor come in short time yah," the nurse interrupted.

She poured some more water into his cup, smiled widely and went to check on some of the other patients.

Later, after Crump had ascertained that it was about eleven, a doctor came to see him – it was the same woman who had seen to him on his previous two visits and he smiled in recognition. A male nurse was with her.

"You again?" she said, shaking her head and smiling.

"I don't know...what...happened..." said Crump, croakily, as the doctor undid the bandage on his head and looked at the stitched wound.

"You were hit by a heavy object, so needed five stitches."

Crump said 'ouch' as the doctor prodded. She then looked closely into his eyes as before, asking him to look up and down, left and right.

"We'll give you some more painkillers – but we want to keep you in for another night. You've got quite a lot of bruising."

"I feel fine," said Crump, "just a bit groggy – not concussed, or I don't think so anyway."

"You've probably built up immunity to concussion by now," the doctor laughed, as did the male nurse with her. "That's a doctor's joke, by the way," she said, slightly embarrassed – they were clearly even worse than teachers' jokes.

Shortly afterwards, Crump had to go to the toilet, so asked a nurse where it was. She brought him a hospital issue gown as he was only wearing his briefs, so he put it on and made his way to the toilets.

It was when he was standing up and pulled down his pants to pee that he saw it – his pubic hair had been trimmed short. Not shaved, just trimmed to about half an inch all over. What on earth was that all about? Had they shaved – or trimmed – him in readiness for an operation? If so, what operation? It was his head that had been hurt and given stitches, not his genitals. They hadn't operated on him *down there* by mistake, had they? He'd heard about things like that happening.

He peed into the toilet bowl – it felt somewhat sore, somehow. He felt his penis – it was sore too, and rubbed slightly raw at the tip. What had happened? Crump's head thumped and he felt a bit dizzy, so he washed his hands, splashed cold water in his face and made his way back to bed as quickly as he could. He was very confused.

If Crump had been able to see what had happened to him the previous afternoon, he would have seen a brick follow a trajectory which ended on the head of a man who was thirty years old on that very day. He would then have seen some burqa-ed Muslim women lift him off the ground and carry him away out of danger – until the bearded Muslim men dragged the women away, that is. Then he would have seen Tracey the security guard, and Marvin the van driver son of one of the department secretaries, under the direction of Edwin Wittering, drag him off the ground and over to the Mandela building. He would then have heard them decide that calling an ambulance was no use as the place was in such chaos that no vehicle would have been able to get through, so they carried him up the stairs to an office where they laid him on the floor. Edwin Wittering would then have said that he would apply cold water to the bleeding wound on the unconscious young man's head and look after him until medical care was available, so Tracey and Marvin could both go back down to see if they could help anyone else.

He would then have seen Edwin Wittering, with his unbearable stench and vile putrid breath, lock the door before undoing the young man's trousers and removing them, as well as taking off his own. After performing some rough oral sex on the young man, Edwin Wittering would then force himself into the man's unconscious mouth and into his throat. After a few gasping moments, he would have seen a smiling and satisfied Edwin Wittering get a pair of scissors from the basin and trim Crump's pubic hair, placing the cuttings in an envelope before walking over to the shelf and putting it in a scrapbook, inside which were very many other examples of the public hair of young males of various ages that Edwin Wittering had 'helped' over the years.

But, of course, the unconscious Kevin Crump saw none of this, so had no idea at all why his pubic hair had been trimmed short and his penis was sore. It was an utter mystery.

With not a little embarrassment and hesitation he asked the nurse if anyone had shaved or trimmed him *down there*. She went to ask others, but came back saying there was no record of that happening, and why would they do that to someone with a head wound anyway? Perhaps they'd done it by mistake and kept no record – perhaps it was all an NHS cover-up? It seemed unlikely, but... It was even more of a complete mystery now and Crump was utterly flummoxed.

It was visiting time from two till four but Crump didn't expect anyone to come. He presumed everything would still be chaotic, so would understand if no-one visited – though he would have loved to have seen the newspapers, just to make sure it wasn't all just a dream and he wasn't going mad, if nothing else. To his surprise, early that afternoon Raj arrived with Athena and they brought some papers with them as well as the obligatory bunch of grapes.

"I'm fine, really," he said to them, lying.

The truth was that it was his mind that was hurting much more than his head, and his real pain was not caused by the stitched wound on his scalp or any bruising. The pain came from what he had witnessed – the riot and the attack on Rudyard Perkins. It was, predictably, all over the front pages.

"But why you are not paying for TV service," asked Raj, gesturing to the overhead screen.

"Just didn't think of it," said Crump, thinking how these days you couldn't escape the digital world of screens and buttons anywhere, even when lying in a hospital bed, "I'll do it later," he lied.

Athena and Raj told him all the details about how he'd been rescued by the Muslim women, and Tracey and Marvin, and Edwin Wittering. The mention of that name made Crump shiver, but he would now have to thank them all for what they did, except perhaps the Muslims – as he knew he had to follow the order never to approach the Abdullah building.

They told him how, according to the latest news, Rudyard Perkins and his driver were now both in a coma in hospital after being badly beaten up, and both may well have permanent brain damage; and also about how there were loads of police around the university campus, as well as news crews from all over the world, and how the riot was headline news, and all over the internet too – there was lots of mobile phone camera footage on YouTube. The university was now, it seems, world famous. The marketing manager would be ecstatic, no doubt, when thinking of all the free publicity.

They also told him how the university was making a big thing of how they hadn't wanted the lecture to take place anyway and that the riot was all the fault of Islamophobic elements and groups, including the police, and not the Muslim community or students, who should be welcomed and valued by everyone. The police were saying the university was irresponsible and how, as usual, they had treated the police as some kind of enemy and had been very uncooperative. Politicians fired insults and accusations around like bullets. Some self-appointed Muslim leaders and media-savvy Mullahs said it was all the will of Allah – a judgement against students for not being devout Muslims and drinking alcohol and tolerating homosexuality and eating pork, not necessarily in that order. Everyone appealed for calm, especially those who seemed to be getting hysterical.

The funny thing was that, from what Raj and Athena were saying, nobody seemed to be blaming fanatical religious people for this at all. In fact, some were actually blaming Rudyard Perkins for 'promoting' his scientific evolutionary views in a 'multi-faith and multicultural university' and for causing the riot, the implication being that he'd deserved everything he'd got – to be beaten to a pulp and put into a coma.

Crump decided he would catch up on all the TV news in detail when he was discharged – probably the next day they told him – so spent the rest of the day reading the papers Raj and Athena had brought, and resting. He couldn't face watching TV – couldn't face seeing it all again. Television was always just too real, somehow, even though he knew most of what was on it was utterly fake and stage-managed. It was, maybe, just his way of reacting to the shock of what had happened.

After dining on some of the rather dull but passable hospital food, he slept well. Considering the notion that he may be in some kind of shock, he knew he had to rest as much as he could. He slept a beautiful sleep amidst the ever-present noise of the hospital ward and was discharged the next morning, after a breakfast of cold toast with plastic-tasting margarine and weak tea, served again by the cheerful African nurse.

Mrs Glidewell was waiting when he arrived home – she was worried that he hadn't been home for two days. He explained what had happened; she said she rarely watched the TV news because it was always too depressing but had heard about the riot on the radio, and they watched a special programme about it on TV together that evening while enjoying a nice shepherd's pie ready meal that she had cooked them.

The programme showed what had happened at the 'religious riot' at Thames Metropolitan University and Crump could even see himself – and Raj – pictured in the crowd as Rudyard Perkins got into the car after the lecture and it drove off. Crump felt a little sick as he watched the footage – though also strangely disconnected. Numb, somehow – as though it hadn't been him at the riot at all, but another man who looked exactly like him. Mrs Glidewell looked more upset than he did watching the programme – perhaps because she wasn't used to watching violence on the TV news every evening.

Unbelievably, the BBC news seemed to be blaming the riot on Islamophobia too – and they were even insinuating it was the fault of Rudyard Perkins himself for offending Muslim sensibilities. They allowed a great many Muslim 'leaders' to express their opinions, and even tried to link the riot to Palestinian issues and the supposed wrongdoing of the 'West', and their vox pops of 'Muslim communities' seemed to express a similar view, as well as the predictable conspiracy theories that the whole thing had been staged by MI5 and the 'Zionists' to make Muslims look bad. Bizarrely, no-one seemed to be effectively challenging this, or even blaming the rioters for causing the riot or violently attacking others.

It was almost unbelievable that such a thing could happen

at a British university, and it looked like there would be a public enquiry about it – not that that would do any good for Rudyard Perkins, whose brilliant brain may well have been damaged beyond repair. Crump knew that the footage of him being dragged from the car would already be all over the internet though, and that some Islamic fanatics would be delighted at the images and probably use them in films promoting jihad against the West and all infidels and anyone who wasn't exactly like them, tolerant-minded Muslims included. A middle-eastern Islamic leader had already made a statement praising the Muslims for fighting Jihad in the riot, and condemning all who co-operated with the authorities or helped the injured – over a hundred people had needed hospital treatment, apparently. It was almost incredible that no-one had been killed.

Earlier, during the afternoon, Crump had called his mum to let her know what had happened and that he was alright, and then he'd called the university. He told them he'd be in soon, probably the next day. There were only just over two weeks till the Easter holiday, and he had a lot of assignments to hand out in his lessons as well as preparation to do for the conferences he was due to attend, and he really wanted to get the benefit of Sandy's experience regarding his research as well. They said that was fine – surprisingly. He spoke to Wendy Webb, eventually, and she told him that, due to added security, he would have to show his security pass at several points all over the campus when he did come in – apparently, a lot of TV people were trying to pass as students to get access to the campus, interview witnesses and take pictures. Crump wasn't surprised – he knew that those who worked in TV had the morality of rats.

But the worst thing to greet Crump on his return home from hospital was the post. There was one birthday card from his mum, and one from Becky, as well as a phone bill. But most disturbing was an important-looking letter in a heavy white envelope. It looked like a legal letter – and it was.

When Crump opened it and read the contents his jaw almost dropped open – it was from the solicitor representing Barbra. The letter stated that legal proceedings would be taken against him for the injury and pain he had caused unless the matter was settled – and it went on to make the suggestion that compensation of circa £20,000 may be considered reasonable.

Was this some kind of sick joke? He had been attacked by, and defended himself against, a violent lunatic and now the mad witch was claiming compensation – for her pain and suffering and hurt feelings? Compensation of £20,000! He knew that Britain was becoming compo-crazy, but not to this degree, surely? What was going to be next – a religious bigot maniac claiming compensation from Rudyard Perkins for the hurt he had been caused by beating his victim up? It was ridiculous and surreal and stupid and...

He decided that, in his state of mind, with all that had happened, and a head still aching both inside and out, despite the painkillers, it was better to do nothing for the time being. So he put the letter by the phone and decided that he'd go into the university the next day to ask the advice of his colleagues. Surely he wouldn't be expected to pay compensation to a woman who had attacked him? Or had the world gone completely mad?

Thinking about the events of the past couple of days, his brain answered him immediately: 'Oh yes,' it said, 'the world has gone completely and utterly mad, and is getting madder by the hour.'

And that, thought Crump, was all there was to it.

CHAPTER NINE

Finding Out

"So you knew?" said Crump.

He was sitting in Wendy Webb's office and could hardly believe what he was hearing.

"I gave you the choice in our previous meeting to either accept responsibility for your attack on Barbra or to contest her allegations through due procedure," said Wendy, "and you chose the former."

"Of course I did," said Crump, "I didn't want to be suspended!"

"Please do not raise your voice at me, Kevin," she said.

Crump sighed – he had to keep his cool.

"I'm sorry, it's just..."

Wendy Webb smiled, perhaps sympathetically.

Now that s/he was a woman – or, at least, a man pretending to be a woman – she seemed to be using her 'femininity' to full advantage. In Crump's experience, men seemed to have less of an issue with direct speaking than women, who were prone to taking offence at anything not expressed in a gentle and sympathetic way. He had even known female colleagues burst into tears if spoken to too directly – thankfully Wendy hadn't done that.

She asked him if his head injury was better. He replied that it was, though his scalp was a bit sore.

"Off the record, I'd suggest that you negotiate with the

complainant's solicitor – £20,000 seems reasonable, considering..."

"But she attacked me," Crump pleaded, "and I defended myself!"

"Not officially. You accepted blame for the attack, in writing."

She was right – he had.

"But I'm innocent!" said Crump.

"Not *officially*," said Wendy, "and not according to your own acceptance of responsibility."

"But...but..."

Crump thought hard, but couldn't think of anything to say. The buggers had got him again. Wendy smiled.

"I'm sure if you contact your union they may suggest you reach an out-of-court settlement."

He did, and they did too.

Crump booked an appointment with a solicitor recommended by the union for the following week. He made a mental note to ask them if there would be any chance of his claiming compensation for being knocked out cold during a religious riot on university premises. Well, if everyone else was getting compensation for everything under the sun, why shouldn't he? He decided he would go with whatever the solicitor advised.

It had taken Crump about half an hour to get past all the security checks at the university – there were a lot of police and TV crews around, as expected. All the rubbish and detritus from the riot had been cleared away and the place looked cleaner and tidier than he had ever seen it – perhaps because so many classes had been cancelled or rescheduled, so there hadn't been many students around. Not one empty drink can or crisp packet lay on the ground – a situation he was sure that would soon be messily remedied as more students started coming back after the vacation.

The first thing he had done when arriving at the university that day, before even going to his office or seeing his colleagues, was to find and thank some of the people who had helped him when he had been knocked out – the security guard Tracey, Marvin the van man and Edwin Wittering. He would have loved to thank the Muslim women too – and especially the burqa girl with the beautiful eyes – but just couldn't risk it.

Tracey was on the door, as usual, and seemed delighted when Crump thanked her for her help.

"Oh it's nuffink mate – nice to see yer back on yer feet innit?" she had said, grinning and laughing her huge wobbly laugh.

Crump had got on well with Tracey since the 'misunderstanding' on the first day and she had even let him in on other occasions when he'd forgotten his security pass, which he'd done more than he cared to remember. Amazing to think it was less than six months since he'd first met her – it felt more like years.

He went into his department. He could see from the foyer that both secretaries were there, so he knocked on the glass door and entered. The secretaries and other admin staff always looked at Crump as though he were some gormless idiot or a dangerous weirdo – probably, he thought, because they were party to all the confidential information about him. It was they, of course, who typed and sent out letters for everything, so they possibly thought he was some kind of sexist, racist, violent fascist pig if they believed what was in his file. But this time they were very pleasant, and allowed him to phone Marvin from the office – one of the secretaries was his mum. Although a bit wary – this was Crump's only conscious contact with him since he'd nearly been knocked down by him on his first day – Marvin seemed friendly enough and thanked Crump for thanking him for saving him.

Marvin repeated the lie that everyone does in these situations: 'anyone would've done the same thing'. Oh no, they wouldn't – and Crump knew it. He just couldn't help his misanthropy any more. Most people would have scarpered and let him get trampled and beaten to death, their actions ruled by the self-preservation instinct. But then he had to admit that on the occasion he'd been hit over the head with a placard the Muslim burqa women had come to his rescue, and when he'd been attacked at Christmas the ambulance had stopped to scare away his attackers and take him to hospital, and now he'd been saved from a religious mob – and by Muslims too, amongst others. Perhaps there was goodness in human nature after all – in some people anyway – it was just that the way he had been treated by the university lately seemed to suggest the opposite.

Perhaps it was just institutions and those in them – or any crowd or group of people – who behaved like that, and the only hope for humanity lay in individual human acts of altruism and bravery and selflessness? If that was the case, Crump thought, humanity was really totally fucked, seeing as every single thing in the 'civilised' world was run by institutions – democratic nations themselves were institutions really, ruled by the will of the mob, otherwise known as 'democracy'. Such cynicism had been bubbling up in him since he'd started working at the university – and now he couldn't get rid of it, even if he'd wanted to.

After steeling himself with a couple of cups of tea in his office, he made his way over to the education department. He was dreading meeting Edwin Wittering again. The man made his skin creep and seemed to have the weird idea that Crump was somehow interested in him – *sexually*. Or perhaps it was all Crump's imagination? Did he give off some kind of gay 'odour' or signals? If so, what were they? Was there such a thing? Surely, Edwin didn't think that seeing him at the GUM clinic meant he would automatically be interested in having gay sex – is that what Edwin thought? If so, why? Or did he try it on with all young men? Crump was thirty anyway – not really *young* – and he hardly had model looks, so why did Edwin Wittering think he was interested?

It was all so confusing, and Crump felt the tight sensation in his stomach that he always felt in such situations – in fact, in most situations involving other people. That tight little knot of anxiety was like a fellow traveller – a friend, or enemy, shadowing him wherever he roamed on the road of life. Either that, or a vile parasitic worm eating him away from the inside and stopping him achieving his potential. Either way, it would never go away and he knew it.

"Ah Kevin," said Edwin Wittering, smiling warmly and leering over Crump as he walked into his office, "Come in, my boy – have a seat."

The stench was disgusting, and Wittering's rank breath blew into Crump's face as he walked past him and sat down. It was all Crump could do to stop himself from grimacing and holding his nose, and he deliberately breathed through his mouth so as not to suffer the appalling smell. Somewhat pervily, he thought, Wittering hovered behind the seated Crump for rather too many seconds before walking to the other side of the desk and sitting down.

"I just wanted to thank you – for the other day," said Crump, trying to sound friendly, "y'know...saving me from...well...thanks..."

Edwin smiled broadly, displaying his yellowing teeth and sickly reddened gums. He licked his fleshy lips like a lizard.

"Kevin, you don't need to thank me," he said, "I was just happy to help a young boy in need."

"You...you all saved me from...well...it could've been a lot worse...I can't remember a thing..."

"Probably for the best," said Edwin Wittering, looking between Crump's legs and remembering.

Crump shifted uncomfortably in his chair.

"Yes, I suppose it is," said Crump.

"Feel free to come up for a chat anytime," he said, "perhaps we could go out for a drink one evening?"

"Oh," said Crump, surprised at the invitation, "I'm...very... busy..."

"Course you are, course you are," said Wittering, smiling, "young chap like you, thrusting forth in your career – but I'm sure we can do it again sometime..."

'Do what again sometime?' thought Crump, frowning. What could he mean?

Crump had absolutely no idea whatsoever that it wasn't only the university that had him well and truly fucked.

* * *

"If I were you," said Raj, "I should be doing whatever lawyer is saying."

"I think that's best too," added Athena, "the law can be very complicated..."

Johnny Wong, who now occupied Kwame's desk, nodded in agreement.

"But it's twenty thousand quid!" said Crump, "and I didn't do anything wrong – she attacked me!"

"World is going tits-up-arse-up crazy!" said Raj shaking his head.

"Raj got a letter," said Athena, sounding worried, "about Barbra."

Raj showed the letter to Crump. It demanded that he report to Wendy Webb to explain his absence from Barbra's diversity training session on the day of the Rudyard Perkins lecture and reminding him that attendance at the sessions was compulsory. It also stated in so many words that he had been seen on campus on that day, and that there was video evidence, and that he would no doubt like the opportunity to explain his absence from the diversity session as there was sure to be a logical explanation.

How typical of the department, thought Crump. Being called in to a meeting with Wendy sitting like a big fat spider in her web wasn't enough – they had to throw in the sarcasm too! Raj looked worried.

"Oh they can't complain about your not being there, surely," said Crump, "especially not after the riot!"

"They should get their priorities right," said Athena, "the diversity training was a waste of time anyway – just role playing disabled people. I was a legless Palestinian in a wheelchair as a result of illegal Israeli Zionist bombing and..."

"But I was telling lie to them," interrupted Raj, "they are knowing this because I was being seen at lecture – and I was missing diversity training, and I am never being absent. Never!"

"Well in that case, you're obviously a racist sexist disablist monster then, and there's no hope for you," said Crump, joking.

Rajdeep smiled weakly for the briefest of moments.

"You had full attendance until then, didn't you?" asked Athena.

Raj nodded. His face seemed to have been swallowed by a big, worried frown.

"There shouldn't be any problem Raj, not for just missing one poxy training session," said Crump, "anyway, it could be worse – it's not as though you're me, after all!"

They all laughed at that. It was good in a way that they were all in a similar, if not exactly the same, boat.

* * *

Later, Sandy was reassuring Crump in his office.

"If the worst does come to the worst, old boy, it's only twenty big ones," he said.

"But I can't afford twenty grand!" said Crump, "as it is, my salary barely pays for my rent and food – I'm practically penniless at the end of each month!"

"Ah to be young again, so poor but so carefree," smiled Sandy, taking a sip of his glass of whisky.

"But I'm not young – I'm thirty," said Crump, "and I'm certainly not bloody carefree."

"Ah, the young have aspirations that will never come to pass and the old have reminiscences of what never happened... so maybe poverty wasn't such jolly good fun after all – maybe it's just my little grey cells turning to sludge eh?"

Crump sipped his whisky too – it was only lunchtime, but one glass wouldn't hurt.

"You know Crumpie, I envy you – I really do," said Sandy. Crump wasn't sure if he was joking or not.

"You're young – and believe me, thirty *is* young – and you're healthy. You're at the cusp, boy, the very *cusp*!"

"The...*cusp*?" asked Crump, baffled.

"Yes, the *cusp* – the cusp of a new era – a new dawn – right at the beginning of your academic career, whereas I, well..."

His words trailed off and he sighed. Crump looked at Sandy, and he did look like a rather old man – balding, red-faced and fat – but he was always so cheerful, carefree and full of energy, that Crump envied him those qualities at least.

"I may, later on, be able to help you make a little money for yourself," said Sandy, slyly, a noticeable twinkle in his otherwise rather bloodshot eye.

"Oh?" said Crump, "how?"

"Just some extra paying work I could pass your way. Anyway," he went on quickly, "plenty of time for a chinwag about that later. You prepared for your conferences then, Crumpie, old boy?"

"Oh, yes, I'm well prepared – thanks for all the help you've given me, Sandy."

It was true – Sandy had spent a long time helping Crump organise his research – so much so that it would only take a little more work to make it into a book. What would Crump call it? 'Representations of the British Education System in 19th and 20th Century Literature and Film'? Too dull. 'Portrayals of the Educational Experience in 19th and 20th Century British Culture?' Maybe – but should he specify 'culture' rather than 'literature and film'? And perhaps 'perspectives' was better than 'portrayals'? 'Perspectives' was one of those fashionable words, like 'issues' and 'values', that academics liked to use to sound 'with-it' and intellectual – usually unsuccessfully – but was it right? Sandy interrupted his thoughts.

"Oh 'twas nothing Crump, I enjoyed it – had an absolute

ball – fascinating subject, by the way. You've worked hard on it, old chap."

Crump smiled. He had. And soon he was going to two universities – two! – to present his paper to real, proper academics as an equal.

"So now you'll be getting something published, and you're going to a couple of conferences too – I do believe, Crumpie, that you're on your way, old boy!"

Crump smiled with pride. It was rare that he ever had anything to be proud or happy about at the university, so he savoured the moment.

"Course it'll take you a while to catch up with Kenneth," added Sandy.

"Who?" asked Crump.

"Oh I mean Kwame," said Sandy, "or Kwame Kwesi Mbagwu to give him his full name – used to be called Kenneth – Kenneth Twinkle – his 'slave name', doncha know."

No, Crump didn't know.

"Anyway, he's off at yet another conference this week – part of some ethnic minority achievement task force or other – all government bollocks of course, but it looks simply spiffing on a CV. It's his seventh conference this year I think. Or is it eighth?"

Crump wanted to scream. He wanted to scream and shout and yell so that everyone could hear how it was *he* who was well-educated and brainy and well-read, not Kwame or Kenneth or whatever his name was – who had only three books on his shelf. Three! And couldn't even speak proper English – let alone write it – and apparently only knew anything at all about hip-hop and rap. In fact, he seemed so utterly devoid of all cultural or literary knowledge that it was a miracle he ever got a job in a Department of Cultural, Creative and Communicative Studies in the first place, and – *and* – he never seemed to do any work at all, he just sat there nodding with his headphones on all day on the rare occasions when he was in the department. What did he do in his lessons? Play rap and hip-hop? Nod like a dog wearing a hoodie and a baseball cap?

How could he succeed so much and Crump struggle just to get through every day? How...? Why...? It made no sense.

"You OK Crumpet, old boy – you look a bit... twitchy."

Crump was livid and could feel his blood pressure rise, and a pulse – probably of envy, sadness and despair – started throbbing in his neck and his temple.

"Just...tired," he said, lying.

Sandy finished his drink in one, and poured them each another.

"That's where it's 'at' these days – diversity this, diversity that – some people make a bloody fortune off the back of it, in their very well-paid careers..."

Crump nodded, but really didn't have the energy for a debate. Sandy shook his head slowly.

"And all those bloody ragheads and tent-women wandering around – beating people up willy-nilly, as though this were some barbaric Islamic state," said Sandy, handing Crump his drink.

"It was the Muslim women that rescued me," said Crump, defensively, "but it was rather...shocking."

"I should coco – we're going be known as the university that turned Rudyard Perkins into a vegetable. Still, good for recruiting the bloody Arabs, I suppose..."

Crump knew this was true, even if it was somewhat shocking. The publicity would have gone all over the world and the university's handling of the issue, and absolute defence of all behaviour by all Muslims, would have been much admired in the Middle East and gone down very well amongst the '*ummah*' everywhere.

"And then there's all those damn suicide bombers," said Sandy, "They think Crumpie, they actually think, that if the blow themselves to buggery as an act of martyrdom against 'infidels' that they'll go to paradise and get to screw seventy-two sumptuously sex-hungry virgins!"

Sandy let rip a great roar of laughter at this. Crump sipped his whisky wearily.

"Seventy-two virgins to shag – seventy-two! Not seventy-three or seventy-one. But seventy-two!"

"It is...rather a specific number..." Crump said.

It was. Actually, it sounded rather like one of the more absurd government targets.

"And how do they know they're all virgins in paradise anyway, old boy," pondered Sandy, "and are they all wearing tents like the burqa babes here? And if so, how does one get in? Is there a...a...flap of some kind? Or a zip?"

Sandy guffawed. Crump shrugged and drank a warm mouthful of whisky. He was sure that if he'd said the same he'd have been up on a charge of racism – or else not celebrating diversity enough, or some other rule. But he wasn't going to argue.

"Seventy-two virgins?" said Sandy, a big grin on his face, "I already get that with my broadband package! These Muslims should try surfing the internet!" and he laughed loudly at his own joke again – and so did Crump this time.

It was good to laugh, after all that had happened – even if it was at politically incorrect jokes at the expense of an ethnic and religious minority. It was better than crying, at least.

* * *

The final two weeks of the Spring term flew by.

Crump couldn't wait to go to the conferences at Easter and present his paper. All accommodation had been arranged, and he'd made a list of what he needed to pack. He felt he needed a break, especially after all the stress of the previous week, and the wonderful thing was, it would all be rather a busman's holiday – he could have a refreshing break whilst building his career profile and meeting academics in his field.

Even better, in Brighton, he would be meeting up with his university friend, Otis, who was back in his home town for a couple of weeks – he would no doubt tell him about the great time he was having teaching English in Greece. There were simply no bad sides to his plans and he was looking forward to the Easter break immensely.

But first, there was business to finish. He spent the final week of term handing out the essay assignments to the students in his classes. As usual, many of them didn't have a clue about what to do, despite having studied the subject for the previous six months, and looked permanently perplexed. But the international students who were extremely weak in English would no doubt be getting someone else to do their essays anyway, so looked rather calm and happy. The students had the whole of the holiday – all of April – to write three essays of a few thousand words each. All they had to do was parrot what they had been spoon-fed and follow the detailed essay plan that had been done for them – no original thought was required at all. In fact, original thought was very dangerous and was to be avoided at all costs, as Crump well knew.

He went through all the question sheets in class, question by question, giving suggested answers for each, with sources to be researched and used. It was as though he was doing all the work for them – the thinking, the planning, the researching – perhaps because he *was* doing all the work for them. But then he was used to this, because this was the way all teachers and lecturers were expected to introduce coursework to school, college and university students these days. He even knew some teachers who did so much of their students' coursework that it had more claim to carry the teacher's name than the students'. It was the same at every British school and college, private or state, and was now true of all universities too.

Crump wondered what it would be like to teach at a proper university, before wondering whether such places existed any more. Education for education's sake was seen as a bit dodgy these days, after all.

Towards the end of term, Johnny Wong invited Crump, Raj and Athena to a Chinese restaurant in Soho. He had some friends visiting from Canada and wanted to introduce them to his new British friends. Crump spent an enjoyable evening in delightful company eating just about the best Chinese food he'd ever tasted, which Johnny had ordered in Cantonese, naturally. He loved the way that the dishes just kept on being plonked in the middle of the large round table for everybody to share – he loved almost every dish he tried, even the weirder ones – and was surprised that Johnny's Canadian friends said they thought the food was just average in quality and not really authentic. The Chinese food in Canada must be superb if they thought this was just average.

Sharing a meal this way was, he thought, just about the best way he knew to make friends with people. There were people of all races and backgrounds around the table, all having a great time – and there was no need for any diversity form to fill in, or strategy to implement, for everyone to get on just fine.

Crump also liked listening to Canadian English and found it a fascinating cross between British and American English, with its distinctive '*ou*' sound and the habit of putting '*eh*' at the end of almost every sentence. He made a mental note to research the origins of Canadian English – it could even be the starting point for future research. By the end of the evening he felt almost optimistic, and he hadn't felt like that for longer than he cared to remember.

In the last week of term Crump went to see his solicitors. From what Sandy, Athena and Raj – not to mention Wendy Webb – had said, he was not hopeful that he would be able to contest Barbra's compensation claim, especially because he had admitted to the assault to avoid the suspension and disciplinary hearing that would have followed a denial. And so it proved.

"We'll negotiate on your behalf but, I would say, their quote's about right for this sort of thing," said the solicitor.

For some unfathomable reason, the solicitor reminded Crump of Rudolf Hess. Perhaps it was that blank, dreamy look which also seemed to suggest deep, dark thinking going on behind the bushy eyebrows. Perhaps not.

"But it's twenty thousand pounds," said Crump.

"You know that's really not a lot of money these days," said the solicitor, "and if we contest the off-the-record offer then they could bring a formal compensation claim in court and then..."

"Then?" asked Crump.

"Well, let's just say then the sky's the limit – six figure claims are not unusual, especially if the claimant can show evidence for physical harm or mental distress that may well lower her earning potential in future."

"But she attacked me!" said Crump.

"Not according to your written admission of guilt," said the solicitor.

Crump nodded his head sadly – he couldn't deny the letter he'd written or the second warning he'd accepted – and wondered where on earth he would find the money.

"I'll get on to her solicitors and start negotiations – I think they'll accept twenty."

"That's something I suppose," said Crump "but twenty thousand! I'll have to...I don't know...borrow it, I suppose."

"There are lots of loan companies around if the bank says no. Twenty-two should cover it."

"Sorry?" said Crump, "I thought you said twenty."

"Twenty – plus our fees, Mr Crump," said the solicitor, smiling, and looking more like Rudolf Hess than ever.

* * *

"I'm hearing negativity and aggression in your voice," said Mandy Pandy.

Crump was sitting in his fortnightly counselling session. He explained to her why he was rather tense: the financial pressures caused by the compensation he'd have to pay, the second written warning, the ending up in hospital – again – the scam that he was forced to partake in as a lecturer regarding cheating and passing students of low levels, the disappointment and disillusionment he had experienced since starting his university academic career, the upcoming fitness to practise hearing at the college... It seemed never-ending.

"You sound very negative," said Mandy Pandy, "do you think you're depressed?"

She sounded as negative and depressed as usual. Crump looked closely at her face. She looked pale and weary, and her eyes were dull and distant.

"No actually, I'm looking forward to the holiday – the conferences I mean," said Crump.

She looked blankly at him, and seemed a little annoyed, probably because he had contradicted her theory that he was clinically depressed.

"I'm presenting my paper at two conferences – getting away from it all for a week or two."

"It's good to get away from it all," mumbled Mandy Pandy, looking at her watch.

It was the end of the session and Crump stood up and went to leave.

"Have a nice Easter holiday," he said, but Mandy said nothing.

Crump had a shock when he stepped into the waiting room. Miss Sharma, the librarian who had falsely accused him of sexual harassment, was sitting there, next to a woman he recognised – it was the bird-like, middle-aged Asian woman who had been on the panel the previous summer interviewing him for his job. He could see immediately that she was Miss Sharma's mother – they looked practically identical – and wondered why he hadn't seen it before. They were both crying, the middle-aged woman rocking back and forth. Miss Sharma looked up – she looked distraught and didn't seem to even recognise Crump. She had the same distant look in her eyes as Mandy Pandy – either that or she'd forgotten to put in her contact lenses.

He hurried out of the waiting room – he was strictly banned from talking to Miss Sharma and didn't want any more false accusations levelled at him. But a spring was in his step – it would be over a month until he'd have to sit through any more counselling sessions and he felt enormously cheered by this. They always made him feel anxious and depressed – which was, quite possibly, the intention.

It was his last day at the university before Easter, so he invited Athena, Raj and Sandy to the pub for a pre-vacation drink at lunchtime. Johnny Wong was at a conference on film in China. It was a pleasant occasion, just the four of them, and conversation was deliberately kept off subjects educational. Sandy recommended that Crump take out a long-term loan to pay the damages to Barbra, and he agreed that this was probably the best thing to do.

"Oh, and have you heard?" said Sandy.

"Heard what?" said Crump.

"That mad old man-hater Cecilia – she's pregnant, old boy!"

Athena smiled. Raj shrugged. Crump frowned.

"What?" he said.

"Y'know – preggers, up the duff, in the pudding club, *with child.*"

"Perhaps she was going to sperm bank," suggested Raj, rather bashfully.

"No idea," said Sandy, "but she already has a wife, as it were."

"Oh?" said Crump, "Who?"

"Didn't you know?" said Sandy.

"I don't tend to...have much contact with Cecilia," he said.

"Margaret No-name."

"No!" gasped Athena.

"Yes," said Sandy, "been together since Christmas apparently – kept it hush-hush."

"She is jolly well keeping everything hush-hush," said Raj, "she is never saying bloody word!"

"No idea who the baby's daddy is, but Margaret said Cecelia's nearly four months gone, so I suppose she might've got a drunken shag at Christmas, just to get impregnated!"

A tight knot of anxiety tightened in Crump's groaning innards.

"But," said Crump, "she hates men, so how..."

They all looked at him.

"And what if it's a boy? He can't have her as his mother – she'd make his life a misery!"

"Still, she's doing rather well for herself is Cecilia – she's becoming a well-respected commentator on women's issues, had stuff published in the Guardian, gets invited on Woman's Hour, banging on about patriarchy and gender stereotypes etcetera etcetera blah blah blah..."

"Really?" said Athena.

Sandy nodded.

"And Margaret No-name, well," said Sandy, "she's got quite a nice sideline writing afternoon plays for Radio Four. I heard one – lots of angry women moaning about men, with a bit of lesbianism and Marxism and multiculturalism thrown in. They love that kind of malarkey at the BBC y'know...'nother drink?"

Crump felt suddenly sick, so made his excuses and left. He would need to be fresh for the fitness to practise hearing in the morning, but over the last few weeks had come to the view that he didn't really care that much if he didn't return to West London College, especially for just the one day a week.

But the main reason he had for feeling sick was nothing to do with the college or the university or his needing to get an early night, and he knew it. After all, he was used to drinking – he had a couple most days of the week, and drank as much as he wanted at weekends. No, the reason why he felt the tight knot of anxiety twisting and snagging in his guts was the awful feeling – the horrible, awful, sickening feeling – that he may, actually, be the father of Cecilia's unborn child.

He had no memory of the Christmas party, but, thinking back, was sure someone had had sex with him. It all made sense now – Cecilia had drugged his drink and used him sexually in a deliberate attempt to get pregnant. Or was his imagination just getting carried away with itself again? Was he making all this up? Was he just paranoid? He didn't know. He had no idea what had happened at the Christmas do – he was sure he'd had sex with someone but really couldn't be certain who. Should he demand a DNA test? He didn't know what to do.

Surely it couldn't be true? And if it was, what could he do anyway? What if that woman – that crazy, nasty, twisted witch of a woman – gave birth to his child – his son? The thought was the stuff of nightmares, and that night he had a dream that Cecilia gave birth prematurely in his office – the four-month-old foetus crawling after him mewling 'why?' as it clawed up his naked body and... When Crump woke up he was covered in sweat. It was three thirty. After two very large whiskies he drifted off to sleep again in the armchair.

He woke up at six o'clock with a pain in his neck and the memory of bad dreams throbbing in his skull.

* * *

Crump decided to wear a jacket and a tie for the fitness to practise hearing at the college. He hated wearing that man-strangling noose called a tie, but he knew how managers could be influenced by good impressions and such superficial, sartorial details. Documents and photocopies of his work and the letters from the university had been prepared. Sandy had kindly written him a glowing reference too.

He was bitter that Elizabeth Clint had, in her evidence – (he had been sent a copy in advance) – suggested that Crump had, on several occasions in previous years, been late and had smelt of alcohol while working at the college. And after the amount of extra work he had done – often unpaid! She really was a nasty piece of work, but thankfully, only her evidence would be presented at the hearing and she herself would not be present.

The door opened.

"You can come in now," said a ruddy-cheeked, obese woman with a squeaky voice and thick glasses.

Crump got up from where he sat in the waiting room, took a deep breath and went into the college meeting room.

There were seven people around the horseshoe-shaped table and Crump sat facing a man who was the chairman and who introduced everyone. They mostly said nothing, except the fat, ruddy-cheeked woman with the squeaky voice who was aptly called Rosie and said she was from Human Resources. Instead, they just gawped at him, in pity perhaps, as though he were some thief standing before magistrates. He hated all of them for that.

"I admitted to the university that I had made mistakes – if I hadn't, I would've been suspended pending a tribunal..." said Crump.

"Like this one?" said the fat squeaky HR woman.

"Yes. My ambition is to follow an academic career at university, rather than at a college, and I was keen not to cause any problems there – so I admitted it."

"Was that wise?" said the balding grey-haired man.

"In retrospect – probably, no..."

The people around the table looked at each other, then back at Crump.

"I don't know – but I can tell you something – I'm not a racist and I'm not a sexist either, and I've always done my best to give my students an excellent education, irrespective of who they are. I also believe I'm a good teacher."

He said it as though he meant it – because he did. But he knew how his denial of being racist and sexist at the university had been used as proof that he was both – so he wasn't exactly hopeful. Some of the people round the table scribbled on notepads.

"Do you have a drink problem?" said the fat, red-faced woman called Rosie.

"Oh," said Crump, slightly startled, and looking around, "no – I like a drink, but..."

"It's just that several people have reported that you smelled of alcohol at certain times when you were teaching."

Crump didn't understand this. He was always careful not to drink on duty, except for a Christmas lunchtime drink, or exceptional occasions. But perhaps some mornings the smell of alcohol still lingered, and then he realised that the fat woman may have smelled the odour of whisky that was lingering on his breath when he'd entered the room, after his couple of whiskies in the middle of the night.

"They must be mistaken," said Crump, remembering Sandy's advice never to admit to anything, ever, "or perhaps *several people* have their own motivations for saying such things."

Remember the two rules – it's just a business and it's just a game. He was playing the game and would deny everything always, even if he did carry the slight whiff of whisky on his breath. And anyway, since when did Britain become some kind of puritanical state where alcohol was banned everywhere and the mere whiff of it was a sin of giant proportions?

"Thank you for coming," said the balding grey-haired man.

Crump looked each member of the panel in the eye, said thank you, smiled as innocently and gravely as he could and left the room. He felt like getting completely and utterly pissed, which he could quite happily do that evening as he wasn't going away until Sunday, so he could spend Saturday recovering and relaxing. It was a relief for it all to be over, whatever the panel decided.

"I'm sure it'll be fine," said Becky.

They were having lunch in a pub round the corner from the college. He hadn't seen Becky for weeks. Now that he no longer lived in the area or worked at the college, they neither seemed able to find the time somehow. That was a shame.

"To be honest, I don't care that much," said Crump, "I've kind of got used to the idea of not working at the college anymore, and it's not as though teaching uninspiring A levels and GCSEs there allows for much real education anyway, much as I miss all the students."

"Oh but I miss you too," said Becky with a jokey wail.

"I'm sure you'll cope," said Crump, smiling, "It's just that I've..."

"Moved on?" said Becky.

"Exactly," said Crump, "I mean, my future's elsewhere now really. Y'know, I put in so many extra hours of my free time at the college, helping the new teachers and everything, and what thanks did I get? None – none at all. I just got suspended for a nonsense spurious reason..."

"I think you're right – I think Lizzie Clint wants a promotion so instigated all this on purpose, like a witch hunt, so she could boost her chances of getting one."

"But she's already head of department," said Crump.

"Oh I think she's after the big one, here or at another college."

"Principal, you mean? Well, she's sly and manipulative enough, and completely amoral too," said Crump.

"She'll be perfect then," said Becky, and they both laughed at this *because it was true.*

* * *

Crump took it easy on Saturday, tidied up his flat a bit, packed his bags, watched a couple of comedy DVDs and went for a walk in the park to nurse his hangover. He had got completely drunk with Becky the previous evening but had really enjoyed himself too – it was good to have someone outside the university to talk to sometimes. Then he did a bit of shopping for Mrs Glidewell before going for a couple of pints in a pub.

She seemed to be managing OK after her stay in hospital – but she was slower, somehow. Older. Wearier. He had fish and chips with her in her flat, and looked forward to an early night.

"I ain't been on holiday for years," said Mrs Glidewell, "last time was Butlins in Clacton, but now me husband's gone there don't seem no point really, all on me tod."

"It's not exactly a holiday," said Crump, "not officially – I have to present a paper, to other academics."

Mrs Glidewell looked blank at this – sometimes academics forgot that their self-obsessed little corner of the world was of absolutely no interest to the vast majority of people, and that what they did really didn't matter very much at all.

"That's nice, dear," she said, "you're a very educated and *articulated* boy."

Crump didn't have the heart to correct her.

"But you be careful of all them teddy boys in Brighton, ducks," and she gave a slight shudder, "bloomin' toe-rags – that's why we stopped goin' – I ain't been there since we was down in 1961, or was it 62?"

"I'm sure I'll be fine," said Crump, "and anyway, I'm off to Colchester first."

Mrs Glidewell frowned.

"Garrison town that is – full of toe-rags an' all – all them squaddies – bloomin' lucky we won the war what with them being tight all hours!"

"I'll try and be careful," he said.

"Course we didn't really win no war, did we? It raises me *shackles* it does what's happened to this country – can't walk down the street without getting mugged or stabbed, drunken layabouts all over the shop."

"I'm sure it sounds worse than it is," said Crump, remembering that he'd been to hospital three times in the past six months through unprovoked attacks.

Maybe Mrs Glidewell was right. He knew he sounded unconvinced by his own argument.

"This country," tutted Mrs Glidewell, shaking her head, "gone to hell in an *handbag* it has, ducks."

Crump nodded and smiled and made them both another cup of tea.

* * *

"Top lecture," said a man in John Lennon spectacles, "an absolute cracker – one of the best I've heard in ages."

Crump had just delivered his paper on 'Perceptions of

Education in 19th and 20th Century British Literature and Film'. It had gone down very well indeed.

There'd been about fifty people there, all academics in humanities, mostly literature and other cultural fields, so he was making some good contacts too.

"Thanks," said Crump, glowing with pride but trying not to show it.

"Such a bloody fucking cunting relief not to have to sit through yet another fucking PowerPoint slide show," said a pretty, demure-looking woman in her early twenties standing next to the John Lennon glasses man.

Crump blushed at her incongruous language – he knew it was illogically sexist but it was still always somehow a shock to hear women swear like that.

Sandy had suggested not using PowerPoint, and instead just speaking from notes with perhaps one or two transparencies on the OHP, and a couple of stills from films, and he was right. Without PowerPoint getting in the way, and although very nervous and not a naturally fluent public speaker, Crump was able to express both his knowledge and his enthusiasm for his subject to the audience without them staring up at a silly simplistic bullet-pointed slide while he read down a list of points they had already read on the screen.

He was beginning to think that perhaps the person who invented PowerPoint – not to mention the dreadful Comic Sans font – should be publicly shot, or at least deported somewhere far far away. Siberia, perhaps. Or Toytown.

Crump made his way to the university bar to have a couple of drinks with Matthew and Lucy, the two enthusiasts who had praised his lecture. They were a similar age to Crump and were also lecturers in English literature and film and cultural studies at new universities. Happily, as it was the Easter vacation, there were no students about, just a few attendees of the conference and several members of some religious conferences taking place at the same time as theirs. They shared the canteen with some Christian youth groups every day, and it was cheering to see that everyone, no matter what their beliefs, shared a healthy disgust at the truly awful food. Crump and others eventually decided to sample the fare of local takeaways rather than suffering the dubious delights of the canteen.

The University of Colchester was an odd-looking place. It was sixties-built, with several tower blocks where students were usually accommodated, and a concrete shopping-precinct-like campus, all built slap bang in the middle of rolling green hills where rabbits hopped around all day long with no fear of either daylight or humans. If you fell asleep and woke up in this place, thought Crump, you might think you'd woken up in Telly-Tubby land, and would half expect Tinky-Winky to skip over the horizon. Crump's accommodation was much like a Butlin's style chalet, painted bright yellow, and it looked like it was made of papier mâché. It wasn't elegant, but it'd do – he was only staying there for two nights before heading off to Brighton anyway.

While at the conference, Crump thought he might as well attend a few lectures by other academics and make some useful contacts. This, as Sandy would have said, is what it was all about – just a business and a game, so play it. And playing the game was what Crump was doing, but there was no reason he couldn't enjoy a few drinks with new friends at the same time.

Matthew and Lucy turned out to be pleasant characters, and both told him about their own universities and the problems they faced – it seemed he wasn't alone in being shocked at the low levels of student ability or the tick-boxy mentality, or the cheating, or everything else that went on. It was the same at their universities. Crump didn't tell them he'd got any written warnings – an admission that he'd been 'done' for racism or sexism could ostracise him immediately from any gathering of the liberal-minded and tolerant – but Matthew volunteered the information that he'd got a first warning too, apparently for making a joke about dyslexics:

"All I said was 'dyslexics of the world, untie!" Matthew said, which Crump thought rather clever, "y'know, *'unite'*...*'untie'*...It wasn't even my joke – heard it on the radio – but then I also used the word 'brainstorm'."

"Can't fuckin' say shit these days – it's such a fuckin' cunt!" said Lucy, one of the most innocent-looking people Crump had ever met, who used the filthiest language he'd ever heard too.

"Coz 'brainstorm' might offend epileptics, apparently," said Matthew, rolling his eyes, "it's 'disablist' language, so they say."

"You gotta fuckin' say fuckin' 'thought shower' – I mean what the fuckin' cunt's a fuckin' cunt wank 'thought shower'? Know what a fuckin' golden shower is though, right?"

And Lucy laughed a laugh so dirtily that Crump had to look again at her face to make sure she wasn't some old East End whore but was actually a pretty and coy-looking English rose of a girl. Crump made a mental note to avoid the word 'brainstorm' in future – he didn't want to get in trouble for being 'disablist' as well as racist and sexist.

After a couple of days at Colchester, Crump got the train to Brighton. As usual, he had a hangover – the university bar was subsidised so it was a shame not to take advantage. He had booked a B & B for this conference via the university and his old friend Otis had agreed to meet him at the station and accompany him there by taxi. They'd been great pals at uni but hadn't seen each other for over three years.

If he had one, Otis was Crump's best friend, and also a person he admired – he was the man Crump would have liked to be if he'd had the choice. First of all, he was good-looking – not stunning, but girls always fancied him, especially with his great sense of humour and his winning smile. Whenever Crump smiled, he rather unfortunately looked as though he were leering like a pervert or some monster of a paedo, full of twisted evil and criminal intent, and people looked at him strangely. When Otis smiled, everyone's eyes lit up and they smiled back, especially women who gave off all the usual primitive hair-flicking, cheek-glowing, lip-licking signs of female acquiescence. He was not only better looking, but also always got higher marks than Crump in essays at university – not by much, but no matter how hard Crump tried he always seemed that four or five per cent behind. They both got 2:1s, but Otis got his with higher marks. And the most annoying thing was, Otis also seemed to do about half the work Crump did to get those higher marks.

It was a shame that Otis had become so disillusioned and fed up with his school-teaching job, because Crump was sure he was a wonderful teacher, and he had been very grateful for all the advice prior to his interview at the university too. Still, now Otis was living in the sunny Mediterranean – teaching English in Crete – and Crump felt sure that whatever his old friend did he'd not only succeed, but excel in, and get to the very top. He was looking forward to seeing Otis again immensely and felt a child-like butterflies-in-the-stomach excitement while waiting for his train at Brighton station.

Crump walked onto the platform and looked around at the passengers disembarking. No Otis. At least, not that he could see. He was usually utterly reliable. What could have happened? It must have been something serious – Crump's mind started to have anxious visions of car crashes and hospital wards when he felt a prod on the shoulder.

"Oi, Crump, have you finally gone blind from all that Onanism?"

Crump instantly recognised the warm, rich voice. He turned round, and there was Otis, smiling.

"You walked straight past me, mate – I can't have changed all that much."

Oh but he had. Instead of the handsome bright young man that Crump remembered, a man in his twenties with a sparkle in his brilliant blue eyes that seemed to signify a deep inner confidence that success could be achieved in everything and anything and would be too – instead of that Otis, Crump saw a shrunken figure of a man, no longer young in appearance, but tired-looking and middle-aged, who even had flecks of grey in his unkempt long hair, with sunken dull eyes staring blankly from a sallow face, sun-stained and with wrinkles and spots that seemed to be holding it in place. When he smiled, Crump saw that he had a front tooth missing. Disconcertingly, his warm and mellifluous voice was exactly the same as it always had been.

Crump had been somewhat shocked when Otis had told him three years before that he had become utterly disillusioned with the education system and the school where he had been working. Otis had said he had gone into teaching in the first place not due to career prospects – although Crump was sure he'd reach the top one day – but because he really believed in education as a force for good and wanted to communicate the joy of learning to school kids and widen their horizons, to help them to achieve their potential. After a few years as a teacher, Otis had said he had realised that there was no 'education' at all in what he was doing, so he had decided to get out and move abroad to consider his options. That was three years ago.

"Otis," Crump said, trying to hide his shock with a rictus smile.

They patted each other on the back.

"You look...well," he lied.

Otis's eyes twinkled momentarily and knowingly at the lie before resuming their dull, distant look. Crump's smile couldn't hide his shock and he knew it.

"We all change," said Otis, somewhat wistfully, looking into his friend's eyes.

"We do," said Crump.

Sadly, he thought, not always for the better. What the hell had happened to Otis? What the bloody hell had happened?

The B&B was on a road off the seafront called Lower Rock Gardens. It was perfect – five minutes from the pier and ten from the main East Sussex University campus building. Otis helped him up to the first floor room with his bags – it was all very pleasant and clean, and was being paid for by the university from funding they had secured.

The conference title was 'New Perspectives: Culture,

Communication and Identity' which, Crump thought, could have meant just about anything, but they had said his paper on education in film and literature would be perfect, especially as whole sections of his paper were on the representation of gender, race and sexuality. They said this would score well in the diversity assessment and add value, and so please university managers.

Later, they went to the town centre, had some pasta at an Italian restaurant in The Lanes and decided to sample the beer in a couple of pubs.

"Graham Greene used to come here to get wasted," said Otis, "See, he got things right – he did three hundred words in the morning, then spent the rest of the day enjoying life, eating, drinking and shagging. Lived till his late eighties too."

Crump smiled as they finished their fourth pints. He knew he drank a bit too much – probably way too much according to government's finger-wagging nanny unit guidelines – but he didn't overdo it. Not like Otis was obviously overdoing it. Crump could recognise the alcoholic hunger in his eyes – that demon, that madness, common to all true addicts – as well as the emaciated frame, the sunken cheeks, the ill-looking and blotchy, clammy skin. He watched Otis drinking and knew he wouldn't be stopping until he was wrecked – but neither would Crump that night. He didn't have to give his paper the next day anyway, but the day after that, so he could afford to enjoy himself – if 'enjoy' was the right word.

"You should come out to Crete," said Otis later, "It's sunny – except for a few weeks of pissy rain in the winter – and it's cheap. Cheap booze," he said, grinning his one-toothed smile, "'specially the ouzo – you could easily get a job in a little language school like the one I work at."

"Really?" said Crump.

"Course – you teach twenty-five hours a week, no flippin' nonsense like coursework or league tables or any of that tick-boxy twaddle – and no need for bullshit lesson plans."

"Sounds like heaven," said Crump.

"You just teach from the textbook – the way they like it over there – perhaps just three hours in the morning and two in the early evenings on every weekday, and you're done."

Otis took a large glug of his drink.

"The rest of the time's your own. Pays OK too – enough dosh to live on anyway."

"Sounds tempting," said Crump, "but..."

"But?"

"I'm just starting my academic career, and..."

"And are you enjoying it?" Otis interrupted.

Crump sighed. Otis smiled. He couldn't hide his true feelings from his best and oldest friend.

"Life's too short to waste it doing something you don't enjoy," said Otis, his eyes warm and concerned.

"I do enjoy it," Crump lied, "or would, if I could just teach – I mean properly teach, to students who were interested and intelligent..."

"Oh you mean education?" said Otis, "You know as well as I do that there's precious little of that in the so-called education system in this country these days."

Otis knew what it was 'all about' these days too – a business, a game and survival of the thickest.

The next day, Crump couldn't stop thinking about what Otis had said. This conference seemed larger and more impersonal than the one at Colchester, and a lot of people there were senior lecturers who obviously knew each other and seemed to enjoy excluding new people from their little cliques in the manner of 'professionals' everywhere. They were just like the worst of the students he remembered from his university days – pretentious, rude, 'up themselves'. Crump decided just to attend a few lectures and presentations and not to bother much with any social event – he'd rather spend time with Otis than with this pompous crowd.

He spent Monday attending several lectures and was bored out of his skull by every single one. They all used PowerPoint and Comic Sans font for a start, and seemed mostly to be about media studies and perceptions of identity in celebrities and similar nonsense. After Crump had sat through the third paper on 'femininity, sexuality and celebrity', and had been forced to gawp at large images of non-entities and bimbos from countless soap operas and TV reality shows, he decided that he may possibly have come to the wrong conference. No-one here seemed to be researching a 'proper' subject at all. His presentation, taking in 19th and 20th century British literature and film, would probably seem rather old-fashioned and academic – not to mention difficult – to lecturers more used to researching Big Brother and Heat magazine. He had a drink with Otis early on Monday evening then went back to the B&B to rehearse his lecture and get an early night.

He presented his paper at two o'clock on the Tuesday afternoon. The hall was large and there seemed to be about two hundred people in attendance. Crump was nervous. Very. That twisted knot of anxiety, that old companion from childhood, started writhing like an eel gnawing at his innards, eating him from the inside out. But he took three deep breaths and used his usual old technique of imagining the audience naked in order to boost his confidence. He also used his other trusty technique for any public situation – he took his glasses off, so gave his lecture to a blur of people, happily unable to see the whites of their eyes.

Crump decided against even a couple of swigs of vodka as he didn't want anyone to smell it on his breath, or to end up slurring his words – although he had to admit that one of the best lecturers he'd had at university seemed to permanently smell of booze, even for morning lectures.

He knew he had to learn to lecture to audiences with confidence and without any Dutch courage courtesy of Mr Smirnoff and friends – and he was getting better at it, he knew. For the moment, though, he would dispense with his glasses – which he only needed to see at a distance anyway, so he could still easily read his notes, and anyway he more or less knew it all by heart now and probably could have given a lecture without them.

The lecture went well and much of the audience seemed impressed, although some looked utterly baffled – Crump had assumed some basic knowledge of literature and culture, but it was clear that many academics in cultural fields such as media studies and related subject areas had no knowledge of literature or culture at all.

Nevertheless, Crump breathed a sigh of relief that it had all gone so well. He had now presented his paper at two conferences and would be able to state this to any publisher who wanted to commission a book about his subject, and he would easily get the paper published in a major academic journal. It would do wonders for his RAE assessment too and, according to Sandy, he could rewrite it several times and publish those papers under different titles as well to boost his score.

That evening he went out with Otis on a pub crawl to end all pub crawls, starting at the Palace Pier and taking in about ten pubs – although Crump couldn't be sure – so it was an extremely hung over Crump who shuffled into East Sussex University the next morning to attend a lecture on sexual identity called 'Email or Femail?' It seemed worth attending for the rubbish pun alone.

"Mr Crump," came a monotone female voice from behind him as he sipped a coffee in the foyer, "could I have a word?"

The short, unsmiling woman standing next behind him was called Nicky Glunt, according to the laminated name badge pinned to her ample chest, and wore bright blue mascara on her droopy eye-lids which made her look rather ill.

Crump thought she was about to congratulate him on his lecture and thank him for coming – and perhaps invite him to the next conference – but instead she asked him to follow her upstairs to a first floor office.

"This is a clear case of plagiarism, Mr Crump," she said, sternly, "and you will be reported for it to all necessary authorities."

Crump's hangover throbbed in confusion, but he couldn't deny that his lecture was almost identical to the text on the piece of paper Nicky Glunt had handed him.

"But, no it's not..." said Crump, trying to think.

Was this some kind of practical joke? His lecture wasn't plagiarised – not in any way, shape or form.

"Yes, it is, as the article printed on the document you are holding clearly proves."

Crump looked at the piece of paper. There was no doubt about it – it was his lecture, printed verbatim on the page. He was speechless and shook his head.

"This was published in a journal six weeks ago, Mr Crump..."

"But it couldn't've been...it couldn't..."

"But it was."

"But I don't understand – that's impossible!"

Nicky Glunt blinked her blue eyelids at him. She went on: "...and it was written by a highly respected academic too – a Dr Sandy Buttery..."

"What?" said Crump, "Who?"

Sandy Buttery! Sandy fucking Buttery! Surely he didn't...? Surely he hadn't...? The bastard, thought Crump, the utter utter bastard! He did – he had – he stole my work! Sandy Buttery *stole my work!*

"I believe Dr Buttery is a senior lecturer in your department at Thames Metropolitan University too. What a coincidence..."

Nicky Glunt rolled her sarcastic eyes at him and smiled, nastily.

"Is he aware that you have stolen his research to write your own paper?"

Crump's brain fizzed and buzzed like a blown circuit. His jaw opened and closed several times but no words came out. He quite simply didn't know what to say.

The bastard, thought Crump, the complete and utter bastard. Sandy had nicked his research and published – under his own name – the paper Crump had written. And all along

Crump had thought Sandy had been selflessly helping him, when in fact he was plagiarising his research paper, using him to do the hard work with the intention of taking all the credit for himself.

Nicky Glunt showed Crump an original copy of the academic journal. There, at the top of the article, was the name – Dr Sandy Buttery. Crump didn't even get a mention! It was common for senior academics to get junior lecturers and PhD students to do the hard work, then get their name put on an article or dissertation as a joint credit for their 'consultation', but Crump's name was nowhere to be seen, and it was surely traditional for the junior lecturer to be informed!

Sandy hadn't said a word about the article and yet it had been published in a journal weeks earlier. And now, perversely, Crump was being accused of plagiarism for delivering a lecture that was entirely his own original work but which had been stolen by his unofficial supervisor and supposed friend. It was, quite simply, unbelievable, but Crump had to believe it when shown the journal, and he knew he couldn't prove it was his own work either – he had allowed Sandy to copy his work onto his computer weeks before in order that he could give him advice about it.

Nicky Glunt slowly blinked her blue eyelids at him. She reminded him of a small, fat and happy pig in shit.

Sandy fucking Buttery, thought Crump – the total and utter fucking cunt!

* * *

"You stole my fucking work," said Crump when Sandy opened the door of his townhouse.

Crump had decided not to stay in Brighton until the end of the week, after all. He had been told that he was not welcome at the conference after his 'plagiarism' had been discovered. He was also told that this invalidated his offer of free accommodation so they would send him a bill in due course.

Later that day, he had a couple of drinks with Otis, told him what had happened, and then caught an early evening train back to London. It would only take an hour or so to get to the city, and he would have time to go home before going round to see Sandy. And he was adamant that he had to see him that evening. As it was, the train was delayed due to a 'jumper' on the line – but he was only half an hour late so could still manage it.

How could Sandy do that? How could he betray Crump? And why? It wasn't as though he needed to steal Crump's work – he was already a senior lecturer perched at the top of the academic tree. It was almost unbelievable – but not really unbelievable, not these days, because if Crump had learnt one thing in the business and the game that was the British educational system, it was that anything – anything – was possible. Any scam, any swindle, any betrayal of trust and any witch-hunt of the innocents – it was all possible, if not probable, at a British university in the twenty-first century.

Crump sat in the plush living room of Sandy's townhouse. He refused the offer of a drink.

"Why?" said Crump, "why did you do it? I trusted you."

Sandy sipped his whisky, smiled somewhat sadly, and shrugged.

"Oh come on Crumpet..."

"And don't fucking call me that, Buttery," said Crump, with a sneer, "how many times do I have to tell you?"

Crump felt like punching him but knew that would solve nothing; also, he knew that, despite the age difference, Sandy could probably beat him up rather badly and with considerable ease.

"Look, if there's been a murder it's always better to hang the wrong person than nobody," said Sandy, "and you're just the wrong person this time – next time it'll be someone else."

"Oh and I'm supposed to be happy about that, am I?" said Crump.

"That's the game, old boy, that's what it's all about."

Sandy finished his whisky and sighed at its warmth.

"It's called teamwork,' he said.

"Yes, *my* teamwork!" yelled Crump.

He felt a rage welling within him. It bubbled and bubbled up in him, and soon he could hold it in no longer – his words spurted out in a loud and angry rant:

"Do you realise that as well as just being expelled from a conference for supposedly plagiarising my own fucking work, which I have been working on for months, I have also been given warnings this year for being racist and sexist and for defending myself against a maniac to whom I now have to pay twenty thousand fucking quid, whilst I constantly have to turn a blind eye to massive cheating by students most of whom have the IQ of brain damaged chimps?"

Crump leaned back in his chair, exhausted.

"Welcome to the British higher education system," said Sandy.

Crump shook his head in despair.

"So you've got integrity, Crump. Great. How much d'you want for it?"

Sandy laughed at his joke. Crump looked at him with either contempt or pity – he wasn't sure which.

"It's not funny, Sandy," said Crump, accepting a glass of whisky when Sandy poured another, "not funny at all."

"We have to be wise as serpents, Crumpie old boy, to survive and prosper in our little jungle," said Sandy.

"But... I have done nothing – nothing – wrong. Nothing."

"I know, old boy," said Sandy, "I know".

"Look at what's happened to me. I've tried my very best to fit in and to be a good lecturer and...everything else... but...but..."

Crump's voice broke and his eyes felt moist. After the anger, Crump now felt an enormous sadness welling within him. Sandy patted him on the back. For some reason, Crump still liked him. Why? He didn't understand it himself.

"Listen, don't let the buggers get you down, Crump old

chap," said Sandy, "and don't worry so much – it'll all work out in the end..."

Crump was too emotional to speak for a few moments but was glad that he managed to stop himself from crying. He composed himself and took a large gulp of his whisky.

"But Sandy," he said, "the whole fucking thing is a complete and utter scam – everything, from the top to the bottom. You, me, everyone and everything – it's all a scam, a mess and a joke. Is that what a university education is supposed to be about?"

Sandy inhaled deeply and shook his head; Crump could tell he'd started drinking long before his arrival.

"Best not to think like that, old boy," he said, "just remember the two golden rules – it's all a business..."

"...and it's all a game. I know," said Crump, "almost the first thing you said to me when I arrived at the university."

Sandy smiled at the memory.

"And as true now as then. Just remember," he said, "you may not be able to polish a turd, but you can roll it in glitter."

Crump smiled at that because it was perhaps the best summary of the British education system he had ever heard.

"I think it's time," said Sandy, "that I let you into a few little secrets about the way the university works..."

That evening, Crump listened to Sandy as he talked and talked and talked. He explained how everything worked, in detail – as though he were unburdening himself of a dark secret.

It was eye-opening stuff. More than that, it was mind-blowing – absolutely incredible what he was being told. Sandy was keen to state that nothing could be proven, so everything he was revealing should be kept quiet – he would deny all knowledge of telling Crump anything if questioned. But he said he felt a duty to let Crump know how things worked and also to give him the opportunity to make some money to improve his 'debt situation'.

"But that's unbelievable," said Crump, not for the first time.

"That's the way it is," said Sandy, "in the game."

It turned out that, in addition to his salary, Sandy ran a website which provided custom-written essays for payment, and which also sold ready-made essays. Crump knew these sites existed – and it was very difficult indeed for anyone to prove plagiarism in a student's work if it was original and had been written to order, because it wouldn't show up on any plagiarism-detection software scanner such as Turnitin.

Sandy said he owned the company with a business partner who ran the business day-to-day and Crump could, if he wanted, write essays for them for extra income. Crump said he'd think about it.

Sandy also said he co-owned a university. Crump didn't know what he meant by this, and at first thought he had misheard, but apparently he and his business partner did actually own a university which awarded paying customers degrees and PhDs, and which was registered in Liberia, a corrupt African state that turned a blind eye to just about everything.

Qualifications at 'St Jude's University' were awarded for 'prior learning', so no new learning or study was required to get a degree. They could even backdate it for you, if you so wished. They charged thousands for a PhD, which was basically just a piece of paper, so they must have been making a fortune. Now Crump realised how Sandy could afford such an elegant and expensive townhouse.

According to Sandy, there were plenty of academics and other prominent people who had bought qualifications from his 'university' and many too who used custom-essay internet companies like his to buy themselves good grades and better class degrees. He recounted a list of some well-known people – British and international politicians, well-known academics and media folk amongst them – who he claimed were former customers.

As the evening wore on, Crump kept refilling Sandy's glass with whisky until he became, though not *drunk* exactly, certainly very tipsy – which was Crump's intention – and he started to say perhaps more than he meant to. Far more.

"Y'know Crumpie, there're several lecturers at Thames Met who bought essays and qualifications from me, even one or two doctors of philosophy," Sandy slurred, grinning, "not me of course – my PhD is absolutely genuine, unfortunately – I spent three years reading and writing all about Dickens, and for what? I could've just bought the bugger off the internet!"

Crump nodded and topped up Sandy's glass.

"Still, Kwame looks set to become lecturer of the year, so s'not done him any harm eh? Course the dumb little fuckwit still thinks the Cutty Sark was a slave ship!"

Sandy laughed loudly again.

"He was one of our best customers ever, old boy – I think we must've done every single one of his essays for his degree and Master's."

So that's why he's only got three books on his shelf and has a barely literate level of English, thought Crump. It all made sense now – Kwame had bought custom-written essays from Sandy's internet company to get his qualifications.

But how many others were there? How many people were teaching at that university and others who had bought their essays, or even their entire degrees? How many in all the professions? And if it went on in Britain, this scam would be sure to be thriving in the less law-abiding countries of the world. How many doctors, nurses, teachers and others were there who'd entered their professions this way? Could anything or anyone be trusted anymore?

But there was more. It turned out that Fiona Windrush, the head of department, had gained her PhD from St Jude's University too, and, bizarrely, it turned out she was not actually black after all.

"Oh no," said Sandy, by now worse off for the best part of a bottle of whisky, "No no no, the lady is not a negress indeed."

He knocked back his glass of whisky in one. Crump looked at him in puzzlement.

"Y'see," he slurred, "she used to be white – daddy was Greek and mummy was a Brit – Londoner I think – but then she realised that if she *claimed* to be black, it'd do her career no end of good. So bingo hey presto, she's black – and according to the concept of self-definition, she has every right to claim to be. Her real name's Fiona Psaradaki – she changed it to Windrush after the boat, y'know..."

"The first passenger boat bringing immigrants from the West Indies in the fifties?"

"That's the fella," said Sandy, swaying drunkenly where he sat, "but there's more..."

Crump could not believe what Sandy was telling him – it was so ear-poppingly explosive – and he started to make notes. Sandy was too pissed to notice or care, it seemed, or maybe he just wanted to come clean – to unburden himself. With a feeling approaching epiphany, Crump realised that now, at last, he was well and truly playing the game, storing information to use for his advantage at a later date – just like Sandy did, just like they all did, in 'The Game'.

Just as Crump was about to leave to go home Sandy, who by this stage was unsteady on his feet, began rifling through a drawer. He didn't see Crump take the record book – the one with details of all transactions – from the table and put it into his jacket pocket.

Eventually, Sandy pulled out an envelope and gave it to Crump.

"Keep this close, Crumpie, my boy," said Sandy, swaying slightly, "This is where integrity gets you."

Crump had no idea what this was all about, but when he was on the bus home he opened it. It was from Freddie Finch, his predecessor, who had drowned himself in the Thames and thereby created the vacancy at the department that Crump had filled. It was addressed to Sandy.

As Crump read it he felt an enormous sadness well up inside his heart. He also felt the pang of recognition in what he was reading, and he read the letter over and over again on the way home. Crump ignored the drunken idiots on the bus and didn't care that tears were streaming down his cheeks. He didn't want to cry but he couldn't help it.

This is what the letter said:

Dear Sandy,

I will be dead by the time you read this. I am writing this to let you know why I did what I did and I hope you can understand.

Since I was a teenager I have wanted to teach at a university. They are extraordinary institutions, places where the quest for knowledge is all, where lively and open thought and discussion are encouraged, where profit is not the sole motivation for life, or so I thought. How wrong I was in my assumptions! What I discovered as a lecturer at Thames Metropolitan University was that higher education these days has become nothing but a profit-making enterprise, and universities places where money, not learning, is all that matters. Have you any idea how that destroyed me inside, the fact that everything I valued, everything I believed in and trusted since childhood turned out to be a sham?

I honestly do not know what happened and why, but I now realise that some kind of cultural revolution has taken place in the university system, some drive towards egalitarianism that has ended up inflicting misery on, and degrading, everybody involved. Everything is a fraud, cheating is rampant, students learn nothing and seem perfectly happy to do so, lecturers turn a blind eye to it all, original thought is discouraged at all costs, and all the university cares about is attracting more students and subsequent funding. They, quite simply, do not care about education because that is no longer the role of a university. It's just like Stalinist Russia, from where my father emigrated as a small child via Germany in the 1930s (you will remember that I told you he changed his name from Finkel to Finch as a young man): all the figures record another triumphant and successful harvest while peasants drop dead of starvation in the fields. We now have a situation where intelligent men and women prostitute themselves to a system in which no intelligent person could believe. In other words they are all, each and every one of them, living a lie.

I am sorry but I have decided that I simply cannot live like this anymore. I cannot live a lie, and there is nowhere else for me to go and nothing more I can do. My dreams have been shattered and both my heart and spirit broken and I no longer wish to stay alive. Everything I believed in has turned out to be fake, a Potemkin village of superficiality and deception, as hollow as an eggshell. There is no other way out of this situation and I know that and accept it, so please do not feel sorry for me. I am doing what I want to do.

I am sorry for any problems I have caused. Thank you for being my friend.

Yours
Freddie

That was it – Crump had made up his mind. He was going to expose the whole thing – the scam that the British education system had become, the corruption at the university, the fake degrees and essays, the bribery, the fraud and the cheating. The lot. He couldn't change the world but he could have a damn good try at making it a bit better. Game or no game, business or no business, career or no career – he had to do it, for Freddie's sake and everyone else's.

He read and reread the letter for the rest of that evening, and for the first time in goodness knows how long he went to sleep feeling, if not exactly happy, then at least not ashamed and disgusted at the life he was living and the man that he had become. In short, he felt what it was to be human again.

It had taken him a long time to find his way back to what mattered, but now he knew *what it was all about*, and he now knew what he would do.

There comes a time when silence is a betrayal. It was finally time to break the silence.

CHAPTER TEN

Burning Up

The summer term – the best of times, the worst of times, and everything in between.

A time when most teaching and classes end, only to be replaced by the seemingly endless marking of coursework essays for staff, and preparation for exams and final coursework submissions for students. A strange time all in all, as the real studying and teaching has been completed by then. A vaguely-defined, abnormal, half-life of a term, and one in which everybody, students and lecturers, is looking forward to the summer, although also dreading exams and coursework submissions and the marking thereof.

Not long to go before all of an academic's energy could go on doing research free from the distracting irritation of teaching ungrateful and ignorant students, and all students' energies could go on doing nothing – i.e. waiting for exam/coursework/degree results, attending graduation ceremonies, applying for jobs and/or preparing for unemployment.

The weather was almost identical to that on Crump's first day at the university the previous September – cloudy, but with shafts of sunshine occasionally stabbing through the chilly early morning air. He blinked through the bus window at the sky and could see dark clouds above. Even the weather's trying to deceive, he thought, what with those little bursts of sunshine fooling everyone into thinking it was going to be fine, and therefore to leave their umbrellas at home, only to unleash heavy showers onto their hoodwinked heads later in the day. You can't trust anything or anybody, he thought, as he made his way to the office – but at least now he knew what he was going to do.

"Where's Raj?" he asked his colleagues.

It wasn't like Rajdeep to be late.

Athena tried phoning him.

"Switched off," she said, "I'm sure there's a logical explanation – he's never missed a day..."

"What, never?" asked Johnny Wong, who occupied Kwame's old desk.

Kwame now had his own office after becoming the department's 'Diversity Champion' and 'Head of Black Culture'. The three books were gone from his shelf and, instead, the shelves displayed Johnny Wong's extensive collection of texts, especially those on Chinese and Hong Kong Cinema, his special area of interest and research.

"I'll try later," said Athena, clicking off her mobile, "So how were the conferences?" she asked.

Crump told her what had happened – though not about what Sandy had told him about the way things worked, or his decision to spill the beans about it. Athena nodded with sad resignation.

"So what will you do?" she asked.

Crump shrugged.

"I'm thinking about that," he said.

She saw his sheepish smile.

"What are you up to?" she said – she knew something was going on.

"Nothing," said Crump, as innocently as he could.

It would be unwise to tell anyone about his plan now, even Athena, though he would have loved to let her know what he was planning.

"Have you guys seen this?" said Johnny Wong, holding up an opened newspaper, "It's terrible, eh?"

Crump and Athena went over and looked at the newspaper. On page nine there was a picture, in colour, of four faces, two of which Crump seemed to recognise, but he wasn't sure where from. But as he read the headline, and the text below, it suddenly dawned on him who they were. They were the two guys who, months ago, he had seen in the computer room when he'd gone to thank Miss Sharma for her help. They were the students who had been pestering the two Chinese girls in the corner and who had been exposing themselves. The article said that these two business studies students had been arrested for a series of rapes and sexual assaults going back over a year, and that they were being remanded in custody until their trial later in the year. Crump felt physically sick.

"Are you... OK?" asked Athena.

Crump nodded, though he had felt the colour drain from his face and felt slightly dizzy. He sat down.

"Makes you wonder eh," said Johnny Wong, "what our students get up to."

Crump knew he should have reported it – what he had seen in the library – but then if he had, what would have happened? He would probably have been up on another charge of racism, accused of making false accusations against members of minority groups. Had the two Chinese girls been raped? Come to think of it, he hadn't seen them on campus for months. Had they returned home? And had they left because they'd been attacked – or raped? Crump feared that would indeed turn out to be the case. And how many other students had there been?

If he'd reported the two students from the library, then maybe – maybe – they'd have been arrested earlier and some of their victims wouldn't have been attacked. If, if, if. It's always 'if' – but the fact was, he hadn't had the courage to report what he had seen, to risk being falsely accused of racism, and he hated himself for it. He was ashamed of what he had – or, rather, hadn't – done. What kind of man had he turned into?

Never again would he turn a blind eye. He would try and make amends somehow, in a small way, by writing the article and exposing what went on at Thames Met. It was all he could do, and he determined then and there that he would make a start that day – he had all the notes from the drunken meeting at Sandy's house so it wouldn't take long to fashion them into an article of a couple of thousand words or so.

The first day of term was the day that all the coursework essays had to be submitted. For some reason best known to the university, students didn't just hand in their work to their own department. Instead, the system was centralised, and all essays, dissertations and assignments from every department were handed in at the registry office on the ground floor of the Mandela building where they were logged onto the central computer. This, predictably, led to huge queues, which led to frustration, which led to frayed tempers and utter chaos. On average it was taking three hours' wait to submit essays, and the queue snaked from the registry, along the corridor and outside the building – all of which meant that classes were massively disrupted as so many students were absent or coming or going during the lesson. Unbelievable, thought Crump, that the university administrators couldn't even organise something as simple as essay submission. Probably too busy attending diversity training sessions...

There was a meeting at four that afternoon in the team room about marking, and everyone had to attend. Crump had, by now, developed such a hatred of just about everyone and everything at the department that he left it to the last minute to enter the room. Fiona 'Windrush' had already started speaking, and stopped mid-sentence and stared hard at him as he entered.

"I'm not late," said Crump defiantly, looking her straight in the eye, and walked across the crowded room.

He sat on the floor by the bookshelf. He knew his watch was right – he had synchronised it with the Greenwich pips on the radio at lunchtime, but the clock on the wall said it was two minutes past four.

Windrush said nothing – she simply stared at him. Crump

looked at the floor – he knew her intimidation technique relied on eye contact, and that slippery mix of steel and charm she always used. So he sat cross-legged and looked at the floor like at a primary school assembly. He could sense that Windrush had noticed a change in him – he would never have done what he had just done a few weeks before. It's amazing what making a decision about one's future can do.

The meeting itself was dull and predictable. Lots of stating the bleeding obvious, as usual, as well as constant reminders to give the students the benefit of the doubt and to be sensitive to their cultural needs – which, as every lecturer knows, meant turning a blind eye to cheating from the lucrative international students.

The newer lecturers – like Crump – were to mark their student essays then hand them all to their supervisors to be checked. All final decisions would be made by the supervisors, as would decisions about whether plagiarism had occurred. All this would be validated by external examiners, Windrush said, and it was all Crump could do not to burst out laughing at this point.

Everyone knew that universities these days were more or less self-regulating and that external examiners simply rubber-stamped their decisions – they were, after all, lecturers at other universities themselves, who did exactly the same thing to boost their own students' marks and turned a blind eye to low standards and cheating. If they marked harder than their colleagues they would surely have to answer for their actions and get into trouble, so they never did, and no-one had the courage of a little boy to point out that the emperor was being stripped of what little clothing he had left. Except in the case of professionally-accredited degree courses such as medicine, universities were answerable to no-one for the standards of their degree awards, because they alone set the exams and the coursework assignments, and they alone marked and graded them.

Crump talked to no-one at the meeting – he wasn't in the

mood. All he wanted was to get back home and start work on his article. He spent much of the time ignoring Fiona Windrush's smooth lecture or Wendy Webb droning on, and instead couldn't take his eyes off Cecilia and the now very visible bump in her belly. Was that unborn life in there part of him? There was always that thought in his head, but what could he do? He couldn't force her to have a DNA test after all, except through legal action perhaps – and anyway, could he face knowing if he was the father? And he also knew he may just be allowing his imagination to run wild by even thinking that she could have had sex with him when he was 'out of it'. But maybe he wasn't. What life would a child born to a woman like her have, though, whether or not the child was his? He was sitting there pitying the life of that unborn baby when everyone stood up. The meeting had ended.

That week, he worked like a demon, writing the article about what went on at Thames Metropolitan University, sometimes working into the early hours. He was careful to use no real names for either the people or the university, and also to leave out certain things, such as Sandy's involvement in the custom essay company and the fake degree factory of St Jude's University, as well as the university staff who had their degrees and PhDs from there – he didn't want to ruin Sandy's life and he also wanted to keep some information back for future possible use, just in case. He made the article objective, so left out his being attacked, as well as details of his specific disciplinary warnings, and also any details about the diversity training – he didn't want to have to pay any more damages. All references to students or staff used false names, although insiders would be able to tell who was being talked about. He would also have loved to expose Kwame for the illiterate he was, though he decided this wouldn't have been fair – he didn't want to hurt anyone personally by writing the article.

Instead, he made everything general, but pulled no punches when he described the low standards, the dodgy dealings with the Arabs and the Russians and the Chinese – (all

299

of whom, he discovered, had been given permission, for a price, to take over the running of certain courses in future in the UK and overseas, and award degrees too) – the strange goings-on at the Department of Islamic studies in the Abdullah building, the ubiquitous plagiarism and the blind eye turned to it by everyone, the 'positive action' policies against white men and the totalitarian rule of politically correct diversity schemes, the witch-hunts against the innocent, and the sheer brazen dishonesty of practically everything that went on as standard at the university. In three evenings it was finished – honed to a sharp and efficient 1200 words from its original 5000, and was, Crump decided, possibly the best thing he'd ever written. It was from the heart and he knew it. It *rang true*.

"I know what you should call your article," said Becky, when he'd called her and told her what he was doing, "University of Lies."

"What, like a pun on 'University of Life', you mean?" asked Crump.

He didn't really like it.

"Why not?" said Becky, "Can you think of anything better?"

He couldn't, so 'University of Lies' it was. A cheap pun, possibly – an accurate title, definitely. But eye-catching and accurate because that was exactly what Thames Metropolitan University was: a university of lies and deceit where nothing – absolutely nothing – was honest, decent, fair or just, and where nothing was ever what it seemed or what it should be.

The truly shocking thing was that Thames Met wasn't some 'rogue university' unlike all the others – it was *exactly* like all the others, both from the post-1992 stable, and from the better and older universities, even the top ones: everybody was equally involved in the same giant scam and no-one was innocent. It was just a business and just a game, and Crump was sure to quote that in the article and give plenty of evidence about why Sandy was right.

He had made a couple of phone calls to journalists that week, and one in particular – from 'The Guardian' – was most interested, so it looked like the article would get published in the national press too. He certainly didn't want the piece hidden away in some obscure journal that no-one would ever read. And, of course, the article would be published anonymously.

Crump had called Becky to tell her what had happened regarding the fitness to practise hearing. He had received a letter that week from the college telling him that the tribunal had decided that he was, indeed, fit to practise as a college teacher, but with certain conditions – he would have to be supervised in any college teaching for the next two years, with regular assessments, and also to agree to undergo any diversity training deemed necessary. When Crump read this he crunched the letter into a hard paper ball and threw it against the wall.

How dare they! How dare they do that to him, and expect him to be happy to be treated like some prisoner on probation – and at some crappy further education college too, and in a crappy part-time hourly-paid job! Why on earth should someone of his ability, education and intelligence put up with crap like that! Why indeed.

He called Elizabeth Clint and told her that he was not interested in teaching at the college ever again. And no, he wouldn't be giving any notice either. He said his talents were being wasted doing such a low-level job. He also mentioned that in his opinion the management of the college was well below standard, and that he felt great sympathy for all the teachers still unfortunate enough to be working there. For the sake of the students if nothing else, he said he hoped that the college management would improve soon, and that he knew Elizabeth Clint was only using the tribunal process to further her own career and that she was a nasty and inefficient manager – and then he put the phone down as she was half way through a sentence. It made him feel *great*. He really didn't care about burning a bridge he never wanted to cross again, and was joyful that he'd never have to deal with that awful woman ever again.

Becky thought it was great that he'd done it too – sometimes, you've just got to tell people exactly what you think of them. He wrote a letter rejecting the college's offer and stating why, as well as saying that he expected an excellent reference for his hard work and dedication over the years and would be seeking a copy of it at a later date. He was sure the reference, if he ever needed it, wouldn't be as glowing as it should be – but, as he detailed in the letter, he had done his job, got good results, taught well, been popular with students, and put in hours and hours of unpaid work in the last year too, so at least it should state that.

Something else he did that week was to arrange a loan – for £25,000 – because, as the solicitor informed him when he called, Barbra's people were now demanding £22,000 and the solicitor's fees had gone up too, to almost £2,500. The bank wouldn't even entertain the possibility of giving him a loan like that – not on his salary and a short term 0.8 university contract – and the unintelligible Scottish woman at the bank's call centre even chuckled down the phone when he asked about one. Instead, he called round some loan companies and took out a £25,000 loan over three years from one of the many companies charging exorbitant interest rates – but it was the best that he could get and would involve paying just over a couple of hundred a month, which was manageable.

He had a great pile of coursework essays to mark but decided to leave all those for his free day on Friday and the weekend when he would hermetically shut himself away for a marking marathon and do the lot. It was far more important to him to revise his article – (he was by this time in regular contact with the journalist at 'The Guardian') – so it could be published as soon as possible.

On Thursday, he turned up as usual for his counselling session, and was shocked and saddened by what the staff welfare office told him. Mandy Pandy was dead. She had apparently committed suicide by throwing herself in the path of a train at the end of the Easter vacation, so all sessions were cancelled until further notice. It was with some embarrassment that Crump asked exactly when and where it had happened, but he always liked to know details. It was with even more embarrassment that he heard that she had thrown herself under the Brighton to London train on the afternoon of the day Crump had returned to London. So that was why there had been a delay. For some ridiculous reason Crump suddenly felt guilty, as though he had killed her, simply because the train he was travelling on had probably been the one that hit her. Images of severed limbs and crushed skulls momentarily bloodied his thoughts. The receptionist said that the coroner had yet to hear the case, but that Mandy had left several suicide notes and that several witnesses had seen her jump off the footbridge into the path of the train, so it seemed a straightforward suicide – if there was such a thing.

"She must've been very unhappy," said Crump, stupidly.

"She should've got some counselling," said the receptionist, equally stupidly.

The witnesses had apparently stated to police that they had seen that Mandy Pandy was smiling as she jumped to her death.

* * *

"You have a nice time away then, ducks?" said Mrs Glidewell.

"It was very... interesting," said Crump.

He had got them fish and chips for two, as it was Friday, and his landlady religiously had a fish supper on a Friday, despite not seeming particularly religious. So he was now eating cod and chips in his landlady's flat with a mug of fresh tea she had made him.

"Expect it's all changed now down at Brighton – 'ere, you didn't have no bother with no teddy boys did ya?"

"Nothing to speak of," said Crump, "but I did meet an old friend – from university. He lives in Crete now – in Greece."

"Greece? Oh too hot for me, dear. But I used to like that

singer...whassisname?... *Dennis Rousseau*...that's it...back in the seventies."

"Think he was a bit before my time," said Crump, some vague image of an obese bearded crooner bubbling up in his televisual memory.

"Very high voice, y'know, for a big fella. When Stanley and me was goin' down Brighton – or Clacton – Ooo we used to have such a knees-up! Strollin' down the prom hand in hand, dancin' in the dancehall, fish an' chips every night – the full *gambit* we had – but then, we was on our hols..."

"You only live once," said Crump, trying not to sound sardonic – or as Mrs Glidewell would probably say, *sardinic*.

"I ain't never been abroad," said Mrs Glidewell, biting a long, floppy, vinegar-soaked chip, "don't think I'd like it though – s'pose it depends what kind of a person you are."

"Suppose it does," said Crump.

Mrs Glidewell smiled at him warmly.

"You're a good boy," she said, for no reason Crump could fathom, "don't you worry 'bout me."

He had no idea why she had said this, but said 'OK' anyway.

"I just like being in me home and that's the end of it. Always have and always will. There's plenty would like to have an home, but ain't got none, so why'd I want to go 'way from mine?"

It was a good point and Crump had no answer. Why did so many people spend so much time away from their homes, as if trying to escape their lives by travelling to other places on holiday all the time? What were they trying to run away from? Themselves?

"Nice bit o' cod this, ducks," said Mrs Glidewell.

"It is," said Crump, because it was.

Crump had spent the whole day marking coursework essays and went back upstairs to continue – he intended to spend Saturday and Sunday doing the same.

It was truly shocking what he was reading – many of the

essays would have easily been considered fails when he was at university. But Crump knew that whatever he said, and however he marked these essays, the senior marker – who in his case was Sandy – would pass them all anyway, even the ones that had been word-for-word copied from the internet, even the ones so obviously not written by the candidates but bought from some custom-essay company, and even the ones written in pidgin English at pre-GCSE level. Even though Crump knew this, he decided he would mark these essays properly, according to the values and the educational expectations that he expected to exist – and which used to exist – in every British university, and so he did.

In the early hours of Saturday, while polishing off a bottle of whisky, he did a rough calculation of the marks he had awarded – he found that about 30% had failed, a further 25% scraped a Pass, 20% were Third Class, 20% 2:2, and only 5% 2:1 level. There were no Firsts.

Crump knew well that these marks – which were accurate, and which he would hand in no matter what – would be changed to reflect the targets the university had set. So, after his marks had been doctored by senior markers and/or 'scaled' by computer, they would look more like this – no fails, 10% Pass degrees, 10% Third Class, 10% 2:2, 45% 2:1, and 25% First Class degrees. He had seen this kind of mark-up going on all year.

And even if a particular department's marks were low, it didn't really matter, because the magic of 'modulation' would mean that they could be lifted to match the level of the more generous marks in other departments, irrespective of how dreadful the standard was. This was a trick used extensively by universities to hide the poor performance of weaker departments. It worked, too – like magic. And nobody ever asked questions if the marks were good.

As regards plagiarism – well, perhaps one or two students would be asked to resubmit an essay if it had been word for word copied from the internet, just as a token gesture to make things look professional, but then everyone knew that resubmitted essays were hardly ever failed. Failure was simply not an option any more in the British education system, and everyone won a prize – the only question was what prize they would get. It was like one of the games Crump had seen on the pier in Brighton – everyone got a prize for paying their pound and having a go at hitting the target – including everyone who lost – but the prize that everyone received would be some cheap tat fluffy toy that was practically worthless. That, thought Crump, was what a British university degree had become – a valueless piece of fluffy toy tat. What a shame.

Crump had thought about it long and hard but had decided that he was no longer willing to be party to the fraudulent scam that was being conducted at his university, and was glad his anonymous article entitled 'University of Lies' would be published in 'The Guardian' the following week.

He knew it was futile, and that the marks of the essays he had assesed would just be raised to hit predetermined targets – and also that these fake results would be approved by external examiners who gave the veneer of respectability to a system that had descended into fraudulent farce long ago – but at least *he* would know that he had marked the essays accurately and properly, and that his hands were clean and his conscience clear. The university wouldn't like it – but then they never liked anything he did, so what difference would it make anyway?

He fell asleep in the armchair having drunk substantially more whisky than he'd intended to, and woke up early on Saturday morning with a painful crick in his neck. Much as Crump believed in the theory of evolution, he wondered whether it couldn't have done a better job of connecting the head to the body – a pain in the neck seemed so common as to merit a rethink, or at least a spring or a cushion instead of the twisted sinews that connected head to body.

After showering and making himself some tea and toast – as well as having a tot of whisky to wake himself up – Crump decided to go downstairs and make Mrs Glidewell a cup of tea.

He always did this at weekends now, and really enjoyed the old lady's company too – she seemed to have so much of what he and everyone he knew had lost, although he couldn't really put his finger on what that was exactly. Some kind of innocence, perhaps – some inherent goodness – and a real sense of home. Love, maybe.

When Crump entered the living room he saw Mrs Glidewell sitting in her armchair with both the light and the TV still on. She looked absolutely still and didn't seem to be breathing, so Crump immediately thought the worst. A twisted knot of anxiety tightened in his stomach.

He approached her tentatively and was relieved to see that she was not only alive but awake, with her eyes open. He spoke to her and asked her if she could hear him, but she didn't respond, although her eyes were clear and focused, and then moved slightly too. It was as though Mrs Glidewell wanted to communicate and speak to him, but couldn't. Her face looked different, somehow. Crump called an ambulance and within a couple of minutes the paramedic arrived.

'Perhaps she had a heart attack," Crump said to the paramedic as she entered the house.

"More likely a stroke," she said, as she assessed Mrs Glidewell and made her comfortable in preparation for the ambulance arriving, "It's alright sweetheart, we're here for you now."

Mrs Glidewell didn't respond.

Crump went to the hospital in the ambulance, and settled down for a long wait in the waiting room. If he'd thought of it he could've brought the rest of his essays to mark, or at least a good book, but as it was he had to make do with an old copy of Heat magazine. It was as Crump was chuckling to himself at the concept that people actually paid good money for magazines which only seemed to contain pictures of fourth rate soap actors in the supermarket, that he heard an unmistakeable voice.

"I am not bloody immigrant just off boat," it said, "and I am jolly well not needing interpreter – except when I am having difficulty understanding damn ignorant indigenous population of UK!"

Crump sprang to his feet and headed for the direction of the voice. Eventually he caught up with a trolley being pushed rapidly down the corridor.

"Please do not be going so damn quickly...this is not race!"

"Raj!" called Crump, running up to the trolley.

Raj looked up at him from where he lay, then looked away, as though ashamed. Crump saw that his wrists were bandaged.

"I had no idea you were in hospital," said Crump.

Raj had called the department office earlier in the week to state that he had flu so wouldn't be in.

"You relative?" asked a nurse with an African accent.

"No, just a friend," he said.

"It is not visiting hours," said the nurse.

"But...Raj," said Crump, ignoring her, "what're you doing here?"

It was only later, and after being persistent in following Raj to his new ward and persuading the nurses to let him have a few moments unofficial visiting with his friend, that he found out.

"But...why?" asked Crump, baffled.

Why would someone like Raj – someone so cheerful, and so able, who seemed so happy in their work and so together in their head – why would someone like that slash their wrists and try to end it all? Why?

"Why not?" said Raj, somewhat snappily, "Why bloody hell not?"

His face seemed to crumple from one of anger and anxiety into one of pain and deep sorrow.

"What is point?" he said, "What is point?"

For a moment, Crump thought he was going to start crying.

"But," said Crump, looking at the bandages around Rajdeep's wrists, "you always seemed so...so..."

"Happy?" asked Raj.

"Well...yes," said Crump.

It was true. Raj had always seemed so keen and enthusiastic and excited to be teaching at a Thames Metropolitan University. It was Crump who seemed to be struggling, to be sinking into a mire of depression, to be in a permanent state of conflict with the university and his place in the world. It was he who had been coming apart at the seams, if not actually disintegrating – not Rajdeep.

"Oh I am hiding my feelings quite brilliantly – always I have been doing so – probably I would even be having smile on face at my own execution!"

"But...compared to me, Raj, you were so...together – teaching students and doing your research and..."

Crump could say no more – he didn't know what to say. Raj smiled at him warmly and sighed.

"When I was boy in India," he said, "I was reading all the day. All of classics! My father was giving me complete works of Charles Dickens for thirteenth birthday, and I was reading them non-stop..."

Raj smiled at the memory.

"I was developing such love for genius of Mr Dickens, and for Britain also, and London – and for idea of self-improving value of education. My dream, from tender age, was to be coming and teaching at British university."

Raj closed his eyes and sighed sadly.

"But that's what you did," said Crump, encouragingly, "you achieved your ambition."

Raj laughed – almost manically – and then was silent.

"Yes yes," he said, "you are right, you are right...or you would be being right if British university education system was what I was imagining it to be."

Raj looked at Crump, and Crump looked back at him and nodded. He understood.

"But we are both knowing that British *education* system is not working like that – there is no education in British education system. Not *real* education, not joy of learning, love of knowledge – most students are not giving damn either. All they are caring about is getting job, and for this they are needing good grades. This is not education system – this is just training system for monkeys!"

Crump had no idea that Raj felt the same way as him or was as disillusioned by the realisation that the education system had been so compromised. They had never discussed it.

"Can you imagine how is it for me to be knowing that everything I was ever believing in – everything I was ever putting faith in, everything that was ever giving me the hope – me, that little boy in India – can you imagine what was it to realise that none of it was being true? I am like priest who is losing his faith in the God. So I was having no reason to live. So..."

His words trailed off. Crump looked at Raj. He didn't know what to say.

It turned out that Raj had also been given a first written warning by the university for his missing the diversity training session and instead attending the lecture by Rudyard Perkins, and this seems to have been the source of shame that had pushed him over the edge. He was also castigated for his insensitivity to people of faith by insisting that the theory of evolution was true, and there had also apparently been complaints from religious students about his 'Islamophobia' and 'lack of sensitivity to those of different cultures'.

It also turned out that he'd had enough of Britain and London and the university, and had decided that, when his wrists had healed sufficiently, he would return to India to consider his future. He could work teaching English to children at a small private school he knew, and needed to be with his family, he said. Crump tried to persuade Raj to stay but knew it was futile, so instead he accepted his decision but insisted that Raj say goodbye to him properly before he left for good. Raj nodded, but somehow Crump knew he would never see him again, and he didn't.

It turned out that Mrs Glidewell had indeed had a stroke

and was undergoing further tests to assess her condition. From what they said it seemed likely that she would have to go into care, though nothing had been decided yet – they'd let him know.

Crump went home and spent the rest of the weekend marking the rest of his essay allocation, drinking copious amounts of lager and whisky, and making phone calls. He just felt like doing that though he usually wasn't much of a phone-natterer. He called his mum in Swansea and had a longer phone conversation with her than perhaps he'd ever had. He called Athena and told her all about Raj. He called Becky from the college. And he called Otis – who was still at his parents' home in Brighton – to say that he would definitely be coming over to Crete for a holiday soon.

But most of all, he spent a great deal of time thinking – thinking about how he had changed since starting his job in September, thinking about how everything had changed since then. The next week would be a big one and he knew it – his 'University of Lies' article would be published anonymously that Tuesday and, despite the fact that it never mentioned people's names or that of the university, it would be easily identifiable as Thames Met to all those who worked and studied there, and he was sure the hunt would be on to find the whistle-blower.

Still, there was no way they could identify him – or, at least, prove it was he who wrote the article – so he would just wait and watch and see what happened. He couldn't and wouldn't back down now. No matter what the consequences were.

* * *

"Do you deny writing the article?" asked Wendy Webb.

She looked flushed and held a copy of 'The Guardian' in her hand, or rather the supplement from inside. It bore a huge headline – 'University of Lies' – and then, underneath: 'The Shocking Truth about British Universities'.

Crump had bought several copies on the way to work and had smiled for the entire bus journey as he'd read the published copy of his article. He had to admit it – he was proud of himself and what he'd done – which was an unusual state of affairs for him. It was clear that the copy of that morning's Guardian had been seen by managers at the university and Crump wouldn't have been surprised if his contact at the paper had tipped them off too, just for fun.

"I neither confirm nor deny anything," said Crump, smiling innocently.

He was getting the hang of the prevarication and bullshit and management-speak that had been spewed at him all year long. He was now spewing it back whence it came – just 'playing the game', as it were.

One thing he didn't understand was why, when he'd turned on his computer that morning, he'd had an email from Wendy Webb asking, very curtly, for him to see her as soon as possible. Neither Athena nor Johnny Wong had been sent one, so he wondered how they could have identified him – if they had – from the anonymous article. It was baffling.

Crump was also sad to see that Raj's desk and bookshelf had already been cleared. Athena said one of the secretaries had done it the previous evening and the books would be sent on to India. Raj had resigned for family reasons, she said, as his father had died – something Crump knew was a patent lie – and had already returned to his homeland. He didn't blame Raj either for the resignation or the lie or for not saying goodbye, and hoped he would be happy. Crump would miss him.

"Of course, but who *did* write this article I wonder," said Wendy Webb.

Crump could see a masculine vein throbbing in her neck and there was sweat on her forehead too, but he could also see that she was trying to appear cool and confidently feminine. She looked very male that morning. Crump enjoyed watching her squirm.

"Probably, a...journalist," said Crump, shrugging his

innocence, "and I'm not...a journalist – so why would I write...an article...for a newspaper?"

"Have you read it?" asked Wendy Webb.

"I may have had a quick look earlier," said Crump, "quite something really – everybody's talking about it, y'know."

"Oh I know," said Wendy, "and I also know that the person responsible will be facing very serious consequences."

Crump smiled at her and she scowled back as they met each other's eyes. She knew. He knew she knew. He didn't know how she knew, but she did. For sure. But he really didn't care. He knew that even if they did think it was him they couldn't prove a thing – not unless the journalist at 'The Guardian' informed on him and he doubted that would happen. Unless he was bribed, of course. Journalists had a nasty habit of being very moral people until they were paid. But it was too soon for that – the article had only been published that morning, after all. No, they were clutching at straws, identifying those people who'd have good reason to do such a thing, and Crump, he knew, was one of them. Let them clutch, he thought. Let them guess. He'd watch them squirm as everybody in the educational world identified the anonymous university in the article as Thames Met. Let the game continue.

Crump had handed all the coursework scripts he had marked to Sandy the day before and was keen to find out what he thought of the article too.

"You do know, old boy, that I can't let any of your marks stand," said Sandy, pouring them each a large glass of Scotch.

It was barely eleven, but Crump had only one lesson that afternoon, to which many students wouldn't turn up anyway as they were busy revising for exams in May, and he felt he deserved something of a celebration after the publication of the article – though he hadn't told anyone that he'd written it, not even Athena.

"Which begs the question, Crumpie," he said with a sparkle in his eye, "why didn't you mark them as you were supposed to? You naughty boy...Cheers!"

"Cheers!"

Sandy grinned and clinked his glass with Crump's and each both took a large gulp of whisky. He seemed to be under the impression that he had been forgiven for his betrayal – a mistaken impression that Crump was happy to let stand.

"Because," said Crump, smiling, "just because..."

"Ah, that old chestnut of a reason," said Sandy, "Mmm yes... just because..."

"Yes," said Crump, "and I shall refuse to change my marks if you ask me too."

Sandy grinned widely and nodded at Crump's defiance.

"So the worm has turned at last," he said, "I wondered how long it'd take you to get a nasty dose of morality, old boy."

As expected, Sandy said that all the coursework essays had to be passed and that about 70% had to be 2:1s or Firsts. There were, on no account, to be any fails. Any essays that were obvious fails (i.e. of retard scribble level) or were obviously plagiarised (i.e. word for word copied from the internet) were to be flagged. The student could then, if absolutely necessary, be asked to resubmit, especially if other modules' marks were just as weak. Often, though, a low mark in one module could be 'disappeared' by a stronger mark from elsewhere – for example, an approved prior learning mark, or modules already taken in a foreign student's home country which had achieved high marks, by fair means or foul. And then there was always the magic of modulation if all else failed.

Sandy said that, as senior marker, he'd re-mark them all himself – and also that he wouldn't say anything to Wendy Webb about Crump's refusal to follow the marking scheme.

"Interesting piece in 'The *Grauniad*' today," said Sandy.

"Really?" said Crump, trying to act innocent but failing utterly – he couldn't help a cheeky smile from twitching at his lips, no matter hard he tried, especially with the warmth of the whisky under his skin.

"I should co-co, old boy," grinned Sandy, "all about this university – though of course it's all anonymous, and no-one and nothing's mentioned by name – but it's all about us, oh yes indeed."

"Oh," said Crump, sheepishly, "what does it say?"

Sandy filled their glasses with whisky again. Large ones.

"Oh all sorts, all sorts," said Sandy, and then continued in a mock Dickensian accent, "can of worms opened, among the pigeons a cat has been well and truly put, young Master Crumpet, and no mistake!"

Crump sipped his whisky and smiled.

"Still, no real harm done," said Sandy knocking back his drink, "a few heads'll be a-rolling down the marble steps though, and a few 'exciting new' initiatives and policies will be introduced. The usual suspects'll bang on about renewal and cultural change, that kind of cobblers – adding value, raising awareness, etcetera etcetera, blah blah blah – and then things'll go on just as they always have forever and ever, amen."

Sandy rolled his eyes upwards and mock-prayed when he said this. Crump sipped his whisky. He knew that Sandy knew it was him, though he had no idea exactly how – perhaps he was just giving off 'vibes'. He'd always been a bad liar, and the guilt was probably obvious from the look on his face.

"It's not as though this place has got a reputation worth saving," said Sandy, "but the irony is, every university in the country's doing exactly the same stuff as us. Shame if anybody gets hurt though..."

"Don't you think a lot of people have been hurt already?" said Crump, "Freddie Finch, for example? Or Raj."

"What's wrong with Rajie?" said Sandy.

Crump had forgotten that only he knew about the suicide attempt.

"Oh... he had to go back to India – family reasons," said Crump – truthfully, according to what the university knew.

Sandy frowned. He knew there was something else and that Crump was lying again – but also knew he wasn't going to be told anything more. He finished his drink with a resigned sigh.

"Reputation, as the bard said, is oft got without merit and lost without deserving," Sandy said, "so it has to be seen who and what survive this...*development*...with their reputations intact... Let's just hope we all survive the gathering storm, my old Crumpet."

"I'm sure...y'know...everything'll be fine for everyone," said Crump.

"That it will, that it will, old boy," said Sandy – somewhat morosely, Crump thought.

Then, as he was leaving Sandy called after him:

"And Crumpie, old boy – beware the sweetness of things..."

Crump wasn't really sure what that meant, but it sounded profound, somehow. Sandy was pouring himself another large whisky when Crump left.

When he got back to his own office he saw that he had an email from Fiona Windrush. It was marked 'URGENT' and stated that he was to go and see her at 2pm.

Obviously, Wendy Webb had referred it upwards, though there was no way at all that anyone could prove he had written the article, so there was no reason at all for him to worry. He did, of course, and that tight knot of anxiety twisted tight inside his guts as he thought of sitting in Fiona's office again. The whisky helped the anxiety a bit but it also meant his breath might smell of alcohol – luckily he kept in a permanent supply of extra strong mints for just such occasions, so should be able to neutralise the boozy smell in a couple of hours.

After a quick lunch with Athena at the staff section of the canteen – as awful as usual but neither could be bothered to go anywhere else – Crump went to return some books to the education department. The teaching he did there was only meant to be for two terms, and he really didn't want dreadfully dull and badly written books on teaching and learning taking up space on his bookshelves any more. With any luck, the pungent extra strong mints would mean he wouldn't have to smell Edwin Wittering's rancid breath too.

"He ain't there," said a passing student as Crump knocked on Edwin's door.

"Fuckin' paedo he is," said the student with her, sucking the air through his teeth.

"He's been arrested innit – in Thailand," said the first student, "for shaggin' schoolboys – p'lice raided the office yest'day..."

"Took away laptop and ting... child porn innit..."

Crump couldn't believe it. Could Edwin Wittering, long-serving teacher trainer and head of the department of post-compulsory education, have really been arrested for underage sex in Thailand? And what did the police find in his office?

There was no other way. He asked the secretary in the education department office – a particularly sour-looking woman – about it but she refused to give out any information. He handed the education books back to her. She didn't say 'thank you' as she grabbed them from him. Luckily, as he was leaving, a young woman – a junior secretary who had overheard his enquiry – ran after him and told him that yes, Edwin Wittering was under arrest in Thailand for having sexual relations with several boys aged eight to sixteen, and that such charges usually led to hefty prison sentences of about ten years.

Couldn't have happened to a nicer man, thought Crump. People like that deserved to be locked up and, somehow, Crump wasn't really surprised at all by this, but he couldn't say exactly why. The junior secretary said that the police had raided his office the day before and taken away several computers and books. Crump thanked her for her help – it was nice to know what was going on for once. It just went to show that you never really know anyone – not really. Never know who or what they are. Never know what dark reality lies behind their outwardly respectable benevolence.

Crump didn't know it, but the detailed scrapbook was filled with samples of pubic hair from boys aged twelve and above – which included the pubic hair Edwin Wittering had cut from

Crump when he was unconscious. It had also been taken away by police and was now bagged evidence that would later be used to investigate claims of abuse going back many years.

On the way out, Crump bumped into Nick Craven and Sandra in her burqa. They were amongst his favourite students – more intelligent than the usual, and both seemed committed to education and passing onto the next generation their love of learning and knowledge. This at least made Crump feel that he had achieved something that year – not much, true, but something.

"God bless you," said Nick, warmly, "go safely."

"Inshallah," said Sandra, through her burqa – Crump knew that meant 'God willing' in Arabic.

Despite Crump's cynicism about religion and dislike for all the hypocrisy, noise and self-righteousness of the overtly religious, at least some of them were polite – he could hear his mother speaking when he thought that, though she would also have said they dressed smartly and had nice short haircuts too. Remembering how rudely and shabbily some people had treated him that year, things like that meant a great deal.

Politeness, after all, cost nothing and made life so much more pleasant. He wondered if anyone had done any research on who was more polite – religious people or atheists. He had seen research showing that levels of optimism and happiness were no different, and also that the mentally ill were more likely to become religious – (or was it the religion that made them mentally ill?) – and made a mental note to seek out more research in the field. It could be an interesting subject for future study, though he'd need to read up on psychology first. And he certainly wouldn't be showing his research to any colleague ever again until it had been published. He'd learnt his lesson there.

As Crump walked back to his department he felt an acid reflux in his throat and felt rather sick – probably a result of all the stress. Just then, as he was approaching the Seacole building he was nearly knocked sideways by a blow to the face

– a hard slap that nearly knocked him off his feet. After coming to, he looked up and saw Margaret No-name walking away from him. She had slapped him. Hard. What on earth was that all about? He rubbed his right cheek and winced at the soreness as he watched her march away. He was too stunned to respond or say anything, so didn't.

* * *

Crump was sitting in Fiona Windrush's office. He smelt of extra strong mints and there was a red mark across his right cheek where Margaret No-name had slapped him. Fiona hadn't kept him waiting this time. That wasn't like her at all – she usually liked to keep people waiting, to assert her power over lesser mortals, presumably.

"Coffee?" she asked as Crump entered her office.

He had noticed the stylish percolator by the large sink area at the far side of the room. Fiona Windrush aka Psaradaki had the best office in the department by far – it was huge and even had an en suite bathroom and shower, and its own cloakroom. The trappings of power, thought Crump as he accepted her offer. She smiled and didn't seem as angry as her email suggested she would be.

She handed him the coffee, sat down on the other side of the desk and looked at him. He sipped his coffee – which actually tasted of coffee, unlike the coffee in the canteen – and looked right back.

"Are you happy here," she asked, "at Thames Metropolitan University?"

Crump didn't know what to say. For a mad moment he wondered if she might have poisoned his coffee in order to bump him off and shocked himself with the rather paranoid thought. He remembered a piece of advice Sandy had given him about coping with difficult students, or those who asked questions to which you didn't know the answer – reply to a question with a question. It never failed.

"What do you mean by 'happy'?" he said.

Fiona Windrush smiled and nodded knowingly. It was probably the answer she would've given in his situation too.

"What I mean is, do you think you...fit in...in this department – at this university – or do you think there may be a mis-match?"

"A *mis-match*?" said Crump.

"Yes, a mis-match," said Fiona Windrush.

Crump thought. No need to rush an answer – take your time before saying anything.

"I...don't know," he said, confidently, "It all depends on..."

"...what I mean by mis-match?" interrupted Fiona Windrush, nodding cynically at Crump.

He smiled back and nodded too.

"I've read today's paper, Kevin," she said, "Have you seen the article in The Guardian by any chance?"

"I had a quick peek," said Crump.

"A quick peek?" she said.

"Yes."

"University of Lies – an interesting title, don't you think?"

She was now holding up the newspaper to show him.

"Interesting? Err...possibly..." said Crump, deliberately noncommittal.

There was a long, still silence. Fiona leaned forward.

"I know you wrote it," she said, in a whisper.

"Oh but I..."

"Don't deny it, Kevin – I'm not as stupid as *you* look," she said, her eyes hardening into a steely stare, "you see, all computers at the university are monitored, as are all phone calls, and emails sent and received."

Shit, thought Crump – he'd sent the article by email from the computer in his office, and there was a copy of it in his desktop folder now. He could feel the blood draining from his face.

"Is...is that legal?" asked Crump, unable to think of anything else to say.

"You're not denying it then? And yes it is legal, as is the random monitoring of all offices. Data protection, health and safety and anti-terrorism legislation make it so."

What did she mean, 'random monitoring'?

"You see, we've been recording all conversations in all university offices for over a year now."

Oh, that's what she meant.

Crump's mind flicked through the snapshots of memory from the past year – every single conversation he had had in the office, every single phone conversation, every single email sent, had been recorded. No wonder she – and Wendy – knew everything that was going on in the department. Crump was actually relieved at this – he had at one stage, shamefully, suspected Athena or Raj of informing on him. Now he knew why.

"Oh," he said.

"Oh indeed," said Windrush, leaning back in her chair and looking smug, like a cat.

Wait just a minute, Crump thought to himself. He had nothing – absolutely nothing – to be ashamed of. He hadn't been claiming government money for more students than existed and bribing people to keep it quiet; he hadn't bought essays to get his degree or bought a fake PhD; he hadn't conducted witch hunts against innocent people, driving them to attempt suicide – and succeeding, in the case of Freddie Finch. He wasn't going to stand for being bullied or intimidated. It was time to raise the stakes.

"I know your PhD is a fake," he said, louder than he expected, "as are the degrees and qualifications of several staff members here, and I also know your real name is Fiona Psaradaki and you're not black at all, but just changed your name to help your career through the positive action policies..."

Fiona Windrush looked taken aback – she hadn't been expecting any resistance. But she soon composed herself. She looked calm and spoke softly without taking her eyes off him.

"You know a lot," she said, snidely, "but then so do I."

Crump looked at her. What did she mean? She told him.

"For example, I know that there have been several other complaints about you and your racist, sexist, disablist language and attitude, and your lack of respect for people of faith," she said, "enough to get you a final warning and end your academic career for good, actually."

There was a tense silence as Crump stared at Windrush and she stared back, like two cats facing each other on a wall. But then he smiled more widely at her and her smile wilted visibly – she knew he had something else. Crump played his trump card:

"And I know about the dodgy deals with foreign universities, the blind eye that's turned to cheating and plagiarism here, the international students let in with fake qualifications, the failed students passed no matter what," said Crump, "and I have evidence to prove it too."

Evidence – that word was the killer blow. Fiona looked flustered, but composed herself quickly and said:.

"We follow best practice and are assessed independently, so your accusations mean nothing, Kevin."

"I also have evidence about all bribes made by you to a certain individual in this department to keep him quiet, as well as records of your name and others in the register of St Jude's university showing exactly when, and for how much, you purchased your PhD."

At that point Crump took from his bag a book of records he had taken from Sandy's house on the night when his host was hopelessly drunk. It was all in there – all the proof he needed, most of which he had only hinted at in the article.

Fiona Windrush looked physically shaken by the sight of it and went pale, which was most unusual for a 'black' woman.

"Show me," she barked, and held out her hand.

She was getting angry. Good.

"No," said Crump.

There was no way he was going to let her get her claws into either that ledger or him.

322

"Oh there could be anything in that book," she said, casually, pretending not to care.

"Yes," said Crump, coolly, "but unless I get what I want I'll be sending copies of it to the authorities, the police and the media – and we'll be able to see whether they find 'anything' in it or not, won't we?"

There was a strained silence, before Fiona Windrush composed herself and nodded. Crump smiled. He had won, and he knew it.

"You do know," said Fiona Windrush, "that a member of staff has accused you of rape, don't you? Off the record, of course."

Crump's smile dissolved into his face.

"What?" he said.

She told him about Cecilia's accusation. So *that* was why Margaret No-name had slapped him earlier! So he *was* right – he *was* the father of Cecilia's baby. Or was he? It was all so confusing and he couldn't trust anything anyone said at all any more.

But someone had had sex with him that evening at Christmas – he would just have to accept it *could* have been Cecilia the man-hater. But rape? Crump a rapist? He knew that was an utter lie despite the fact he had no memory of the night in question. The thought of having sex with Cecilia was enough to turn his stomach.

"Cecilia?" he asked.

"So you admit it," said Fiona Windrush.

"No I most certainly do not," said Crump crossly, "In fact, I rather expect it was she who raped me – do you seriously think I'd want a baby with a woman like that?"

"That's what she says," said Windrush, "though she hasn't made a formal accusation – yet..."

"I have no objection to a DNA test..." said Crump.

"...and we must take all such claims seriously, especially as the alleged offence took place on university premises."

"And what does she stand to get out of it?" asked Crump, "Money?"

She'd also get attention and sympathy of course, automatic credibility for her filthy lies, and an excuse to hate men even more than she did already.

"There would be compensation paid by the university – or, rather, a goodwill payment for compassionate reasons admitting no liability."

"And I suppose I'd be suspended while the matter was investigated?" said Crump.

Fiona Windrush smiled and nodded. She thought she had got him. She hadn't.

"Well, I'll fight it," said Crump, "I'll fight it all the way, and I'll take all this to the police as well."

He held up Sandy's book of records. Fiona Windrush's face fell. She had expected him to crumble, not fight. She wasn't used to people standing up to her – in the education system, it was very rare for any teacher or lecturer to ever stand up to a head of department or senior manager. Crump knew he was winning. He spoke his mind:

"I have no faith in you or this university or the British education system, but I do have faith in British justice. If Cecilia wants to report any supposed crime to the police then that is her right – but I'll fight her every step of the way – and I'll win too."

And with that, Crump stood up and made his way to the door. His hand was on the handle when she spoke:

"Wait," said Fiona Windrush.

Crump turned round and looked at her.

"I'm sure we can...come to some arrangement..."

He walked back to the desk and sat down. He was just playing the game, and he had played it well. He knew – and she knew – that he had won and could now get what he wanted.

Crump smiled at Fiona – he knew victory was his, even if it had been achieved by a little 'blackmail' here and there. All part of the game, Crump thought, all part of the game. Adversity was a good teacher, after all.

* * *

"So how much was it exactly again?" asked Athena, a week later.

They were sitting in the expensive pub by the Cutty Sark where he had taken her and Raj for lunch on the first day they'd met – which was rather fitting as this was Crump's last day at the university. And he didn't mind paying the exorbitant prices this time either.

"Thirty thousand," said Crump, "as a goodwill payment, but most of it's spent already."

He had still told no-one what he knew about corruption or bribes at the university, or the fake PhD Fiona Windrush held. He had handed over Sandy's ledger to her when the cleared payment had been received in his bank account – though he'd made a couple of photocopies, just in case. He had then paid off Barbra's damages and the solicitor's fees and was still five grand up on the deal! Willingly, he had donated a thousand of that to the children's educational charity mentioned by Freddie Finch in his will.

"Wow," said Athena, "so you're rich!"

"Hardly," said Crump, "well, not financially anyway..."

"I'm going to miss you," said Athena, sadly, "and now Raj has gone too – I'll be all alone!"

"All things must change," said Crump, "and anyway, Johnny's there in the office, and there'll be new lecturers next term too – all bright-eyed and bushy-tailed."

Athena nodded. Crump knew from his experience at the college that teachers who left were pretty soon forgotten, and there were always new recruits to take their place.

"So they're paying you till the end of term anyway?"

"Yep, and giving me a good reference too. I leave Thames Metropolitan University on good terms – or better terms than I expected."

"I have no idea how you managed it," said Athena, and it was rather remarkable, thought Crump, that it had gone so well, "but *bravo!* Good for you!"

"Yes," said Crump, "good for me!"

They raised and clinked their glasses.

"To us," said Athena.

"To us," said Crump, and they drank their extortionate lager thirstily.

"So come on then, teach me some Greek – I'm going to be there in just over a week!"

It was true. He had decided, after getting the 'deal' from Fiona Windrush, that it would be the best thing for him to do – to take Otis up on his offer and to go off to Crete for a year – at least – and teach English to kids in one of the small language schools – there was a summer school too, so he'd be working soon after he got there.

It was a shock at first to realise that he was being asked by Fiona Windrush to leave the university, but he also knew he simply couldn't face the thought of doing another year at Thames Met, or applying to any other university either. Not yet, anyway. And it was great that he'd managed to get the £30,000 out of them – he'd at least have four thousand to keep him for a year on top of his basic teaching salary. He needed a break – that was for sure – and after what Sandy had told him he was glad to walk away from that sham of a so-called university and never return.

At first, Crump didn't believe it, but Sandy said that it was almost certainly true, though he had no proof and was speaking 'off the record'. It seemed, however, that Crump – and before him Freddie Finch – may well have been employed simply and solely in order that they could, as white men, be investigated for racism and sexism and thereby sacked, in order to make the department, and its senior staff, look as though it were enforcing its diversity policies vigorously. It seemed absurd, to specifically employ white men with the intention of conducting a witch hunt against them for being supposedly racist and sexist, and persecute them for their supposed crimes. It was certainly amoral. But it seemed all too plausible that they would use him and others like him as playthings to enforce their proactive diversity policies and gain kudos for it – and the more Crump thought about it, the more he thought that that was what must have happened. How else would an open-minded and tolerant man like him have got into so much trouble? He'd been set up right from the start.

He had no proof, but knowing what he knew now, he really wouldn't have been all that surprised if he and Freddie Finch had been employed solely so they could be sacrificed on the altar of political correctness and so-called equality. Incredible, really. But then, so much else that had happened that year was incredible too, in a way. But it had happened, nevertheless – so why shouldn't that be true too?

"If wishes were horses," he said after finishing another pint.

"Beggars would ride," said Athena.

And they were both right. It was an expression that Crump's mum always used and which Athena had learnt from him. And it was true, too.

They wandered from pub to pub – although he was drinking much more than she was, including a few shots of expensive whisky. Athena did try and teach him some Greek, though not very successfully – he was rather slurring his speech by the end of the evening – and promised she'd write to him to let him know about any developments at the university.

He had already heard Baroness Bloodstone in a radio interview saying how they had 'rooted out' the individuals responsible for the irregularities at the university – and he supposed that she meant him, and Sandy of course, who had been the biggest head to roll, though apparently all that meant was that he would retire one year earlier but with a full pension too, which was what he'd always wanted. Sandy had confessed to Crump that his business partner for his custom essay business and the fake degree awarding St Jude's University was, actually, a subsidiary of a subsidiary of the media company belonging to Baroness Bloodstone's husband, though Crump had no proof of this and he was sure the trail leading back to him would be well-hidden. It was hard to tell what was true sometimes at the University of Lies, so sometimes it was better just not to ask any questions. If you challenged anything – if you didn't play the game according to their rules – well, they would try to destroy you. Simple as that.

Crump was so drunk by the end of the evening that he was seeing double. Athena had to leave him to get the tube back to her girlfriend's house, but, before that, they wandered down to the Cutty Sark in the half-light of a soft summer dusk. Athena hugged him under the figurehead and gave him a kiss on the cheek. They would have been so good together, thought Crump, but he knew it was impossible. Athena wouldn't have been Athena if she'd been straight, after all. She had tears in her eyes as they waved goodbye to each other. Crump would miss her.

It was a beautiful and mild May evening and was only just getting dark, and Crump enjoyed just standing there alone, taking in the sights and sounds of London – the City with its tower blocks and twinkling lights on the far side of the river, the noise of revellers in the High Street on the south side, the Cutty Sark in front of him, majestic and elegant. And always the river, flowing past silently – but not silently either, though with nearly no noise. It made strange music – especially to drunken ears.

He looked up at the Cutty Sark and remembered how Raj had loved it – how excited he'd been when he first saw it, like a child. It truly was a beautiful boat. Crump looked up at it and thought about how his life, and all lives, were a journey, as exciting and beautiful and sad and happy and risky as any trade mission to the East that that beautiful ship had embarked on in the past. But then he was rather drunk, and he always got both a bit romantic and a bit maudlin when he was so pissed he could barely stand up straight.

Suddenly, he saw something glint in the corner of his eye, and something that looked like a shooting star flew through the air near him. He looked over and tried to focus his blurry eyes through the darkness onto what he was seeing.

There were, as far as he could make out, three figures standing some way off – all in hoodies – who were...doing what exactly? They seemed to be...no they were...lighting something – setting some objects on fire and then...and then...throwing them at the Cutty Sark! Even as drunk as he was and at that distance he could see what they were doing.

Just then, the deck of the Cutty Sark exploded in flame. Another Molotov cocktail hit the deck, then another, and then another. Within seconds the whole ship was ablaze. The orange light from the fire lit up the whole area and felt hot on Crump's face.

"No!" he shouted, "Stop!", and one of the balaclava-ed masked figures turned around and looked straight at him.

The growing, glowing flames on the deck illuminated the scene in the darkness – he could see the three figures and they could see him. One of them started to approach him, walking slowly but purposefully towards where he stood. Crump froze. He was only a few feet away now. His eyes were bloodshot – stoned perhaps – and were full of hatred and anger. Something in the figure's hand glinted in the firelight. It was the blade of a knife. Crump didn't – couldn't – move.

"No!" called a voice, and the figure with the knife stopped.

The man paused, turned back, then started walking away from Crump towards the two other figures. And then they ran, leaving Crump alone watching the burning ship.

This was not the place for a drunken man to be, he knew – watching a fire like an arsonist – and the police would probably arrest him if he stayed. They may just assume it was him who'd torched the ship.

He looked one last time at the Cutty Sark – it was now an inferno – and then ran. It had taken only about a minute for that beautiful ship to be utterly engulfed in flames. And for what? Did those idiots actually think it was a slave ship? Even as he ran, Crump could feel the heat of the fire on his back. The flames shot high into the air, the old wooden beams cracking loudly in the heat.

Crump could hear sirens wailing. By the time the fire engines had got there it would be too late, he knew. No-one and nothing could save the ship now. It would just burn and burn and burn through the night until all that was left was a blackened, smoking wreck.

If he stayed at the university, he thought, he would end up much the same – burnt out, burnt up, and utterly destroyed. He looked back in the direction of the Cutty Sark one last time – he couldn't see the ship directly but the sky glowed orange all around and embers of burning ash floated up into the darkness with the smoke. Funny how beautiful destruction could be, he thought. Crump never looked back again after that.

This was perhaps the end of one chapter of his life – and maybe the beginning of another. But he knew he'd never go back. Never.

He had no regrets, and he was happy to be going home.

The game was over, at last.

EPILOGUE

Crump got himself another cold bottle of beer from the fridge.

The heat of the afternoon was stifling and sweat dripped off his brow and wetted his scalp. He sat on the bed exhausted, held the bottle against his hot face for a moment, then took a long swig from it and sighed.

It was now six weeks since he'd arrived in Crete and he was sharing a small, spartan flat with his old friend Otis in Heraklion, near the port. He was teaching English to kids of all ages in a small private language school, in the mornings and the evenings, with a five-hour gap in between. The teaching was very book-based and traditional, and the kids were OK by and large, though noisy as hell like everything else in the country – and, happily, there was no requirement for detailed essay plans or reports or any institutional nonsense of any kind. He went in, taught from the book, set and marked compositions for homework, and that was it. It wasn't exactly interesting and inspiring work, but it certainly wasn't any less stimulating than teaching at the university. The pay was basic, but enough to live on if you were careful, and the cost of living was cheap, especially the alcohol. Crump was taking full advantage.

The last thing he had done before leaving London was to go and see Mrs Glidewell. It had been decided that it would be for the best if she went into long-term residential care, and the house was to be sold to pay for it. The nursing home was situated in a leafy and quiet part of Eltham and was pleasant as far as these things go, but Mrs Glidewell's severe stroke had left her unable to speak. Crump could tell when he saw her that she wanted to, and also that she recognised him. He could also see how frustrated she was that she was unable to communicate, but he could see in her eyes that she understood him.

He told her about how he had left his job at the university and was going off to teach in Greece – about how there'd be lots of sunshine and how he'd probably travel around the islands at some stage and visit Athens too, where Socrates and Plato and Aristotle created the foundation for Western Civilisation and its education system – as it used to be, anyway – and about how he would say hello to *Dennis Rousseau* if he saw him. She understood, he could tell, and she reached out and held his hand and attempted to smile as he said goodbye. He kissed her on the cheek and said he'd send her a postcard. But he knew he'd never see her again and he didn't. Mrs Glidewell died in her sleep a month later.

It was amazing how much Greek he'd learned too in such a short time too, although most people spoke some English. He spent most evenings drinking and talking with Otis so picked up a lot from him. They talked of the past, and the future – of what they could do, and what they should do, and what, supposedly, they would do. But Crump knew that Otis would do nothing but drink himself silly every night and, for the time being at least, Crump was happy to join him. As well as cheap bottles of beer, there was also cheap whisky and extremely cheap and deadly ouzo to enjoy, although the hangover from that was the worst he'd ever had.

They were going to go island-hopping, but Otis said it was far too hot in the summer, and anyway, the islands were so expensive – they would explore some of the coast of Crete later in the year, and maybe spend a week or two in Athens too. But for the summer they would stay in Heraklion, teaching and drinking and sweating – or 'chilling', as Otis ironically called it.

Crump had sent postcards to various people but had had no replies. It was expensive to phone the UK so he didn't bother, except to tell his mum he'd arrived safely. He was starting to think that his friendship with Athena was not as close as he thought, when one afternoon there was a knock on the door. It was the old toothless lady from an apartment in the next door building, and she gave him a bundle of letters – it seems the postman had been mistakenly delivering letters to the neighbouring building for weeks and the lady had just found them all in the communal hallway.

There were letters from his mum – who he knew had written – but also one from Becky and three from Athena. He decided he would have to call them both later, despite the cost, and explain what had happened and why he hadn't replied.

Athena talked about how an enquiry was underway at the university, led by Baroness Bloodstone – predictably – which would identify weaknesses and bring about 'cultural change' and 'renewal' with a raft of 'exciting new initiatives'. Or, in other words, 'pass the buck'. Nothing would change, and they both knew it.

Fiona Windrush was leaving to take up a post of head of department of cultural studies at a top British university. Wendy Webb was to be the new head of the Department of Cultural, Creative and Communicative Studies at Thames Met. Sandy had, of course, been forced to retire – Athena had attended his leaving do. She said that he was now almost permanently under the influence, and that she'd seen him wandering round Greenwich in the evening clasping a whisky bottle and as drunk as a lord. It was as though the purpose had gone out of his life – despite his full pension, his beautiful house, his successful business and pots of money.

When Crump told Otis all about this later, he said, perhaps mockingly:

"So he got what he wanted, but lost what he had – just like Elvis."

Crump didn't disagree, and Otis began drunkenly singing 'All my trials Lord will soon be over', as something of a tribute.

Sandy had been a good friend – once. He was also an

experienced teacher – but then, in his case, experience was what was left when everything else had been lost. Crump would never forgive him for deceiving him and stealing his work.

Sometimes – just sometimes – Crump could see in Sandy the man that he must once have been, a man who believed in real education, in the pursuit and transference of knowledge, before the cynicism and the dishonesty rotted him away from the inside like a dead fish. Was that his fault or the fault of the system? Would Crump become like that if he remained a lecturer at a British university? He didn't know, but from what Athena was saying he did know that Sandy wouldn't live very long into his wealthy retirement if he continued drinking like he was. It was terrible what shame could do to a man.

Athena also told him how Kwame (aka Kenneth) had resigned from his post as Diversity Champion and Head of Black Culture at Thames Met and had decided to go back to being a junior lecturer again whilst studying for another Master's degree. Apparently, he had undergone some kind of transformation, Athena thought – a religious conversion without the religion – and now was heavily involved in campaigning against knife and gun crime, especially amongst black boys. He was also very involved in promoting racial integration rather than segregation, and had even been part of starting a campaign against African-American-style separatist black-only organisations and attitudes, such as the push for a separate black history and culture curriculum. This had meant that he had come in for terrible insults and bullying from black pressure groups and to his being called a traitor, an Uncle Tom and a 'coconut', but Kwame was determined, so Athena said, that integration and non-violence was the only way forward. Crump hoped things would work out for him.

They had worked out OK for Crump, all in all. Yes, his job was way below his capability – yes, he was drinking too much – yes, Crete was a pretty backward kind of place. Crump had even been told by the school-owner that he was not allowed to say anything about religion or politics, or anything good about Turks or Albanians or gays, as parents may complain – ironic really, as the Ancient Greeks had practically invented gays in the first place. Sort of. And yes, he would just have to put up with that nonsense, just as he put up with the nonsense at Thames Metropolitan University.

All he knew was that the nonsense of his life now was less than the nonsense that his life used to be, and that was progress of a sort, at least. It was all a business and all a game, wherever you were, and that was what it was all about – in Greece, in Britain, and probably on the Moon too.

All he was doing was playing the game – just like everyone else – but at least now he was doing it on his own terms. He'd think later about what he was going to do after the summer – and for the rest of his life.

It was an hour before Crump had to go out and teach his evening classes that day, so he had a cold shower, made himself a feta and tomato sandwich, and turned on the old TV with the grainy picture in the corner of the room.

Usually, Crump let the dreadfulness of Greek TV wash over him, and didn't pay much attention, but he always liked to look at the news every couple of days, so as not to live completely 'under a tub', as his mum would say.

As he watched, he saw images of London. Familiar images – places he knew. He turned the volume up. There had been some sort of explosion – or explosions – there were images of people and police and ambulances. It was a while before he realised that all this had happened the day before – on the Sunday, which he had spent staying in getting drunk, listening to music and playing cards with Otis in the flat.

And then he saw it. They were showing a video – the kind of home-made terror porn suicide bombers make before their missions, with uniformed figures set against the background of green cloth and Arabic slogans. He could just about hear the words in English, past the Greek commentary – the threats against the 'West' and the 'Crusaders' and the 'Infidels' – and he recognised the voice that spoke them.

For there, in the video, was Nick Craven, the trainee teacher from his education class, who was supposedly a born-again Christian, but was now wearing a head covering and was angrily issuing threats on behalf of the *'ummah'* – all the world's Muslims – against the Jews and the Christians, the blasphemers and the Zionists and the infidels in the West. Had he been faking being a born again Christian all along? Had he actually converted from fascist to fundamentalist Muslim instead and kept it hidden, playing the part of a peace-loving Christian instead? If so, Crump could only admire his acting skills. It seemed unbelievable really, but, as he well knew from painful experience, nothing was really unbelievable and anything – anything at all – was possible.

Next to Nick Craven were two women in burqas. He recognised them immediately from their gaze. On the left was the trainee teacher Sandra, and on the right, the burqa girl who had helped him when he had been attacked – the girl with the beautiful, sad and frightened eyes.

They were now all dead, having blown themselves to pieces on buses and tube trains in London, together with several other 'martyrs' pictured on the TV. There were over two hundred people killed in London, they said, and all European transport networks were on a state of high alert. Crump watched open-mouthed in horror. He could hardly believe it, but there it was on his TV screen – the evidence. This, he knew, would change everything even more – in fact, much more – than the religious riot at Thames Met had done. London – and the world – would never be the same again.

That familiar tight knot of anxiety started twisting in his stomach like a worm, gnawing at him and laughing, it seemed, at his naivety and stupidity. How could he have missed that? How could he have not realised that they had been planning this all along?

He was sure that the Centre for Islamic Studies in the

Abdullah building would be implicated – it would probably have been where everything had been planned, where they had got the money, perhaps even where the bombs had been made. He was sure that the university could have done something – *should* have done something – monitored what was going on, at least tried to put a stop to the extreme and radical Islamist views that seemed standard amongst Muslims at Thames Met.

Surely, the religious riot and beating up of Rudyard Perkins should have been a warning? Surely, someone at the university should have acted, at least after that? Or were they all such cowards, never daring to criticise anyone or anything for fear of being branded racist or Islamophobic, and damaging their careers? Was that really what it was all about, in the end? And what were they all so afraid of? Ending up like Crump – out of the system and out of the game?

The TV continued to show scenes of destruction and carnage in London, with smoke spewing from tube stations and buses ripped open by bomb blasts.

Crump sighed, wiped the sweat off his brow, put the bottle of lager to his lips and drank.

It was going to be a long, hot summer.